VERTICAL

CODY GOODFELLOW

Michael Foster, Cam Buckley and Maddie Acosta—all former activists in the infamous urbex crew Les Furies. Together they scaled buildings, broke into the spaces no-one else could, and chased a rush that still haunts them.

Now though, Michael is stuck recovering from an injury, coding in a dead-end start-up, But Les Furies cannot hide forever. A journalist has uncovered Michael's identity and he is being sent anonymous videos of his time in the crew.

When he discovers that Cam and Maddie are planning on reuniting the crew one last time, to scale the Korova Tower in Moscow, he is sceptical. But the tower has never been scaled before. Breaking into the world's tallest building on Russia Day is too good an opportunity to pass him by.

But Michael is about to discover that the vertical city has another purpose, one far more sinister than he could have imagined, and this one final ride for Les Furies might well be the last thing any of them ever do.

9781803363998 • 26 September 2023 • Paperback & E-book
£8.99 / $16.95 / CA$22.95 • 336pp

PRESS & PUBLICITY UK
Olivia Cooke
olivia.cooke@titanemail.com

PRESS & PUBLICITY US
Katharine Carroll
katharine.carroll@titanemail.com

VERTICAL

CODY GOODFELLOW

ALCON
PUBLISHING

TITAN BOOKS

Vertical
Print edition ISBN: 9781803363998
E-book edition ISBN: 9781803364001

Published by Titan Books
A division of Titan Publishing Group Ltd
144 Southwark Street, London SE1 0UP
www.titanbooks.com

First edition: September 2023
10 9 8 7 6 5 4 3 2 1

A CIP catalogue record for this title is available
from the British Library.

Printed and bound in the United States.

*For Butch Carter—outdoorsman, horticulturalist,
news junkie, my dad.*

They say that when you're about to die, your life flashes before your eyes. Now, he knew this was only a myth. But as he fell from the top of Korova Tower, Igor Marinov found he had plenty of time to reflect on how he'd come to be thrown off the roof of the world's tallest building.

They say that   ashes before
four   as the fall
from the   and he has
longest   thrown off
the roof of the

PRELUDE

Igor long suspected that "the Boss"—his *Avtorityet*—knew of his strong aversion to high places. Why else would he have gifted Igor the "honor" of being that night's official greeter; stationed like a common valet at this temporary rooftop helipad 190 floors above Moscow? This was either a deadly serious message, or just the Avtorityet messing with him for sport, as sadistic fucks like him were wont to do.

It was almost 3:00 a.m., the witching hour. And tonight's coven would be arriving not on brooms, but rather combat-ready helicopters direct from the Kubinka military base. When you really wanted to impress, having the army on speed dial was a potent flex.

Perched on opposite sides of the roof, ten-story construction cranes faced each other like twin sentinels, silently beckoning to the approaching aircraft. Great effort had been made to ensure that tonight's guests wouldn't encounter each other prior to their arrival—be they old rivals, outright enemies or, worst of all, potential conspirators. None of them had more information than any of the others, and perhaps because of that, or just plain FOMO, all had immediately RSVP'd.

The helipad swayed slightly underfoot, jolting Igor with a sharp bolt of panic. He gasped hard, stricken by the reminder that he was nearly a kilometer above solid ground. But this was nothing compared to the slow-burning fear which had gnawed at his consciousness for months now, making it seem like there was no such thing as solid ground anymore. At least, not for him.

The first chopper emerged from the darkness without running lights, its shrouded rotors eerily muted. *Whisper tech that actually works?* Thought Igor. Taking a deep breath, he stepped back to watch the large craft touch down with a jouncing thud. *So it begins.*

Four men emerged, flanked by a quartet of armed security. Each wore an impeccable black or gray suit, all specially tailored to accommodate their snakeskin cowboy boots.

Keeping his eyes down, Igor offered each guest a special custom-made earpiece. The devices would translate in real-time whatever the wearer heard into their native languages. The AI-assisted software was still in beta, but Igor wasn't worried about that end of it; the presentation itself—a slick video package—already had all the necessary language options.

The chopper dusted off and Igor ushered his charges onto the semi-exposed service platform that passed for an elevator—hastily installed at the top of this giant lightning rod, like the conference room itself, for tonight's entertainment. The next helicopter was already approaching.

With his stomach twisting into tighter and tighter knots, Igor managed to greet seven more VIP parties, all pretty much the same—rich and dangerous. Hiding behind a respectful smile, he diligently checked their earpieces before escorting the guests over to the lift.

With the last chopper drifting off like a specter into the moonless sky, Igor felt a wave of relief, however brief. *Now the hard part*, he thought, checking his watch during the lift's slow descent to the 183rd floor. Once it had settled, he raised the safety gate and headed toward the conference room and its gauntlet of aggressively nondescript men in bulky black suits, earpieces and wraparound sunglasses—which Igor knew featured starlight and infrared sensors.

Two of them administered a rough pat down, acting like they'd never seen Igor prior to this moment, despite his working there all day. *God, these fucking guys.* But he mutely played the humble *shestyorka*, a nobody with nothing to hide, and thus was nothing to worry about. He almost believed it.

With security behind him, Igor entered the hub of business suites and strode to the small tech room where he'd be running the presentation. Opening the door without knocking, he entered his control lair, a dimly lit room the size of a jail cell that adjoined the main conference space.

But instead of finding Feliks the audio tech bent over the mixing board and pretending to work, Igor was met by another *obshchak*, this one probably on loan from Wagner Security, who, being as large as he was menacing, easily took up most of the room. Feliks was practically cowering in the far corner by a metal cabinet, eyes wide. Igor felt his sense of authority pooling around his ankles like warm tar. *Fuck me, now what…?*

Igor flinched when the man leaned in close. "Igor Marinov," the operative said, not really asking.

"Yes," Igor managed, his senses returning. If the obshchak's job was to keep everyone on their toes, mission 100 percent accomplished.

The man handed Igor a black plastic snap case the size of a fat paperback. He knew what it was and snapped it open, revealing a trim silver Faraday bag. To Igor, it shone like an enchanted ring. Snug inside was a pair of military-grade USB drives—A & B, for the sake of redundancy.

Carefully removing drive A, Igor slotted it into the DLP video projector he'd field-tested earlier that day. The machine blinked to life, system diagnostics booting up. A few tense moments later, its LEDs blinked to steady-green—the program file, the Digital Cinema Package, was fully loaded and ready to play.

"Good to go," confirmed Igor in English, giving a quick thumbs up. He carefully removed the thumb drive and handed it back to the obshchak. After the man had returned both drives to their plastic coffin, he then turned and left the room without a word, closing the door firmly behind him. Igor and Feliks exchanged looks, both deciding not to comment.

Situated near the projector was Igor's air-gapped laptop, configured for controlling the lights and any other theatrical aspect of tonight's presentation. After checking that it too was "good to go," Igor stepped to the small observation window and scoped the conference room. The VIPs were warily enjoying themselves, their security teams deployed around the perimeter. Hopeful Miss Russia contestants circulated with silver trays, serving glasses of Bollinger and small-batch artisanal caviar. *So far, so good,* thought Igor. Everything appeared on schedule.

An Influencer DJ was stationed at stage right, mashing up classic club tracks, nothing too radical. When a runway-ready ingénue, surely another of the Boss's girlfriends, took the low stage at the far end of the room, the DJ gave her a nod of recognition and seamlessly segued into a backing track as good anything he'd been playing that evening. With sincere K-pop vibes, the woman broke into a sugary club song, riding the DJ's beat. *Not without talent,* Igor noted.

Shooing Feliks from the mixing console, Igor again rechecked the projector and laptop. He needed time to think, and busy work freed up mental bandwidth. But he knew the really important decisions had already been made, most of which he hadn't even been aware of at the time. It was the money that had led him here, but once he'd learned the project's ultimate purpose, he'd been plotting a way to get out without being murdered. To not act would make him worse than the people he was working for. Now he had to find his nerve and see it through…

Her song concluded, the singer scampered off, Ig a lurid hug along the way from the Avtorityet as he took over the stage.

Flashing a wide toothy grin, he swiped a lock of hair out of his eyes and deployed a few well-honed smutty jokes, fortified with topical references. Igor had to admit, the Boss was really killing it.

With Feliks busy tracking down the source of a faint impedance hum, Igor surreptitiously copied the encrypted DCP, along with the digital key to unlock it, from the DLP unit onto his own military-grade USB drive, a much smaller one with better shielding. It hit the bottom of his pocket just as the Wagner operative appeared in the control room doorway and fixed Igor with a grim look. Feliks made a small sign of relief—the vague hum was now gone.

"Igor Marinov, be ready for my signal," the obshchak said, stepping to the observation port. He peered out at the ballroom of VIPs, adding, "When I tell you, lower the lights and start the projection. But when I tell you. Understand?"

"I know the cues," Igor muttered. "There's no need to—"

The man turned to look Igor full in the face. "Do you really want the responsibility?" At that moment, Igor realized that this scary monster was actually cutting him a huge solid, shielding him from any blame if the show didn't start on cue.

"Uh… no," confirmed Igor sincerely. "You tell me when."

From the stage, the Boss theatrically called for the house lights to go down. Igor stared at the security man, letting him know he was on full alert, ready to start.

"Go now," the man announced.

Igor tapped the Enter key. Instantly, the presentation started, turning down the lights and starting up the video projector. Not to be left out, Feliks adjusted the sound level slightly; the hum was still gone.

Satisfied, the obshchak gave Igor a slight nod, like they were a team now, and silently left the room. After thirty seconds of awkward silence, Igor coughed. "OK, Feliks, looks like we're good here," Igor said. "I need a smoke after all this… excitement. And good job on that hum problem."

"Thanks, but don't take too long," said Feliks. "If that fucking gorilla decides to come back, I don't want to be here alone. Besides, he seems to like you."

"Don't worry, I'll be right back," replied Igor, on the way out the door.

In the hall, the security gauntlet was now just two dark suits. They barely reacted when Igor said he'd left his phone at the helipad. As the elevator took him to the rooftop, he knew there would be more than just his acrophobia to deal with.

Igor been working for "the Boss" for less than a year. What was once a lucrative IT-light side hustle had taken over his life. The money was too good, best he'd ever made, legally. All he had to do was troubleshoot company systems and keep his head down while doing it. All in service of "the project." Before long, Igor knew more about it than anyone outside of the Avtorityet's black-suited inner circle.

If only I'd known…

He'd naively thought he knew what he was getting into. After all, he was an adult, sanguine about the ways of the world, where honest men went to jail and connected criminals prospered. But when Igor finally understood who he was actually working for, what he was helping to create, he had impulsively reached out to Razbit, a covert group that protected *osvedomitels*—whistleblowers.

Razbit, Russian for "smash," employed classic analog spycraft—mail drops, book codes, flowerpots in windows, and enigmatic meetings with high-signs and counter-passwords. It was a bitter joke that Russian *osvedomitel* laws only applied to those calling out government corruption or malfeasance, as if the hen could trust the farmer. And if the farmer was also the fox? Razbit's old-school dissidents promised to fully protect Igor if he could deliver hard proof, actual documentation for the world to see.

He knew he was being watched; his phone and other devices surely were monitored. And he knew what would happen if he even appeared to be acting like the very kind of citizen that the true boss had made a career of pursuing when he was in the FSB.

You were a fool, Igor Arsenyevich Marinov. Why had he reached out to Razbit in the first place? Where did this new martyr complex come from? Clearly, he hadn't been thinking straight for quite some time. *Am I really a patriot—or simply delusional?* He wondered if there was much of a difference.

By now, cold sweat had plastered his shirt to his back, and Igor stiffly exited the elevator and stepped out onto the roof. With tonight's the guests and guards two stories below, the helipad seemed deserted, and he shivered in the whipping arctic wind. He checked his watch: two minutes until the presentation ended. *Had something had gone wrong? Surely not!*

Igor became aware of a high thin whine coming from out of the darkness. He took a deep breath. *Is two minutes enough time?* The approaching quadcopter was skillfully piloted, navigating the lashing updrafts off the tower's façade with ease. The drone crested the edge of the helipad and came to settle beside a cluster of electrical conduits.

Desperately glancing at the elevator and the surveillance cameras, which were supposedly disabled tonight, Igor crossed the helipad and crouched over the drone, the last guest of the evening. Looking back one final time, he took the thumb drive out of his pocket and secured it within the small weatherproof capsule on the drone's underbelly.

He rose up and flashed a laser pointer towards the northwest and the Federation Tower, once the pride of Russia, but from this height little more than a footstool on the face of the city below. The drone came alive, launching back into the wind, heading south. If it wound up smashed on the ground, could it be traced back to him? Why had he ever believed in this plan?

With the quadcopter gone, Igor also made to leave; the presentation was just about over. Remembering to retrieve his phone from the concierge's kiosk, he was surprised to find his spirits were lifting. *I'll grab a bottle of champagne, and see if one of those Miss Russias has a laptop with a malware problem...*

There was a crack of thunder out of the cloudless sky. *A gunshot?* Igor knew it was. His heart sank.

The elevator was gone. No, it was returning—he hadn't noticed it was gone. Backing away, he looked everywhere, but knew there was nowhere to go.

The Avtorityet, one Dimiter Zamyatin, the deputy finance minister of the Russian Federation, stepped from the elevator platform, shadowed by two grim security guards. Igor immediately recognized them, but not the special forces operator in full fatigues, cradling a tricked-out sniper rifle with a starlight scope. *Undoubtedly the best long-range shot in Mother Russia.*

Zamyatin smiled like a shark as he approached, speaking in a casual, chummy way that froze Igor's blood. "Igor Arsenyevich, I thought you were afraid of heights." He used Igor's patronymic—his father's name—something he'd never done before. And never would again, Igor was sure.

"I beg your pardon, sir," Igor said, holding out his hands to show they were empty. "I only stepped out for a breath of fresh air. This night has been very stressful, making sure there were no mistakes, which there weren't..." He knew he was babbling but couldn't help it.

Zamyatin's cold smile grew wider. He and his men approached, crowding Igor back up onto the helipad.

"Completely understandable. I, too, want no mistakes. And it is always good to face one's fears. Do you know what I fear? It is but one thing."

Igor had a pretty good idea, but he only shook his head.

"It should be obvious. A man in my position, who has dared all, fears only betrayal. To lose all I have struggled to accomplish, and because of a little man with small dreams and outsized fears."

Igor could only shrug expansively, head down, absorbing this pearl of wisdom, ashamed that he could not begin to apply it to himself. "Forgive me for taking you away from the presentation…"

"Not at all," Zamyatin said with a dismissive wave. "I have brought it with me. I believe I owe you this special time. You know, Igor… I have long admired you." He donned a pair of black leather driving gloves as he strolled around the helipad. "A man of few questions, a man who simply makes things happen. In this, you are like our dear friend… our *Pakhan*."

Igor swallowed hard. The Avtorityet only paid compliments as a preamble to punishment, and there was no higher compliment than invoking the Pakhan—the *Krestniy Otets*, boss of bosses.

"Russia looks at him and sees a man of destiny," Zamyatin continued, "a man who writes history, a man restoring our strength. But the world, the West, sees only a thug with no real vision for the future. When he falls, they think Russia will fall, and good riddance.

"Those who know him realize he has worked hard to entertain the West's error. He has always been a pawn of Russia, a tool stronger than the others, tempered by fire and ice, but a tool nonetheless, one that Russia wields to build herself anew."

As he spoke, Zamyatin's voice became ever louder, grander. The howling wind itself seemed to take notice, calming as the Avtorityet herded Igor towards the far edge of the helipad.

"They say that it's more important how you correct mistakes than the mistakes themselves. What do you think?" Zamyatin's dead eyes bored into him.

Now it comes…

"No opinion, friend Igor?" Zamyatin prodded. "No matter. We can test this theory, see if it's true." Now he spread his arms out, in full orator mode.

"Only God and his angels can unmake what is being built

here." He seemed to gesture toward the two cranes, the tower beneath their feet, like a patriarch bestowing a blessing.

"So, I ask you, Igor *Arsenyevich*, and I beg you not to lie to me... Are you an angel? A *fallen* one, perhaps?"

Igor simply stared into Zamyatin's eyes in an ecstasy of terror and dread. He'd known from the moment the Avtorityet stepped off the elevator, that he was beyond hope. *It's a strange taste, the breath of stolen air. Strange to feel one's heart beating when one is already dead.*

"Sir, please let me explain... This is all a mistake."

Zamyatin shook his head sadly. "I only wish there was time, comrade. But I suppose I can give you one last chance." The Avtorityet smiled, and for a moment, Igor believed in this chance. He would make the most of it. Convince his boss nothing untoward had ever occurred. Or confess everything. Give up Razbit. He would enjoy that bottle of champagne, the girl too...

But then he looked around and saw that the rooftop was crowded with people. The VIPs surrounded the helipad, intently watching this demonstration of the Avtorityet's keen management style. Igor saw Feliks among them, staring at him as if to say, *Who's the kick-ass tech guy now,* brodyaga?

The Boss's favorite girlfriend, Miss Urals, sashayed towards Igor. She carried a magnum of champagne; the cheap stuff, this time. But she held it up with such a sparkling smile that Igor let himself imagine she was offering it to him. That all was forgiven.

"Prove you are not a fallen angel," Zamyatin said.

Igor opened his mouth, though he had no words. The Avtorityet's gloved fist clipped his chin and Igor bit his tongue. Then he was seized by the same security goons who had hassled him all day, even the one who was on his team, and before he could scream, they tossed him off the roof.

For a heartbeat, Igor seemed to dance on the gusting winds. Like an angel. But then he was simply falling. The dream was over.

The wind buffeted him with invisible fists, flattening his features into a mask, stealing a long, horrible howl from his skinned-back lips. It was worse than his worst night terrors. Endless. And he couldn't even close his eyes, the wind prying them wide. Through streaming tears, he could see the lights of Moscow, its buildings reaching up like fingers. Below, the brilliant but cold halogen lamps of the construction site, the flashing lights of the security patrol cars speeding away through the open gates, the tiny dot directly beneath him that resolved into a matchbox, then a shoebox, and finally as an oversized refuse bin half-full of scrap metal and plastic.

It took Igor eleven seconds to fall the first three hundred meters. Time enough to reflect, to pray, to beg or curse God, to vow revenge, search for some consolation, or simply die of fright. Or maybe to believe he was an angel, after all. But he kept accelerating.

And then, a miracle—

The tumbling had stopped. Igor found himself splayed out, lying prone on the wind. He felt the terrifying descent slowing, if not arrested, by his body's position. His clothes bulged with trapped air; his cupped hands were like rudders. He began to swim on the violent night sky.

Igor struggled against the terminal wind resistance, striving to bring himself in line with the horizon, to find that providence that would allow him to soar away. What would the Avtorityet make of that? Watching him borne aloft, landing safely on the ground, an angel after all. Perhaps then the Boss would realize all his schemes would be similarly undone. And who was the architect of his ruin...

But wait...

Igor was defiantly screaming Zamyatin's name when, traveling at fifty-four meters per second, his body entered the dumpster with nearly a quarter million foot-pounds of force. An image of his mother flared in his mind just before his body burst, torn apart by the metal debris.

The assembled guests on the roof only faintly heard the bin ring like a gong with the impact. They clapped anyway. Even the Iranians and North Koreans were fully engaged now.

"I wanted you to witness this, my friends," Zamyatin told his rapt audience. "I know it's cold up here, but you must see that none will dare interfere with what we have created. None will know our name, until all the world speaks it as they would the name of God. We call this mighty edifice the Cow. A simple name, bucolic, but with it, we shall milk the world, wringing every last drop from her shriveled tits!"

Knowing from experience how to shatter a real magnum, Miss Urals unleashed a two-hand major league swing to smash the large bottle on the lip of the helipad, christening the tower to hearty applause. The guests then retreated to the elevator—it was fucking cold up there.

Feliks became aware of the bad taste festering in his mouth like a poison frog. He spat his guilty feelings downwind and followed the crowd toward the lift. *Poor stupid Igor,* thought Feliks. *How could he think I didn't know?*

In the distance, the returning helicopters were like a string of stars floating in the night sky.

Miss Urals snuggled under the deputy finance minister's arm. He was beaming.

Igor had indeed made sure that the presentation was perfect.

FIRST MOVEMENT

"MONEY, NOT MORALITY, IS THE PRINCIPLE
OF COMMERCE OF CIVILIZED NATIONS."

—THOMAS JEFFERSON

ONE

Click the link, look at the screen, and you're falling—
You're sprinting across an industrial rooftop, springing from chimney to ventilator hood, leaping over jagged holes in rusty sheet metal, scrambling for the edge and dropping to a fire escape, then soaring out into space over an alley, tumbling onto a steeply pitched roof...

You're free-climbing the concrete stanchion of a suspension bridge, attacking the vertical surface with naked fingers, scrabbling for seams and cracks until the pillar terminates under the cowl of the abutment. Pivoting and kicking away from the bridge like a spider, you hurl into the air and dangle from thrumming steel cables high above expressway traffic. A thundering commuter train passes overhead...

You're riding the El over Canal Street, but on the roof—doing cartwheels and handstands, high-fiving your friends. Then you flatten against the graffiti-strewn deck, whooping with nervous laughter as it enters a tunnel...

Running from two cops on a busy downtown street. You juke right, vaulting over a trash can. One cop makes a diving tackle, but he goes down in a flurry of White Castle wrappers as you slice through the crowd waiting at the curb. Sliding over the hood of a cab, you reach the opposite curb a split second ahead of a crosstown bus...

Popping a manhole cover, dropping into a sewer, shining your flashlight on a wall mural more beautiful than anything you've ever seen in a museum...

Hacking the rooftop LED screen on a financial giant's Wall Street tower so your video message blazes out, loud as any billboard overlooking the stampeding bull statue. Now disguised as a swaggering, entitled stockbroker, you slip out amid the delicious chaos...

You're zip-lining off a skyscraper. Wind and acceleration fold you into a bullet. Racing over a blur of city blocks, speeding towards a high-rise parking structure, you follow your crew dropping off the line, popping parachutes, fatal velocity arrested. They swing weightlessly on the night wind.

But *your* chute becomes tangled, collapses into a nylon shroud. You plummet, spinning fast toward the unforgiving asphalt below...

Michael Hong squeezed his eyes shut. Underneath his feet the rocking floor fell away and a harness seemed to lift him up on a ripping wind. Only to crumple, sending him tumbling into empty space again...

Fighting the waking nightmare, Michael asked himself *The Questions*, said the words that would arrest a full-blown panic attack.

Where are you?

I'm on a train... *inside* a train...

Who are you with?

I'm alone, but I'm good. I'm good...

What do you see?

He opened his eyes. Soupy gray dawn broke through stacked June gloom clouds over Millennium Park and the Art

Institute. No commuters were staring at him. Nobody could hear his heart hammering against his sternum.

The video finished playing on his phone. FURIES/ GREATEST.HITS: *Watch Again?*

A drop of sweat ran down the bridge of his nose and spattered on the screen. He thumbed back out to the text directory. An unknown sender with an unlisted Vimeo account; surely an instant *Delete*. But he was hovering over the *Reply* button. Whoever sent it must have serious game to bypass his spam filters. A moment later he pushed the message into the holding folder for unwanted bits of reality that he didn't want to deal with yet couldn't fully delete.

Closing his eyes again, drawing stability from the rocking of the train, he took stock of the situation. The jerky, head-mounted GoPro images, the dizzying speed, the total disregard for safety or gravity, would give anyone vertigo, but that wasn't the problem. Only a lunatic with a death wish would do stuff like this.

That lunatic used to be *you*... Michael Hong.

Get a grip, he told himself. Look at it like a programming bug. Go over it like lines of code. Ask yourself the questions to get the answer. *Don't panic.*

Who sent this?

Who made this?

Why did they send it to you?

Who *knows*?

Asking the questions didn't put him at ease because he had no answers. Anyone could've done it, of course. The videos were easily found online, shared to death these last few years. No mystery there... except for the last one.

They never shared *that* one. For obvious reasons. Only one person could have uploaded it, but Michael couldn't believe he'd do it.

Couldn't you, though?

Looking around the train, he noticed several people staring

at him now. He took refuge in his phone. But still, he was unwilling to look at it. It could open up and swallow him if he did.

TWO

The gym was gridlocked, every machine on the floor churning, anonymous bodies drifting from one station to the next like self-assembling robots. Michael was crushing the rowing machine, jacking up his heart rate and working his core before meeting his trainer. But his mind was a million miles from his workout.

Most likely, the video didn't mean anything. That was the simplest explanation. He would ignore it… until he couldn't. What if it meant he'd been sold out? The thought turned his earlier anxiety into righteous anger. He threw himself harder into the rowing, surging ahead of his neighbors' lockstep dance floor rhythm.

Trainer Curt clocked in for his insurance-mandated legwork torture session and Michael was soon too busy to dwell. But he hit a wall halfway through the workout, all the muscles in his right leg turning to liquid fire, refusing to work.

"Come on," Curt barked. "Fight through it."

Michael stopped mid-set. Clamped in the elliptical's grip, his right leg quivered and twitched.

"That's it?" Curt shook his head in disgust.

"My leg," Michael said, wincing at the weakness in his voice.

"Gotta work through. Quit being such a pussy bitch."

The crude psychology almost worked. "Yeah, yeah," Michael muttered, but he started heading for the showers.

"Good effort," called Curt, sensibly dropping the drill-sergeant act. "Same time next week…"

Limping out of the shower, Michael's leg sang grand opera all the way to the locker room. Leaning on the wall, he planted his foot on a bench and kneaded the grievous bulge of scar tissue on the inside of his calf.

He'd been less than thirty meters off the ground when he fell, but it was like being hit by a car going fifty miles per hour. Compound fracture of right tibia and fibula; shattered patella, replaced with ceramic and steel inserts; spiral fracture of femur. Cracked tailbone and lacerated rectum. Three surgeries, two months in traction, four months in a body cast, and six months and counting of grueling PT.

He was lucky to walk without a cane, and doubly-lucky not to have had a colostomy. His physical therapist had admitted that Michael would never have full function again. Of course, he was dedicated to proving her wrong, but it was becoming harder to keep the faith.

In the lobby, he glanced at the wall-mounted flatscreen playing a viral helmet-cam video of a wingsuit flyer swooping down the canyon of a metropolitan center, soaring like something never meant to touch the ground. He caught himself staring until the streamlined form shot a narrow gap between twin skyscrapers and finally pulled the rip cord, the tapered ramjet chute unfurling. After the flyer was safely on the ground Michael, let out his breath and hobbled out of the gym and into the bustling street.

With the foot traffic's urgent tempo prodding him along, Michael jammed in his earbuds. Despite the raucous dystopian din of Negativland's *Escape From Noise* album in his ears, the rumble and mutter of the street forced itself into his thoughts, leaving him isolated but never alone. Another mote of worry in a rushing torrent, Michael tried to let himself be absorbed, but something always pulled him out.

A deeper noise was overwhelming him. Tingling vibrations crept up his unsteady legs. Hot, dirty wind rose around him. The roar of an elevated train swelled in his ears, bearing him away as he fought to untangle his fouled parachute before the pavement came rushing in...

Michael stood frozen at the foot of the steps, struggling to control his breathing, his fear, his reality. Ill-tempered commuters colliding with him, he fell in step with the racing mob, letting it sweep him up to the platform and onto the train, its endless, mindless pressure carrying him away from himself. Still, he knew that one way or the other, he was going to have to face this before it swept him away for good.

But that meant talking to the last person on Earth who would understand. And that would suck major.

Making his way to his desk on the development floor of Macrosync, Michael was increasingly aware that this flimsy startup was nine-tenths hype and vaporware, the rest old-fashioned corporate stinginess. All the young coders and number crunchers toiling away around him were freelancers, free from the burdens of health-care enrollments, 401k plans or vacation time. In spite of Michael's pivotal role in the project, he was no closer to clinching a long-term, ironclad employment contract. The company promised that everything was going to change once the app launched, but these assurances only stirred up the blood everyone was smelling in the water.

Logging on to the company server, Michael dutifully checked his email and reviewed the dozen open tabs on his screen. After plotting out the day's goals on the in-house productivity app, really an employee monitoring program, he felt his phone vibrate. A new voicemail awaited.

"Good morning, Mr. Hong, this is Rich Weka from Belmont Student Loan Consolidators. Please return my call at your earliest convenience so we can discuss the repayment options regarding your student loan—"

He frowned, deleting the message, cuing up one that he'd somehow missed. *Must've come in during my post-workout anxiety attack.*

"Heeeey. It's Maddie. Just checking in. Haven't talked to you in a while. Scoped out this building yesterday. Nothing crazy, just an old-school place-hack. Too bad you're not here. I think you'd like it. Anyway... hit me up."

Long after the message ended, Michael sat lost in thought. No way this was a coincidence. No word from either her or Cam in almost six months, and Maddie's breezy tone sounding as forced as his loan officer. He bit his thumbnail, eyeing the *Call Back* button, only to crank up his music and retreat to a window filled with lines of code.

Despite all the bullshit, the job offered a kind of solace, because the job was basically all numbers. And numbers were reliable, delivering the results you put into them. They never crumbled under stress or buckled under pressure. *They weren't a fucking parachute.*

But today the numbers only held Michael's eyes for a minute or so before he felt someone staring at him. *What the hell?* Looking across the jungle of cubicles, he saw a beautiful woman with glossy black hair in a loose ponytail and striking Arabic features, maybe ten years older than him. She was perched on one of the chairs where the prospective hires sat. With an open laptop on her knee, sporting an understated charcoal-gray blazer, pencil skirt and a cream-colored blouse, the woman presented a commanding air that was both focused and casual.

She'll probably get whatever job she's angling for, Michael imagined, and hoped that it wasn't his. He saw her fritter away at her laptop or glance up as various workers or visitors passed by; all of her attention seemed to be on... *him*. WTF?

Then she caught Michael staring and tipped him a wink.

He turned back to his work, grateful to have a place to hide.

THREE

Cam Buckley planted his cleats with aggressive confidence. The other golfers laid down their drivers to watch him wind up and smash his dayglow orange ball off the roof of the forty-story London House tower. It sailed into the brilliant early summer sky, soaring high over East Wacker Drive and the wide green gutter of the Chicago River. Cam's audience *oohed* and *aahhed* when his ball smacked a patio table on the twelfth-floor observation deck of the monolithic building some three hundred yards away.

"Trump Tower! You see that?" Cam's entourage hoisted their glasses and cheered, then returned to their own driving, firing the balls into the river with varying levels of skill. So far, pelting the tour boat moored on the north bank was the closest anyone else had come to beating his record.

It's fun to have fun, but you have to know how, Cam reminded himself, quoting his guru, the philosopher Theodore Geisel, better known as Dr. Seuss.

There seemed to be no shortage of newly minted and fairly dull one-percenters who had no idea how to play with their new toys. To service their self-image as genius bad-boys, they reveled in whatever juvenile outlaw activity Cam came up with, like today's golfing on the roof of a building housing the Turkish consulate, a boutique hotel, and a sensor imagery corporate headquarters.

When they'd groused about the place being too safe, he'd told them about the photographer who fell to his death here while taking pictures only last year, which made them feel a little more like daredevils. That Cam was the only black guy any of them knew socially probably didn't hurt, either.

LH Rooftop, the upscale penthouse cocktail spot at their backs, was shut down for the break between brunch and dinner, but he'd charmed the manager into opening the bar on the sly to keep his playboy daycare lubricated.

One of Cam's less inspired side hustles, but it kept him solvent while he cultivated more promising ventures. His time with the Crew already seemed so long ago, but soon he could put aside all this dude-bro nonsense and get back to being what he was always meant to be. Speaking of which, his phone started to quiver in the pocket of his linen chinos.

"Mario. *Qué pasa, guey*?" Cam answered.

The voice on the line was like a hornet in a soda can.

"Calm down," Cam cut in. "What do you mean, I'm 'out of money'? Explain how that's possible. And do it slowly."

The voice slowed down, but the volume and pitch went up.

"Of course, I'm not worried—that's what I over-pay *you* for. Well, you're obviously not skilled at your job."

The guy next to him—Chuck or Chet or Chad, he honestly couldn't remember—sent his hot pink ball soaring and hit the T on the façade of Trump Tower. Cam dutifully gave him a fist bump. "Dude, nice follow-through. Seriously, bro. Respect."

He let the warmth drain completely out of his voice as he turned back to his call. "What? No, I'm here. Hang on, I'm going to put you on speaker."

Shrugging the tension out of his shoulders, arms, and hands, he knelt and rested the phone against the tee hammered into the coping of the roof.

Mario continued his report. "...Unless you can generate

immediate and significant cashflow, we're not going to survive long enough to launch."

Chet and Chad were watching, slurping their Mai Tais. Now was not the time to go off-brand.

"OK, well... let me hit you with something." Cam stood up, raising his voice so everyone looked up from their own tees. "And this is just, you know... spit-balling."

"I'm listening," Mario replied.

Cam swung the club, putting every ounce of his trim and toned 165 pounds behind it. Epic follow-through. The phone turned to a spray of sparkling plastic and glass, a pinch of fairy dust settling over the honking traffic below.

"*Bro!*" Chad or Chet crowed.

"*You're a maniac!*" Chet or Chad shouted.

Trying to remember which of these dumbasses gave him the "hot inside tip" that just gutted his portfolio, Cam graciously accepted their high fives. Before the round of drinks had come, he'd schemed five different ways to get revenge, or at least righteous justice.

FOUR

M addie Acosta was late for work at 8:30 p.m.

Very late, she reminded herself, striding into the lobby of Aon Center. Sipping a latte with a weary but determined expression that complemented her smart H&M skirt-blazer combo and Saucony running shoes, Maddie had used this flavor of corporate camouflage before. *I'm being dragged back to the office to put in unpaid overtime on a hellish HR audit, so if you try to stop me, I'm going to raise Hell and then start rage-crying and you'll really be sorry...*

The security guard picked up what she was putting down, smiling briefly as Maddie steamed past the front desk, then turning back to the sports page and the various monitors. Rubber soles squeaking on the Carrara marble floor, she eyed the grand glass elevators in the northwest corner of the lobby.

The new observation deck atop the eighty-three-story tower was not yet open to the public, making the gala that was in full swing there all the more exclusive. The two nearest elevators were shuttling the local glitterati, their access overseen by a corporate hostess with a tablet and two guards in serviceable sharkskin suits, taking names and checking IDs.

Across from the elevator banks, Maddie scoped it all out without appearing to notice any of it, clearly submerged in her own problems. Few of even the most renowned urbex boys were any good at this aspect of the game. Fearless and nimble they might be, but even if you took the hoodies and suspicious climbing gear away, they still presented as sketchy hood-rats up to no good. Sometimes it was fun to play hide-and-seek, but whenever she could, Maddie relished looking her adversary right in the eye and becoming invisible and simply showing them exactly what they expected. The power of profiling; few could resist it.

She hurried to fall in step with another, similarly attired woman who took a hologram-stamped glittery smartcard out of her handbag as she approached the bank of elevators. The doors whispered open and the woman stepped aside to let Maddie go first, then tapped the reader with her card and punched the button for the eightieth floor.

"Same floor. Right on."

The woman threw her a skeptical look. Smiling with gratitude, Maddie made a show of fishing for her own keycard. "Amoco loves hiring temps for all the dirty jobs, right?"

The woman bit her lip and nodded. Maddie knew that Amoco was using accounting temps to carry out algorithm-based solutions to thinning the herd of mid-level executives; more humane, according to HR specialists. The woman was at least ten years older than Maddie and was probably burning the midnight oil to stay ahead of the axe. The ride passed in silence and the women exited on eighty without comment.

Maddie watched her go, silently wishing her luck. Ducking into the stairs, she jogged up two flights to the locked door at the top. The NO ROOF ACCESS warning proved wrong—the alarm easily disabled by tugging on a loose wire. There was always some dedicated smoker on one of the top floors with a firm preference for a rooftop view, rather than a long elevator ride down to the street.

Stepping out onto the roof, Maddie enjoyed a deep breath of the rushing wind off the river, and beyond it, Lake Michigan.

She took out her camera and snapped a few pictures with her toes perched on the edge, savoring the rush of the vertigo-inducing perspective.

She hadn't been up on Big Stan—as native Chicagoans still referred to the old Standard Oil Building—in a couple years. Not since the Furies. It felt weird, but good. Certainly, she'd never experienced it like this... Looking around the roof for cameras, she slipped out of her blazer and skirt, then tugged her blouse down until the hem touched her knees, revealing a smart, if slightly wrinkled black D&G cocktail dress. Then she cursed, forced to grab cover behind a ventilator chimney.

A pair of security guards came around the massive bank of air purifying and exchange units. They were definitely looking for somebody. *Maybe for me.*

Flattened against the exhaust ducts, Maddie was close enough to hear the pair commiserating about the Cubs' dismal home stand last weekend. A flashlight beam swept her feet. Her toes were still curled when she heard their footsteps recede into the windswept murmur of the city far below.

Moving from cover to cover on stocking feet, Maddie crossed to the northwest corner of the tower, where the observation deck loomed over the rest of the roof. Looking over her shoulder for the rent-a-cops, she threw herself at the marble wall and effortlessly scaled it, then stepped over the waist-high glass railing.

The well-heeled crowd was thin at this end of the observation deck, but she only had time to drop a pair of secondhand Jimmy Choo heels on the floor and dig her ruined stockings into them before a waiter appeared with flutes of champagne. Smiling, she took two.

"Can't seem to find my date anywhere!" Maddie said, before hustling off to mingle with some of the richest stiffs in Chicago. Mixing with the small group that encircled a stunning blonde, a local TV newsreader, she checked her bag and tucked the Sauconys out of sight. *Time to get to work.*

FIVE

When everyone else had finally gone home, Michael saved his work to the server and looked up from his laptop.

Mystery Lady was still there. Nearly every time he'd checked, she was reading a book or pecking at her phone, and if she wasn't, she reappeared within a few minutes with a fresh cup of coffee or plain water.

Eventually, the game had worn thin and Michael had to put her out of his mind, working doggedly, if not single-mindedly. But vague feelings of guilt began to penetrate his concentration. He couldn't begin to pin down quite why he should be so bothered.

But with the other odd developments today, it was too much to ignore. A hoary chestnut of wisdom from a James Bond novel swam up in his thoughts when she finally stood up and began to cross the empty room towards his desk. *Once is happenstance, twice is coincidence, but three times is enemy action.*

But who was the enemy? Even in his wildest imagination, he couldn't feature a cop coming after him. After all, he was a law-abiding taxpayer, a contributor to society. Nobody could prove any different. *And even if they could...?*

Besides, she didn't look like a cop or a federal agent, but maybe somebody who played one on TV. Her caramel complexion and subtly tinted hair looked well cared-for, but there was something in her eyes, in the way she moved, that betrayed a familiarity with danger. She had a *readiness* about her, a sort of glamour that Michael rarely saw in people who hadn't stared eternity in the face. When she finally reached his desk, her bashful smile brightened and her open hands came up, making a big show of not carrying a weapon.

He offered her a noncommittal look and tried to appear busy. But he knew he was done, and it showed. Sweat rings under his arms, circles under his eyes, and he couldn't imagine what his breath must smell like.

"What are you working on?" She hovered behind him, close enough for an unfamiliar herbal fragrance to push away the burnt-coffee and stale ozone of the workspace.

Her accent was posh British, at once precise and lyrical. Totally intimidating. Perfect for bending service workers to one's will.

"What?" he managed.

She raised her voice with a still-brighter smile. "I said, what-are-you-working-on? What is your job here?"

"Oh uh, just an app, you know. Cross-platform type... thing..." He shrugged and looked back at the screen, but he didn't need to see her reflected over the opaque wall of code, now she was in his head. "Supposed to be this 'game changer' for dating."

"Dating. Sounds interesting," she said, clearly not caring if he knew she was lying to his face as easily as reading a menu.

"Oh, it's not. You got me there." He winced. She laughed a little, which Michael found helped a lot. *I am so screwed.*

"So, you're a coder. That makes sense. Seems to me like all you freelancers are either writers or coders. Sort of the same thing, I guess."

Was she flirting with him? He could almost never tell. "Sure, yeah. Coders are just as creative. Can be. Like regular writers. The good ones..."

Her shoulders went up and her hands fanned out expressively. "I can't read code, but I assume that you are one of the good ones."

"So, what do *you* do? When not waiting around."

She cracked a smile. "I'm a writer, as well. But with words. Though words are a form of code, I suppose." Michael winced. He knew this wasn't just a random encounter with a nice stranger. He tried to make it clear he still had work to do. *Time to wrap it up*.

"Amara Massaid," she said, holding out her hand. Reflectively, Michael took it.

"Michael Hong." The moment dragged, and he wondered if he'd have to explain why he didn't quite look like a Hong. Some people had to be told that he was mixed-race, that his father was second-generation Chinese American... Then he realized she was waiting for him to talk, trapping his hand in hers until he did. "So, you write what, like stories? Anything I might have read?"

"Perhaps." She surrendered his hand, but blinked slowly, holding his eyes. "I'm a journalist. I actually just came back from Al-Raqqa."

Enemy action.

Michael balked as his internal alarms went off, opting to deflect until she came clean. "Oh yeah, that's in uh, Michigan, right?"

She laughed, giving it a bit more than the dumb joke deserved. "Syria, actually. The civil war there has fallen off the world's radar, but it's still very much a thing..."

He felt a little foolish, so he tried again. "Isn't that like the most dangerous place in the world to be a journalist?"

She tried to shrug, but her shoulders stayed tense. Eyes darting away, searching the darkest corners of the office with a haunted expression. "Not my first rodeo. I spent six months of my rookie year in the DRC, and I covered the proxy war in Libya after that."

"Doesn't it scare you, traveling to places like that?" He felt a twinge of guilt at his insensitivity, but relief that they weren't talking about him. This woman faced the kind of real peril that made his adventures with the Furies look like a frivolous, narcissistic hobby. In spite of himself, he was a bit fascinated.

"Once you've been there—seen the elephant, as they say— you're never the same... but I had to get the story. I guess you could say my curiosity outweighs my sense of self-preservation. I mean, it's all programming, isn't it?"

Intrigued, he leaned closer, meeting her gaze. "What is?"

"Fear. It's genetically hard-wired. Factory setting."

"Fear keeps us alive."

"Yeah, it can," she allowed. "But it can also paralyze."

"Deer in headlights," he muttered, feeling a bit like one now.

"One hundred percent." Her expression brightened as she dropped the other shoe. "I'm working on this piece right now. Young urban post-millennials. Like you."

"Hate it already," he said, with less of a humorous spin than he meant to.

"I know, right? But that's the thing... Millennials aren't afraid. They literally think they can do anything. Like these kids I'm writing about. Type T. Thrill-seeker-adrenaline-junkie-types, know what I mean? But they don't scale mountains... they scale cities. Like it's all their own private jungle gym."

Michael's tension came back big-time. The whole day—the mysterious video, the passive stalking—began to make sense. If she noticed his discomfort, she was too wrapped up in her spiel to let on.

"I mean, I get it, I guess," she went on. "Why be the ten thousandth guy on top of Everest when you can be the first to summit the Burj Khalifa?"

Now it was his turn to tense up and look away. "Sounds dangerous."

"I think it's cool. There was this one crew, called themselves

Les Furies, for no particular reason since they weren't French, but they killed it. One time, they climbed this financial building in New York and hacked its LCD ad-wall. Instead of spewing the usual corporate propaganda, they had it playing a loop from Renoir's *Rules of the Game*. You know, the hunting scene where the rich people kill all the rabbits? So amazing, yeah."

She had his number and was just playing with him. Now he had to steel himself against reacting to the memories she was stirring up. *You're falling—*

"And they didn't get caught. Supposedly, they dressed up as civic services workers and walked right out. That video got a million hits in like a day. Surprised you never saw it."

He took a swallow of the only fluid on his desk, the cold, gray dregs of his last coffee. It stuck in his throat. "So, what happened to them?"

"That's what I've been trying to find out. Three-and-a-half million followers on socials and then they just evaporated. People talk, of course; that one of them fell, got killed. Or they're all rotting in foreign jail somewhere. Been trying to track them... haven't had any luck." Her eyes caught a glint of light off his monitor and turned it into a mischievous twinkle. "Until now."

He let the dramatic pause draw out, waiting for her to elaborate, for the right words to throw her off the trail. He only managed a lame smile. "That's quite a story."

Michael snapped his laptop shut and stowed it in his satchel, coiled up the power supply and slipped his arms into his windbreaker.

"So that's it? We're done?" she said.

He waved his hand at the empty office. "Early day."

He felt her eyes on his back all the way to the elevators, but she didn't follow him. *Bro, you sure put her in her place*, he told himself. He only used "bro" in his head when he was really pissed at himself.

Despite lingering pain in his bad leg, Michael took the stairs, hoping to work off the nervous tension. He burst into the lobby just as Amara got off the elevator. Passing her, he shoved through the revolving door. The wind shoved back, shockingly cold for June. He walked into it, pulling his lips back in a grimace. He could catch the northbound bus on Dearborn to the train back to his apartment in Greektown, but it wasn't due for almost ten minutes, and he decided against getting buttonholed at the bus stop.

She trailed a few steps behind him, shouting over the traffic noise and wind. "You guys were at the top of your game, but then you quit. Why?"

He kept walking, ignoring her, trying not to draw attention. His eyes darted to the row of dodgy rental scooters. He briefly considered making his getaway on one, but with his luck, his card would be declined.

"They changed the regs around buildings in practically every major city because of your crew."

He turned around, walking backwards across East Madison, arms up in a placating gesture. "That's not me," he said, tilting his hands emphatically to push her away. "Sorry. No comment."

Amara finally stopped chasing him, muttering "fuck" under her breath, her words cutting through the street noise to reach him as he turned away.

SIX

Michael picked up the pace, heading north up Dearborn, but he barely saw where he was going. All the implied threats and nagging enigmas of the day receded behind the real question. *Why did I react to being outed that way?*

Would it be the worst thing ever if the world discovered that he used to roll with an infamous urbex crew? All they'd be on the hook for were a few misdemeanor trespassing and safety violations. Any one of the companies they'd pranked could've done what Amara had; ferreted out their true identities and sued their smug, self-righteous butts off. But no one had come looking; clearly, no one really cared at this point, if they ever did. All the things they'd done had gotten a lot of attention, but it was fleeting—they'd never really changed anything.

Still, Michael had abundant cause to dread going public. He wasn't running for political office or anything, but his gig as a freelance coder was tenuous at best. Though he preferred it to the full commitment of a salary job, did he really want to risk what little stability he had? His insurance provider would certainly sue if it came to light that he'd incurred his grievous injuries in a BASE-jumping stunt; not falling off his roof while trying to fix a satellite dish, like he'd claimed at the ER. He might even be prosecuted for fraud.

And there were plenty of "respectable" people in the BASE and urbex communities who despised outlaw show-offs like the F.U. Crew for bringing the wrong kind of controversy to their sports, and used shunning, heory, vandalism and even "blanket party" beatings to punish them.

No, the reason he balked was exactly the reason anyone else would've proudly owned up to it. Cashed in with book and movie deals, maybe a sweet gig as a Hollywood stunt consultant. He was never in it for the notoriety, the perks, the groupie action.

Then why did you do it?

It was a question he was even less prepared to answer.

The Furies used to talk endlessly about the rush and the freedom, and "value" of their political pranks. The "statements" they were making. But Michael thought he was doing it to explore the world and find himself. He'd learned more than he ever wanted to know about both, just in that last disastrous outing alone.

When he saw those videos this morning, his other life captured, distilled down to a super-cut highlight reel, he'd felt locked out of it, unable to relate to the wild-eyed maniac with the camera strapped to his head. That last clip had done the trick, though, putting him right back to where it all went wrong. That part, he couldn't escape, no matter how he tried.

He only then realized that he was running.

Crossing East Washington like a wide receiver going deep to snag a pass, he darted through the sleepwalking knots of pedestrians, moving so much faster than the grinding rhythm of the foot and vehicle traffic. He jumped the curb at a dead run, pushing himself harder than he'd let Curt push him at the gym. His perceptions narrowed to a tactical scale, plotting a path through the obstacle course of the street. The pain of his leg fell away, his brain concentrating on the mission in front of him.

Smiling now, he juked left to dodge a large, loud party spilling out of a sidewalk café, pivoting and springing off a mailbox and hitting the sidewalk sprinting. Someone behind him shouted, "Holy crap, did you see that?" and someone else yelled, "Go get 'em, Spider-Man!"

He reached the next corner and turned east onto Randolph. He let himself run the next couple blocks so fast his mind closed off the past and admitted only the narrowest window on the future. The next obstacle, the next opportunity. Crossing State, Wabash and then Michigan Avenue, he threaded a zigzag path between honking cars and crossed into Millennium Park.

A gaggle of cyclists cut Michael off at Millennium Monument Plaza, forcing him to either stop or dive over a park bench. Long-suppressed reflexes chose the latter, but when he dug in with his right leg, it just gave out on him. No snap or tear; it just wasn't there. His unsupported weight sprawled into the bench and cartwheeled over it to face-plant on the lawn.

Someone laughed and took a picture. "And the agony of defeat!" More snarky snickers followed.

Michael sat up, torn between angrily cursing the passerby and their ancient cultural references, and joining in their laughter. He was sore, but he still felt pretty good. The run had purged his nervous energy, and his lingering doubts, as well.

He lay back on the grass, looking up at the handful of stars bright enough to shine through the city's gnarly light pollution. What he'd told Amara was the truth. *That "Type-T" guy in the Furies, that guy in the video clips, it's not me. Not anymore... if it ever was.*

Back then, he'd only just joined a parkour group that practiced here in this park. That was when he first met the ones who became his best friends, his crew. He learned a lot from them, but what did he really take away from his time in the Furies, besides that he couldn't cut it?

He recalled their first jaunt together at Chicago's notorious Damen Silos. How he'd almost fallen into a smokestack and broken his neck, telling himself he was never going to do this crazy shit again. But then...

Never mind. You've got a job to do, a life to live. Let the old one go. He picked himself up, brushed the dirt and leaves off his chinos and picked up his satchel. It was barely in his hand when someone swooped down on him as if on silent wings and took it from him.

Pulled off balance, he staggered a few steps, staring at the retreating mugger in total disbelief. Then took off after him.

"Stop, damn it!" he shouted. "That guy mugged me!" The other people in the plaza jumped out of the thief's way as he circled the fountain and the colonnade, hurtled over a bench and took off under the trees.

Save your breath. Then he was moving too fast for thought, the heat in his muscles turning to electricity. His lungs, still outraged from the punishing run, seemed to expand to fill his chest. His brain surged with adrenaline; his perceptions deepened.

The mugger wore a hoodie and track pants, good cross-training sneakers and climbing gloves. This last detail pinged his suspicion even as he dogged the mugger's steps through four lanes of speeding traffic across Randolph.

The mugger juked right and ran up Stetson, jumping the hood of an oncoming yellow cab, going over the roof and leaping off the trunk before the outraged cabbie could hit the brakes or honk his horn.

Stunned by the skill he was seeing, Michael still managed to cut in front of the stalled cab and follow the mugger across Aon Center Plaza. A more ornate imitation of the Millennium Monument, complete with a grand fountain and fancy Italian-style brickwork, the plaza seemed a weak choice to try to lose him, for it also boasted very hands-on security systems and high visibility to CPD patrols. Still, the mugger charged north, skirting along the esplanade that encircled Old Stan, clutching Michael's satchel under one arm like a football.

Michael noticed the mugger's head swivel right just a moment before he turned east, letting Michael gain a few steps on him. The thief cleared the skyscraper's base, then turned and launched himself at the sheer wall, scrambling ten feet up the city-dingy marble facing and hurling himself at a projecting single-story turret that jutted out of the northwest corner of the skyscraper.

Racing straight into the wall himself, Michael could only try to follow.

He hit the wall and dug in with his left foot on the ground-floor windowsill, converting his forward momentum into much more costly vertical lift. The mugger had managed to spring up onto the turret one-handed, but Michael barely got his center of mass over the edge before it started to rise into the air underneath them.

The mugger threw out a hand and pulled Michael up onto the roof of the glass elevator. It ascended so quickly, Michael felt his blood slosh out of his brain and pool in his rubbery legs.

Watching the street fall away so precipitously, Michael scooted backwards away from the edge, nearly hitting the speeding wall of the building as it rushed past.

The mugger grinned, teeth shining out of the shadow of his hood. Beneath them, the elevator continued to accelerate, the city dwindling at their feet.

Gasping for breath, Michael held out his fist to bump knuckles. "Damn it, Cam. Couldn't you just call?"

SEVEN

"You've still got it, bro," Cam said, smiling and nodding. "Have to admit, had my doubts…"

"Gimme my bag, asshole." Michael busied himself getting his flask out, keeping his eyes off the view, which made his head swim with terminal vertigo. They were sitting on a phone-booth sized projectile that was racing up the outside of the third tallest building in town. Cam removed his hoodie and track pants, balling them up before tossing them into the wind.

"When did they put this thing in?" Michael asked.

"All brand-new," Cam answered. "Tallest glass elevator in North America, and the fastest. China still holds the record, but Bailong is in a lousy national park. How about that view, amirite?"

"Don't," Michael said. Still catching his breath, he looked from his old friend and rival to the skyline, now an abstract lattice of light and shadow far, far below. Planes taking off from O'Hare looked like fireflies. Low clouds over the lake looked like ice on a puddle. And still they rose…

Revolted and exhilarated, Michael's stomach was caught in the sickening pull of gravity and seemed to draw him towards the edge. He could imagine some ancient god of gravity hungering to consume him…

The elevator jolted to a halt. "Last stop," Cam said. "Watch your head."

They rolled out from under the elevator's massive mechanical boom. Cam climbed onto it and reached down to pull Michael up.

For just a moment, Michael felt the old rush, the confidence. Wasn't he as safe up here as on the pavement, a thousand-and-some feet below?

Under Cam's mugger disguise, he wore off-white cotton slacks with a burgundy silk dress shirt. Michael felt a whole new suite of anxieties join the ones already sluicing through his nervous system.

He felt underdressed.

Climbing up on the roof of Aon Center, Michael found himself dragged into the last thing he would've expected to find here.

The old functional rooftop was almost entirely taken up by a swanky new observation deck, currently hosting a VIP cocktail reception. Clusters of local socialites and celebrities were mingling, enjoying their own magnificence. Occasionally, one or two took in the view.

"Jesus, Cam, what the fugghhh…"

"I know, right? Look what they did to it. This was our playground…"

"Are you seriously quoting Madonna songs at me right now?"

Cam dead-panned, "Don't make me go Elton John on your ass…"

"Yeah, we played here," Michael answered. "When we were kids."

"Oh, so when you fell down, you grew up. That's sad, bro." Cam sauntered into the midst of the cocktail party, eyes dissecting. "Well, I hope you didn't grow up too big to play with us."

"Us?"

Out of the crowd came Maddie in a stylish cocktail dress, holding three flutes of champagne, none of which seemed to be her first. Passing them out, she threw her arms around Michael's neck and hugged him, hanging her slight, taut weight from his shoulders for just a moment. His leg protested, but he told it to mind its own damn business.

Just as Michael touched her back returning the hug, she broke it off and punched him in the arm. "Asshole... you don't return my calls."

"I know," Michael admitted, buying time with a sip of champagne. "Work..."

She gave him a dubious nod. "What are you doing now?"

"I have this thing... big deadline... I was going to try and knock it out tonight, actually, when I got mugged." He cocked an eyebrow at Cam.

"Black man invites you to a party, and you call it a mugging. I see how you are."

"I *know* how you are," Michael shot back, smiling in spite of himself.

"Yeah, there's a word for people like you... It's on the tip of my tongue."

"I prefer the term *douche connoisseur*," Michael retorted, not feeling the joke, but his friends laughed anyway. "So, you were following me, though..."

"I prefer the term *stalking*," Cam deadpanned. "I watched you shoot down that foxy lady who chased you out of your day job... Seriously, man, your game needs work."

Michael groaned and looked around for the exit. "What my game needs, that lady hasn't got. But seriously—seriously, kids—"

"*Seriously*. No work tonight," Cam proclaimed. "We're drinking." Downing his champagne with authority, Cam looked around for the nearest waiter.

The next few rounds were very serious indeed, with only minimal conversation breaking up the old pattern of silently soaking up the atmosphere, of enjoying being invisible in plain sight, waiting to see if they'd be found out.

As if on cue, two security guards emerged from the service elevator. Sporting discreet dark suits, the pair circled the observation deck, eyeballing the guests. Someone might've reported the noise and extra weight on the glass elevator, or this could just be SOP for a ritzy party like this.

Cam leaned in close to Maddie and whispered something in her ear. She laughed uproariously. Michael refused to feel excluded and jealous, or tried not to. *Best not go there, OK?*

They became one with the crowd until the guards gave up and left. Now, they could enjoy themselves for real. Maddie went to the hosted bar for something more substantial than champagne. Michael and Cam staked out a table. Anyone who might get their nose out of joint at the trio's presence simply assumed they must be rich enough to behave like peasants, and gave them a wide berth.

They let the silence settle over them. When Cam finally spoke, Michael realized he'd been watching Maddie wait at the bar with the kind of expression he probably shouldn't display in public.

"I said, 'How's the day job?'" Cam repeated with a knowing grin.

"It's... you know."

Cam nodded, smiling crookedly. "Still working on that stalker app? What's it called? In Your Face or something? How's it work again?

"It's a mobile imaging app," he said, feeling like a dork. "You take a person's picture and it pulls up their social media profiles."

"Right. No way is that a creepy stalker app."

"No, listen. Governments and law enforcement use face-recognition all day long; that's the reality of modern life in today's terrorism-based economy. Why shouldn't average citizens enjoy the same tools? It's a game changer. Besides which, most people put their lives on social voluntarily."

"It *is* a game changer. *For stalkers*." Cam nudged Michael, busting his friend's balls until he stopped frowning. "You look good. Last time I saw you, you had that thing…" He gestured vaguely, like he didn't know the word in English.

"A limp."

"I was gonna say 'a *walker*,' but yeah."

Michael punched his thigh. It was still sore and mildly twitching from the run. "Getting better. Still far from one hundred percent."

"I hear you."

"Speaking of things, how're you and Maddie? That still going strong?" Now it was Michael's turn to offer the smarmy smirk.

Cam looked away, affecting deep personal hurt for about half a second. "You're such a dick."

"No, it's just I know you."

"True, true. I keep asking her to marry me."

"Yeah, well… I'm sure one of these days she'll weaken."

"Already has."

Michael took a moment to process Cam's coy smile as sincere, and another to wait for a punchline. He looked over at Maddie chatting up the bartender, oblivious to their discussion. For a moment, he felt himself cracking in half. Finally, he picked up his drink, crashed it into Cam's and took a swig.

"Congratulations, man. That why we're here? Celebrating?"

"Yes, we are. We're celebrating a liberation."

"Not sure I follow. Where does the marriage part come in?"

"No, not *my* liberation," Cam said expansively. "*Yours*."

Cam just let his cheesy grin go stale on his face until Michael got the picture. "No," he said. "Absolutely fucking not."

"Korova Tower," Cam went on. "*The* tower. They're calling it the world's first starscraper, for real."

Michael wracked his brain, but came up empty. "Have I heard of it?"

"Sure, at some point; just didn't register. It's not finished, not much publicity. But when it is, it'll be the tallest. And now it's all ours."

"Stop saying words. I don't want to hear about it."

"You don't want to hear about The Vertical City? Man, we're going to climb it."

"We who... you and Maddie?"

Cam shook his head, smiling. "We're getting the band back together."

"The F.U. Crew?"

"Who else? What do you say?"

Where the hell was Maddie with those drinks? "F.U. to that. I have a job and a life and I plan on keeping both."

"You're a code monkey, pilgrim."

"Software engineer."

"That doesn't actually sound any cooler, bro. Besides, I know *you*. You can't quit. Not yet, anyway."

The champagne went sour in his stomach. "You hit your head? Forget what happened?" *Was he shouting?*

"We had a mishap."

"'We?' The ground kicked the shit out of *me*, bro! *You* were fine."

"Look, dude... you *survived* it." Cam toasted him with his empty glass. "You beat the Reaper. Own that shit."

Michael shook his head, and he could almost feel the drunken blood infusing his brain, sloshing around. The flash of anger he'd felt quickly burned itself out, leaving a sharp sadness. "Nah, we pushed it too far. I was lucky." *You were luckier*, he thought. *You and Maddie.*

"That's what we do," Cam insisted. "We push things. It's always been about that. Not ones and zeroes. That's *them*..." Waving a disgusted hand at all the gala guests, going about their by turns dreamy and desperate lives in willful ignorance. "They paid a fortune to come up here and enjoy what we take for free. This was our view, our city, our world, Michael... not because we paid for it, but because we conquered it. That's still who we are. That's still what we *do*. As the man said, 'The Earth belongs to the living, not to the dead.'"

Christ, quoting Jefferson at me now? Michael felt genuinely torn. He tried not to let his trepidation show, but Cam could always read him.

Leaning in for the final sales pitch, Cam stage-whispered, "It's going to be huge. I'm talking about the biggest crew doing the biggest place-hack anyone's ever seen. It's just sitting there for the taking, no one's done it yet."

Michael sighed. There was no talking him out of this. "It's not like it was before. They're cracking down. We get caught now, in some other country... And where the hell *is* Korova Tower, anyway?"

Cam shrugged. "It's, uh... in Moscow."

Michael sat back in his chair. *I should get up and walk away.* "If this is another prank, you can stop now. It doesn't even sound real. Aren't we pretty much at war with Russia?"

Cam shook his head. "We're not... technically... and with all the sanctions, they can't afford to kick money out of bed, which is all they'll see when they look at us. As long as we don't act or look like journalists. Not kidding."

"How would we even get there, never mind how would we get out—"

"Let me worry about that," said Maddie, returning with the drinks.

Michael threw her a look, searching for some sign Cam was just screwing with him. He couldn't find it. "You too?"

She reached across the table, taking him by surprise as she placed her hand on his. "We want you to be there."

He looked down at her hand, noticing the engagement ring on her finger. His throat was like a wet paper straw, barely wide enough to fit the shot of whiskey Cam set in front of him.

"No BASE jump," Cam wheedled. "Just a straight climb, that's all. We go out with a splash."

"Figuratively."

Cam shrugged, knocking one back and corralling another.

Michael grabbed his other shot and held it up between them. Looking from Maddie to Cam as they beamed at each other, Michael proposed the only toast he could without his voice cracking. "To the Furies."

"F.U. Crew rides again!' Maddie and Cam shouted. They clinked glasses and laughed loudly until everyone around them felt acutely overdressed.

EIGHT

The next morning, Michael was at his desk on time. He logged in and immediately spaced out, replaying and re-examining last night's events, chugging water to ease his mild hangover.

He'd tried everything he could to dash their hopes. Begging off early just before they parted ways at the El station on Wabash, he pointed out how Cam must've seen him crash and burn hopping the bench with his bad leg.

Cam wasn't having it. "Yeah, that was epic. You should've seen the look on your face! Oh wait, here you go." He took out his phone and shared an action pic of Michael kissing the grass in the aftermath of his ill-advised parkour stunt. The look on his face was, indeed, nigh meme-worthy.

"Nice," Michael had said, "but there it is. I wouldn't be any good to you there, even on a straight climb."

Maddie stepped in before Cam could make it worse. "It's not your leg that's holding you back, Mike. It's your mind. You hesitate now when you take risks that used to come naturally. Something bad will happen every time if you set yourself up for it. But once you reconnect, it'll all come back. I want that for you."

Of course, he knew the accident had damaged his mind as

much as his body. He broke out in a cold sweat just thinking about the crazy things they used to do, but he'd never given any serious thought to seeing a therapist about it.

His father was an engineer at an orthopedics company and a second-generation immigrant who passed on the impassive masculine expectations of his Chinese heritage without any actual heritage. His mother taught critical thinking and debate courses at the local community college. Both highly educated specimens of the superficially open but emotionally remote Midwestern stereotype. He was raised to treat ideas as signals and emotions as noise, and to push through negative feelings as one would a mild sinus infection.

Friends recommended stuff like meditation and hypnotherapy, pointing out how many pro athletes used it to come back from traumatic injuries. But he wasn't sold. Results only seemed to come when you believed in it completely, which to Michael felt too much like the placebo effect. And if it did work, did he really trust anyone messing around in his head when he wasn't conscious? He firmly believed he couldn't be hypnotized anyway, for the same reason he couldn't sit still long enough to meditate. His brain had no *Off* switch, and he couldn't see the upside in finding one.

He hadn't said anything. If he was only a little more drunk, if Cam wasn't there, he might've said everything.

Michael realized he was staring at his laptop screen without seeing it. He looked around the bustling office space, his gaze drifting to where Amara had sat all day yesterday, watching him. She was, of course, gone.

Outside the windows, a braver man than Michael swiped the glass with a squeegee while his partner power-washed the urban grime off the limestone facings. Their platform was only a few feet wide, yet they worked on, oblivious to the danger, to how easily they could fall. He realized he'd been staring, instinctively certain that something terrible would happen to them the moment he looked away.

Closing the suite of development tools on his desktop, he opened a browser and searched "Korova Tower." If it was a prank, Michael concluded, then Google was in on it, too. But they weren't trying too hard...

At first, he found only a few bland articles from European and Russian business websites, all at least two years old. These outlined the proposal to rehab Moscow's dilapidated Presnensky District into the International Business Center. A vague public/ private partnership overseen by the Russian Finance Ministry was the backing entity. No surprise there.

The flagship project was a world-beating skyscraper that combined high-rise luxury living with an immense commercial space dedicated to leading a renewable energy revolution, which sounded like so much PR boilerplate. Russia had never been interested in renewables and it was unlikely they'd suddenly gotten religious about global warming. But after that announcement, the tower dropped off the front page with such authority that someone must have declared a blackout. The articles he found in the US and British press were no more helpful, larded with speculation that the whole thing was just more fake news, crafted by the people who perfected it.

A more recent, weirdly terse *Russian Times* piece noted that a deputy finance minister and the board of directors of an unnamed company was slated to cut the ribbon on Korova, a 190-story mixed-use "starscraper" rumored to cost upwards of $35 billion US in about three months, although "some critics" alleged that Moscow's Vertical City was a colossal fraud, or as one "critic" put it, a "next-gen Potemkin village." Michael had to look up the reference.

This worried Michael enough that he followed up on the article's "critic" and uncovered a rat's nest of conspiracy theories.

Masha Zworykin, a gadfly blogger who once had a popular TV show during the Yeltsin era, clearly had an axe to grind with the current regime. She regularly accused the president of having her banned from the airwaves and putting her life in jeopardy.

While the government never dignified her allegations with a direct response, they were goaded to provide the tame state media with a slick video presentation on Korova's innovative engineering and safety features.

Plenty of western media coverage followed, with features in *Forbes* and *Business Insider* and a segment on the History or Discovery Channel, but Michael couldn't help but notice how all the video clips seemingly all came from the same official source, suggesting that no one from the outside world had set foot inside this shining edifice of innovation.

The vacuum of hard facts about Korova Tower inflated a bubble of paranoid conjecture around it, from rumors that it would be revealed as the fabled Trump Tower Moscow, to speculation that it was some kind of antenna for Tesla-inspired free broadcast power or weather control—Russia's answer to the HAARP project. It wasn't like the Bermuda Triangle or Atlantis, but when it came to the soon-to-be world's tallest building, there was so little of substance about it that Michael still wondered if it truly existed.

And then there was the peculiar absence of urbex videos. That alone was cause for suspicion. Moscow was *the* hotbed for place-hackers, BASE jumpers, tagging, and parkour crews. Why were they being so coy? After all, the Federation Tower, the reigning tallest building in Europe, had been hacked on video long before its completion. With such a monster going up in Moscow, there should be hours of footage of lanky teenagers in hoodies and sneakers scaling the skeletal superstructure like a jungle gym, getting run off by armed security guards. But there were only a few furtively shot tourists' views of the tower looming over the otherwise flat, sprawling city. Uniformly, they were all captured from a great distance, shaky with the fear of being intercepted by the police or private security teams.

And getting arrested over there was something to have nightmares about. With the Kremlin embracing the hostage business, there was little chance of simply getting off with a trespassing charge. If they found an excuse to pick you up, you'd quickly become a political pawn, and the State Department was basically indicating that if you went over there, you were on your own.

Michael was hardly the news junkie he'd been before the accident—his doctor had told him to ignore all media for his own health—but he was aware of what Russia had done in Chechnya, Syria, Georgia and now Ukraine, of course. Also, what could The Furies hope to accomplish in the face of such dire events, sticking their heads in the bear's mouth for a goofy stunt? Ill-considered, tone-deaf, arrogant, privileged—take your pick.

Cam had shut down Michael's concerns with a bravado that was stunning, even for him.

"Just don't bring a vape pen," he'd shrugged. "Is that a problem for you? We're gonna play it cool. Don't give them an excuse until we pop Korova's cherry, and then we'll bug out before they know they've been played."

It was way too weird to take seriously, wasn't it? When he'd started doing this stuff, it was exactly the kind of mystery hack that Michael had hoped for. Much as he loved the physical challenge and the odd opportunity to punch up at plutocrats, what got him hooked was the thrill of going off the map, into places the world tried to hide. The parkour, the place-hacking, were just a means to an end. It had gotten sidetracked when he became one of the Furies. If Cam had concocted this whole shenaniganza to pique his interest, then Cam knew him a lot better than Michael would've given him credit for.

Whatever the truth was, they were serious about this, about bringing back the Crew and facing down the Evil Empire. So much so, he somehow never got around to asking Cam just how Amara got the video clip of his accident.

A lot of unknowns and blinking red lights, but Cam and Maddie were going, with or without him.

And they were getting married...

No matter how he looked at that, it felt like an ending. He imagined his friends jumping off a cliff without chutes, going where he could never follow.

From that first meet-up at the Damen Silos, they had become tight as family. From one exploit to the next, others had drifted in and out of their crew, but the three of them were a consistent core, the element that made Les Furies more than just a club for amateur daredevils. So many of the sites they hacked were high-rise mausoleums, bearing the names of dead or moribund companies. The Furies felt compelled to force the point that these titans of industry happily took government bailouts before laying off their workers and shipping operations overseas. Dying capitalism destroying its children.

Together, they brainstormed leaving cheap digital projectors running provocative images and slogans up where the whole city could see them, which became their trademark and gave them a rep as not just rogue athletes, but as legit street artists, as well as a valid voice of the so-called resistance.

Nobody remembered who came up with the idea for the stunt that sealed the Furies' hometown notoriety. When a Chinese equity firm put in a bid to buy the Chicago Stock Exchange, even as many traded companies were winding down operations and shuttering factories throughout the Midwestern states, pedestrians on South LaSalle Street went into a panic when a host of human bodies in business suits leapt from the roof, only to float unnervingly above the street, suspended by golden helium-balloon parachutes.

The army of balloon-men, hastily inflated and shoved off the roof by the giggling trio, became a local symbol for the stark inequality baked into the system. Some people called them terrorists after that, but they were just kids at play. Snarky pranksters in the Abbie Hoffman tradition.

Maddie once proclaimed that the three of them made the perfect couple, and while she was pretty loaded when she said it, it was truer than any of them knew. They just fit.

When Cam and Maddie took it to the next level as a couple, Michael never really felt like a third wheel. He accepted it as inevitable, and kept his doubts to himself. If he was being brutally honest, they needed each other enough to mistake what they shared as a rarefied strain of true love.

Cam thrived on chaos, always needing an audience. He could do a handstand on high steel a hundred stories off the ground, but he got antsy when things got normal or quiet. Maddie always needed to feel validated for what she could do, not just how she looked.

Was being a complement to each other's baggage a form of love? The two of them never stopped to rest, and neither could function too well alone, but Michael seemed to thrive on it, as they often reminded him. Didn't mean he enjoyed it, though it was how he got his best work done.

It was hard not to ponder how it could have turned out differently, if not for the accident. If Michael would have told Maddie how he felt, when the time was right for it. *Don't kid yourself, bro*, he thought. *You write apps, not rom-coms.* For better or worse, Cam and Maddie were meant for each other, and he resolved that he would be happy for them. One day he might even believe it. They were headed off for an adventure, and he—

An email pinged his Inbox. He scanned It absently, rubbing his forehead.

We're really digging the new interface for the app. I think we're close. We have a couple of notes we'd like to run by you when you have a sec. Thing's going to be a killer!

Cam's words returned with a vengeance. *Don't sell yourself short, bro. It's a creepy stalker app, period.*

Michael reminded himself that this is what he'd gone to school for. To learn to make bullshit at a dead-end job, so you could afford to pay back the assholes who financed you learning how to make bullshit. That was the trap he was in.

It was a bitter but unsurprising irony of late-stage capitalism that with so many industries dying and the middle class shrinking faster than the rainforests, the transfer of wealth from the young to the ruling gerontocracy was fully ingrained and fiercely protected government policy, crushing dissent and activism well before the Occupy movement. Holding predatory student loans and the threat of unemployment over the heads of young people with no other way to make their voices heard. It was a pit that he'd jumped into with both eyes open, yet still blind to reality. Now he knew that even if he never ran with the Furies again, he'd be looking over his shoulder until the distant day when he paid them off. Interest never sleeps.

Michael looked around. His fellow worker bees were beginning to pair up for lunch or hunker down over their monitors with ramen or leftover take-out, gulled by dreams of that private office and a week's annual vacation time they'd never get to take.

Michael stood up and closed his laptop, stuck it in his bag and put on his jacket. He strolled towards the elevators, nodding at various people whose names he never remembered, but just short of the elevators, he turned and instead took the stairs.

And instead of going down, he went up.

Michael ascended to the top floor, taking the steps two at a time, becoming almost hypnotized by his own rhythm. He reached the top floor but paused at the door, unsure whether it was locked. He'd never been up there, and wasn't quite sure if he wanted to go through it. So he'd let fate decide. He twisted the knob, felt a resistance strong enough that he almost let it go and went back downstairs to work...

The door opened.

He stepped out onto the roof. The sounds of the city swelled like an orchestra tuning up. Corny, but that's how it felt—charged with potential, tensed to unleash something great. Noting the change in himself, that he'd come up with such an image, maybe he should write rom-coms, after all.

He walked out to the edge, his brain racing in a dozen

directions at once. He looked across the street at the stacks of office windows filled with people just like him... but not really. Slowly, ironing out any tremble of nerve, he climbed up onto the ledge, balanced the balls of his feet on the edge of the coping, flexing his toes in his scuffed brown loafers. He closed his eyes, letting the unseasonably brisk wind wash over him and carry away all the shit he was drowning in yesterday.

Then he looked down.

The people on the street weren't quite ants... maybe beetles. Even though it was only fifteen stories, a fall would surely kill him. People would say he must have cracked under the pressure of the job, and maybe he had, but the last thing he wanted to do right now was die.

Michael's dad used to tell him about when he saw that nut in a Spider-Man costume scale the old Sears Tower and plant an American flag at the summit on Memorial Day, 1981. As an adult, Michael read about the climber Dan Goodwin and how he took up urban mountaineering after he tried to sell the Vegas fire department on a rescue plan that could have saved people who died in the MGM fire in 1980.

The substation fire chief who told him to go climb a tall building meant it as a screw-you, but once he caught the rush, Goodwin was possessed to scale every skyscraper, dodging police and firemen to summit the John Hancock Center, the Renaissance Tower, and Two World Trade Center. An outlaw in a superhero's tights, by 1986 his climbs were sponsored publicity events, and he was a color commentator for CBS Sports.

Urban climbing was just rediscovering a tradition mapped out earlier by the old human flies and other outlaw daredevils who proved that humans, at least some of them, needed this kind of challenge and danger. And the rest were compelled to watch, which some perceived as a threat to public order. They always tried to forget these people or buy them out, to stop others from getting the same idea, to keep everyone down on the ground and behind a desk.

His fear was still there, but It had retreated In the rush of excitement, the pure connection to his own capability. Nothing else came close to this. He was hooked.

He needed to go.

"Whatever it is, buddy," a voice shouted over the wind in his ears, "it isn't worth it. Come on down now."

Michael looked around and saw two security guards crossing the roof towards him. One of them had his hands out in a placating gesture. The other one actually had his stun gun drawn. Michael cracked a smile, realizing what this must look like. He broke into helpless laughter.

Michael looked down the façade of the building to the street, obligingly lifted his arms in surrender, shouted, "I'm sorry, guys. I quit."

And stepped off the ledge, into the wind.

NINE

Maddie could tell the influencer was about to fall.

The woman's right leg was straining to take her weight as she fumbled for the next foothold with her left. She clung to the handholds, pressing her face against the sheer surface of the climbing wall. With her legs about to give out, she was panicking, forgetting she wore a safety harness. If this kept up, she might actually hurt herself.

Serves her right, Maddie thought. *I should've gone solo.* But she'd agreed to spot the woman because there was nobody else in the gym at this hour, and they wouldn't let you climb the wall alone. The on-site trainer was glued to his phone, which he'd drop the moment the influencer called out for help, but right now, she was too scared to draw breath.

What was her name? Rhonda, that's right. Rhonda who just got back from Cannes, where she partied on a movie star's yacht, and the star wasn't there, but Maddie knew who was, because Rhonda told everyone she knew on her phone while on the treadmill next to Maddie's.

Rhonda had breezed in at the start of her workout and changed the TV channel from BBC World Service just as they teased a segment on Moscow's mysterious new "starscraper." Changed it to some daytime network crap where a coven of pampered celebrities whimpered about the news as if rich white people's ill-informed opinions on current events were a vital natural resource. "Were you watching that?" Rhonda had asked, but was already back on her phone before Maddie could answer.

The relationship went downhill from there. Maddie was fighting to keep her continental breakfast down by the time Rhonda asked if she wanted to be climbing buddies, but even the Rhonda-drama was a welcome distraction from all the other things she'd rather not think about.

Maddie came to the gym to purge herself of useless thoughts and feelings, to push herself as close as she could get in captivity to the zone where they couldn't catch up to her. A five-star people zoo: that was how she thought of the gym, but she couldn't risk going out on the streets and rooftops alone, and couldn't get Cam off the phone long enough for a real workout.

Her fiancé was upstairs, pacing and talking, working the angles, nailing down the financial alliances needed to pull off this stunt. "All things going to plan," was all Cam would say, but Maddie saw how tense he was lately. He wouldn't tell her why, which was making her angry, but she knew that asking was a trigger and would just make it worse for both of them. *Better to let him deal with it alone. For now.*

Cam Buckley had grown up watching his dad, a straight-up *master* of the Hustle. He'd gone from driving a truck on the South Side to running his own shipping logistics company out of the garage, taking on federal contracts to haul freight down the Highway of Death in Iraq. Dad was always too busy to play, but he bounced his son on his knee as he got over with clients, generals and politicians until he got himself in so deep he had to go over there himself, and one day never came back.

Without his father's unique charm to grease the wheels, the company had been ripped apart by government oversight wonks and devious creditors. Cam and his mother lost their house. The Furies became Cam's way of striking back at the system that took away his dad, but mostly, he was out there using that magic Buckley charm to turn people into things for him to play with.

She thought again about why she didn't call Michael or just turn up at his place. She had been looking forward to seeing him again, to the reunion of the old crew. But now some inconvenient feelings had been stirred up, ones she thought she'd outgrown.

For the same reason, Maddie didn't go visit her family, see the old South Side neighborhood again. Why be scrutinized by the people who still called her Magdalena and thought they knew her back in the day; have them judge her for that most unpardonable sin—Forgetting Where You Came From. That would be just too much.

Maddie wasn't out to impress anyone. She drove herself to the limit, letting her performance speak for her. She and Cam had just come back from France, too, though the trip's highlight was exploring forbidden passages in the Paris catacombs with their new friends. *This probably wouldn't impress Rhonda much.*

She hated that she hated Rhonda for making her self-conscious, making her feel like she had something to prove. Staying in this hotel wasn't helping much, either. But one of Cam's bad-boy millionaires owned the place, so they didn't have to worry about room charges for twenty-dollar bottled water.

And the gym's climbing wall *was* kind of awesome.

A four-story surface with a demanding convex slope near the top at the expert end of the wall, so you had to dangle almost upside-down to nail the summit. When Rhonda had condescended to invite her to spot her climb, Maddie had clocked the trainer taking a selfie for Insta and scrambled up the wall without benefit of the spring-loaded harness, then just as quickly scaled the wall to get back down. The astounded Rhonda had asked her if she wasn't a professional athlete.

Damn it, Rhonda, even your compliments sting.

Somehow, it hurt when people mistook her for a professional

because she probably could've been. At least if her parents could have afforded the right schools for her, or if she could drop the dead-end jobs she'd had to work after high school to train for the X Games or the Olympics. *I could've been a contender*, she thought. Dripping with endorsements and magazine spreads, all that.

Drop the pity party, she told herself. She'd done pretty well. She didn't need a Mountain Dew sponsorship or a bougie medallion to prove her worth. Put her in danger, and there wasn't anyone in the world she'd trade places with. Certainly not Rhonda up there…

Speaking of Rhonda…

"Just let yourself drop!" Maddie shouted, before attacking the wall herself. "Hold on," she said as she climbed to Rhonda.

The place where Rhonda was stuck was way beyond her capabilities. And it was Maddie's fault. She'd said it was a lot easier than it looked.

Maddie came up alongside Rhonda and made her voice soothing and calm. "You're OK. You can let go. The harness will catch you—"

"I'm afraid of falling," Rhonda sobbed. "I told all my followers I was going to do this. I look like a total idiot."

Too late for that, Maddie thought. "Nobody here but you and me," she told Rhonda. "You can get up there, but you need to jump."

"I'm afraid…"

"It's fine, just…" She tried to get Rhonda to stretch for the next foothold with her right foot, but her legs were rubbery with exhaustion. *Just let her fall*, she told herself. *Let her figure out that not everything can be bought.*

But instead, she climbed past her, springing to the last row of handholds, letting herself dangle from the inverted lip, then easily throwing a leg over the edge and reaching the top.

"Where'd you go?" Rhonda wailed. "I can't hold on…"

Maddie reached out, nearly falling off the edge before she

caught Rhonda's safety cable. Balancing herself when the pulleys in the ceiling took up the slack, she hoisted Rhonda up the face of the climbing wall by her harness.

"Thanks, you saved my life," Rhonda gushed.

Maddie shrugged and said, "*De nada.*" But Rhonda was already taking a selfie from the top of the wall, her fingers in a victory salute.

Shaking her head, Maddie dropped off the ledge and speed-crawled to the floor nearly as quickly as she would have fallen. Throwing a victory salute of her own, she grabbed her towel and headed for the showers.

"Hey!" Rhonda called from the top of the climbing wall. "How'm I supposed to get down?"

TEN

Cam didn't hear Maddie come in because he was neck-deep in four arguments, and winning three of them.

Pacing the suite, he barely saw the room, and had moved the furniture out of the way. He visualized the people on the Zoom call standing in front of him and spoke to them as if they were face to face. Take away the remote anonymity of being a voice on the phone, make them *feel* you, and whether you won them over or wore them down, you'll win. Something he learned from watching his father.

He was running the table on three of them, but the one he was losing was with himself.

Maddie swept into his camera-view and waved. Cam muted his mic. "Hey, babe. Didn't see you. How was the workout?"

She shrugged and went into the bathroom. Kicked the door shut. He heard the shower start up and thought about joining her, then remembered he had some people on hold and a few more blazing up his text messages. He sighed, trying to regain his flow.

Back in the day, all you had to do was post on a message board, pick a target, pack a knapsack and go. How complicated everything had gotten...

Welcome to the next level, he told himself.

On Zoom, Pascal, his new IT wiz, was telling him the whole plan was insane and unworkable. Relaying a barrage of troubleshooting texts from his Russian counterpart, Serhiy, Pascal had highlighted problems with their in-country web-hosting client, their relay cams, the bandwidth of the Moscow telecom system, and their legal coverage in the not-so-unlikely event of an international incident.

Cam hadn't known him for more than a few months and they'd only met in person once, but he had the coder's number. Pascal liked to hype the obstacles to play up his own prowess in overcoming them. No doubt he'd already resolved all the issues and just needed a good ego-stroking to coax them out. People who accepted compliments as currency were Cam's favorites to work with, because when it came to hot air, he was a billionaire.

"Relax, player, you got this," Cam said in a sunny-yet-somber voice, injecting sincerity and gravitas into his tone until it squirted out the sides of his mouth. "Yes, this is unprecedented, and yes, the obstacles are formidable. If I had any doubts you were the only guy on Earth who could pull it together we wouldn't be having this conversation."

"No shit," Pascal said, stifling a burp and slurping a Monster Energy drink in Cam's ear. "But Serhiy says the worldwide feed will be subject to shutdown at a moment's notice—"

"Do you give a shit what Serhiy says? Is he smarter than you?"

"Hell no!" Pascal rose to the bait. "But it's not Chicago or LA. He's my eyes and ears over there, and he says—"

"That it can't be done. Meaning that *you* can't do it. Is he right?"

"Course not. It's just… it's a lot to keep track of. Like, a lot, a lot. You know?"

"What I know is that you're the man, Pascal. Don't make me lose faith. We're doing the hard part; you don't even have to get out of your chair, my man."

On the phone, Mel, the crew's new publicist, wanted him

to relocate the stunt somewhere else. Mel was a harder case to crack than the tech guys. Whatever objections they threw up, they all wanted to do something dangerous and legally shady. People like Mel, besides taking more of his money than he could afford, were there to ward off bad publicity, and every new idea Cam had gave her a fresh headache. She also liked to put Cam on hold while she had whole conversations with rival clients, so Cam had no problem returning the favor.

"I just got off the phone with a dear friend who's shooting a magazine layout in Jakarta," she said. "You should think about restaging there. I could get sponsorships—"

"You know that's not what we're about, Mel. It's locked."

"There's no upside to Russia. But Jakarta is really hot right now."

"You must have a strange understanding of that term. They don't have a building any kid couldn't scale and share to YouTube. Listen, Mel, I love you, but you're not a voting member here. I'm gonna give you the news, and you're going to make sure it gets traction. Please, Mel, just do your job. OK, babe? Don't worry about it."

"What I am worried about is you being seen or heard from again. And don't call me 'babe,' bitch."

"It's not the Evil Empire anymore," he retorted, laying it on so thick, grateful she couldn't see his face. "They're all capitalists, now."

"Who's understanding is strange now? They're straight-up gangsters. And not the fun kind. Look, if I can't talk you out of this—"

"You can't…"

"Then I'll do what I can to get word out without giving away the game. The press releases will be so light on details they won't get pick-up in the mainstream outlets."

"They'll catch up. Trust me."

Cam hung up and checked his text argument with Yuri, his new security consultant.

Though officially based in Israel, Yuri worked extensively in Russia helping businesses plagued by Mafiya protection rackets, kidnap rings, and terrorist threats of various flavors. His track records and connections were impressive, so Cam wasn't too worried about operating in Moscow now that he had Yuri fully signed up.

My cousin is a good interior decorator over there. Fresh paint, wallpaper. Exotic. African, French accents. Not cheap. Please advise.

Cam shook his head. Yuri was a deeply paranoid dude, but his talking-in-code game needed work. He was trying to say the forged passports were in process, just in case they were identified and had to flee the country. These docs would be good enough to fool customs, but they wouldn't be American IDs; a lot tougher to fake. New Zealand sounded good. He assured Yuri nothing would go wrong and even if it did, all they could be nabbed for was trespassing. It wasn't like they were going to steal a political poster in North Korea or something. Nonetheless, Cam had agreed to them, so perhaps Yuri's paranoia was contagious.

Cam removed his earbuds and closed his laptop. Massaging his temples, he shook off the various masks he had to wear to pull this thing off. He thought again about joining Maddie in the shower, but still had one last argument to deal with. And he was still losing it, inside his head.

Michael would turn them down. Cam practically counted on it, but still had to make the effort. And yet, while he was hatching plans within plans, considering every eventuality on this stunt, he hadn't made any serious moves towards choosing Michael's replacement.

I got nothing but love for the man, he thought, *but he was never really cut out for a life of adventure.* That first time at Damen Silos, when Michael nearly fell to his death, Cam pegged him as a bad luck charm. He could feel the fear coming off Michael like a fever, but damned if he didn't pull through.

For someone like Cam, who just didn't feel it, Michael was something of an enigma. He didn't lack the nerve, but he had way too much imagination, with little or no control over it. Yet, throw so much at the dude that he couldn't overthink it, then he was a steely eyed badass.

Cam had bonded with Michael over their shared experiences, becoming like a brother to him. They challenged each other to go bigger, further, faster. Michael's curiosity took them to a lot of places; perhaps short on video-friendly danger but drenched in lost history and esoteric mystery.

Their trip to the Washburne Trade School Building—six stories of über-creepy art deco ugliness that eventually fell to the demands of progress once landmark status had been denied—was one of their biggest hits thanks to Michael knowing its colorful history. When they crashed the Chicago Stock Exchange, Michael had been the one to point out how Richard Nickel, the local godfather of urbex, had died photographing the grand old ruin back in 1973, trying to save it from the wrecking ball. And it'd been his pictures, his sacrifice, that moved the powers that be to preserve some of the Louis Sullivan-designed structure.

Cam truly loved the dude like a brother. But always in Michael's eyes, you could see that mote of doubt that made you think he was going to panic and sabotage himself, and maybe take you with him. *Hurts to even think it, but that's the stone truth.*

Yet he had to invite Michael. He was part of the crew. He was in its DNA. Without him, it might have turned into something else, or ended up going too far too fast. The viral videos that got millions of hits, of kids blithely traipsing on ledges and catwalks high above the city obscured a deeper, darker truth.

People snuffed it all the time doing what they did. Those were the videos that didn't get shared. Michael had skated out to the ragged edge and almost gone over. The light in his eyes, the fire, was gone, probably for good. Last night, he'd seen that, and more importantly, Maddie had, too. *Maybe now, she'll get her head right and move forward…*

Cam scrolled a list on his phone, shaking his head at each entry. None of them checked all the boxes, and as he thought about Michael, it just didn't feel right. Several old friends who'd gone on a few Furies excursions had balked at the invitation once they heard where they were going, and he'd kept the whole thing on the down-low to avoid getting his inbox flooded with kooks and noobs. There was a backup plan, naturally. Had to be. Something else he'd learned from Dad.

Screw it… He closed his eyes and jabbed a button, only opening them when the phone started ringing. Hobart Carruthers was kind of a douchey trust-fund brat, but he'd helped them whip up the balloons for the stock exchange stunt, and he was almost completely fearless. *Destiny is calling, Hobie…*

"Oh my God!" Maddie's scream came from the bathroom. Cam turned and reflexively shouted, "You alright, babe?" It wasn't her *upset-at-something-on-the-internet* voice, or *I-hurt-myself-come-quick* scream. She came out of the bathroom in a hotel robe with one hand over her mouth and her phone thrust out for him to see. He canceled his call and looked at her phone.

It was Breaking News. LOCAL MAN LEAPS FROM ROOFTOP, read the chyron below shaky phone footage of a man standing on a ledge at the top of a fifteen-story office building. A reverse angle from a rooftop security camera showed him step off the ledge and disappear from view. The man's face was never shown, but Cam knew just by how the figure moved.

It was Michael.

"Asshole…" Maddie said, turning the phone to look closer.

Cam's head was spinning. What would make Michael do something like that? Was it him? His offer? Was it the job?

"Let me see," Cam said, but Maddie hogged the phone so he had to use his own.

The newscaster had an inappropriate smirk as she delivered the news.

"An unidentified man jumped from the roof of the Macrosync Building this morning... but landed on a window-washer's platform and lowered himself to the ground, eluding security and escaping on the roof of an elevated train. Police have not released the man's identity, but Hollywood, if you're listening... Chicago might have your next Spider-Man."

"Son of a bitch," Cam said admiringly.

Just then, both their phones chirped with an incoming text message.

It was from Michael.

I'M IN.

SECOND MOVEMENT

"EXPERIENCE HATH SHEWN, THAT EVEN UNDER THE
BEST FORMS OF GOVERNMENT THOSE ENTRUSTED
WITH POWER HAVE, IN TIME, AND BY SLOW
OPERATIONS, PERVERTED IT INTO TYRANNY."

—THOMAS JEFFERSON

ELEVEN

Two weeks later, Michael shuffled out of the Terminal A baggage claim hall at Sheremetyevo—A.S. Pushkin International Airport. It was Friday morning. He rubbed his eyes at the brilliant sunlight.

Wednesday night's eight-hour red-eye flight out of O'Hare had deposited him at Charles de Gaulle just in time for lunch. He used the nine-hour layover to train into Paris, take a brief sightseeing tour, and enjoy a *croque madame* at a café outside the reopened but still fire-scarred Notre-Dame. This was where tightrope artist Philippe Petit had cut his teeth, walking between the iconic cathedral's square gothic towers before going on to conquer New York's World Trade Center.

It was Michael's first time in Paris. The bustle and rampant beauty had proven more exhausting than the flight itself.

Some instinct managed to steer him back to the airport; full consciousness didn't kick in until he was approaching customs. Fortunately, he breezed through, just in time to learn his flight was delayed. After napping in a chair at the gate, he caught the four-hour Air France connection to Moscow.

Arriving fairly rested at Sheremetyevo shortly after 4:00 a.m., Michael navigated his way through passport control. Here, he faced a much hairier eyeball at customs than in Paris. Then he picked up his battered but still rollable suitcase, which he'd packed light, leaving out any specialized gear or clothing that might mark him as something other than a casual young tourist from the States. Everything the crew needed would be sourced locally.

The last thing they wanted was to raise suspicion. And if he had to put his initial impression of Moscow into one word, *suspicious* would cover it.

Sure, de Gaulle International had soldiers with machine guns strolling the terminals and elaborate bollards and checkpoints outside the departure lounges, but every Russian citizen he passed warily checked him out the same way the soldiers did: with deep suspicion, as if specifically warned about him. When he smiled at the passport control lady, her cold, taut expression had tightened into a scowl. Whatever illegible marks she made on his form had led to a thorough search of his bags.

Somehow, in spite of following the weather reports, Michael realized he'd expected the weather to be biting cold, this being Russia and all. So yes, the sticky heat was definitely a self-inflicted surprise. But there was bitter cold of a different sort—in every pair of penetrating eyes that regarded him as he shuffled through the protective barriers.

Maybe people stared at him like this at home and he just didn't notice. Macrosync had threatened legal action after his provocative resignation stunt. Ultimately, they decided that it would reflect badly on them, so they didn't press charges or cooperate with the police. He'd negotiated a month of PTO, and in return bashed out the fixes they wanted on the project. He'd also ramped up his physical therapy to prepare for whatever the hell he was doing here in Moscow.

By the time he stepped out into the rosy dawn light, he was shaky and tired, wanting only real sleep in an actual bed.

But then he saw his friends.

Or rather, they saw him.

"What," shouted a familiar voice from the throng waiting

at the greeting area barricades, "you can't spot the only black man in Moscow?"

Maddie threw her arms around him while Cam squeezed his shoulder and took his suitcase. They laughed as they manhandled him, and he immediately felt more refreshed.

"How was your flight?" Maddie asked.

He showed her the T-shirt he bought on the Champs Élysée, showing a tiny figure wire-walking between the spires of Notre-Dame. "Bite-sized Paris was nice. But I'm really feeling that lost day."

"Too bad! We've got schemes to scheme and plots to hatch." Leading them out to the curb, Cam flagged down a taxi van. "We took the Metro out here, but we won't put you through that."

Cam threw his suitcase into the back and the driver, a garrulous older man with a yellow cigarette in the corner of his downturned mouth, opened the loading door for them. Just as they were about to shut it, an old woman in a mangy fur coat and hat inserted herself into the van. *Classic babushka*, thought Michael as she planted herself on the bench seat beside him without any acknowledgment. While the three friends looked at each other awkwardly, the driver harangued the old woman in rapid-fire Russian. She merely repeated her destination, her clipped growls like a soldier facing interrogation. The driver threw up his hands and got behind the wheel, then hurled the battered van into the swirling scrum of traffic.

Maddie snorted, trying to keep from breaking into a giggling fit. The babushka snapped at the driver, who told her in universally comprehensible tones to shut up, but she wasn't having it. This went on as the van wound its way out of the airport maze and on to a broad, surprisingly empty expressway. Finally, Michael had to ask. "Excuse me. What's she saying?"

"Oh, it's nothing. Old women, you know, they live to complain."

"What about?" Maddie put in.

"Oh, nobody respect the old traditions, nobody look out for the elders, all the foreigners coming—they don't like it. We like you fine, no worries…"

The babushka snapped at him again, went into an extended tirade.

"What was that about?" Michael asked.

The driver scowled. "She say government kick her out of her home."

"Really? Why?"

"They make many new buildings. Russia is biggest country, but they knock down old factory districts to build new… how you say, cloud scratchers."

The three of them looked at each other as the old woman went on. If she seemed angry before, now she struggled to fight back tears.

The taxi driver translated. "Building she live in was burned down. She had to move."

"No shit? Is that true?"

He shrugged and unconvincingly shook his head. "Is illegal, but very common. When USSR went away, was very bad time. Things better now. Not like before. Thirty, forty year ago… maybe."

"It's very nice," Michael said, fumbling as he added, "Back home, they make it sound like Chicago in the 1920s. You know, with all the gangsters?"

"No, is not like that," the driver vigorously shook his head and wiped the idea out of the air. "We have rules. Laws, not so much, but if you follow the *rules*, nothing bad happen. You are here for Russia Day, yes, no? All the concerts, fireworks, parades. All the wrong people celebrating all the wrong things."

Michael didn't quite get that last part, but let it go. The taxi pulled over at the mouth of a monolithic apartment block and dropped off the old woman. She might've been a witch who took their tongues with her, the silence in her wake so profound.

For the rest of the ride, Michael let his face remain glued

to the window, taking in Moscow. The buildings were either brutally drab or cheaply modern, the streets sparsely populated with old European cars, the sidewalks crowded with harried-looking people, all hurrying somewhere. It might've been Detroit without, as Cam pointed out, any black people. Fifteen miles out from the city center, everything was new, but somehow slapped together.

He looked over and saw Maddie nestled cozily against Cam, who had one arm wrapped around her, looking at his phone in the other. The fine hairs on her arm turned to gold against her bronze skin in the morning light. They were playing a game where you had to come up with a Russian custom or point of etiquette, and the other person had to guess if it was true or false.

"Never wipe your feet when visiting a Russian home," Cam said, affecting a solemn reading voice, "for luck."

"False," Maddie said. "If you don't take your shoes off, they'll kick your ass. Um… Don't ever smile at a stranger in Russia."

Definitely true, Michael thought, turning his gaze back to the city. As they passed out of a tunnel, a gargantuan shadow fell across the highway, eclipsing the pale, rising sun.

Twice as tall as the cluster of gleaming spires around it, Korova Tower looked like a ladder to the stars. Its 190 stories dominated the skyline, surmounted by a forked crane that made the already imposing tower look like it had horns.

He'd digested every scrap he could find about Korova and its neighbors, but seeing it in the flesh… nothing could've prepared him. He risked another glance at his partners and saw Cam looking at him with a smile. "You ready for this?"

"Is big, no?" the cabdriver said. "Soon, the world will respect Russia's strength again. Like old days, but better. That area there, Presnensky District, was shameful—old apartments, gangs, children in streets drinking. Now, tallest building in world going up. Move aside, old woman. Russia is rising again."

All of them were thrown halfway out of their seats. The driver stomped the brakes and spat a curse at the waves of pedestrians crossing in front of the van. But this was no ordinary foot traffic, Michael realized. Many wore bandanas or masks, and carried banners with furious-looking slogans in hand-painted Cyrillic. They filled the cross-street, the grand Boulevard Ring that circled the old city center, weaving among stranded cars, shouting and banging on the sides of the van as they passed. Half the shop windows facing the street were already boarded over in anticipation of the weekend. Armed private security patrolled in front of the others.

"What's this all about?" Maddie asked.

"You see?" the cabdriver said, waving his hands at the protesters. "Everyone is free to run wild in streets and complain. Cowards won't go to Ukraine to defend homeland. Shame, but this is freedom, no? Too much freedom... Is chaos, maybe."

TWELVE

I f Michael was still getting acclimated to the city, the hotel was a culture shock in itself. He thought they must be picking up another passenger when they pulled into the turnaround of the palatial Ritz-Carlton. "Yup, this is us," Cam laughed.

The building looked like a Tsar's treasure box, squat and gaudily ornate over every inch of its ten stories. A glaringly modern three-story addition was perched on top like a black glass crown. The Russians weren't nearly as precious as the French about preserving the historical integrity of their vintage buildings. Just across the street, the onion domes and crimson minarets of the Kremlin and sundry cathedrals and museums reminded him that maybe history needed something more radical than a remodel.

Michael felt like a vagrant turning his beat-up old suitcase with the crooked wheel over to the bellhop. In the elevator, he could hold it in no longer, when Cam punched the button for the penthouse. "What the hell, man? How can we afford this?"

"All will be revealed, my friend," Cam said and smirked all the way to the top floor.

"Later, maybe?" Michael said. "I'm exhausted, man. Really need to sleep."

The door to their suite clicked and Cam held it open for

Maddie and Michael to enter. The bellhop fussily ushered Michael's suitcase inside, refusing to leave or allow him to touch it until he'd extracted a tip.

"Holy crap," Michael said, turning around and around, taking in the sumptuous furniture, the tapestries and oil paintings on the walls, the view—

"What seems to be the problem, sir?" Cam asked.

"This is the penthouse suite at the Ritz-Carlton."

"Yep," Cam kept a deadpan expression, as if this was all ordinary. "Welcome to Base Camp."

Michael strained to get a handle on it all. "Isn't this a little... ostentatious?"

"I assure you," Cam replied, "we deserve it."

"I mean, if we don't want to attract attention, maybe setting up a command center at the top of the fanciest hotel in town isn't such a good idea...?"

"It's perfect, actually. They're going to watch us no matter what we do, but they're more likely to lay off following us around town if they think they have us pegged. They'll see what they want to see, and we'll help them with that."

The grand imperial drawing room looked like it had hosted the signing of an international treaty. Now it was a staging area, with heaps of gear and tech, a blinking server tower and a row of laptops. Completing the scene were hills of rope, folded tents, sleeping bags, climbing tools and prepackaged food.

"How'd you get all this crap up here without tipping off the law?" Michael asked.

Cam shrugged affably and rubbed his fingers together. "Bribes, my good man. Bribes and lies. The hotel staff may or may not think we're shooting a porno up here." He waggled his eyebrows. "So, act accordingly."

Several people Michael had never seen before were nestled in the riot of gear.

"Everybody here?" Cam did a quick head count.

A pair of young hipster punks sat on a love seat, playing cards in rubber animal masks. The ostensibly male one wore a parrot's head and a Pussy Riot T-shirt. His partner, in a pencil skirt and an "Orgasm Addict" Buzzcocks shirt, sported the face of an adorable pug.

The most perfectly jacked human specimen Michael had ever seen stood shirtless behind the bar in white cycling shorts, making a protein shake in a brand-new blender.

Another guy, obviously Russian, sat behind the row of laptops—middle-aged, balding and reeking of cigarettes. Scratching his jowls and pecking at a phone, he looked suspiciously at Michael, then returned to his computers.

Cam made a show of searching out the last member of their group, but Michael noticed her first, standing before the window, almost eclipsed by the plush tumble of velvet curtains.

"Hello, Michael," said Amara, approaching with her hand out. Michael pivoted, took Cam by the arm and dragged him out onto the balcony, Maddie in tow.

"Impressive, right?" Cam said. "Like *Mission: Impossible*, in there…"

"You invited a reporter to tag along because… and I can only assume… shit wasn't hard enough already?"

Cam shook his head. "She's not a reporter." He looked away from Michael, caught Maddie's skeptical frown. "She *sometimes* freelances…"

"You said we were getting the band back together, not expanding into a full-blown orchestra. You 'omitted,' *bro*."

"Yes, I did omit. And I own that. But I also said this was going to be big, and I meant it. We're about to hit the Mount Everest of place-hacks and someone like her, a risk-taking Lois Lane with a committed Twitter following, is only going to be a force-multiplier, exposure-wise. She's a rock star."

Michael pointed at the twins. "What about them?"

The masked hipsters had grown bored with cards and were now frolicking out the window. The pug pirouetted on the hand's breadth of windowsill while the parrot shot her with a selfie stick, hanging alarmingly far out the window himself.

"Who are they?" Michael asked.

Maddie replied, "The parrot is Rene and the pug is Zoe. Twins."

Michael stared at them as the parrot climbed out onto the ledge beside the pug. "I don't see the resemblance."

"You remember the two kids who crushed the Statue of Liberty climb?"

"Tried to reclaim it for France or something, yeah…" Thinking for a moment, he came up with it before Cam had to explain. "No. They're anarchists, man. For them, getting caught is like a good thing."

"They have a million YouTube followers… which, for us, is totally a good thing. They're actually really smart."

The parrot was mooning Red Square. Michael let that speak for itself.

Maddie put in, "Rene's a structural engineer."

"Oh, *is* he?" Michael let the sarcasm fly. "And he's the…"

"Parrot," Maddie said.

"Right," Michael and Maddie made pained faces at each other.

"They have a following, they know their shit, and they bring the flavor. Besides, we're all anarchists, you haven't figured that out yet?"

Michael strolled closer to the window to watch the big guy, doing arms-only push-ups, which really just looked like he was humping his elbows. "What the hell am I looking at?"

"That's Bhumi," Cam said, like you'd tell a child, *That's the ocean.*

"Oh…" Turning to Maddie, he pointed and affected his best Cam imitation. "That's *Bhumi*."

Maddie smiled, which made this madness a little easier to take.

"That cat is one of the top two wingsuit flyers on the planet.

If not the best." Cam was beginning to sound a little exasperated with his old friend.

"So, we're not omitting anymore, we're straight-up lying."

Cam took a step closer, the humor gone from his eyes. "I didn't lie."

"You said we weren't going to BASE jump."

"*We're* not. *He* is. And wingsuit flying is like a totally different thing anyway, so…"

Michael pointed out the guy behind the computers. "And who's that?"

"Oh, that's just Yuri. Don't look at him, he's not here."

"No problem," Michael said, drizzling on the sarcasm. Cam's attention was already elsewhere.

The twins now danced on the ledge as the parrot belted the lyrics to a Joe Dassin love tune, "Et heor n'existais pas."

Michael watched them move, disarmed by the carefree fluidity of their dance. "You're sure about them?"

Cam smiled. "No. They're fucking nuts—but hella loaded. Daddy's a billionaire, finances like a quarter of the movies in France with the spare change found in his couch."

"Ahhh…" Michael sighed wearily.

"What? You think *I'm* paying for all this? The suite, your ticket out… all the expendables and bribes… plus if we get caught, that includes legal expenses. How's that for a parachute?" He mugged at Michael's lip-biting grimace. "Too soon? Sorry."

The parrot was now dangling freely by the pug's wrist as he swung out over the hotel façade, waving the selfie stick and singing into it like a microphone. Maddie chuckled and took out her own camera. The parrot continued to serenade Moscow and the crowd outside finally began to take notice, their cries and shouts floating up from the street far below.

"They're not even gonna survive long enough to make the climb," Michael said.

"That's a valid concern," Cam said in a humoring voice.

"And the FSB won't look at all this twice? Why, exactly? And be specific."

"Because of them. All part of our cover. Spoiled Eurotrash rich kids scouting locations for a vanity project music video thing. We see the sights, drop a ton of coin in the clubs, we go home. Yuri's got decoy reservations for a video crew to fly out for the actual shoot next month and ads placed for backup dancers and whatever, so it all looks legit and they think we're coming back, so they'll be a lot less suspicious."

"Ah, like that old Ben Affleck movie," Michael said. "Classic. Kinda makes me wonder, though, why you still need me."

"It wouldn't be the F.U. Crew without you, bro." Cam smiled and squeezed Michael's biceps. Then, as if it just occurred to him, he added, "But if you need something to do, there is one more little chore…"

Here it comes, Michael thought. The inevitable other shoe. "Yeah…?"

"So, dig it. The site we're hacking is in this big development, right?"

"Moscow International Business Center," Michael chimed in. "I know. What about it?"

"Well, they've got security…"

"We've dodged rent-a-cops before."

"It's a little more complicated than that… I was actually thinking you could help, since it's your department."

"And what department is that, Cam?"

Cam led him over to the computers, where Yuri was relaying a Russian news site through some bespoke translation app. "Y'see, they're running this facial recognition deal all around the business center site, and we were hoping…"

"Hoping what? I can hack it for you? I'm not a hacker, and I don't speak Russian…"

"I am not hacker, either," Yuri said indignantly, brushing ashes off his sweaty shirt. "I am security expert. Skill-set totally different." He pointed to a table lamp with a clear plastic dome over it. "Counter-surveillance."

"Say what now?" Michael asked. "This place is bugged?"

"Of course, bugged!" Yuri snapped. "And cannot simply unplug or destroy. We must enclose and feed. False audio, video loops. Misinformation."

Michael leaned in close to the enclosure box. He could hear a tinny voice chattering away from the chunky Android knockoff phone resting inside, propped against the lamp base.

"We recorded two days' worth of dummy pre-production meetings," Cam said, clearly proud of himself. "Audio and video. But anyway, this is in your wheelhouse, bro, trust me. It's what you do. And it's not in Russian. Check it…"

Michael leaned over Yuri's shoulder to skim the *RT News* item about the security innovations at Moscow International Business Center, which included a new facial recognition system that would scan all passersby against a list of known security threats and foreign nationals. It omitted that there were all kinds of ways to defeat the software, as anyone who followed tech news understood. Every failed ID sent an alert to the on-site engineer for review, so to beat it, you'd have to get access to the network. And to do that, you'd have to know the software.

He got all the way to the bottom of the article before he realized what an asshole his best friend truly was. "The advanced face-recognition system was designed by an American company, Macrosync…"

"*Told* you that app was creepy," Cam said.

THIRTEEN

That night, Moscow put on its best face for them.

They had a five-course supper at Metropol No. 4, one of Moscow's oldest restaurants, then adjourned to the Beluga Bar for caviar, smoked sturgeon and astonishingly smooth vodka. Then, still bloated and swooning from the meal, they went to Duran Bar, a loud, packed meat-market scene where the crowd bounced to blistering Slavic hip-hop. Mercifully, they didn't stay there long.

Michael lost track of the places they went, after that. Cam, acting like a Catskills *tummler*, hustled them from one destination to the next with jocular energy. He'd order rounds of drinks for the crew and anyone in their path when the place was proper, or quickly evacuate them from overpriced, crowded clubs with a hearty, "*Yebat eto der'mo!*" A cabbie told them that this translated as "*Fuck this shit!*" so they went with that.

Every time they piled out of a place to caravan to the next, Michael found himself searching the street, looking for the inevitable tail, and was both gratified and unnerved when he spotted one. A black Mercedes with tinted windows paced them everywhere they went, hanging two or three cars behind, but always lurking down the block when they hit a new spot.

By 1:00 a.m., they finally settled in at Icon, currently the most high-end club in Moscow. Located in Red October, a converted chocolate factory on Bolotny Island, Icon rumbled and flashed behind convoys of bulletproof Bentleys and Mercedes SUVs, chain-smoking bodyguards, and the dreaded bouncers.

Men paid a hefty 20,000-ruble cover and still had to pass the withering judgment of the "face control" at the front door. Dressed in his charcoal gray job interview suit, minus the tie, Michael struggled to emit the required confidence and nonchalance. He fully expected to be turned away. Cam hustled the craggy golem blocking the entrance as if they were bosom chums, somehow cutting through the throng waiting at the door and securing them a table in the VIP area where champagne ran to 14,000 rubles a bottle. Michael was impressed with their set-up, then noticed the tiers of balconies overlooking the dance floor.

"What's the deal with the private boxes?" he asked Cam.

"Oh, that's just where wealth beyond our mortal imagination waits and watches, scoping out the action from the shadows."

Michael shivered. "So, they're the spiders and we're the flies?"

Cam shrugged with a leer, letting Michael know he was being hopelessly I.

The Icon club was an introvert's nightmare. A tony international crowd packed the two thousand-deep dance floor, writhing to blaring Russian dance pop, corny remixed crap in heavy rotation because old rich guys called the tunes. Rene and Zoe immediately disappeared into the surging crowd. Amara went the back courtyard to take a call, while Maddie followed Cam to the bar. This left Michael sitting across the table from Bhumi, who was impassively scanning the crowd and saying nothing.

Michael fell into the role, as he often did, of observer. Looking past the other tourists, the crowd fell into a weird pattern. All the Russian men in sight were at least thirty-five, and none of the women past twenty-five. These creatures were among the most breathtaking females he'd ever seen, utterly unlike the models back home, with wide-set, haunting stares and effortlessly contemptuous expressions. They skillfully worked the older, obviously rich guys for drinks and other favors transacted out of sight. He wondered how many of them were the fabled oligarchs who supposedly controlled everything around here. Any younger guys on the scene appeared to be bodyguards.

I do not have what it takes to make it in this town, Michael thought without a molecule of regret. He'd read up on the scene here, seen ads for gold-digger academies, where young, beautiful *tiolki* ("cattle") could learn the secrets to snagging a powerful "Forbes" who would set them up in an apartment, buy them a car and shower them with gifts until they got too old, usually by age twenty-two, and were swapped out for a newer model, or actress.

Studying the crowd, he noticed Cam and Maddie arguing. He couldn't make out what they were saying, but their body language made it clear that Maddie was angry. When she stormed off, Cam returned to their table and plucked a frosty magnum of champagne from a silver bucket.

As if on cue, the sound system seemed to have a seizure. When it recovered, a souped-up version of Plastic Bertrand's "Ça plane pour moi" blasted out of the speakers. The crowd split open to circle round the Jardin twins as they jitter-bugged at the center of the floor.

Michael drummed his fingers on the arm of his chair. He was past pissed at Cam about the face recognition issue, but now wasn't the time or place. "Thought you said those two were twins?"

"Yeah," Cam said, rolling the icy champagne against his sweaty brow. "Why?"

They watched as Rene lifted his sister high over his head and caught her in a close clinch, poised nose to nose, way too close for a standard filial relationship.

"Dude, they're French." Cam distractedly emptied the bottle into a water glass and got up out of his chair. "Excuse me," he barked before heading off towards the floor.

Again, Michael was stranded with the annoyingly enigmatic Bhumi. Of all the new additions to the crew, Bhumi baffled Michael the most because he was either much more or much less than he appeared. His annoyance turned to astonishment when he saw that a swarm of fawning women, particularly Asians, had descended upon the athlete, asking for his autograph, offering up their private numbers on napkins.

Of all the things Cam had thrown at Michael, wingsuit flying was the one on which he'd taken a hard pass. It was just too sketchy in an urban environment.

Since the barnstorming days after World War I, daredevil air show "batmen" had tried to fly on ribbed canvas wings, but few achieved any real lift off them, and fewer still survived their first serious field tests. Even when they deployed their parachutes, the silk got tangled in the wings. The French skysurfer and skydiver Patrick de Gayardon was the first to successfully test a wingsuit that could not only allow one to actually "fly," but to land without a parachute—sadly, he gambled his life and lost, like so many others.

Michael was a little in awe of anyone who could do it. In his research, he'd come across one common factor that bound together the wingsuit flyers from the barnstorming days to the present—nearly all of them were orphans.

Intrigued in spite of himself, Michael moved close enough to shout in Bhumi's ear. "Yo, what's your deal, man? How do these honeys all know you?"

"People over here go crazy for wingsuit flying. In Asia, it's even bigger. They host the World Championships in China."

"No shit. You ever compete?"

"I won it," Bhumi affably yawned. "Not much of a competition, really."

Michael rolled his eyes. *This guy...*

He spotted Cam next to Amara at the bar, his hand on her lower back. Strange. Bhumi sipped his water.

During a pause in the autograph session, Michael had to lean in again. "You don't drink?"

"Alcohol, caffeine, sugar, gluten, dairy…" Bhumi counted them off on his fingers, balled them up and threw them away. "I never allow any such toxins to enter my body."

"Not even on special occasions? I couldn't live without coffee," Michael said.

Bhumi, silently looking off into space, might've been an enlightened guru on a mountaintop, attempting to educate a clueless lesser being. "Attachments are dangerous. A road that leads only to pain."

"Yeah," Michael joked, "I get the headaches, too." Why couldn't he resist busting this guy's chops? Maybe for the same reason Bhumi couldn't just get over himself and drop the warrior-monk bullshit.

Bhumi sighed, sipped his water. Wasting his wisdom. "Any time you free yourself of a thing, you're better for it, my friend. Surrender of the self. Change is the ultimate reality. The only constant."

Michael patted his pockets. "Hang on now, let me write this down."

"The self is the only thing you have control over." Bhumi's laser-guided attention wandered to the crush of hungry-eyed models waiting for a break in the conversation. He arched an eyebrow at Michael. "Think about it logically… if you're a part of a larger whole that's always changing, then attachments can only bring suffering."

Michael frowned. Vodka never brought out the philosopher in him. "Adapt or die, something like that?"

Bhumi shrugged. "Something…" The models would not be denied a moment longer. Bhumi tensed in his chair.

"And this," Michael said, indicating the wall of women, "what is this?"

"Surrender of the self," Bhumi said tightly. "You mind?"

Fed up, Michael vacated his chair. Two models quickly squeezed into it, pressing cocktail napkins and pens into Bhumi's hands.

Enlightenment looks exhausting, Michael thought. He realized he'd forgotten to ask Bhumi if he was an orphan.

Michael wandered through the jostling crowd of club-goers. Rene and Zoe were still tearing it up on the floor. He saw Cam leading Amara by the hand, no doubt going somewhere more private. Michael finished a drink he didn't need and deposited the glass on a table as he passed by. *God, I need to get out of here.*

Eventually, he found himself leaning on the railing on a rooftop terrace packed with smokers. Like a diver surfacing from icy water, Michael inhaled the sultry, smoky night air. He spotted Maddie sitting at a table, a bottle of vodka for company, or a protective force field. He went over and sat beside her.

"Seen Cam?" she asked. Her voice sounded tight and tired. Had she been crying?

Michael considered telling the truth for a fleeting moment, but brotherly duty prevailed. He checked an empty glass for cigarette butts before pouring himself a stiff dose of Russian courage. "He's floating around somewhere. You know him."

Maddie picked up the bottle and filled her glass, took a shot and winced. "Yes, I do." She didn't have to explain to him, at least.

Looking around for any change of subject, he spotted the silvery eminence of the solitary skyscraper lording it over the western horizon. "That her? Russia's glorious challenge to western hegemony?"

Maddie forced a smile. "Yes. It's a whole lot of vertical."

Bathed in spotlights that silhouetted its crown of cranes, Korova Tower looked almost alive, as if it were assembling itself in the dark, impatient to be completed. Beside it, the once-mighty Federation Tower looked like a footstool, and the whole city looked shrunken.

"Jesus," he murmured, "that's no skyscraper, that's a sky-violator."

She laughed. "The dick-measuring contest is over. They won. Russia clearly has the biggest dong."

Cheered by the sound of her laughter, he added, "Not the only thing about this outing that's getting too big. The cloak and dagger stuff is a big distraction."

Her eyes narrowed. "What do you mean?"

"You haven't noticed we're being followed everywhere tonight?"

"Oh, that." Maddie waved a dismissive hand, though her expression betrayed a whisper of unease. "Relax, they're ours."

Michael did a double take. "We have bodyguards?"

"Cam's not taking any chances with the locals. Mafiya kidnapping rings are a thing here, apparently."

Michael didn't think that was who they'd need to worry about, and doubted if a couple of hired goons could stop the full weight of the Russian intelligence service swooping on them on bogus espionage charges, but he didn't belabor the point. "I just feel like we're in over our heads…"

"It's the same old game," Maddie said, "just a higher level. You know Cam… he never stops playing."

"But *attachments bring misery*, according to Bhumi. He might not be wrong." Despite his fairly spot-on Bhumi imitation, the comment came off heavier than he intended.

"Climb, conquer and quit," said Maddie. "Wasn't that one of our mantras?"

"I thought it still was," said Michael. They both smiled, any residual levity drifting away with the cigarette smoke, leaving Michael floundering for something else to say.

"The new crew. What do you think?" asked Maddie, having switched channels without Michael noticing.

"Rene and Zoe are nice…" He took a big swig of vodka to stop saying anything else.

"Twincest?" Maddie blurted.

Michael practically spat out his drink. Vodka surged into his sinuses, scorching his face from the inside out. Sensing his helplessness, she leaned in close and did a fair imitation of the twins' slinky, creepily intimate dance in her chair. He waved helplessly at her to stop.

"What?" Maddie demanded. "Those two are way too tight."

When his coughing fit subsided, he wiped tears from his eyes. "No, that's just, you know, brotherly-sisterly love."

"It's *some kind* of love."

"Well… I read or heard that identical twins identify both bodies as their own, so it's not sexual… unless touching yourself is sexual…?"

"Thanks," Maddie said, toasting him with her glass. "That makes it, like, twenty percent less creepy."

They cracked up again, the laughter igniting pleasant memories of old times. She relaxed, leaned her head on his shoulder. He tried not to throw an arm around her. "Still glad you came?"

He exhaled loud and long through pursed lips. "Honestly, I don't even know why I agreed to join this circus."

"Sure you do." She turned and looked deeply into his eyes. Michael tensed up. *Did she know?* By now, she had to…

"Cam asked."

Not the answer he expected. He smiled harmlessly and looked away. "You still get those dreams? Remember we used to talk about…"

"Flying."

"Yeah. Yeah…" He suddenly felt morose and somber. *Must be the vodka*, he thought, hitting it again. "Now when I close my eyes, it's like… falling. All the time."

She sat up, enervated, making him regret what he'd said. His shoulder, where she'd touched him, felt like part of a happy person. "How long have you felt like that?"

"Since the accident. Maybe a little before." Looking away from her, then away from Korova Tower, he went on, "I thought coming out here… I don't know. I don't know what I thought.

I miss when it was just the three of us exploring. Wasn't about proving anything. It was about finding something that was yours, and only yours. The second we started sharing that with everybody... I don't know, it just changed. Does that make sense?"

Maddie put a hand on his shoulder. "I think... that you think too much."

"Think so?"

"Yeah. Instead of living life, you're too busy..." She poked the side of his head, not ungently. "Thinking about it. Gotta get outta your head, son." Her Cam imitation was a lot better than his.

"I think too much, huh? Maybe you're just used to being around Cam." He nudged her playfully.

She smiled. "Shut up. No, Cam... you're right, Cam lives *entirely* in the moment. Which can be tough, especially when you're trying to plan a future with someone. But that's what makes him who he is. Most people spend their entire lives never really doing anything. Cam has vision. A plan. He goes for it... you know?"

Michael didn't say anything. She was conning herself, imitating him now without realizing she was doing it. "You're gonna marry that fool, huh?"

She punched him in the arm. "He's your best friend..."

"He *is* my best friend, but I wouldn't marry him. Just sayin'."

"Guess we're both a couple of suckers," she said. For a moment, she leaned back against him again and he felt a rush of blood fill his face. He almost said something, when a chorus of cheers and shouts erupted from inside. Maddie got up and went to the railing overlooking the dance floor and called out, "Awwwww shit... Get it, Rene!"

Inside, Rene was busting an epic acrobatic move on the dance floor when he bumped into a big guy who just had to be someone's bodyguard, knocking a drink out of his hand. They sized each other up, Rene bowing as if inviting the goon to dance. The meathead gave Rene a hard two-handed shove.

Rene flew off his feet and crashed into a circle of women, but before the goon could press his advantage, he caught a right hook to the jaw from Zoe, who kept coming after him like an avenging angel until his buddies intervened.

Michael and Maddie pushed back inside the club and forced their way across the crowded floor, through shoving bodies and dazzling laser flashes. The crowd had opened up to watch the brawl, which was in full swing with not a bouncer in sight. Rene was shoved back on his feet by the women he'd fallen on. Bowing gracefully to them, he launched himself at the meathead grappling with his sister. Two of the bruiser's friends were circling, looking for an opening to separate the twins, eyes red with roid-rage.

Michael waved down the rest of the crew in the VIP area, cupping his hands and shouting, "Cam!"

Cam jumped up on his chair, searching the crowd, then saw Michael motioning to the brawl. "Oh shit!" He waved his arms like a conductor, trying to flag down the bouncers, who... stopped and turned their backs.

Michael tried to get between the Russians and the twins and walked right into a flying fist. A million-watt laser show went off in his skull. He staggered into someone who shoved him back, trying to catch up to his feet, ducking a haymaker punch more by luck than skill, when someone else caught him and stood him upright.

"Surrender the self," Bhumi said in his ear, and pushed him out of the way.

Bhumi calmly let the knuckleheads charge him, then threw his water glass at the big Russians' feet. Twisting to avoid the flying glass, one planted a foot on an ice cube and stumbled face-first into the big athlete's perfectly toned, expertly positioned knee. Bhumi stepped aside to let the big guy collapse, then went toe-to-toe with his comrade.

The bouncers finally arrived and formed a wedge to drive all the combatants towards the exit. The original bruiser had multiplied into a gang, trading punches with Rene while Zoe fended them off with high, sweeping kicks. One of them backed into a flying tackle from Cam, who yanked the hulk's blazer down to trap his arms and rode him like a roped steer across the floor, raining blows on his head and shoulders.

Michael backed away from a wall of swinging fists and raking nails, still stunned from the shot to his dome. Now the missing bouncers began sweeping the floor in force. Maddie grabbed his hand and tugged him towards the door as Cam bellowed over the cacophony, "Marines! We are leaving!"

The crew shouted back, "*Yebat eto der'mo!*" and made for the exits.

No cabs stopped for them on the street, but it was almost 5:30, so they caught the first Metro of the morning back to Red Square.

Considering how they were one of the best-preserved features of the Soviet era, the Metro stations were something of a surprise. Built in the post-WWII boom that Eisenhower used to create the interstate system at home, Stalin's subway networks boasted chandeliers, lavish architectural ornamentation and grand Classical columns. Michael figured the idea was to give every peasant in the workers' paradise the thrill of storming a Tsar's palace on their morning commute.

Slouching on the seats at the back of a train car crowded with morning commuters, they rode in silence, each wrapped up in their own thoughts, aches and pains.

Michael looked up and caught Cam smiling at him, sharing that mischievous grin and beaming with... yes, it was pride. No point wondering not if, but how much, Cam bribed the bouncers to let this little team-building exercise run its course. Before he could resist it, Michael's own face lit up with a grin when he looked around, all of them were smiling and laughing, then at the disapproving scowls all around them, they laughed even harder, and when Cam held out his fist, every member of the Furies leaned in and touched knuckles.

FOURTEEN

Dawn broke over the capital, the surfaces of Korova Tower gleaming like scaly skin in the rosy light. The blue glass inserts covering the building's lower two-thirds threw off sparkling flares, contrasting with the upper third, a fluted wand of naked concrete and high-tension steel, a fluttering of shadows.

Covering a whole city block, all around its foundation were rows of trailers, heavy equipment, generators and stacks of windows and other building supplies, which would one day host a plaza and park. Chanting protestors with blaring air horns were less than a mile away, a telling contrast to the stillness of the site.

A lone surveyor in an orange vest and hardhat took laser readings from a series of points around the building, then crossed the field of red-gray earth to step inside the front entrance.

From the window of a vacant office building a few hundred yards away, Rene and Zoe, bleary-eyed from the night before, slurped coffee and took notes, sharing a pair of binoculars. Scattered all around were sketchbooks, fat markers and a folio of mylar stencils, which Rene had been cutting by hand with a penknife. Nearby on the windowsill sat a tripod-mounted video camera, rigged with an impressive telescopic lens.

They watched the surveyor enter the exterior construction
elevator and punch a code into the touchscreen console before
riding it up the side of the tower. Rene inclined his head just a
few degrees. Zoe noticed and went to the video camera, rewound
it a bit to watch the playback. Rene turned and sleepily quirked
his mouth in lieu of asking in words.

Zoe smiled and nodded.

Her brother made a pantomime gesture to suggest striving
vainly to keep his heart from leaping out of his chest, making
her laugh.

In his room at the Ritz-Carlton, Cam lounged, gobbling Advil
and hot soup on a bed where American presidents had slept.
He was eavesdropping on a recorded conference call between
two of the developers of Korova Tower and the contractors
tasked with completing its construction.

Cam skimmed the English transcript. "With the decision
to increase the structure's area by another ten percent," said
one of the contractors, "we were effectively building bigger on
the existing foundations. We all know that the pour was never
designed to for an additional load like this. To accommodate
this unplanned expansion, we were forced to reduce the size
of the core walls. In theory this was sound strategy." And here
the speaker paused, no doubt to focus everyone on his next
words; Cam certainly was. "But in reality, the practical result of
this adjustment has, in effect, caused the building to…" Another
pause. "Tilt."

Everyone took a beat, silently processing how their
responsibility for delivering a leaning building of this size
and importance would affect their individual futures. There
was already a story going around. One of the developers'
spokespersons broke the communal meditation. "Surely this
occurrence was anticipated…?"

The lead contractor cleared his throat a bit nervously. "One doesn't build a structure with the assumption it won't stand up straight, but there are always contingency plans. We have the most advanced 'active alignment' systems in place. So yes, we can course-correct, but even with state-of-the-art megastructure stabilization technology at hand, we will have to place tower construction on hold until after the load discrepancy has been fully accounted for. You must understand," concluded the contractor with no small amount of genuine passion as he warmed to the subject, "that this exigent circumstance directly impacts the building's structural integrity."

Cam could imagine the developer scowling. "You mean it could collapse? You've seen too many disaster movies."

"Perhaps you haven't seen enough. We need to address this situation without delay. This is what I am telling."

Another pause. Cam imagined them all staring each other down.

"Speaking of delay," said the developer, choosing to ignore the last vigorous exchange. "In light of our current accelerated schedule, how might this affect opening day projections?"

"Well, I'd be lying if I said it wasn't going to be a race to the finish…"

Cam was beginning to think he was wasting his time, no matter how worried the contractor sounded. Probably just a ploy for another kickback. There was a huge folder of this shit, and Cam hadn't begun to dig into it until after their inside man had gone dark two weeks ago. Serhiy, their local IT guy, assured him that Igor was just on a long, overdue vacation, which Cam knew was sketchy, even potentially fatal, if it wasn't resolved soon. Even so, he decided to dump the illicit audio files on Rene; he had other priorities. If Rene found something worthwhile in the endless Russian jabber, all the better, and if there were any big surprises, he'd be sure that Cam was the first to know. Finding out that the face recognition deal was sourced from Michael's day job was pure gold. *It's a small world after all, bro…*

Cam yawned, skimming the translation, popped another Advil, and dozed off humming the *Mission: Impossible* theme.

Michael blended in with the tourists, just another passenger on a nondescript boat tour meandering down the Moscow River. Like everyone else, he snapped pictures and listened to a translated tour on his earbuds. But unlike everyone else, he was there on recon.

He watched the scenery drift by, his brain throbbing in equal measure from last night's vodka and the punch he'd taken. More annoying and painful were the guilty thoughts about Facial.

What had he been thinking, helping to create that monster? Even Dr. Frankenstein must have thought he was building an *Übermensch*, right up until it opened its eyes. Michael didn't do it all by himself, of course, but he was responsible for the code that compared varieties of photographs to authenticate the submitted image. This was the central element to the app's effectiveness.

The truth was even worse, though. He hadn't really been thinking at all. Needing a distraction from his painful recovery, he'd buried himself in work and looked at it as a series of challenges. In a few reflective moments, he told himself that the app would empower people who were being harassed, assaulted, or robbed. He'd bought the company line about people-power and didn't look any deeper than he had to.

He didn't push back against his boss's shaky arguments that stalkers, creeps and sex pests had other resources for targeting their victims, while innocent people had almost none. He wasn't proud of what he was doing, but he didn't walk away, even when the marketing VP began to pivot and talk less about young urban professionals and more about contracting with police departments and government agencies.

This was worse than any outcome he could've imagined, but it shouldn't have come as a surprise. Because Facial searched multiple databases, it consistently outscored competing face recognition Ais, especially on darker-complected subjects, so it would be a leap in quality over most public surveillance systems. His contract explicitly entitled the company to exploit his work worldwide at their own discretion, but he always assumed any rollout abroad would be the same type of app for regular people's phones. If another country didn't allow their citizens to have such apps, they wouldn't do business there.

The thing he'd helped build was being used to monitor and tag pedestrians at special locations like Korova, but soon it would blanket all of Moscow, Saint Petersburg, Minsk and beyond. Surely, it would spread to every totalitarian regime that could afford it.

He wasn't surprised Macrosync had kept it a secret, but to find out from Cam only rubbed salt in the wound. *How could you be so blind?* He'd let himself be led because it was easier than taking charge and thinking for himself. *And how is that any different from what's happening now?*

He had to pull his mind out of this negative feedback loop. The looming structures off the starboard bow did exactly that. The tour was approaching his target.

The guide held forth at the front of the boat in her native tongue. That the canned translation in his ear was more or less in sync with the live recital was a vague source of relief to Michael.

"In 1980, there were no skyscrapers in Moscow," explained the tour guide, "while today we have nearly as many as New York, with almost a quarter of the world's steel and cement being put to use. On the embankment just before you is Federation Tower. At ninety-seven stories, it was once the second-tallest building in Europe. To the left, of course, is the newest centerpiece of the expanded Moscow International Business District... the Korova Tower.

"Dubbed 'Vertikal'nyy Gorod,' or the Vertical City, almost a full kilometer in height, Korova officially holds the title as the tallest building in the world, eclipsing the Burj in Dubai and even Saudi Arabia's Kingdom Tower. Designed by renowned Italian architect Alfonso Ziggura, who said his desire was 'to create a ladder to the heavens'... a motif he cleverly implemented into the building's design, as you'll see when it officially opens in September."

Michael observed and took notes alongside his jottings gleaned from the 'net. The tower was being built by the Korova Corporation, a Russian venture capitalist firm—so, basically, another bunch of oligarchs playing with stolen money—at an estimated cost of $35 billion. Even in broad daylight, it felt like a phantom, a—what was the phrase?—a "vertical Potemkin village."

Moscow was a vast city of fifteen million, but even given the crush of density towards the center of the capital, there was little impetus to go high-rise in a country that sprawled across eleven time zones. Yes, there was some real "big dick energy" at work here, just as Maddie had observed. The biggest dick... or the smallest...

"The skyscraper was designed for mixed-use occupancy, with plans to open the first five floors, which feature a world-class concert venue, for occupancy in July... making Korova also the largest building ever to open while still under construction.

"The tower will boast its own underground Metro station and is equipped with state-of-the-art fuel cells to meet the building's clean energy needs. For the first time ever, a skyscraper will be able to generate its own renewable power, and even feed the excess into the surrounding area... a beating heart at the city's center—"

"You are American, no?"

Startled, Michael took an earbud out and looked at the woman beside him on the bench. Maybe thirty years older, studious, with big eyeglasses and dowdy outfit more concerned with blocking the sun than accommodating the heat. "Is it that obvious?"

She nodded. "How do you like Russia?"

"It's great," he said, a raft of empty pleasantries on his tongue. "Loving all the history, but I'm surprised at how..."

"Modern?" The woman arched an eyebrow at him, making him fumble and laugh at himself.

"Yes, you could say that. This new tower... Really impressive..." That sounded lame enough, if he was dealing with a spy. In the Soviet era, KGB agents followed foreign visitors everywhere, and why would the country's suspicious nature change, with a former KGB agent in charge? Would they send a woman who looked like a college professor to follow him? And if so, would she just call him out?

Suddenly, he didn't feel like much of a spy. Nobody over here knew his name or would have any reason to suspect anything, but Michael wasn't a dummy. He'd followed the stories about Americans being arrested for espionage in response to the election meddling accusations back home and NATO support for Ukraine, but the Furies weren't trading in state secrets or Soviet-surplus weapons. He'd never really thought he had anything to worry about. In spite of his mission, he was just a tourist plotting an unauthorized outing. All it was, really, was particularly reckless trespassing. And Russia wasn't North Korea; at least not on the surface.

"Russia's pride," the woman said, and chuckled darkly. "You know, not everyone here is so proud of what we've become."

"I, uh, noticed, the... the marchers..." he fumbled again, wondering where this was going.

She leaned in close and put a hand on his knee. Startled, he sat frozen as she whispered huskily in his ear. "That is why they march. We dream of beating the West at its own game... the capitalism. The democracy, not so much. Today, they march against dissident groups being excluded from elections, and reporters jailed or shot or poisoned, tomorrow for the conscripted being rushed to the new Western Front. But most are resigned, if not perfectly content. While there is Putin, there is Russia, we say. But when there is no Putin, there will be no Russia…"

"You're a big country," he said. "I'm sure someone—"

"You don't understand, do you? The oligarchs are thugs with no plan. They run the casino and rob it both, trusting that benign fate will keep the lights on. But with that tower—they call it Korova. Do you know what that means? It is the Cow. Through which we will milk the world. When it opens, there will always be a Putin, so there will always be a Russia, until there is nothing else."

"You're right, I don't understand…"

"You will," she said, "when it is too late." She got up off the bench and made for the gangplank as the boat nosed up against the pier to conclude the tour. Michael started to go after her, but then shook his head and laughed. He didn't need to try to understand. *If that's the best you can do, Russia, maybe I am a pretty good spy.*

He stood up and fell in step with the other tourists, balling his fists up in the pockets of his windbreaker. Then he felt a small plastic object in his pocket. It had to be a thumb drive. Furtively, he palmed it, snuck a glance sideways before opening his hand. Confirmation. He felt an unseasonable chill as he looked around, studying the faces for someone else who might be following him, who might have noticed the strange interaction.

You're not a spy at all, bro, he told himself.

Because that *was a real spy, and she deputized you into their secret fraternity, bro… Holy shit!*

FIFTEEN

Maddie sat on a bench in Gorky Park, busy on her laptop. Mel the publicist had done a fair job of wrangling the socials for the Furies, but Maddie couldn't resist getting into the trenches herself.

LES FURIES ARE BACK. F.U. CREW GOES WORLDWIDE WITH MOST MASSIVE HACK TONIGHT. WATCH LIVE!!!

She shared the banner headline on each of the stacked tabs on her browser, cracked her knuckles and braced herself before wading into the comments.

Even with VPN protection she worried about her encryption being cracked, about being shut down. And if those responsible for monitoring them figured out that she was a member of the Furies and was posting from Moscow, thus putting them on a heightened alert, they couldn't possibly take a harmless social media stunt that seriously... could they? All those "ifs" were eating at Maddie's stomach lining.

Posting under the alias *madsk!llz312*, she'd been teasing a major announcement for the past three weeks, hashtagging the site that would host their streaming video and updates. Chat-groups all over the world lit up over the news. Excited Likes and Loves abounded, but she zeroed in on the trolls who called the crew "fame-hungry, commercial sell-outs" and a "disgrace to urbex."

Sour grapes, most of it… but were they wrong?

If anyone in the urbex community wasn't starving for exactly the kind of fame they were courting they kept to themselves and nobody knew their names. If they were angry at the crew's political bent they were kidding themselves that urbex—at its core about reclaiming forbidden spaces—wasn't by definition a political act. All those people faulting them for trying to make a living doing what they were good at must surely love their own day jobs.

Weird to be world-famous while also totally unknown. *Hello, Banksy.* From their first amateurish jaunts, they'd worn bandanas or particle-filter masks. They were either breaking the law or stirring up asbestos and worse; then they'd collectively decided to keep their identities secret. If they were just the Furies, they remained mysterious, known only by their audacity and their activism, invisible until they sprang into action.

Though she sometimes longed for the respect that fame might bring, *infamy* was, she had to admit, way cooler. When people know your name and your face, they think they know you, and if they buy what you're selling, they think they own *you.* Maddie was more than content to lurk and play sock puppet as the world wondered who they were and where they would strike next.

Even your worst enemy can give you the gift of truth, and haters, as the lady said, gonna hate. Maddie was still hungover. The free-floating angst from last night—what did she say? What did she do?—merged with the nagging doubts over the fight with Cam. It stirred up her anxiety so badly that only flaming fools on the 'net could lay it to rest.

When he says he's doing all of this for us, Maddie thought, *does he really not see how we're really doing all of this for him?* She knew that Cam would see just what he wanted to see, just like she had, especially being jazzed about the crew reuniting, seeing Michael back on his feet, the travel, and yes, the posh hotel. It all felt like a dream, and she'd gotten so into it, she dared to dream that Cam might... *What?* Stop being "Cam"?

As long as she'd known him, Cam's charm had been legendary, but she had to get engaged to him to uncover how much effort went into it, how he could never turn it off. A master of "getting over with" people, Cam sized up everyone he encountered like an obstacle course, spotting handholds and slippery places. He charged at them, stunting right over them like they were made to be climbed, had them falling all over themselves to make him happy in return. Maddie had seen him turn it on for security guards who'd caught them red-handed, how he'd get them posing for selfies before letting them go.

Sure, she was pissed at how hard he was still working Amara. Cam had said he only wanted to make Amara feel like part of the crew, but she'd seen them dancing together, and when she'd called him on it, he'd just blown her off. Told Maddie not to worry. To grow up, and respect the Hustle.

This morning, Maddie didn't know how she felt. She was so in love with Cam just yesterday, but sometimes, when she examined her feelings, she felt like she was just another victim of the Hustle, and everything he'd said or done started to fall apart.

Like with Michael.

If not for the fight they'd already had, she would've lit into Cam about dragging Michael along, coercing him when he wasn't ready. But Michael was an adult, and if he was still seduced by Cam's line of anarchist alpha-male bullshit, was it really her job to wake him from that beautiful dream? Maybe he really needed it right now, even if it meant a gulag in the near future...

Michael wasn't that dumb, though, was he? What other motive would take him halfway around the world to risk his life on this stupid stunt?

Maddie added some Emergen-C to the brackish tap water in her flask and bolted it down, wincing at the gritty aftertaste. Popping her knuckles again, she vented her anger hating on some haters.

SIXTEEN

Saturday afternoon, the group reconvened for a final briefing at a secret location. Each of them returned from their individual tourist activities to rendezvous on a bus south of the Moscow River. Cam nodded at each of them as they boarded, but they stayed apart until Pyatnitskaya Street, where they all jumped off to catch the tour that Cam had arranged.

The Street of All Fridays was a refreshing break from the rest of Moscow, a sleepy antique avenue mostly overlooked by the rampant development devouring the rest of the city. Two-story mansions and little shops of pre-Soviet vintage, rich with ornamental flowers, lions and bears molded on the façades, shed an air of decaying whimsy on the street, even as it was being destroyed. Across from the bus stop, they saw a construction site where a group of protestors in Pinocchio masks gathered to mourn whatever local landmark once stood in the spot.

They walked for several blocks with a jocular tour guide who took a swig of vodka from a silver flask at each historic site. Cam scanned the street behind them every so often, relishing the espionage game. None of them had observed anyone following them, but their phones could be tracked, and this country had invented street-level spycraft. You had to assume they were there, that they watched.

The police, or anyone claiming to be police, could demand your passport at any time, and custom demanded a crisp 1,000 ruble note folded within, if you didn't know the arcane etiquette for tendering a bribe. Even locals had to present their papers on demand and could be fined or arrested if any of the required registration stamps were missing or expired.

The tour crept on until they passed through a courtyard with an outdoor bar. Cam detoured into a narrow doorway at the back of a decrepit mansion, half-consumed by fire. Even this precious neighborhood was subject to a plague of arsonists, the guide had told them, developers intent on eating up this last remnant of the old Moscow.

The crew followed Cam through blackened, roofless halls to a small, smoke-damaged room overlooking a courtyard rife with wildflowers. All their gear was assembled on a long table that looked like it might once have hosted banquets. Curtains were drawn and Yuri went over each of them with a scanner before declaring them clean.

Cam picked up Bhumi's thermos, filled with some mystery liquid, giving it a whiff. "What is this?"

Bhumi looked annoyed. "That's my piss."

Cam recoiled, setting the thermos carefully on the table and wiping his hand on his shirt. "What the hell? Why is it in a thermos?"

"For when I take a shower," Bhumi replied, screwing the lid down on the thermos and sticking it in his pack. "It's good for your roots."

"You put that in your *hair*?"

Bhumi looked both offended and disappointed. "Of course." Tilting his chin at Cam's hairline, he added, "You might try it. You're kind of thinning on top."

Cam laughed uncomfortably. "Thought maybe you drank it."

Bhumi shrugged. "Oh, that too."

Cam's laughter died in a gasp. "What's that good for?"

Bhumi shrugged. "It's good for drinking."

Cam stood by with his arms crossed, while Maddie, the logistics boss, told them everything they still needed to know.

"As Russia Day festivities are beginning this morning, all of Moscow is taking the weekend off. All work is halted, so security's going to be minimal. And because of the protests, the police are stretched even thinner than usual."

"It goes down tonight," Cam said. "We've been maxing out the online outreach, but all of you can help. Get the word out. The F.U. Crew is back on the scene and something big is about to go down."

"Rene and Zoe locked down the schedules," Maddie continued. "Construction crews, security guards... when they check in and check out. How many are there, and where they're posted... 8:00 p.m. is our sweet spot. The third shift comes on then. The entry point is the southeast corner of the site."

Zoe jumped in, speaking with a pungent French accent. "The past few days they've been working with only the skeleton crew. Even before the holiday..."

"Well, that's even better," Cam interrupted.

"Hold up," Michael said, "they pulled the construction crews, maybe there's a reason for that." He looked to Maddie, who turned to Cam. "Anything from your guy on the inside?"

"We're good. Typical contractor bullshit. They're delaying over a design hiccup from when they upscaled the building. Nothing for us to worry about. They're just holding out for more money."

Michael sat up in his seat, still feeling like something wasn't right. "Let's talk more about the building itself." *Like, what's wrong with it?*

Rene read the building specs off his iPad, speaking in French while Zoe translated. "One-hundred-ninety floors of mixed concrete and steel frame surrounding a concrete core. Only the lower third has been completed, but they energized the entire building about a month ago. So, while it's still a long way from being finished, it's got significant functionality."

"So what's the problem?" Michael asked.

"If you're afraid it's going to fall over, you can relax," Zoe said. "Near the top, the tower houses one of the world's most sophisticated mass-damper systems. It's built around a 150,000-gallon water tank that acts as a stabilizer against the building's harmonic vibrations."

"What does that mean?" Amara asked. "Sounds celestial."

Zoe began to answer, but Maddie cut her off, looking pointedly at the reporter. "It's pretty simple. Any structure that's taller than it is wide has to flex, or it'll fall over in a stiff wind or an earthquake, right? For something this tall, they need a counterweight, like a big pendulum that rocks to cancel out the sway of the building, so it doesn't get out of control and shake itself to bits. That about right?"

Rene shrugged and lit a cigarette. "More or less," Zoe added.

Maddie went on, "We've got the codes for the construction elevators, but if Michael can get us through the front door—"

Michael blushed, but nodded.

"Great," Cam said. "Go ahead and walk us through that."

Michael threw up his hands, starting to get out of his chair. "Do I need to do it from there? Or should I…?"

"No, you're good. Just use your outside voice."

Michael took a deep breath. He'd had to scramble to come up with fixes while everyone else followed the program. This was starting to feel like the job he'd just quit. "OK, so… your typical face recognition AI looks for matches against a list of known IDs to spot bad guys. China, the UK, Dubai, all have it, and Russia is next… But… our software is a little different."

He went on, warming up to his subject in spite of himself. "Brand X authentication positively matches everyone against a master database—national ID cards, driver's licenses, et cetera. If it fails to get a match, it flags the failure for an on-site engineer to review, and sends live security to go check them out.

"It's fairly effective, but it gets a lot of missed matches because image capture doesn't always catch a full face, and it tends to draw a blank on any complexion darker than Rihanna. But our app mines social media photos for comparisons." He rolled his eyes as Cam mouthed, *Creepy*. "And it's an equal opportunity authenticator. I could ID any of you and pull up your profiles and vital stats off a snapshot in worse light than this, and the cameras around the International Business Center are set up to take advantage of the floodlights.

"Now, to defeat the cameras, all you have to do is block them with lasers or infrared, or obscure your face... a scarf, a balaclava, a mask, hell, even face paint. There's this whole weird style of cosmetics based on dazzle ship camouflage from World War I, that baffles the algorithms, but it looks pretty goofy, and it won't stand up to close inspection by live security, and there is a lot of it, on foot and in cars, around the site.

"So, we're going with these..." Michael held up a baseball cap he'd scored from a street vendor and altered with components from an electronics store, all bought with cash. He'd affixed a row of tiny LEDs on the underside of the bill of each cap. "These throw off an infrared beam invisible to the naked eye, but it creates a blurry flash artifact for the cameras. It won't be able to match your face to your passport photo, but it will run up a red flag for the engineer..."

"But you got that part, right?" Cam asked.

Michael let him dangle for a painful, delicious moment before cracking a smile. "Of course, I got it. I can usurp the engineer's access on my phone using a generic password and dismiss the red flags before someone comes looking."

"My man!" Cam crowed, and offered a high five. Michael had half a mind to leave him hanging. "So, what about the other one?"

"Well, the front doors have a full positive authentication scanner. It won't open for anyone who's not on an approved list—"

"But it will open for someone who is, right?" Cam wheedled.

"Of course, but you'd have to be one of the contractors, security or the developers to get in that door…"

Michael trailed off when he noticed Cam smiling indulgently, like he couldn't wait to rip the rug out from under Michael's feet yet again. "Not good enough."

"Well, in that case, we're back to square one," Michael said, tossing the baseball cap aside. "Unless you've got a better idea…"

"I do." Reaching into his knapsack, he unwrapped a stack of silicone masks with eerily fleshy features, and passed them out. "We got a tricked-out 3D printer in the suite to grind out these sweet replicas based on the site safety inspectors. No reason they'd set off alarms, since they're going over everything again, anyway."

"Like I said," Michael cut in, "we still need to get past on-site security… We can't let them get too close, or they'll clock the masks and nail us."

"I've got that sorted, baby," Cam said. "We just need you to hack their mainframe, or whatever."

Michael was getting tired of being used like a temp. "It's a little trickier than that… But I got it covered."

"Great," Cam said. "Now, in the interest of operational security, there will be no phones… I repeat… no phones on the site. Before we enter the building, Yuri will take our phones for a ride, so we have an airtight alibi… but we will have these for routine communications." He held up a portable Baofeng UHF/VHF two-way radio unit. "Channels are already set, they're simple to use, but get to know them, if you don't already."

Michael asked, "I get it, we don't want to be traced, and they'll run down any cellular activity off the site if they think someone's up there, but—"

"Would you relax?" Cam held up a cheap phone. "We will have one, and only one, locally sourced burner phone, to be used only in the unlikely event of an emergency."

Maddie snatched it out of his hand. "So I'll be carrying it."

"OK," Cam said. "Then we're going to just take the stairs to the upper floors. See?" Cam mugged at Michael again. "Easy-peasy."

"What about when we get there?" Michael asked. "It's going to be dangerous, or we wouldn't be doing it. What about *her*?" He pointed a thumb at Amara.

"What *about* her?" Cam shot back.

The reporter shrugged elaborately where she stood by the window. "I'll just be there as an observer."

"What if something happens to her? Who's responsible?"

"Seventeen-year-olds do what you guys do," Amara replied. "I think I can handle it."

"It won't be that simple," Maddie put in defensively. "We do this, we do it *stealth*. GoPro that shit to the top so Bhumi can do his thing, the rest of us get in disguise, walk out when the construction crews roll in. We've got coveralls, vests and helmets, but you'll all have to bring them in, so allow for that in your packs. We want the world to know we were there, just not *until* we're there." Mouth pinched in a cynical smirk, she turned her gaze on the twins. "Think you can handle that?"

The twins whispered among themselves, laughing. Finally, Zoe said, "Yes, we can handle that."

When the meeting had run its course, everyone suited up and checked their bags.

Zoe had the smallest knapsack, while Rene, with a full backpack with stuff tied to the outside, had the biggest. Michael assumed Rene was chivalrously carrying his sister's load, but a quick glance at Zoe's showed a full complement of urbex gear, so what was the parrot packing?

Maddie had the contents of her pack spread out on the floor beneath the windows, doing a final checklist when Amara picked up her GoPro. Maddie snatched it out of her hands. "Do you mind not touching my shit? Thanks."

Chastened, Amara returned to her own packing. Michael watched Maddie, the fiercely focused attention betraying how angry she still was. But at whom? For what? They wouldn't be alone to discuss it until this was all over.

After going over his own bag once more—ultra-thin sleeping bag and insulator pad, walkie, headlamp, GoPro with extra cards and batteries, spotlight, disposable gloves, chemical hand warmers, Handi Wipes, particle-filter mask, sunblock, insect repellant, glucose gel, freeze-dried snacks, water flask, toilet paper, first-aid kit, glow-sticks, and a pair of Sanford Mean Streak permanent markers—he tucked the thumb drive from the boat tour into a side pocket. When he'd checked and rechecked everything, he approached Cam and took him aside. "This thing has… a lot of moving parts. If something goes wrong…"

Cam grabbed him by both shoulders and pulled him whisper-close. "Dude. We're going. It's *done*."

He looked over Michael's shoulder and blurted, "Don't drink that!"

Maddie swallowed the sip she'd just taken from Bhumi's thermos. "Why not? What's wrong with you?"

"But it's… his… um…" Cam looked around the room, feeling like an idiot as everyone else, even Rene, busted out laughing at him. Bhumi looked on owlishly, his mouth quirked in something almost like a smile.

"It's herbal tea with just a touch of ginseng and CBD," Maddie said. "Good for your nerves." Michael shook his head. She held the thermos out to Cam. "Have some."

Cam took it, realized everyone was staring at him, and took a quick swig.

"Let's blow this popsicle stand!" Maddie called out. Michael followed the rest of the crew out of the mansion as Cam led the way, humming the *Mission: Impossible* theme until the rest of them joined in.

SEVENTEEN

From the window of Serhiy's apartment, you could see most of Korova Tower, from the glossy glass foundations to the blinking red and green lights on the rooftop cranes. With the sunlight fading in the west, Masha Zworykin sipped a mug of cold tea and peered at it through the foil-lined curtains. It was hard not to see the black tower as a spear driven into the heart of her beloved city, a derrick pumping the last heart's blood out of Russia. Not even the fiasco of the Ukraine invasion and all the new sanctions had been allowed to slow its runaway construction, this malignant weed that starved the city to feed itself.

"They have no idea," she murmured, "what they're getting into."

"You tried to tell them," Serhiy shot back. His wheelchair whirred as he backed out of the nest of computer hardware that dominated the room.

"Sure. And if someone had tried to tell you what you were getting into in Chechnya, would you still have gone?"

"I had no choice. They do."

"Everyone has a choice," she sighed, setting down her tea and turning from the window. "You thought you didn't, but you did."

Serhiy shook his blunt, shovel-shaped head, lit a cigarette

and tossed the chrome Zippo lighter into the detritus on his desk. "They like to think they have 'agency', as the academics say, but they are woefully mistaken. Americans," he spat with a cloud of sour smoke like a wordless curse.

Serhiy didn't have to be conscripted into the Russian Army. Like many young Russians in the early Putin years, he joined eagerly and fought with valor—and lost both legs in Chechnya in 2004. Masha first met him as an interview subject, relaying his account of war crimes he witnessed in the tragic Beslan school siege. The report changed nothing except to make him a target, and he'd gone underground. In the intervening years, he'd become a tech expert, an infamous hacker who brokered encryption schemes, rootkit exploit tools, and black-market bandwidth.

When the Razbit collective had debated strategies to break the veil of secrecy around Korova Tower, Masha had come to him with the idea after a number of local urban explorers—climbers or diggers, as they were known in Russia—went missing; but Serhiy had been the one who found Cameron Buckley online and sold him on the plan, all the while letting him think it was his own idea.

Serhiy rolled into the room. "You're worried about them. That's so nice, but you should worry about us."

"Not a day goes by that I don't worry about us," Masha shot back. Brushing her hair behind her ears, she ran her fingers over her cheeks, tracing the deep creases that two decades of mortal terror had carved into her face. "At some point, you stop looking over your shoulder, knowing they will inevitably come for you. Every day that they don't feels almost as bad, because you know you're not worth the trouble."

Serhiy checked his phone. "They're moving, finally."

Masha went back to the window. There was nothing to see, of course; the Russia Day fireworks were not due for several hours. But by morning, the world would see what she saw when it looked on Korova. "You're sure the live stream will be relayed?"

"Boris is a coward," Serhiy replied, "but he likes to think of himself as the resistance personified. He'll comply with the shutdown if and when it happens, but by then..."

"If everything else goes according to plan..." Her wiry eyebrows arched as if to acknowledge the infinitesimal likelihood of *that* happening.

"If they don't change their minds, after what you told them..."

They'd been over this. She had told him repeatedly that if they knew a little, they would be more motivated; perhaps they could even be made to see that this cause was worth fighting, even dying, for. That was ridiculous, she knew, especially when dealing with Americans.

"What I did was foolish," she admitted. She'd dedicated every hour of her life to the cause for so long, she'd grown blind to the obvious truth that others might not be so quick to join them. Even before she was driven into the resistance, her nemesis had not been tyranny, but the inborn apathy and national pessimism that invited a parade of monsters from Ivan the Terrible to Vlad the Defenestrator to tread upon their faces and seduced them to love the taste of the boot. She'd thought these Americans—that one, today, at least—might be different.

"It will change nothing," Serhiy said. "Where they would not risk a night in jail by any kind of direct action, they would brazenly throw away their lives out of sheer ego. How like children they are, and how easily led."

They sat quietly now, lulled by the police band scanner's periodic chirps and squeals. The local authorities had been augmented by several hundred cops from neighboring districts, and while no violence had broken out, the police were trying to keep the protesters kettled at a handful of parks across the city, well away from the Russia Day festivities and Red Square.

Masha was reminded of the last time they waited like this, of watching the drone with Igor's hard-won intel take off from the tower's rooftop, to crash in the Moscow River. Serhiy was watching through high-powered binoculars. He saw what happened next, Igor plummeting, screaming all the way down. Even if they'd been lucky enough to recover the thumb drive from the downed drone before the security forces, the world would never take heed, unless Razbit forced them to. For better or worse, the world could never be allowed to ignore an American in trouble.

The plan called for the crew to stream clips from their grand stunt show to Serhiy's site, which would in turn be mirrored globally by Pascal, his counterpart in the United States. The live stream would commence at 7:00 a.m. tomorrow, if they got that far.

Relax, Masha reminded herself. Everything always goes according to plan, when you're trying to get *into* trouble…

Something in Serhiy's jumble of electronics warbled. He turned his wheelchair and scooted over to it. Opening a new window on the largest monitor, he beckoned her over.

"Look at them," he said, pointing at the screen. "Tell me they would still help us, if they knew."

The jumpy live video feed showed a handsome African-American man's smiling face. The image then swooned woozily as he strapped the tiny camera on his head. It panned across the Metro subway car, taking in two hangdog European twins; an arrogant Adonis with braids thrown over one absurdly broad shoulder; a striking young brunette with a puckish smirk; a darker, older woman occupied with her own camera; and finally, the callow-looking Asian-American boy she'd followed and recklessly contacted on the boat tour, only this afternoon.

"Perhaps it will not be necessary," she said.

"You were never in real war," Serhiy grated. "But now you are. And in war, the general is only a soldier who must send other men to die."

Masha swallowed hard her last sip of cold tea. Looking away from the monitor, she told herself that, one way or the other, her war would be over soon.

THIRD MOVEMENT

"THE NATURAL PROGRESS OF THINGS IS
FOR LIBERTY TO YIELD AND GOVERNMENT
TO GAIN GROUND."

—THOMAS JEFFERSON

EIGHTEEN

The seven of them came up out of Vystavochnaya Metro station just before 8:00 p.m. and walked in a loose group. They all wore matching sports caps emblazoned with "Moscow" in Cyrillic letters. They looked like what they were, a group of young, energetic tourists out seeing the sights, goofing around in matching merch.

The Metro ride had been pure chaos, which provided excellent cover. Half of Moscow was headed to or coming from Russia Day festivities, the other half regrouping from or returning to the protests on the Boulevard Ring. They saw bellicose drunks shouting nose-to-nose with masked activists, beer and worse staining pro-democracy picket signs, eyes red and streaming from tear gas, blood and bruises from police clubs and boots.

They couldn't ask for better cover, but it got Michael thinking more deeply about what they were doing. He wasn't any kind of resistance fighter—that was Cam's deal, though Michael knew it was mostly a pose. But he still got a rush out of their more political stunts, striking symbolic blows against the people who'd commodified and fenced off their world, then expected them to pay just to exist in it.

But context was everything. A harmless stunt at home could mean a whole lot more somewhere else. Even if a conga line of Russian kids had already planked Korova Tower, for an American group to blunder in on its national holiday and live-stream it could be taken as a declaration of war.

In the brief time since Michael and his friends had been alive, Russia had gone from being the Evil Empire to a gangster state that invaded its neighbors, meddled in other country's elections, and liquidated critics of the state, whether they be dissidents, politicians, reporters, or even fellow kleptocrats. It was late-stage capitalism with the brake lines cut. Michael had assumed he knew all he needed to about Russia after a few books and podcasts, but now he realized he could put everything he really knew about this country and its people into a thimble, and still have room for a thumb.

What was this stupid stunt supposed to prove? What were they saying besides, *Hey, look at me!* A self-indulgent ego-flex before heading back to the United States and the privilege of throwing it online and getting momentarily famous off it.

They liked to play at being badasses by monkeying around at great heights. Dangerous for sure, but people here lived in fear of their own government yet they were taking to the streets with no hope of being more than a soundbite on international news. Would *they* be impressed by the Furies mooning them from the top of their new skyscraper?

What was it that weird Russian lady told him on the tour boat? *We'd understand when it was too late.* He'd taken a look at the thumb drive, and found it taken up with a huge file of unknown format that he couldn't open, along with a folder of dodgy editorials and videos with machine-translated subtitles accusing the Russian mafia state of everything from false flag attacks on Moscow apartment blocks to killing stray dogs in Sochi for the Olympics. Many of them bore Masha Zworykin's byline. For all he knew, the weird old lady on the tour boat was her. *That tracks*, he thought.

The most recent picture of her online was from when the president kicked the last of the independent journalists out of

NTV back in 2001. The shot of the poised but shattered woman walking in a line with her fellow sacked employees, carrying a large, framed portrait of herself, was almost iconic, but what could she possibly want from him? It was silly to keep thinking about it, but something about the meeting had felt anything but random, like she knew what he was up to. And if she knew, then who else?

He hated this feeling, but he had to admit, he also loved it.

He caught Maddie looking at him and smiled. She mouthed, "You think too much," and blew him a kiss. He caught the kiss and held it in his hand for the rest of the ride.

They walked along the embankment between the Federation Tower complex and the Korova site, Michael scanning for and seeing domed surveillance cameras sprouting like parasitic growths on the lampposts. He saw two teams of security guards at all times. An unmarked car circled the sixty-hectare business area, with traffic bollards to keep all other cars out.

Foot traffic out here was slight, mostly tourists strolling along the Moscow River or posing for selfies as the skyline began to light up, the gritty workaday face of Moscow donning its nighttime finery. Guards were rousting a few skateboarders, which kept them on the far side of the plaza until the Furies had crossed it.

Michael checked his phone and the portal into the Macrosync network running the ID captures. Sure enough, they'd tripped off fourteen alerts already. Any minute, a live engineer would review the queue and flag them as obscured faces in need of human verification. The security guards would get a ping on their phones and leave off hassling those skater kids and come shake them down.

This part was, in its own nerdy fashion, as thrilling to Michael as any place-hack. Using a generic admin password and temp ID, he'd taken over the on-site engineer's duties without letting him know it. So long as they didn't notice the brimming queue dwindling down to nothing as Michael canceled each ticket, nobody would ever be the wiser, and he'd never heard of an hourly admin who raised a fuss when their workload got lighter on a Saturday night.

It was like crossing a digital minefield, but when they'd negotiated It, Yuri took their phones, stowed them in a valise and went back the way they'd come, heading for a waiting taxi. So far as the cellular network knew, they were out on the town again.

Stopping across the street from the perimeter fence, they looked upon the tower as if it had cast a Mount Doom-like spell on them, and they couldn't move.

It was imposing from miles away; up close, it was truly awe-inspiring. A pristine, bluish-silver curtain wall, subtly curved to give the illusion of waves or wind, enfolded the base of the building like a glass skin, marking the extent of progress by the glazing crews, up to about the eightieth floor. Beyond that border, the midsection was an exposed honeycomb of concrete and steel skeleton for about another hundred stories. Near the top where the 190-story building tapered towards a vanishing point, the concrete gave way to naked steel framework supplemented by cranes and hoists, which added yet another ten stories of altitude. The building's innards exposed for all the world to see, like an unfinished creature trying to crawl out of its chrysalis... something beautiful and horrifying at the same time.

Cam waited for the security guard to roll past in an up-armored SUV. He looked at the others, tossed his baseball cap in the trash and strapped on a GoPro camera as he crossed the drive. The crew followed.

They filed in under the sidewalk scaffolding, a wood barrier blocking off the perimeter of the site. Cam strolled casually until he rounded the southeast corner, out of sight from the plaza, his back to the river. Zeroing in on a narrow sliver of an opening where the plywood panels didn't quite meet the scaffolding, an entry point they'd cased earlier, he turned, winked and threw his bag over the fence, then climbed up on the handrailing and jumped headfirst into the gap.

For just a moment, his legs kicked in the air, and then he was gone. One by one, as quickly as possible, they scrambled through that opening in plain sight, pushing their bags through separately. Michael, last to go, heard the growl of an eight-cylinder engine rounding the river drive. Swallowing hard, he jumped up, scraping his knuckles on the top of the barricade. He cleared the fence just before the security car rolled into view.

NINETEEN

About a hundred yards of open ground separated the perimeter fence from the front entrance of the tower. Filled with construction equipment and building materials, the area was harshly lit by halogen floodlights. Rene and Zoe had confirmed that security guards walked the building's perimeter on the regular, though none were in sight now. Guard huts were at the vehicle entrances on the north and east sides of the fence.

The crew separated and swooped across the space, moving from cover to shadowy cover, doing parkour flips and vaulting off the maze of obstacles—stacked floor slabs, pipes, propane tanks, mullions, steel beams, glass panels, air compressors, pile drivers, loaders, dump trucks, and disposal dumpsters. Making scarcely a sound, presenting only flickers of movement, they made like urban ninjas.

Amara lagged behind, snapping pictures of the crew in action. She was caught flatfooted when a security guard appeared at the end of the narrow avenue between stacked pipes and a cargo container, shining his flashlight into the shadows.

The crew took refuge anywhere they could, inside pipes and between bales of tie-rods. Michael hid in an empty dumpster. Peeking over the rim, he spotted Maddie perched atop a cargo container about twenty feet away. She urgently pointed behind them and mouthed "Amara" before rolling off the top of the container and was gone.

Amara stood frozen, looking through the viewfinder of her camera. The flashlight beam swept the legs of her cargo pants. Incredibly, the security guard hadn't seen her yet, but he would in a moment if she didn't snap out of it.

Shit! They weren't even inside yet and they were about to get nailed. As the guard came nearer, the reporter finally got it together and backpedaled out of sight. Michael expelled a gust of breath he didn't know he'd been holding.

Amara bumped into a cart of steel rods, sending a shivery *clang* echoing through the construction site. Michael's heart leapt into his throat.

The security guard called out in Russian. He was pushing retirement age, with a pot belly and a serious smoker's wheeze. He was also armed with a pistol, which he drew as he started again in Amara's direction.

He was almost upon her when Maddie stepped into view just behind the guard, dragging one foot in the gravel to make a faint noise, then sprinted away on her toes. The guard spun and took the bait, chasing after her.

Amara just stood there, horribly exposed in the bright light. Michael flung himself out of the dumpster and ran in a crouch like a soldier in a free-fire zone, grabbing Amara by the hand and pulling her in the other direction.

The security guard shouted again. They flattened against a portable toilet, breathing hard and fast. Surely, everyone must hear them. Amara whispered something, but Michael hushed her, watching Maddie work.

Go, baby, go—

Maddie moved through the construction site so quick and quiet, the guard wasn't even sure what he was chasing. She vaulted over a chest-high stack of coiled copper wiring and shot into a two-foot diameter concrete tube a split second before the guard came around the corner of the cargo container.

He looked around and spotted the tube, went over and shone his light inside it just as she popped out the other end and speed-crawled across open ground. The nearest place to hide was a good fifty feet away.

Through no fault of her own, she was going to be caught…

One by one, Cam, Bhumi, Rene, and Zoe darted out of cover or made a tiny, isolated noise to draw off the guard. Working together, they soon had him spinning in all directions. Michael nodded to Amara and led them into the shadowed alcove near the front doors of Korova Tower.

It was a great game and they played it well, until another guard appeared. At a glance, he looked fitter and sharper than the first sentry. Maddie ran for a steel staircase amid a mass of scaffolding for the glazing platforms. She climbed two stories up the outer wall and found herself at a dead end. While his comrade let himself get drawn further and further away from the building, this fresh guard made directly for the scaffolding. Had he seen her? Was it already over?

With only seconds to spare, Maddie stretched across the arch over the blocked staircase and spider-walked up the steel struts, then swung by her hands and slung her body into a gap between them, all without making a sound.

Even to someone who'd watched her move for years, it was pretty impressive.

The guard ran up the stairs and stopped short at the dead end, looking around in confusion, never noticing Maddie dangling thirty feet above his head. He came back down, flashing the light around with more anxiety than urgency. What was he doing wasting his time out here? Only when he had passed out of sight did Maddie carefully caterpillar back down.

The two guards met out in the open, looking around with obvious frustration. One seemed to insist they keep looking, but the other was having none of it. Now they both turned and continued their patrol, heading clockwise away from the tower's front entrance.

Amara watched wide-eyed beside Michael, her pulse slowly beginning to settle. He hoped this would be a "teachable moment" for her. One by one, the crew assembled beside them to watch the guards pass out of view. Maddie arrived last, still breathing a bit hard, equally pumped and salty over the cause of her workout.

"Thanks," Amara said in a throaty whisper. "I felt it would be good for the story to capture the sense of danger—"

Maddie's eyes almost rolled out of her head. "Oh, I did it for the story, too. Hope you got some good snaps out of it. Next time, I'll let 'em catch your ass while *I* take the pictures."

Amara turned away, looking wounded. Her glib explanation had been a cover-up for real fear. He could see it in her eyes. *Takes one to know one*, he thought. Michael wanted to say something mature, but he couldn't stop smiling, amused by Maddie's cattiness.

Maddie nudged him, still rolling on the adrenaline spike. "See me ninja that shit? You can say it."

Michael adopted a stony expression. "Not gonna say it."

"'Maddie's a badass bitch.' Say the words, come on."

He looked away, as if a bigger badass might show up at any moment. "You're half-right, I'll say that."

She gasped in mock offense, then squinted her eyes and jabbed a finger in his face. "When you least expect it." Then she mouthed *ninja* and drew a finger across her throat.

"I'm not afraid."

"You fucking should be."

"I'm a *little* afraid."

Taking this as her due, Maddie gave him the *eyes-on-you* gesture and took a drink from her flask.

Michael realized that once again, everyone was looking at him.

Oh yeah, he realized. *The tricky part...*

TWENTY

O K, Cam thought, as he watched the crew rifle through their bags. *Bust out that serious Mission: Impossible shit...*

Peeling the backings off the adhesive patches on the inside of the mask, he pressed it to his forehead, cheekbones, nose, and jawline to ensure that it clung to his features. Looking around the circle, it gave him an uncanny valley shiver to see the scowling faces of six recently embalmed-looking Slavic safety engineers.

The likenesses came from Cam's mysterious IT guy, Serhiy. Yuri used them as references for the silicone masks, which the twins had fabricated and painted in the hotel room. Once again, Cam marveled at how complex their little hobby had become.

It was an elegant solution, but it didn't cover all the bases. Naturally, the entry would still be logged and anyone who cared to check would find that the engineers had elected to inspect the tower on a Saturday night, but nobody would look at the logs unless something else went wrong or once the place-hack went public, and by then, they'd either be on their way home, or they'd have a lot more to worry about.

Of course, if it didn't work, their vacation would be over really fast—

"You sure this'll work?" Cam demanded.

Michael shrugged, still fussing with his mask. "Fine," Cam said. "I'll go first."

Cam walked up to the central doors with his eyes on the flagstones beneath his cross-trainers, his other hand out to touch the doors. If the camera flagged him as a *No Match*, there wouldn't be any alarm here, but the security guards would get an immediate *ping* and the doors would remain locked.

When he reached them, he laid his hand on the latch. The others were right on his heels. He risked a quick glance over his shoulder and nearly choked on his own spit. They looked ridiculous; this was never going to work...

The latch clicked and the doors swung open before him.

"Let's milk this cow," Cam said in a fair Tom Cruise imitation, peeling the mask off his face.

The unmasked crew crossed over the threshold into a gigantic lobby: three stories high, all creamy marble, tinted glass and fluted columns stylized to resemble ladders and spiral staircases, with escalators descending into an underground parking garage and Metro station and ascending to galleries overlooking the lobby and a two-thousand seat concert hall.

With the power and interior security systems offline, escalators not running and the only light coming from the floodlights outside, the lobby had a haunting quality of hushed anticipation, as though hundreds of people would come boiling up out of the stairwells at any moment. An eerie fusion of cathedral and train station, it elevated the movement of people and wealth to metaphysical realms, made salvation feel like a product you could never afford, made upward mobility seem as holy, yet unattainable, as heaven.

"If the Tower of Babel had a lobby," Cam smirked, "I figure it probably looked just like this."

While Amara took pictures, the rest of the crew rehydrated and double-checked their gear before the ascent. Rene went over to the bank of elevators and pushed the *Call* button. Nothing happened, naturally. The others looked at him.

"*Quoi?*" he asked. "*Je devais essayer. Pourquoi ça ne devrait pas être facile?*"

"We might as well be shooting off flares. They're still going to be looking for us," Michael griped. "They'll nail us if we go around pushing buttons."

"Would you *relax*?" Cam said, his voice louder than he planned. "They didn't see us. They're not gonna come play hide-and-seek up here, unless there's a good reason to, like an order from their boss. I got aces I haven't even played yet, so just enjoy the goddamn game."

While the others explored the cavernous space, Maddie found the stairwell. The lush décor abruptly terminated at the first step, giving way to naked concrete, girders, exposed conduits, and ducts. Clearly, whoever designed the place figured the elite would never have to take the stairs.

Cam bumped into Rene, who had stopped in the doorway. The goofball pointed at a slot on the right side, a recessed place for a steel door worthy of a bank vault to seal the stairwell. He looked at Cam significantly.

The stairwell might be an ugly necessity, but the captains of Russian industry had taken an honest look at the world and decided it was more important to seal off the stairwells so people couldn't get *in*, than to keep it clear for people to evacuate.

"Says a lot about their priorities," Cam said. "Hey, Maddie, check this out—" He tried to get her attention, but she just squeezed past him and started climbing. *OK, be like that.*

They hoofed it up twenty stories of concrete stairs with metal rails, ascending an endless loop interrupted only by the rising numbers printed at each landing. The first ten-or-so floors were part of a gargantuan shopping-entertainment-spa complex, with galleries of shops and nightclubs stacked like drawers in an enormous, glittering file cabinet. But all of it was locked behind roll-down cages and infrared tripwires, so they avoided it and kept climbing.

No sound but the slap of rubber-soled shoes on concrete, the plosive breaths of working bodies. To break up the monotony and try to repair the breach with Maddie, Cam blurted out a factoid, a game he and Maddie had begun playing after Michael left. Michael had always been the group's Mr. Know-It-All, so maybe it had started as a way to pay tribute, to fill the silence he had left. But mostly, it was a way to egg each other on through grueling workouts. You could call for a break only if you came up with a unique factoid that stumped your partner.

"You burn point-one-seven calories every step you climb," Cam said as he stopped on the fifteenth-floor landing. "That's one calorie for every ten steps... Climb this whole building, that's still not even a decent cheeseburger."

Maddie kept going, but muttered, "Tired already?"

He sprinted up the steps, passing her on the next off-side landing and stopping again at the sixteenth-floor door. Opening it, he took a peek inside and shuddered. It was the kind of open-plan office space Michael worked in.

"Climbing stairs two at once doesn't burn more calories," Maddie said, not meeting his eyes. "More energy is expended over time by taking things steadily." Refusing the water he offered, she went on past him.

Amara came up to him and took his water, drank off half of it. "Can anyone play?"

Smiling slyly, he nodded.

"Vitruvius designed the standard for stairs still used today, with a thirty-seven-degree pitch, in the first century B.C."

Michael went past him and said, "You burn more calories climbing stairs in high heels."

And that was the end of the game.

Every few floors, one of them would open the door and check out the building, but the view was always the same—barren boxes of concrete and glass, exposed ductwork and disconnected electrical lines. Soon, they would be filled with workstations and people plugging away at propping up the oligarchs high above them, struggling to climb the ladder themselves, or avoid being crushed by random whim.

Maybe, he thought, they wouldn't fill in these floors at all. Maybe they were just empty bricks to get the height required for global bragging rights. Did the building actually need to have anything in it? *Probably not, really.*

"Fuck me," he heard Michael blurt out from the landing above. Cam jogged up to where his friend stood. "Look at this shit, man."

Cam looked over Michael's shoulder into the floor. "'Fuck me' is right, buddy."

This floor was anything but empty. Rows of servers filled the space, connected by thick pipes and bundles of braided fiber optic cable.

"Those are OC-3840 SONET interfaces," Michael said.

"Elaborate on that," Cam prompted.

"Top-tier transmission lines. In the States, the internet is pretty much fifteen data centers owned by four big companies. Just at a glance, the capacity here is bigger than all of that. These babies run up to 200 *gigs* per microsecond, and this many freon-cooled servers... Russia is a pariah state, locked out of the global community, so what do they want all this hardware for? Whoever's setting up here isn't just looking to run an ISP. You could run black-market cryptocurrency exchanges, stage a massive AI op, and still have the bandwidth to host a whole national data network right here—control or influence what everybody on this continent sees and thinks. And not just here. They practically chose our president in 2016 with a handful of troll farms. With all this... D'you have any idea what that means?"

"Just that nerdspeak is a universal language," Cam said, shutting the door, "but I don't speak it."

"Then you better learn, dipshit. Seriously, Cam. This is important. This is... troubling." He tried to catch Cam's eyes, make him understand.

"You done?" Cam gestured at Michael like he was holding a remote and desperately changing the channel. "Beat your feet, bro."

Michael backed away, wanting to explain something else Cam didn't need to know, but he abruptly gave up and resumed climbing.

Cam realized the rest of the group had gone on without them and took a hit off his flask before running to catch up, when he heard a strange whirring sound like a generator—no, a lift engine, coming from the other side of that door. The elevators were shut off, he thought, so no worries. He pressed on.

Just as the door hissed shut behind him on its air brake, a construction elevator ascended into view and stopped on the floor. The cage opened and the two security guards, still wound up from chasing their tails outside, stepped onto the floor, flashlights darting with manic energy.

Looking for the crew.

TWENTY-ONE

The monotonous climb continued until the Furies reached the fortieth floor. The placard on this landing had a lot more text than the others. What was so special way up here? The group came straggling up the stairs: Rene wheezing, Amara glistening with sweat, Michael favoring his bad leg. Cam's own legs were burning and shaky, though he wasn't about to admit it. With Maddie taking point, the crew filed through the door and found themselves in one of the skyscraper's generator rooms. The sign wasn't lying; this was worth special attention.

A forest of tubes, ducts and bundled cables connected the electrical substations, air conditioners, plumbing reservoir tanks and pumps, water heaters and telecom relay switches. Against the far wall, a row of diesel-powered backup generators stood ready. Alongside were stacks of electrical storage batteries for the collection and distribution of the ballyhooed renewable energy Korova promised to generate. The walls were clad in shiny grills and louvered vents instead of floor-to-ceiling glass, the panoramic view replaced with a claustrophobic jumble of reflections. Cam had to remind himself they were forty stories up, not deep underground.

He called a short break. In a hushed, uneasy circle they sat or squatted on the floor, sipping water and munching snacks.

The room made an impression on the crew, totally different from the lobby vibe, yet just as impactful.

Rene said something in wistful, breathless French, which Zoe dutifully translated. "He says that this building has many hearts, and now we are inside one of them." He went on and Zoe, blushing but smiling, added, "But if this building is a prick, here, also, are its balls."

Cam nodded but told her, "You really don't have to translate *everything* he says."

With new urgency, they attacked the stairs for another forty floors before trying another door. Cam came around the landing and was greeted with a gust of bracing night air. Already higher than the next tallest building in the city, the country, the continent, they had finally climbed above the glazing, and the unfinished floor they stood upon was open to the night. Large hung sheets of transparent plastic rustled and snapped in the breeze.

Maddie inspected one of the exposed vertical shafts running through the concrete core of the building, which would eventually house an express elevator. A laser level stood by itself on a tripod beside the elevator, where some absent-minded surveyor must've left it after taking readings on the shaft.

Bracing against the door frame, she leaned out over the five-hundred-foot drop to look up and down the shaft, taking in the wicked Droste effect of the seemingly endless recession of the floors. Like the infinite space between two mirrors, it was almost hypnotic. She took out a coin and dropped it, listening, but it vanished in the void without any discernible sound.

She whistled. "Just goes on forever…" Stepping out of the core, she turned and crossed the vacant space to stand on the outer edge of the floor, taking in the sprawling metropolis at her feet. "Like this city."

Cam wanted to take her in his arms, but he knew better than

to get in her way. She was focused on the act and playing to the cameras they were all wearing, which was all he could ask for. Once they'd settled in upstairs, he'd make it right.

Michael sat on the steps, his head hung low. Dude looked ready to quit. Maddie swept past Cam like he wasn't there and knelt beside Michael. Predictably, she was using Michael as a prop to make him jealous. And just as predictably, it was working.

A little too easily, perhaps.

"You OK?" she asked.

"Just feel like something hit me," Michael said. "Something in the food... I don't know."

His skin looked clammy in the glow off her shoulder-mounted flashlight. They weren't high enough for altitude sickness, but that's what it looked like. She touched a hand to his head. "You're freezing. You should've said something earlier."

She rifled through her bag and handed him a bottle of water and a couple Tylenol.

Cam went over to the edge and sat down, letting his legs dangle over the windowsill. The wind in his face was nothing like the swampy warmth closer to the ground. Rolling out of the Arctic over a thousand miles of tundra, it chilled him to the marrow, forcing him to zip up his windbreaker and skin his hands into a pair of climbing gloves.

He noticed a whirring *click* and saw Amara on one knee, taking his picture. She lowered the camera and smiled at him. The pinched look in her eyes told him she was dealing with the tension, maybe even learning to like it.

"Come over here," he said.

"No, thanks. I'm good right here."

"Come on, Amanpour. Don't tell me you're scared."

"If I fell from here..." Her voice trailed off, almost hypnotized by the danger.

"How long would it take? Maybe sixteen seconds. Plenty of time to reflect on your life choices. Relax, I got you."

She gave in and walked over, cautiously taking a seat right next to him, legs dangling freely. Maybe there was a shade of cruelty in it, but he loved to watch people deal with the fear for the first time; to see it through their eyes revitalized his own respect for the game. That first taste and how they took it told you so much about a person, and what they were made of.

Once her fear subsided, she smiled, clearly loving it. She looked out, then down. *Down* usually got people if they could be gotten, as the possibilities festered and ran amok in their heads. They were as safe as on the ground, but some people reacted as if the height itself was a vicious predator that would come for them. Being too careful could kill you just as surely as being careless.

He leaned In a little closer, looking into her eyes. "Yeah?"

"Oh, yeah." Her face didn't light up, but her eyes smoldered as she let herself feel the danger and handle it. Her mind seemed to go to a dark place for just a moment, but then she pushed it away.

"And this is nothing. Wait till we get up *there*." He pointed up. "If you're gonna fall, that's the place to do it."

She snapped a photo straight down the side of the building, her white Feiyue sneakers in the shot. Then she turned to him, poised to take his picture again. Or do something else...

"Do you mind if I interview you a bit, here?"

"What? Sure..." Momentarily taken aback, Cam put on his game face and slid into character.

She switched the camera to video and began recording. "Why do you think people in your world are so attracted to skyscrapers? What is it?"

He thought about it for a second. "It's Edmund Hillary, right? Like conquering a mountain. Only harder."

"Really? You believe that? I mean... Somebody obviously had to come up here to build this... and we did take the stairs..."

He smiled, nodded. *Point taken.* "One, it's illegal. Plus, if you really want to climb a mountain, all you need is a fat wad of cash and a Sherpa to carry you. Want to know what it really is? Branding. Cities use skyscrapers to say to the world, 'We're a developed country.' Same as corporations. A way for them to plant their flag and say, 'Hey, we're here.'"

"Isn't that what *you're* saying?"

"In a way. Yeah." He looked off into the distance, letting in his face go slack, lowering his voice to a somber purr. "What they do is misdirection, though. Something pretty to look at, take your eye away from what's really going on; 'cause somewhere underneath all that shine, there's always something rotten."

"Sounds ominous." He couldn't see her eyes behind the camera to tell if she was humoring him.

"I know, right? Somebody should cue some music." He smiled again, but it felt forced. "Next question?"

Bhumi called out, "Hey, guys." Standing at the edge on the far side of the floor all by himself, he beckoned to them with one hand as he looked out to the west. There was no sense of urgency in his voice, but everyone headed over to where he stood, including Rene and Zoe, who left off tagging the core wall with graffiti. Even Michael grudgingly got up and came over, Maddie guiding him by one arm like he was an invalid. All of them fell in line at the edge to watch the last glimmering rays of a perfect golden sunset die away, surrendering the darkening sky to a grinning full moon.

TWENTY-TWO

After the break, the crew resumed climbing up the stairwell, only to find it blocked, ten floors up, by a red gate with a burly padlock. Nothing like the monster vault door downstairs, but sufficient enough to keep the riff-raff construction teams on the business floors downstairs from mixing with the bespoke contractors working the elite residences on the upper floors.

Maddie gave the gate a good going-over. Besides the formidable lock, it was sturdily inserted into the wall with recessed hinges and no gap above or below. Without giving him so much as a glance, she yielded to Cam, who was still practically arm in arm with their embedded correspondent.

Is that why I'm pissed at him? But she knew Cam was goofing on Amara precisely *because* she was pissed. It had already ruined the thrill of the hack and was starting to get between her and her performance.

Michael wasn't looking any better, though he said he was just waiting for the Tylenol to kick in.

Maddie sat on the lowest step, her back to Cam and Amara, but thanks to the acoustics in this huge concrete tube, she could still hear them all too clearly.

"You don't see this on all the YouTube videos…" Amara's

posh limey accent lilted flirtatiously. Maddie knew she was just fishing for a juicy quote, but… *ugh*…

Leaning in so the light from his GoPro camera shone on the padlock, Cam worked it with a set of locally sourced picks. After too many jaunts ended like this, he'd ordered a lock-pick set and devoured a marathon session of instructional videos until he could defeat any off-the-shelf padlock. "Strictly speaking," he admitted, "this is sort of against the code."

"Aw, yes. 'Take only pictures, leave only footprints.'"

"That's actually the National Park Service," Cam noted. "We don't usually force our way in, and we never take anything. Why give them an excuse, right? Don't damage or steal their precious property, and what can they really do? What we're taking with this experience, they can't put a price on, and that's all they understand."

"Les Furies… cut down by a little red gate, though. That's how my story's gonna end…?"

Cam's voice tightened, the rattling of the lock becoming almost frenzied. "Just a slight… inconvenience… I promise you…" His hand slipped off the lock and he crushed his knuckles against the gate's wire mesh, so like a cheese grater. "Fuck me," he muttered. Turning to watch him sucking on them, Maddie thought, *Poor baby*, and cursed herself for being just as childish as he.

"What does that name mean, anyway? Les Furies. I assume it stands for more than just the F in F.U.…."

Cam puffed up and took his bloody knuckles out of his mouth, ready for his close-up. She could almost hear him thinking about how, when this became a runaway hit web documentary, this would be the clip to lead the trailer. "In Greek mythology, the Furies were the 'angry ones.' That's us. Indoctrinated from the get-go. Go to school, you know? Get good grades so you can go to college. Get that degree. And then what? Massive debt. Student loans. Who profits? The banks and their stooges in government. Can't afford to pay? Go to grad school. Get that Masters. More student debt. Like slaves in perpetuity. *My* generation? We don't want to play their games just to fit in a box that was made for us. It's like... being in a coffin."

"The Erinyes, yes," Amara said, a touch condescendingly, "*that under Earth take vengeance on men, whosoever hath sworn a false oath.*"

Cam sucked on his injured fingers again, staring blankly at her.

"*The Iliad*," she explained. "The Furies whipped their victims with brass-studded scourges. How does what *you* do bring the pain?"

Cam knocked her softball question out of the park. "By occupying their space, for a start, but that's just a game to get the world's attention. The real invasion, the real resistance, is rhetorical. See, they colonize our minds so we think as they want us to, define our desires by their products, so we surrender to their mind control and end up playing ourselves.

"But the Furies disrupt their control over the discourse. We get people to look up and see that these assholes are only masters of the universe because we let them be. If we marched and signed petitions and all that, they'd just ignore us. If we stole from or directly attacked them, innocent people would get hurt, and the cops would mow us down. But we're fighting them in their own arena, and in the long run, we're gonna make them wish we just had whips."

Even Maddie was impressed, but she bit her tongue.

"Your generation seems to have redefined activism," Amara said. Dear God, was the reporter actually falling for this crap?

"That's why they call us Gen Y. We question shit."

Amara smiled. He was hardcore flirting, doing that thing guys do when they look into a woman's eyes and hold eye contact, mirroring and amplifying her excitement. And she was eating it up, or pretending to, like any good journalist.

"Full of shit, more like." *Who said that?* Did Maddie say that out loud? *Oh well...*

Cam broke eye contact, shifting nervously. Maddie got up

and climbed the steps, stepping over or around the crew and their dropped gear, to stand between Amara and Cam.

"He got it from *The Warriors*," she said. "The gang with the Yankees uniforms and war paint. It's his favorite movie. Do you mind?"

Amara didn't need to be told the interview was over. She stood and went up to the next landing.

Cam played indignantly clueless. "What? It's for the story."

She wasn't going to get into that in front of the crew. Lowering her voice to a stage-whisper, "I'm a little worried about Michael. Not looking too good."

Cam made an exasperated sound and went back to work on the lock. "He's fine, he's just wimping out a little bit, that's all."

Now they were getting to why she was pissed. "The Furies were all women... by the way." She went back down to the next lower floor, checking on Michael as she passed.

Hunched over away from the others, Michael wiped his mouth like he'd just vomited, but he gave her a hearty thumbs-up.

Bhumi came to stand over Michael. Maddie was about to leave, but Bhumi was the least known variable in the crew. She was still trying to get a read on him, so whenever he deigned to interact with others, she paid attention. "You know what I think could really help you? Meditation. You should try it."

Michael knuckled his eyes and vigorously shook his head. "Man, shut up... Seriously, just *shut up*."

"Dr. Amit Ray says suffering arises from a detachment with the inner soul. Meditation helps reestablish that connection." Maddie still couldn't tell if he was heroically patient or just totally up his own ass.

"Oh, 'Dr. Amit Ray says...'" Michael rolled his eyes. "You ever think maybe we *need* suffering?"

"How so?"

Exasperation, at least, put a little color in his cheeks. "How're you supposed to grow, if you've never felt pain?"

Bhumi seemed to genuinely ponder this. Then a look of

humble solemnity stole across the taut expanse of his face. "I was doing a BASE jump off Table Mountain once. Misjudged it. Clipped the rocks with both legs. *Pow!* You know? And for a second, I'm spinning... I'm not thinking about my busted legs, if my chute's going to open. I'm thinking about how I might never get to jump again... and how I'd rather be dead."

Michael flinched. He looked earnestly into Bhumi's eyes. Maddie leaned in too, seeing for the first time the vulnerable mortal man in Bhumi, not the steely, godlike exterior. A possible kindred spirit who could share his own fear.

"What happened?"

"What do you think? I stuck the landing. *Pffft.*" He tossed his braids as if affronted by the prospect of failure.

Michael simply shook his head in disgust.

Maddie stepped out onto the ninetieth floor. It resembled the lobby of a hotel. Probably the business and concierge center for the residences above, she concluded. Zoe and Rene hung off the edge of the building, taking selfies.

Just as she turned to go back upstairs, a bird smacked the cement at her feet, briefly spasming before going still. It had fallen at the foot of a hastily stenciled graffiti mural of a winged monkey, the paint still wet.

Rene was urinating off the side. He laughed for the camera in his hand, yelling, "*Regardez! Ma pisse se heorye!*"

So much for the classy Europeans, Maddie thought. She couldn't stay mad at everybody. They were just being who they were. *But who are you, girl?*

Her private horror stories didn't involve near misses or failures in the field, but she had them. When she was standing on a ledge, climbing a wall, she felt no fear, nothing but the exhilaration of controlling risk, conquering danger. No, when she closed her eyes, the visions that haunted her were of being trapped, waiting for her father or one of her brothers to wreak havoc on their home, for the people who were supposed to love and protect her above all others to try to hurt her again.

Maybe she was in total control when she was most in danger, but when she stood still and stopped to think, she succumbed to the creeping feeling that maybe all the trauma and drama she'd put behind her was still driving her choices, making her stick with this crew when she could've turned pro, making her stick with Cam and letting herself be used, all for the childish desire for a man's approval.

No, she thought. *No place for that, no time for that, here.* She had to keep moving, they had to keep moving "What the hell is the hold-up?"

A flash of scarlet fire flooded the open floor, followed by a resounding detonation that rolled across the city below, rattling the exposed fixtures of the tower. Maddie looked up, fearing some new disaster.

Fireworks.

More pyrotechnics shot up from Bolotny Island to the southeast and a dozen other locations around Moscow, exploding almost at eye level with their perch. Blue, white, and red were a heavy recurring motif in the Russia Day program, obviously, but watching it end-on, the barrage of chemical fire and smoke merged into a mercurial nebula, like a galaxy being born.

Maddie sat down, apart from the twins, to watch the magnificent display. Michael sat beside her, leaning against a column a cautious distance from the edge.

Bhumi came out, too, but he just stood on the ledge with his arms crossed, then turned around and lowered himself until he dangled over the void by his arms. Amara took pictures while he did pull-ups off the side of the building. Maybe he was restless, or maybe he just hated being upstaged, even by fireworks.

Maddie almost said something, but thought better of it. That was exactly how Wu Yongning, the famed first Chinese urbex star, fell to his death, but Wu was a skinny guy, not a musclebound behemoth. Watching out the corner of her eye until he pulled himself back up and strolled away as if he'd just dropped a deuce in the corner, she caught Michael's disbelieving gaze and made a *pfffft* noise just like Bhumi had, which made him crack a smile.

When she looked back into the recesses of the building, she saw a familiar silhouette standing in the stairwell doorway, watching her.

A salvo of fireworks painted Cam in a spree of colors but made his face an impassive mask. She raised a beckoning hand to him, but he ducked out of sight, presumably to go attack the lock.

As always, Amara hovered and took pictures. She snapped Michael and Maddie together, silhouetted by the light show, then turned to Rene and Zoe, who were not watching the display at all.

The twins were tagging yet another wall with graffiti as the fireworks display surged to a frantic finale. Amara snapped the artists and their work bathed in light.

Maddie laughed when the fireworks illuminated it. Monkeys wearing business suits, crowded around each other and staring back at us with their arms crossed. *Laughing* at us. *Who do you think you're fooling?*

Amara took another picture and then walked over to the Jardins. "Just out of curiosity... how many walls have you tagged since we got here?"

The twins looked at each other, then adopted painfully innocent expressions. "Just this one."

Maddie stifled a giggle. She hadn't been keeping track, but she had spotted their art on each of the floors they'd explored. They worked fast, filling in the stencils and adding freehand touches with the deft efficiency of veteran vandals. And they were quite good, to be honest... not all of them political cartoons, but with a mischievous spirit that gave Banksy a run for his money.

Maddie turned back to Michael and tried to make sense of the pent-up expression he was laying on her. "Glad you came yet?"

He swallowed hard, pushing down the illness and the anxiety, looking like he was about to say something he'd been preparing for a while. "You know, I thought a lot about why I did come—"

Just then, the whirring of a motor grew as loud as an approaching car. They hadn't noticed it before, their ears ringing from the fireworks, but they heard loud and clear when the work elevator came to a hissing stop and a gate slammed open with a resounding clang.

"Shit," Maddie hissed, grabbing Michael's hand and pulling him towards the stairwell. Rene and Zoe grabbed their art supplies and ran for it, too.

TWENTY-THREE

Michael was clueless as to what was going on, then looked over Maddie's shoulder to glimpse a security guard stepping out of the construction elevator just as they cleared the stairwell door.

"*Cam*!" she stage-whispered.

"I know, I know…"

"No, you don't! There's—"

"Relax, I got this." Abandoning any pretense of stealth, Cam snapped the padlock open and tugged the bolt out of the gate, threw it wide open. The crew grabbed their bags and raced up the stairs, too panicked to stop and shut the gate, let alone fit the lock back in it.

No sooner had they cleared the next landing, they heard the stairwell door below swing open. Headlight swinging crazily around the pitch-black stairwell, Maddie led them up to ninety-one. The door was locked, with a warning sign featuring a big skull-and-crossbones.

Cam passed her like a track star, taking the steps three at a time. He was holding open the door to ninety-two when Michael came stumbling up. "Get in there, man…" he whispered, grabbing Michael by the strap of his bag, and throwing him over the threshold.

The floor was tiled, as were the inner walls. The vast room had sunken floors—no, they were swimming pools—a lap pool, a kidney-shaped play area with honest-to-God waterslides and a wave machine, and an Olympic-size racing pool.

He was still standing there marveling at this epic absurdity when Cam shoved him from behind. "Snap out of it, Mike!" Cam snarled as he ran past. Michael followed the others into the shower area just as the others came back out.

"Dead end!" Maddie gasped. She pushed by him, headed for the windows. Michael hesitated, trying to draw breath to call out to her that ends didn't get any deader than where she was headed. But Maddie and the others charged at the window and slipped through the fluttering plastic curtains, and dropped out of sight.

"Oh my God—" Michael ran to the edge, heart thudding off-kilter in his chest, stomach clenched like a fist. There had to be more to this than what he saw, there just had to—

He noticed the catwalk extending out from the edge and heaved a sigh of relief—but where was the crew? His throat practically closed, his imagination filling in details until he almost saw the broken scaffolding that must've sent them all spinning off into the sky.

But it was intact, and it took his weight when he stepped out onto it, then reflexively pressed his back against a column. A steel-and-fiberglass catwalk, not four feet wide, encircled the floor. He figured it was going to be a balcony so the swimmers could work on their tans. Below and beyond, there was only soupy, gray mist, while the stars in the sky above were achingly clear and bright. They were above the clouds, for Christ's sake.

Where the hell were his friends?

He heard the stairwell door bang open, heard clopping, hard-soled shoes crossing the waterpark floor at his back, at the same time that he heard them.

"*Michael...*"

"*Miiiiiichaaaeeel...*"

"Where the hell are you guys?" He looked down and saw them hanging by their hands from the edge of the catwalk with their bags dangling from their shoulders.

"I can't believe you assholes…"

The footfalls were growing louder and more urgent, the security guard coming closer. Cursing, Michael skinned on a pair of gloves and knelt at the edge of the catwalk. *Take a deep breath, take a moment*—but he didn't have a moment. Another second and he'd be caught; they'd be *lucky* if they got caught and didn't plummet to their deaths.

His pulse pounded in his ears. It would have been impossible, actually, if not for the cloud layer to hide the view. Just hanging out with friends, *hyuk hyuk*—

Planting his hands on the grip-taped catwalk, he turned and lowered his legs over the edge, then let his torso go until he was hanging with his chin resting on the walk. He could see the guard's light, so the guard could probably still see him.

"*Miiiiichaaeeeelllll…*"

Damn it. He lowered himself until he was dangling from the edge of the catwalk by his aching, cramped fingers. He found himself between Bhumi and Zoe, with Rene, Cam, Amara, and Maddie in a neat little row on the other side.

He looked down and saw only swirling gray emptiness beyond his feet. He looked at his friends and the light in their eyes, the utterly mad grins lighting up their faces, and for just a moment, he felt the old rush, and the fear went away…

The security guard stepped out onto the catwalk, his heavy tread making the steel tremble in Michael's hands. He looked at the others as the guard shuffled by overhead, muttering a prayer. When he was out of earshot, Cam started in again.

"*Miiiiichaaaael…*"

The others joined in, all repeating his name, overlapping, doing their best Kiefer Sutherland.

"Seriously, cut it out," Michael said. "He's still up there…"

"Don't be afraid, Michael," Cam husked, and let go.

He dropped. The cloud engulfed him.

Michael had to fight the instinct to help his friend, but his own arms had gone numb. He couldn't hold on much longer, couldn't even pull himself up on the catwalk without help.

One by one, they all let go and disappeared. The cloud closed over them and swallowed whatever sound they made, as they fell.

"Oh God, please..." Michael tried to pull himself up, but his muscles were saltwater taffy. He wasn't going anywhere but down...

From just below him in the cloud, he heard them. "Michael, you're one of us... Come with us, Michael..."

"Screw this." His fingers cramped and he lost his grip and uttered a short, breathless scream as he fell off the side of Korova Tower.

He sucked in a breath to do the only thing left, to scream—

And landed less than ten feet below the catwalk, in a heavy nylon safety net.

The others were laughing, standing at the edge of the ninety-first floor. Cam reached out to help Michael up.

"That wasn't funny," Michael gasped, which made them laugh even harder. He accepted a flask of water and sucked it down. Before he'd finished it, the crew was on the move again.

They crept swiftly through a maze of machinery—pool pumps and filters, chlorine tanks and water heaters, then rows of washing machines, dryers and folding tables. They passed through a cubicle farm with beds and toilets, like open-air prison cells—servants' quarters, Maddie observed. No wonder a skull-and-crossbones was on the door.

"We should abort, man," Michael said. "The guards are on to us. They won't stop until they run us down."

"Didn't I tell you I got this?" Cam said incredulously. Taking out his walkie, he switched channels and said, "G.I. Joe to Ivan... Can you dig it? Repeat, *can you dig it?*"

"What the hell?" Michael asked.

The reply came back, weak and buried in static. "*Ivan is go.*"

Cam just smiled and pocketed the walkie, and led the rest of them to the open exterior walls.

The clouds still obscured the view, the glow of the floodlights barely discernible about a thousand feet down. It gave him a queasy feeling, reflecting on what he'd just done, and how close it came to disaster, all because of one guard. Was not getting caught worth dying for?

"What are we doing?" Bhumi asked.

Cam said, "Wait for it," and as if on cue, they heard a faint crash and a *bang* way down below, like a big door slamming open. Not very discreet, Michael thought. An air horn went off, the kind of thing only the most obnoxious guy at a rave or a hockey game thinks to bring out in public. The blaring honk skirled throughout the city, cutting through the clouds. Off in the distance, he heard tires screeching, a siren, more bangs and the faintest echo of mad, childish laughter.

A moment later, they heard the hum and rumble of the construction elevator as it passed their floor, going down.

"You can all relax now," Cam said.

"What the hell was that?" Michael demanded. Maddie didn't look any more clued in than the rest of them.

"I tapped some locals to stand by in case we needed a decoy. Parkour group, just punk kids, but they've been waiting in the Metro tunnels since we broke in. When I gave them the go-code, they came up through the new Metro station they're putting in…"

"Pretty sneaky," Maddie said.

"Why the hell didn't *we* come up through the Metro station, then?" Michael asked.

"Can't do it without setting off alarms. Infrared beams, motion detectors, all that shit. These kids make us look like old folks on walkers. They'll draw security off after them, they won't get caught, and they'll fade before the cops get here."

Michael still had doubts, but apparently, he was the only one.

"I told you," Cam said. "I won't let anything go wrong. From here on out, it'll be smooth as glass."

TWENTY-FOUR

Alexei and his friends loved a challenge.

Collectively, the CHUD-Moskovskaya Digger Crew would never turn away from any stunt, so long as someone assured them they couldn't do it. The law was irrelevant. The American had shrewdly cozened them into throwing in on this precisely because of the danger involved, but Alexei had to convince the others not to let the crew down.

Still, it was almost more than they could bear, to have to sit still for so long.

The group had played their role in the plaza, kickflipping off the benches until security made a big show of confiscating their skateboards and running them off. The guards were salty ex-military; brusquely haranguing the kids not to come back, taking their pictures and snapping their boards in half. The CHUD kids endured this mistreatment while the Furies breezed through the plaza and penetrated the Korova construction site.

Playing the defeated hooligans, Alexei and his four friends had shuffled back to Vystavochnaya Metro station and waited, glued to the radio for the Furies. At the Americans' signal, they jumped the turnstiles and dropped off the platform, then donned matching sewer-mutant masks and popped road flares to find their way to the new tunnel loop that went underneath Korova.

Piotr was the oldest and ostensibly the leader, but even he wouldn't have to figure out how to dodge national conscription for another year. Alexei was the most experienced, in more ways than one. Not quite seventeen, he was already an accomplished petty thief and father with an infant son at home. He'd brought Piotr and the other three—Mischa, Arkady and little Maxim—in on the caper. Piotr had taken some convincing, but Alexei knew how to wind him up. Just say, *Yes, you're right to be scared*, and you had him.

They poked around the unopened Korova Metro station, but no one shot any videos or selfies. None of them would say it, but even being this close to the tower felt like the wrong kind of danger.

The CHUD Crew was at home down in the subways. Like the mutants in the cheesy American movie from which they took their name, they were uniquely adapted to the labyrinths and ruins beneath Moscow. As veteran diggers, they knew the totality of the underground, not just the active lines on the transit maps. They had even penetrated Metro-2, the legendary secret subway network Stalin created beneath the civilian Metro to carry ordnance for the capital's defense and provide an escape route for politicians fleeing the next invasion or revolution.

But one didn't brag openly about one's outings in this town. Dropping detailed information would attract tourists; noobs would tag and trash the place, or attract the serious authorities. The Americans had sought them out because they were the best and the boldest, but even they wouldn't go up on Korova.

There were plenty of stories going around about the tower, but nobody knew anything firsthand. It was always a friend of a cousin who had been run off the site after a vicious beating, or had simply disappeared.

Nobody knew for sure what happened to Piotr's mate Vadim and his crew, but last anyone heard, those diggers were intent on summiting Korova as soon as the steel superstructure was completed, three months ago. If they succeeded, nobody saw proof; but soon after they'd dropped off the face of the Earth, someone pulled all their old snaps and forum posts off the 'net, scrubbing away all evidence they'd ever existed at all, so it was no idle rumor.

Though it was never officially pronounced, even the most hardcore digger outlaws knew: *you don't fuck with Korova.*

Too bad nobody told the Americans...

The radio on Piotr's belt clicked and the strange language came purring out of it. "*G.I. Joe to Ivan... Can you dig it? Repeat, can you dig it?*"

Piotr grabbed the radio and hit Send. "Ivan is go." Alexei chuckled at the reference to the ancient American gang movie, but it was no less than he expected. He and his friends all talked shit about America while eating up gangster rap and Hollywood movies. The Furies were different—their stunts were next-level, their style totally *kruto*. Piotr maintained they were posers, just glory-hungry clowns, but even he was all-in, tonight. Being this close to whatever the Americans were doing up there felt more than real, like in an action movie.

Piotr gave them their orders with dramatic commando hand gestures. Alexei went over to the nearest of three padlocked revolving doors and drove his pry bar into the chain. Maxim, a skinny kid who stuck to him like Gorilla Glue, shifted from foot to foot like a dancer waiting for the DJ to drop the bass.

Alexei looked up the motionless escalators into the cavernous lobby that was the underbelly of the tower. Leaning back and bracing one rubber-soled boot against the doorframe, Alexei wrenched the chain apart. The padlock spun off like a spent shell casing. He gave the revolving door a hard shove to send it spinning. The moment it began to turn, piercing ultrasonic alarms went off throughout the station. Flashing strobes ruined his night vision. His friends shouted at him to come on, but he waited to see if someone was really coming.

His heart knocked on his sternum, his face tingled, but he wasn't going anywhere with Maxim standing there biting on his thumbnail, looking in his eyes, measuring his own courage against Alexei's.

He couldn't hear a thing with the alarms screaming, but he could feel them coming an electric moment before he saw the bulky torso in a white uniform blouse stampeding down the escalator ahead of three more. His leg twitched, every instinct telling him to run for it, but Maxim just stood there, too dumb to move on his own.

Alexei jammed the pry bar into the revolving door, wedging it in place just before the first guard crashed into it. Cursing, the guard threw all his considerable weight at the door, but it refused to budge. The other three guards skidded to a halt in the blocked vestibule. Alexei took out the air horn and blasted the guard point-blank with the deafening honk of doom.

Laughing, Maxim took a picture on his phone.

Shoving Maxim ahead of him, Alexei shouted, "Beat it!" Maxim sagged and fell at his feet. Alexei tripped over him and spun around, grabbing the dumb kid. "Move!" he shouted, but Maxim was dead weight.

Alexei flipped him over and noticed a smoking black hole in his face, just below his left eye. Blood sluiced out of it, not squirting like in the movies. It was impossible, he hadn't heard any gunshot, but his ears still rang from the air horn. Even when he looked up and saw the security guard pointing a pistol at him, it took a second for Alexei to process what was happening.

This is not how it's done, he silently screamed. *This is not the way—*

He remained frozen in disbelief until a bullet whizzed past his ear and ricocheted off the wall beside him. Galvanized, he sprang over the locked turnstiles and raced for the platform, screaming, "Run! They're shooting us—"

Piotr, Mischa, and Arkady leapt into the tunnel the moment

he came into view, hooting and laughing. Alexei tried to tell them about Maxim, but he couldn't get breath into his lungs. Hurling his body after the others, pushing them along, shoving them down the tunnel, towards the light—

Train coming!

They had no warning because of the ringing in their ears. The train came around the bend in the tunnel and barreled down on them almost before they could get off the tracks. Alexei hit a wall and spread out his hands, feeling for a service door recess in which to hide. The train's headlights blinded him even through his closed eyelids. The hot, grimy wind of its approach washed over him, filling his mouth with ashes.

He felt a pair of hands seize him. He struggled, but Piotr dragged him Into a doorway. He shouted Maxim's name in Piotr's ear, but the roar of the train stole his words. Soon as the train had passed, Piotr pushed him out back into the tunnel. Alexei looked over his shoulder but saw no sign of Arkady or Mischa. Flashlight beams raked the tunnel in the retreating train's wake, converged on a bright red smear on the spotless concrete wall opposite the platform.

Alexei followed Piotr up the tunnel, running for all they were worth. After a few hundred meters, it forked into the main route, a wider tunnel with multiple tracks. Alexei saw the lights of Vystavochnaya Station ahead and redoubled his efforts, pulling ahead of Piotr, who ran looking over his shoulder for the rest of their crew.

Alexei hit the platform and hopped onto it, reaching for Piotr, but his friend easily leapt up on the platform and ran past him.

The station was oddly deserted, but there was no time to reflect on their good fortune. Piotr hit the escalator and used the handrails to hurl himself upward faster than his feet could carry him. Alexei was only halfway up the escalator when a security guard stepped into view at the top and shot Piotr in the chest.

The sound was less than a sneeze. The barrel of the automatic in the guard's hand had a fat silencer screwed into it. Piotr came tumbling head over heels down the escalator, tangling up Alexei before he could reverse course. The cold steel grooves of the escalator treads bit into his elbows and knees. He threw his hands up over his head, riding the terrible fall all the way back to the bottom.

Stumbling away from Piotr, Alexei ran back to the platform. He reversed course when he saw a train stopped on the opposing track. Its doors closed just as he hit the platform and it began to accelerate away. Alexei jumped, throwing the toes of one boot into the handrail outside the sealed doors, vaulting onto the roof of the train car just before it set off into the tunnel.

Alexei slid backwards on the speeding train. His scrabbling fingers found a grip on the seams of the roof and he pressed his cheek against it. Hot compressed air washed over him and he felt the concrete ceiling of the tunnel racing by less than a foot above his head.

They wouldn't follow him this far, he told himself, but nothing made sense anymore. They *killed* the others; they evacuated the station and shot Piotr down in cold blood...

He'd jump off at the next station and hope they weren't waiting for him, and then... what? He would do what he did. Run and jump and run, never thinking of the next move until he was making it.

The next move came before he was ready. The train was approaching Mezhdunarodnaya but showed no signs of slowing down. People on the platform jumped back as the train actually sped up heading through the station.

They must know he was on the train, and they were high-balling it to the rail yard. He had no choice.

Rolling off the roof, he soared over the heads of a pack of shocked Saturday night commuters, who had only a split second to dodge the unexpected flying kid.

Alexei landed on one leg that snapped like a twig under him, and collapsed at the feet of a transit policeman.

The cop planted a boot on his chest and pointed a gun in his face. Alexei was too exhausted to put his hands on his head, let alone try to escape.

"Arrest me," he gasped, "you fat bastard..."

TWENTY-FIVE

The Furies made camp on the 111th floor to sleep for a few hours.

To Amara, who had summited Kilimanjaro and hiked Mount Ararat with her father, it was just like camping on a mountain, with sleeping bags, lamps and a tiny stove. Some of them—Bhumi and Cam and Maddie, each for their own reasons—even brought their own tents. Pop bottles and junk food wrappers littered the floor all around them, but no alcohol, she was relieved to see.

After their misadventure with the security guards, the crew was too shaken to continue tonight, opting to stay where the solid floors and vestigial walls gave them some cover from the wind. Cam acted like it was the plan all along; his bravado was so forced, his ego so big, but ultimately so fragile. In spite of all common sense, Amara Massaid had to admit she was a bit infatuated with him.

She was the last one awake, the others having nodded off about an hour ago. She admired their ability to sleep anywhere, even after what they'd just been through, like soldiers in wartime. But she was still too stirred up to sleep. She passed the time making a rough cut of the brief interviews she'd managed to squeeze out of the crew after they set up "camp"—all except Bhumi, who solemnly told her he never did interviews right before a wingsuit dive, though he'd be happy to give her an "exclusive" as soon as they were back at the hotel. His unselfconscious hubris was such a turnoff, it negated everything else he had going for him.

She wasn't here to cavort with the subjects, she reminded herself. She couldn't help but recognize their feelings, though, couldn't avoid using them as a means to an end, the story. But *she* was part of the story now, and had done everything they were doing. What else would be part of the story?

As a rule, Amara tried to be an invisible conduit, but she would never have pursued this story if not for her own history. Before Libya, she was drawn to the thrill of dangerous assignments, but something she'd learned about herself while covering the civil war in her estranged homeland had shaken her deeply. All that she'd witnessed and been forced to do there had been a matter of survival. She'd surprised herself by what she was capable of, but lingering trauma still threatened to shake her to bits long after the danger had passed. These invincible young punks blithely courted danger as a hobby, and seemed completely untouched by fear or trauma. To discover their secret would be far more than a professional triumph.

But this isn't about you, is it? She deftly shut down that train of thought as she would any unproductive line of questioning.

Editing helped clear her head of all it had absorbed and focused her mind on how to attack tomorrow. Weaving what she'd been told and what she'd witnessed into a cohesive narrative centered her and shielded her from things she'd rather not think about.

Adjusting the gain on her earbuds, she wound the counter back to 00:00 and started the rough cut. Michael appeared on the tiny screen in a tight head-and-shoulders shot, looking somewhat guarded with the night sky and a raw, unfinished column in the background. He'd sat for the interview in spite of his illness, which he still insisted was food poisoning, and it'd taken some doing to draw him out.

She felt pity for him as he frowned, taking in her first question. "Can you remember your first time 'exploring?'"

Michael replied, "It was at this old factory they stopped using back in the 70s..."

"Abandoned?"

His blank expression, curling up into the merest shadow of a mischievous smirk, was answer enough.

Cam appeared on-screen. His big, warm grin was a striking contrast to Michael's introverted vibe. He was proud as hell of what they'd just gotten away with, and he loved talking about himself.

Amara threw him a curveball. "How many times have you been arrested?"

"How many times have *I* been arrested?" Cam's bemused expression threw off the slick flow of the cut, but she adored it, and left it in. "Like... in my life or—"

"For trespassing."

"Oh." He laughed, a little nervously. "We actually prefer the term 'place-hacking.'" He nodded, daring her to argue with him.

"So, a lot?"

"I don't know... it's like 'number of people you've slept with.' At a certain point, counting gets to be *malapropos*, know what I'm saying?"

Depending on how she felt tomorrow, she might axe that last bit. The camera cut back to Michael, letting him finish his story. "Oh yeah. I mean this place looked like something out of those old World War II photos..."

She'd seen the Damen ruins for herself as background research. The fifteen-story grain silos had been rendered useless by an explosion in 1977, and were nobody's idea of a historical landmark, but the unsightly gray heap persisted as an unofficial playground and training center for young urbex enthusiasts.

"Like one of those German cities they firebombed, only this

was like right outside Chicago. Everyone just forgot it was there, you know? But that's what made it cool. If everyone knew it was there, then it would suck. They'd probably tear it down for condos."

Michael seemed to genuinely care about the history of the forgotten spaces. His eyes went remote, reflecting on it. More than the danger, this was what he loved about what he did.

"So, correct me if I'm wrong, but one thing I've noticed about urbex crews is how they seem to provide a back door to intimacy with a place for immigrants, mixed-race folks and other outsiders... and an identity..."

Michael looked askance at her. "We're all outsiders... what's your point?"

Maybe cut that part?

Over to Maddie.

The girl certainly shared the boys' resistance to accessing her inner feelings. Staring daggers at Amara, rocking from side to side on the balls of her feet, making it hard to keep her in frame, she was the heart and soul of this little team, and Amara was torn between hating her back and liking her most of all.

"How would you characterize *urbex*?" Amara winced at how she'd loaded the term, the way Americans spat out a word they held in contempt and clearly didn't understand, like *socialism* or *refugee*. But it did its job, and Maddie started talking.

"Urbex is basically this umbrella term for all types of urban exploration. Rooftopping, place-hacking, infiltration... they all fall into a certain culture that happens when you pack millions of people together in one place."

As Amara had hoped, Maddie soon forgot who she was talking to, and warmed up to her subject. "I think the general feeling—at least this is the way I felt—is that you start to feel like rats in a maze. Naturally, people will find different ways to break free of that structure and express themselves."

Cut back to Michael...

"What got you into it?"

"Me?" he asked blankly. She imagined he probably looked just like that, when he was hanging off the edge of the catwalk. "There was a girl…"

Michael spaced out, but she could almost see the girl in his eyes, perched precariously way out on a crane, an entire city at her feet. Her braids billowing from inside a hoodie, her face turned away, which only increased her allure. Something about her said she would do anything for you, if you could only keep up with her…

She seemed to embody everything he wanted, but couldn't have, couldn't be. She seemed free.

She let the reverie last longer than her editor would allow before jogging him out of it. "Care to elaborate?"

Michael offered a sheepish smile, let out an uncomfortable laugh. "Not really."

Cut to Cam. Same question:

"Boredom."

Cut to Maddie. Same question:

"I saw a Reddit post asking if anyone wanted to meet up and go exploring. And I was like… Exploring? What does that mean… *exploring*?"

She let Michael answer Maddie's question.

"When you explore, you leave the normal world behind. See the unseen."

"Unseen," Amara repeated the word—a standard tactic that got him to think a little more deeply about his glib answer—while she filed away "Unseen World" as a prospective title for whatever this became.

"Yeah. I mean, we live in these cities, right? Only, nobody really *sees* them."

Cut to Cam: "Abandoned buildings, bridges, tunnels… rooftops. Any kind of space that's off-limits."

Maddie: "More and more people started doing it, and it just sort of became this thing…"

Cam: "Suddenly these crews started to form. It was like

bragging rights to see who could explore the sickest places. Who could get the most hits."

Michael: "Abandoned sites were the easiest, but you start to run into other explorers and the sites get trashed or locked up tight... the unknown started to become commonplace..."

Cam: "So we took on more live sites. It was just more exciting, but also, just by going in there, you're making a statement, you know?"

Maddie: "Once people started posting pics on top of skyscrapers, that changed the game."

Michael: "Took it to a whole new level."

Cam: "Viral."

Michael: "And the more hits we got, the more we felt like we had to top ourselves. It was like a drug."

Maddie: "A drug."

Cam: "And the more we did it, the more invincible we felt."

Michael came back on-screen, looking a bit more comfortable, engaged. She almost felt bad about this part. "Tell me about the accident."

He just sat there, thinking about it, maybe reliving it.

She cut to Maddie. "It was an urban zip line into a BASE-jump exit. Pretty hairy, but we'd done it before..."

Cut to Michael, trying to pick his way through an emotional minefield. "The parachute twisted..."

Maddie: "It was scary." The profound tension in her face more than made up for the banal remark.

Cut to Cam. "When I saw Michael hit the ground, I thought... that was it."

And back to Michael, popping sweat and looking over his shoulder as if he just realized he's illegally on top of a skyscraper in a less-than-friendly foreign land.

"What was that like?" Amara asked, hating herself and feeling proud of her commitment to go there, anyway. "To feel invincible one second, and then have that happen to you?"

For a moment, she thought he'd just get up and bolt out of

frame. But instead, he took a moment to search inside himself, and then he cracked a sad smile. "What'd it feel like? It felt like gravity. Sooner or later, everything's gotta come down, right?"

As always, she fretted about her own bias coloring the story. Some authorial voice and prejudice was inevitable, indeed necessary. She didn't write for Reuters or AP. Her editors wanted her unique insight in her stories, but she knew that here, her prejudices would get in the way of the hook that would sell the story.

Amara was too young to remember much of Libya, having emigrated to the UK with her family when she was only six, but she realized later how it set her apart, and not just as the new kid in school. Her father, a respected attorney, voracious reader and insatiable hiker and mountain climber, took her with him on many of his jaunts. She recognized in his need to explore and conquer how he was pushing back against some inner turmoil, not to say trauma. His own parents had died in an American air raid on Tripoli in the 80s, and though he didn't harbor a grudge, he was clearly more wounded by the loss than he ever let on.

People who would watch and read this story at their desks or on the bus to work wanted to know what it felt like to live without fear. To build up these kids as daredevils driven by some extraordinary X factor, she had to put aside her own perception that it wasn't what they had, but what they were *missing*, that gave them the ability, if not the compulsion, to do this crazy shit.

None of the kids in this crew seemed to have been touched, really touched, by death—their nonchalance was so proactive that it had to be a front. The videos of kids turning cartwheels on rooftops were ubiquitous, but you had to look a lot harder for the ones where someone died, because no one wanted to be reminded they were mortal, just like the news could be filled with stirring images of war without ever showing what a bullet or a mortar shell could do to a human body.

Much as she loathed to admit it, the crew reminded her in too many ways of the child soldiers she'd encountered in far too many wars. Invincible in their innocence, until it's too late.

Michael came the closest to honestly feeling the fear, and her heart went out to him for his courage, even as she felt bad for him. He'd had his fragility rubbed in his face with almost fatal authority, and his body was threatening to shut down in the face of doing it again, yet here he was.

She felt a twinge of guilt for reminding him of why he was here, but she hoped it was what he thought it was… Even if his hopes were bound to be dashed by Maddie, he might just make it home.

She looked up from the screen, squinting at the dark, and saw Michael sitting up in his sleeping bag, looking at her.

Speak of the devil.

"How are you feeling?" she asked.

"Better," he replied. "I think whatever I had must've passed." She saw that he was still dealing with nerves, and knew better than to call him out, knew better than most how real those symptoms felt.

She looked out at the view. Cloud cover swallowed up the whole city now, with only the tops of the half-dozen or so other skyscrapers in the International Business Center area poking up through the clouds, which were charged with an enchanting silver light by the full risen moon. There might be no city down there, at all. It felt oddly serene. "We are officially on our own. It feels weird. Like… breathing." Flinching at the clumsiness of her observation, she reminded herself to stick to asking questions.

But Michael seemed determined to pry her open, if only as revenge for the interview. "Compared to the places you've been to, this can't be all that exciting."

"Yeah well, maybe I've seen too much *excitement*." She surprised herself at the vehemence of her reply. Where did *that* come from?

Once again, it worked on him. He dropped the subject. But

he wasn't done. "Hey, Amara? You know Cam and Maddie... don't mess with their thing, alright?"

What a gallant and childlike thing to say, she thought. *Maddie will probably never even know how you really feel.* "Something tells me you're a much larger threat to their *thing*, than I am."

"Hey, I'm not a—I mean..."

"You don't have to convince me, Michael," she said. "But you should watch what you say... Those GoPro cameras you're all using have an internal cellular antenna, so you're broadcasting live to an audience of who knows how many. I'm using my own, but I looked at Maddie's. So, everything you say is part of an interview."

That took the wind out of his sails. He shook his head, looking at Cam and Maddie's tent, then turned away to sleep, or pretend to.

She hadn't cut the other footage into the sequence because the Jardin twins weren't charter members of Les Furies, but the interview cried out for its own segment. They stole any show they deigned to appear in, and they knew it.

When she had asked them to sit still for her questions, Rene was unpacking a small, reinforced steel case, such as very expensive mobile electronics might be stored in. He asked her to wait, but told her she would want to see this.

She waited as he took out almost a hundred tiny drones, each the size of a big butterfly, set them on the floor beside the edge, and activated them from a tablet.

"Does Cam know you have that?" Amara asked. The Frenchman just shrugged. The drones swooped out into the open air like a swarm of dragonflies, and disappeared. Then—

No, she thought, wonderingly. *Fireflies...*

The swarm lit up with red lasers as they danced in front of the building. Nobody in Moscow could see it unless they happened to be watching from the roof of Federation Tower, but passengers flying into Sheremetyevo or Vnukovo airports might notice that the world's tallest building was sending them a secret message.

Amara had heard that drone swarms were becoming quite popular in China, as a mandatory substitute for fireworks because of air pollution and fire concerns.

"It's very beautiful, but what does it say?"

By way of an answer, Rene held up his tablet, which showed an eagle's eye-view from a stationary drone hovering outside the formation circling in front of Korova Tower.

It alternately flashed, LES FURIES and F.U.! in crimson letters that looked like a metal band logo.

Finally, when Rene and Zoe put away their toys, they sat down for the interview. Shoulder to shoulder, they rocked and moved in perfect unison. The cut began when Zoe, hands wrapped around a cup of hot milk, twitched her shoulder just a bit. Without looking away from Amara or otherwise seeming to notice the tiny gesture, Rene scratched her shoulder on the exact spot where it itched. Zoe took no notice of the little miracle, which must happen a hundred times a day.

Amara asked in a scolding tone, "Why are you such jokers? Isn't this activity dangerous enough for you?"

Rene spoke quickly, like a café philosopher with an invisible cigarette in his frenetic hand, while Zoe, sedate and languorously cool, interpreted. "Death takes itself too seriously, so you must laugh at it," she said. "The daredevil doesn't defy death, but only their own desire to die."

Amara asked incredulously, "Doesn't everyone want to live? If you wanted to die by suicide, why not get on with it? Why make a game of it?"

"Why not? Every one of us," Zoe translated, "every living thing, carries the death urge. Most of us feed it with bad food, drink, smoke, drugs... little suicides, death on the installment plan, no? Some of us can resist it, but we all feel it."

She repeated another phrase then, that she didn't translate. "*L'appel d'vide.*"

Amara dusted off her rusty French. "The appeal of the void?"

"Yes. Have you never felt it, when you stood on a cliff or even a sturdy balcony? That pull towards the edge and over it, that feeling in your bones that you *should* fall, or that your perch would dissolve beneath your feet?

"All of us feel it, especially those who risk their lives on this foolishness. If you do not feel it, we do not want to play these games with you, because you are not truly alive."

Taken aback, Amara found herself floundering. "Surely not everyone experiences this strange feeling," she countered.

Rene answered, "Ah, but look at this magnificent tower. It is all but designed to fail and fall. To build such an arrogant structure so quickly, in defiance of physics and sane engineering, shows that whole societies, too, feel the appeal of the void."

It would have been a profoundly stirring clip, if only she could've persuaded them to take off the parrot and pug masks.

TWENTY-SIX

The next morning, the sun itself might've been hung over from the night before, opting to take the day off. High clouds the color of bruises, swollen with rain, passed with eerie speed over Moscow, borne out of the southwest by a jet stream that collided at an oblique angle with the prevailing north wind, creating almost ideal conditions for a thunderstorm. Few in the workaholic capital who had any choice would get out of bed before noon.

An hour before dawn, the Furies awoke and broke camp, bagged their trash and shared a meager breakfast. Rene and Zoe made tiny cups of coffee and crêpes for anyone who asked, but the crew seemed sore and snappish, much more drained than when they'd stayed out all night drinking. The unseasonable cold, the wind howling through the exposed recesses and ducts of the unfinished tower, sapped their vigor and preyed on their nerves.

Michael stirred at the smell of coffee but couldn't get out of the sleeping bag, which was uncomfortable, but still warm. He hadn't slept well, in fact he didn't remember sleeping at all, just a nerve-wracking in-between state plagued by lucid nightmares and nagging, repetitive thoughts.

Bhumi passed close by, almost stepping over him, as he

confronted Cam. "The wind's too strong," he said. "I can't jump in this."

Cam made a noise like someone who'd never actually laughed trying to imitate it. "What good are you, if you can't do the jump? That's literally the *only* reason you're here."

Michael wrapped his windbreaker over his head, but it did nothing to keep out the noise. His chest hurt like he'd been doing wind sprints all night. His heart felt like a ball of clay.

"You can keep your ten percent," Bhumi snapped.

Michael sat up bolt upright. Had he heard what he thought he heard? "Ten percent of *what*?"

"Dude," Cam said, "we're almost at the top. We're right there."

Bhumi shook his head so his braids fluttered in the wind as he walked away. "Sometimes you gotta pull the plug."

"Pull the plug?" Cam blew up. "What is *that*?"

Michael had to shout to be heard. "TEN PERCENT OF WHAT?"

Cam bit his lip, turning to look at his old friend like a stranger he hadn't invited. "The channel. *Our* channel…"

Michael, wobbly but enraged, staggered out of his sleeping bag. "You *monetized* this? We said we were never gonna—"

"I know what we said, but that was before it blew up. Even when we were on hiatus, bro. We were leaving money on the table!"

"You weren't going to tell me—"

"I knew you'd freak out! And I was right!"

Michael was about to blow up, reminding him who he was talking to, when Cam abruptly dropped the mask. The Hustle. He looked like a little boy. "I needed the capital, man. I'm *busted*."

Maddie came away from disassembling their tent. She didn't say a word, didn't have to. This was all news to her. Her arms crossed, she shifted from foot to foot.

"Every company goes public at some point," Cam said, the stroking tone creeping back into his voice. "That's how the real world works, whether you sit in an office all day, or leap tall buildings in a single bound. We're anarchists, man, not communists. Nobody's a communist anymore except you, I guess. You can always sit this one out."

"Everybody sells out," Michael said. "That's what you mean. When did we become *your* company, Cam?"

"Don't lay that shit on me. *You* sold out, man. *You* left us. If I hadn't come around you'd still be down there, sitting in some café with your computer. This isn't about money; it's about you being *afraid*."

The silence became a wall between them. Michael couldn't respond, and Cam wouldn't take it back. Shaking his head, Cam turned and walked up on Bhumi. "How much?"

"What?"

"For you to do the jump?"

Bhumi scoffed and went back to packing his gear.

"I'll up your share another five points."

Now he had Bhumi's attention. The bigger man stood up, using his height and the full weight of his presence to augur into Cam's ego. "Ten."

"Six."

Bhumi picked up his pack and threw it on.

Wow, Michael thought, stumbling into his clothes. Just… *wow*. He had to find out from Amara that all along they'd been starring in a potential snuff livestream—and now this bullshit. *Well, Cam said this would be a game changer*… but Michael was still astonished at how much the game had changed behind his back.

Cam returned and stood over Michael as he rolled up his sleeping bag. In a lower, but still tense voice, he asked, "We good?"

Michael could barely look at his friend. He just shook his head. "Was that ever a choice? You didn't really need me for the face recognition system, you just found a way to rub my face in it. Why'd you drag me into this, Cam?"

Cam knelt down so he was right in Michael's face, so only they could hear what he said next. "Maddie wanted you to come, idiot. *She* needed you here, but nobody else does…"

Michael was about to let loose a fiery retort when Cam checked his watch and threw up a warning hand. He plastered an insincere grin on his face just before strapping a bandana over it.

"And we're live in three… two… one…"

Turning back to Michael, Cam gave a vigorous thumbs-up, got in his face and launched into another of his patented F.U. Crew rants. It took Michael a moment to realize he was not speaking to Michael at all, but to the GoPro camera strapped to his head.

TWENTY-SEVEN

They climbed.

An endless, exhausting slog as tedious as PT at the gym, and every bit as taxing. Michael kept his complaints to himself, but it was all he could do to keep up. Everyone was tired, tense and wrapped in their own grievances. Except the twins, who had donned their animal masks again and kept up a lively, chattering conversation in their shorthand French dialect.

At the 120th floor, they passed through another mechanical room like the one below, with similar heavy equipment, though much of it was not yet connected. Even above the hum of the transformers, they could hear the wind through the louvered vents like an endless, frigid breath.

Above 120, the tower became even more vestigial, as if they were not merely ascending, but traveling backwards in time. The stairwell was just a hanging lattice of textured steel risers that rang with their footfalls. No concrete slab floors, just steel I-beams with plywood and fiberglass platforms connecting the most well-trod paths. Everywhere you looked, there were gaps and pitfalls through which you could see the swirling clouds outside. Wind sliced through the tower, playing it like a colossal instrument. Strange, haunting music surrounded them, drowning out the meager shreds of conversation they tried to keep up. As the tower tapered, its footprint shrinking with each passing floor, it seemed to vibrate ever more fitfully in the inclement weather.

By the time they reached the 180th floor, the wind was blowing freezing needles of rain into every corner of the tower's steel skeleton. Coming out of the stairwell at its terminus, they found themselves in a large, bare room taken up almost entirely by a massive cylinder suspended on hinges mounted in the walls.

As they circled around it in search of an exit, Michael distinctly heard a deeper, more ominous sound through the rain coming from within the cylinder. Like water sloshing. He put a hand, then an ear, against the wall of cold steel. It was like that sound you hear when you put your ear to a seashell, if the seashell was the size of a house.

As if he'd disturbed something within, the cylinder slowly tilted a few degrees, just enough to make Michael recoil from it. The sound of water within shifted and sloshed louder.

Rene was looking at the cylinder in awe and mistrust. He said something to himself, but Michael prodded Zoe until she translated. "It's the mass-damper, for stabilizing, no? Thousands of gallons of water flow back and forth between two Olympic swimming pool-sized chambers within, to counteract the tilt of the building."

Michael thought he'd felt the whole building swaying under his feet, but assumed it was just vertigo.

The rest of the crew came back without finding a way up. "Dead end, everybody," Cam said.

"What happened to the stairs?" Amara asked.

"Stairs?" Cam cried out in a hammy voice. "Where we're going, we won't need stairs!"

The steel walls extended for thirty feet, but the contractors had not yet hung a ceiling, and the top floors and even slivers of sky showed through the maze of beams and ducts.

Without a word, Maddie donned her gear and went to work. Free-climbing by stretching between the sheer wall and the mass-damping cylinder with no harness, nothing to save her if she fell. Michael could only watch with the others, throat clenched in worry, but heart pounding with pride for his friend.

Faster than climbing a ladder, Maddie scaled the wall and threw a rope around the mast of a construction elevator, which ascended from the 183rd floor up the empty throat of the unfinished stairwell and continued all the way to the roof. Locking a carabiner to a harness on the rope, she lowered it down so the rest of the crew could be lifted to her perch.

From there, as Cam predicted, there were no stairs. The only way to the roof was up a crude ladder attached to the mast of the elevator. The rain came lashing in at such volume that it was like having glasses of ice water constantly dashed in your face. Michael's windbreaker was waterproof, but rain forced its way into his hood and up his sleeves as he climbed, aggravating his chill. He shivered and shook, losing his footing and taking his full weight on his trembling arms.

Halfway up, amid a dizzying maze of steel frames and platforms and empty, icy space, he slipped and barely caught himself. His feet struggled for traction on the slick rungs, but they were too weak to carry him any higher. "I can't do this..." he mumbled, barely loud enough to hear himself, "I can't do this..."

Farther up the ladder, Maddie pivoted to cling to the bolts fusing two lengths of steel conduit, so the rest of the crew could pass. "*Michael!*"

He looked up to see her watching him and struggled to make an effort, but it just wasn't in him anymore.

He hugged the ladder for dear life, his feet shaking. She looked up and locked eyes with Cam, shaking her head, then she climbed down until she was right next to him.

"How you doing there, kid?" She laid a hand on his forehead, so much warmer than he felt. He couldn't think of anything to say, could barely think at all. The look on her face verified his worst fears, but she still tried to charm him out of it.

"Hey. This is easy. We've done worse than this before."

He shook his head. "It's not the same." He hated being the weak link, but he'd been as strong as he could, for as long as he could. Forcing himself, he looked into her eyes. *I'm not the same,* he thought, and knew she could see it.

"Maddie! Come on!" Cam shouted from the cathead of the elevator tower.

Making a pleading gesture at Cam with her hands, Maddie took a moment to center herself and ran her fingers through the fine hairs on the back of Michael's neck. "Maybe you should head back, yeah? It's insane out here." She'd never touched him like that, not even when he fell. It made him feel like a beloved dog, about to be put to sleep. Michael just nodded solemnly. There was no argument, and he couldn't bring himself to ask her to help him get back down.

"Maddie!" Cam shouted again. "Babe, leave him! Let's go!"

She looked at Michael for a moment, pressed her hand over his and gave it a squeeze, told him to be careful, and then started climbing again, effortless in spite of everything the tower threw at her. Even now, he wished he could follow her; but he only threw her a last searching glance before he began his long descent.

TWENTY-EIGHT

The rain finally eased up, but the wind seemed to blow harder, in vicious, piercingly cold gusts that tried to pry them from their perches. The crew was resolute, moving painstakingly up the construction elevator's mast.

Maddie kept her focus on the next rung, the next handhold, her movements precise and spare, feeling none of the joy that should be filling her, right now. This was everything she'd dreamed of and worked for, but all she could think about was how badly she wanted to get to the top, and drop-kick Cam off of it.

The coldness with which he'd just ditched Michael when he couldn't go any further... was that who he really was? All that talk about getting the crew together, when Cam just needed him to beat the face recognition; all that bullshit about getting Michael back on the horse when he was in no shape for something like this. He'd thoroughly used his best friend and then thrown him away. It made her livid, but also sick to her stomach, when she considered who else he must be playing.

Bhumi arrived first, stepping onto the roof and throwing down his pack on a helipad beside an uncompleted stairwell head. He'd started to unpack his wingsuit when Cam came up to him, shaking his head and pointing up. "What are you doing? Don't uncork the champagne yet. We go all the way."

Bhumi looked where he was pointing, at the twin ten-story cranes. Anchored directly to the concrete core, they each extended a hundred-foot jib out over open space. Bhumi shrugged and shouldered his pack, a weary expression on his face.

Carefully avoiding Maddie's fiery gaze, Cam split them in two groups. He, Maddie and Amara would scale #2, while Rene, Zoe and Bhumi would climb #1. "This is the big payoff," Cam shouted over the wind. "This is our moment to shine. Who even knows how many millions of people are watching right now… So don't blow it."

Maddie bit her lip. It didn't hurt their numbers that the video of Michael's fall got leaked a few weeks ago, but it brought a totally different energy. A lot of the people out there watching wouldn't be fans rooting for them, but morbid assholes, anticipating another accident.

Be safe, Michael, she thought, willing precious energy to her friend, wherever he might be.

After they'd stashed their packs at the base of #2 and broke off into groups, she sidled up close to Bhumi and told him, "You don't have to go."

He just looked at her like she was the dumbest form of life he'd ever seen and sauntered over to the base of #1.

Just getting to the cranes was pretty tricky, crossing an 18 inch-wide I-beam slick with half-frozen raindrops. Despite the danger, the twins recklessly horsed around, jumping up and down and dangling each other over the edge. Maddie moved as if it were a crosswalk, avoiding Cam's hand when he reached out to her from the concrete abutment at the crane's base, not looking back to check on Amara.

They climbed into the cage of the crane's mast and filed up the ladder. In spite of the heating pad-lined climbing gloves, her hands were numb, clumsy, and throbbing with the chill. She'd taken off her engagement ring and hung it on a chain around her neck, under her windbreaker and sweater. As she had several times already, she checked on it. Still there, though she had half a mind to give it back.

Don't do anything rash, she told herself. Cam was under a lot of stress, and she knew he genuinely loved Michael, but this thing had gotten out of control. Nothing about it felt right, but it was almost over, and there would be time to sort out her feelings when they were safely back on the ground.

But that was the thing, wasn't it? She'd always felt as safe up here as she did on solid sidewalk; so why did this place, this whole thing, feel like it was about to turn sideways underneath them?

When they first became the Furies, it'd been like having two big brothers who weren't overprotective and condescending. It was so amazing, having these two guys to play with, who respected her skills and challenged her to go further and faster, that she'd dreaded the inevitable moment when one of them would hit on her. But it never came. Cam always flirted with her, but he flirted with everybody. Michael, more reserved, guarded, obviously carried a torch for her, but he never pressed it.

And how did she feel about him?

She loved him like a brother, and if the moment came, she might've fallen for him, but it just didn't work out that way. She had to tell herself that, because any other explanation made her feel fickle and fake.

When they'd taken Michael to the ER, Cam and Maddie stepped back as if they'd committed a crime and would soon be arrested. They each visited him in the hospital, but not together. Cam called her a week later and asked her out on a place-hack. He was shaken, overwrought. He broke down crying, saying the whole thing was his fault.

Up until then, Maddie had thought of Cam as a lovable bullshit-artist. She adored his bravado and his total commitment to the crew, loved how he made their stunts meaningful. Seeing him like this, hearing how he really felt about Michael, about the crew, about her... It shook her, turning her harmless crush into something more, and she hadn't asked herself if it was anything less than the Real Thing.

Until now.

Maybe Cam had used her the same way he used Michael. Maybe he didn't even realize it. Maybe he believed he really did love her. That was the most depressing thought of all...

So, stop thinking it, pendeja.

Seriously, she chided herself in a voice that might've been her mother's, but with more swears. She and Cam had been an item for almost eight months, and it'd been heaven. Life with Cam was an adventure. They traveled, they never stopped playing and exploring, they had excellent sex... but was any of it real?

She didn't even know what the word meant anymore.

This *is real*, she thought. *This ladder you're climbing, this crane you're on, this building you broke into, this crazy, screwed-up country you may soon have to escape...*

Don't worry, Cam has a plan. Doesn't he always?

She stopped on the ladder. Her blood sugar must be low. She dug in her pocket for a glucose pack, but the contents were all tangled up—earbud cords, ChapStick, sunglasses, and who knew what else. She impatiently ripped the glucose out of her pocket and a bunch of other stuff came with it, tumbling past her and raining down on Amara.

"Ow, nice," Amara said. Something more solid than the ChapStick had fallen with it. She patted herself down, shaking her head in disbelief.

Oh shit, she thought. It was the phone... their only phone.

"Sorry," Maddie said, feeling humiliated. They were almost done, almost out of here. They wouldn't need it, and they'd laugh about it later. They'd don workers' coveralls and just walk out...

But not if she didn't get her head together. *Keep climbing*, she told herself. *Be here now...*

They reached the top of the crane at last, climbed over the

slewing unit that housed the motors and out onto the jib, while Cam opened up the operator's cab and climbed in.

She could see Rene getting into the cab on the other crane, and Bhumi strapping on his Birdman wingsuit. She wished she had binoculars. He looked like a flying squirrel, with the quilted webbing from arms to legs.

The wind still ripped through the superstructure, but the rain seemed to have stopped. Through the thin metal grate where they stood, she could see the tapering shaft of the crane and far below it, the entirety of Korova Tower, the tallest building on Earth. She looked around for someone to share the moment but there was only Amara, who smiled diplomatically at her and then snapped a picture.

The whole crane lurched, and the metal shivered as the motors ground to life. Cam worked the levers and the crane pivoted towards the tower even as Rene did the same on #1, swinging them round and extending the jibs until they almost touched. A mere ten or twelve feet separated them—barely a crack of space on the scale of the building, but a perilous chasm, when you got up close, as they began to do, now.

Maddie's radio chirped, and Zoe's voice came out of it. "Do you feel that? The steel is humming."

"Repeat that?" Maddie said. She put her hand against the nearest strut on the cage around the jib and felt a weird, shimmying tension, heard a low groan that might or might not be a natural response to the high winds.

"It stopped," Zoe said. Maddie felt it, too, but didn't know how to react. That was a *good* thing, right?

"Keep going," Cam said. "Almost there…"

They continued out to the very end of the jib and waved to Rene, Zoe, and Bhumi. Shouting, whooping, taking selfies, they poured out all the tension of the last twelve hours at the tops of their lungs. Pumping their fists in the air, they felt like they'd won the Olympics. They were, quite literally, on top of the world.

Rene busted out a selfie-stick and shot video of himself and his sister, then of the crew on the opposing jib, with the crane arm, the tower, and all of Moscow so far below them, you could almost tell yourself you saw the curvature of the horizon.

Cam pulled out his walkie and waved it in the air for the others to see. Screaming into it, "Is this sick or what?!" he let out a long, loud whoop of pure joy. If she wasn't already Maddie could've fallen in love with him, right then.

Rene screamed back over all their radios, "*C'est absolument incroyable!*"

"OK," Cam said. "Now for the tricky part."

And he jumped.

TWENTY-NINE

Detective Lieutenant Vasily Sterankov did not rise to his current position or hold it for as long as he had because he was a good detective. Oh, he was excellent at taking down cases, but the most critical facet of his criminological abilities was the ability to know when to close his eyes, plug his ears and detect nothing at all.

Vasily had seen the men who trained him railroaded out of the force for doing their jobs too well, for serving the wrong master. Sometimes it could not be helped. Sometimes, you stepped into what appeared to be a murder investigation, only to find the body, the weapon and then the case itself vanished into thin air, or worse, to find yourself the prime suspect.

The older cops like Vasily, the last holdovers from the Perestroika era, tried their best to help the younger ones, but those who came up before the Russian spring of the 90s always ended up in the worst jams. The new ones, men who'd lived their whole lives under the current regime, needed no one to tell them when to look away, and when to put out your hand.

The media reliably underestimated the crowd sizes as under ten thousand, although two thousand cops had been bussed in from nearby cities to keep order. This Sunday morning, Sterankov should have been at his *dacha* in the country, seeing to its chronically leaky roof, but all hands were called in to process the hundreds of protestors who'd been arrested.

Orders from on high were to round up anyone suspected of membership in pro-democracy groups, especially those with international backing. The message was clear; the state wanted proof that foreign agitation, not broad popular support, was behind the protests. Never mind that these were the biggest demonstrations the city had seen since the last presidential election, when the president extended his own term from four to six years. Never mind that with the conscription call sending hundreds of thousands to war, even ordinary people were braving the crackdown. Even so, half the country still hoped that he'd give himself a lifetime term when he won again.

Whenever you thought you couldn't take it anymore, you could always find comfort in knowing that next year would be worse.

Everybody else in the office was sucking down coffee and stepping away from their desks twice an hour for smoke breaks. Last year, Vasily had painfully weaned himself off tobacco. He didn't miss the grim miasma of smoke that still stank up the warren of day rooms, interrogation cells and corridors, but without strong coffee his mind was sluggish and prone to morbid despair.

His wife sent him to work every day with a bottle of herbal tea to "cleanse" him of "impurities." Horrible stuff, like something steeped in a moldy tree stump, it came in an unwieldy glass bottle, because plastic or metal containers polluted the body with free radicals, whatever those were.

At first, Vasily took it to humor her and poured it down the sink, but she caught him out. She could smell it in his sweat when he cheated, and broke down crying when he came home smelling of coffee and cigarettes, so he tried to show willing. Marina seemed to believe that if he merely abstained from all pleasure, he would live forever.

Forever, doing this...

Sipping the unspeakable tea, Vasily reviewed the reports that had piled up since he'd left his desk a mere six hours ago. Intrigued by one arrest report in particular, he had this punk Alexei Betrozov brought up from the holding cells in handcuffs.

Now he looked at the battered and tatted-up teenager hopping on one foot to his chair in the interrogation room and wondered if it was a joke, an unwelcome distraction, or that third thing that one must always be on guard for, that camouflaged trap in the floor that could open beneath one's feet at any moment.

This punk kid was no protestor. Clearly didn't care about any political situation, not even his own. Vasily clocked his tattoos: from a street gang, but not even a good one with territory and income, just a bunch of clowns who pulled pranks and stunts to see themselves on YouTube.

And yet the boy sat posing like a crusty old *vor* with the president's hotline number on speed dial. Didn't ask for his cuffs to be removed, didn't try to beg a cigarette. Clearly, the punk had scored some painkillers while in custody, but that wasn't what got Vasily's goat.

Fleeing private security from the International Business Center, the teen had fallen off a subway train at Mezhdunarodnaya, where a transit cop arrested him. The security patrol told police he was part of a group, but the rest got away. He had not asked for a lawyer. With a crushed nose, black eye, and broken ankle, he had made no request for medical care.

Vasily took a swallow of tea and set it down in disgust. "You're a hard boy, no?"

The kid just shrugged. He had a few prior arrests, but only nuisance stuff; he wasn't yet a serious hoodlum. Someone had attempted to contact the boy's mother, but she had an extensive rap sheet herself, and had shown no interest in picking him up.

"Those pills you're on are already wearing off, aren't they? Another day in solitary, where you can't get any more, will do for you."

Vasily didn't expect this to break his nerve, and it didn't. "Well," he cracked his knuckles, checking the rap sheet, "Alexei Ivanovich, I'll pay you the compliment of being blunt. We don't care what you were doing when you were caught. You were only trespassing, no? Doing your tricks. I only want to know one thing, then you are free to go... with notice to appear, of course."

Vasily sat back, letting his offer settle over Alexei. After a long beat, and no apparent response from the kid, he tried again.

"Is only a misdemeanor, no? No reason to rot in jail with those animals. The cell you were in was full of demonstrators, but you are welcome to stay in the Petting Zoo. Filthy place— 0 of 10 on Foursquare. Would not recommend. Such unspeakable things go on there, but we'll never tell. So far as your friends will know, you were most cooperative snitch."

Alexei Betrozov blinked at the clock. "I don't know anything worth knowing, *chek*. As you say, I just got mad skills."

"Such skills will prove useful, dodging bullets in Ukraine," Vasily admitted. "Sixteen or no, you'll be conscripted before you're even tried. The Grandfathers will break you into a whole new way of earning a living. A sweetmeat like you will attract more pricks than a pincushion."

Vasily almost hated himself for using such ugliness, but the kid had to know what awaited him at the front. When they weren't stealing everything not nailed down, the army's dreaded Grandfathers—gangs of senior recruits and non-commissioned officers—ruthlessly hazed and sexually assaulted new recruits, even turning them out as prostitutes in boot camp. *Such monsters are supposed to win us a glorious war,* Vasily thought. He wanted to shake the kid for putting himself in such jeopardy, for making Vasily send him there, but in the end, no one's choices came to anything, against what Russia wants.

Vasily tried a new tack. "Your mother must be very proud.

She hasn't called or come to pick you up, by the way. Perhaps you have a new father."

Alexei rolled his eyes. This wasn't getting them anywhere.

Vasily had no reason on paper to suspect this kid was anything more than another glory-hungry idiot. But the kid was running from the International Business Center, and there'd been reports of some kind of light show on Korova Tower shortly after Alexei and his friends fled the area.

In a city where unruly punks were everywhere underfoot—breaking into buildings, tagging walls, stealing everything not nailed down—the International Business Center had become the quietest district in Moscow since construction began on Korova.

A couple of kids had fallen from the building when it was still a steel skeleton a few months ago. Nothing showed up in the news, but Vasily interviewed the security guards, and came away all but certain the kids had been chased, if not thrown, from the building. Since then, nobody messed with it; or if they did, nobody called the police.

It reeked of the third kind of trouble, the kind that swallows you whole. Everyone with a badge knew the project was government-protected, the stink of an FSB black bag operation all over it.

This kid clearly knew nothing but enjoyed acting like he did, no doubt trying to run out the clock. If the local parkour crews had overcome their fear of the building, someone must be paying them very well. Whoever uncovered such a conspiracy to meddle in the government's business would be playing with fire, but it could mean a promotion or even better, a chance at the kind of job you don't have to show up for. A *political* job...

"As you know, today I have bigger fish to catch. All I want to know is who I must call to post your bail and get you out of our way." Vasily picked up the desk phone handset, his other hand hovering over the keys.

Alexei couldn't completely mask his reaction. His eyes

widened a bit, he clamped his thin lips on a sigh of relief. He grunted a number.

"Pardon me? Who am I calling?"

"Yana," he mumbled.

"And who is she? Your special lady-friend?"

Slouching in his chair, the insolent punk made a *get-on-with-it* gesture. "I have many…"

"But this one is special. She will go your bail, no? Maybe she believes you will marry her someday."

"If getting too much ass was illegal, chek, I'd be Public Enemy Number One."

"Don't want to waste my time, *mal'chik* . Your own mother doesn't care about you, why should this one?"

"She's the mother of my son."

"Oh, that's lovely! How old is he?"

In spite of himself, Alexei cracked a smile, picturing his little boy. "Almost a year…"

"You must be very proud, Alexei Ivanovich. Tell his name."

"Ilya Alexeiovich," Alexei said, almost reverently. Rolling up the grimy sleeve of his tracksuit, he displayed a tattoo on his forearm—the boy's name and birthdate in Gothic gangsta script, above an impressive photo-accurate rendering of an infant's angelic face, albeit with gold chains, wraparound shades and a halo and devil horns.

It should be a crime, the detective thought. If we lock these useless ones up for rubbing each other out, how much more should we punish them for multiplying?

Vasily set down the phone and took out a plastic evidence bag, sliced it open with a box cutter and took out Alexei's phone. Suddenly, the boy came alive.

"Hey, give that back! That's my property."

"All you have," Vasily said in a menacing growl, "belongs to the state."

As with all phones taken with arrestees, Alexei's had been inspected by Gribkov, the precinct's property officer and unofficial phone hacker. Sending it to Division to be stripped was a crapshoot, the phone, just as often as not, disappearing. The department budget didn't allow for Vasily to sniff around the punk's phone or 'net usage logs without cause, and he had none, beyond his own perverse curiosity.

But Gribkov had told him the password on this model was a six-digit code. These clowns could barely remember their own digits, so the password would be something easy to remember even when wasted, a name and a number.

Vasily thumbed the password in and got an error message. He considered the familiar variations on Ilya, but then remembered how this generation did things, and entered *I1ya18*—the kid's name and birth year.

The lock screen disappeared. Alexei reflexively lunged across the table, but Vasily stood up and backed away. Looking at the *Recents* on the phone, he saw a couple texts to the aforementioned Yana and various friends and acquaintances, which should help stitch up the rest of his gang. Then he opened the browser and looked at the history.

Several visits to a US domain piqued his interest right away—a site for something called the FU Crew. Wasn't there something in the report from last night about a light show spelling out that name around the tower? Yes, the security guards claimed to have searched and cleared the building, finding only some minor vandalism and graffiti, but this website was streaming video of several young hooligans climbing a crane overlooking an unfinished skyscraper that loomed over all of Moscow. The time signature showed it was a live stream.

They're still up there, Vasily thought, which meant this nonentity before him was only a decoy, and the ones who were up there were, in all likelihood, Americans. The fools were not just trespassing in a place where no one should go; they were advertising their recklessness to the world.

Vasily's hand shook as he put down the phone. "Boy, you will tell me who hired you to lead the guards away from Korova

Tower. Tell me where to find these Furies... and we'll forget about you and your gang."

Alexei did not look so smug now, but neither was he forthcoming with any honest answers. If a lifetime spent grilling bad men was any kind of teacher, underneath the hardboiled veneer, the kid looked scared out of his mind and close to tears. "I am the last of my gang. You can't help me, chek. You should be wondering who's gonna help you..."

Vasily leaned in close and whispered, "Tell me. I will protect you."

Alexei looked down for a moment, then cleared his throat and spat on the floor.

So much for him.

Vasily grabbed his files and headed for the door. He would get Gribkov to strip the data off the phone; then he would have to decide whether to alert the FSB about a possible international incident, or just kick the dirt back into the hole he'd dug, and hope to hell that nothing came of it.

He never reached the door. Beneath his feet, the floor shuddered, rolled and flung him across the room. The ceiling shook itself to bits, acoustic panels and fluorescent light fixtures raining down on his head as if the room itself had become a mouth to chew them up. He barely registered the sound of shattering glass, and rolled away from the one-way mirror set into the wall.

When the earth stopped moving, Vasily could not see or breathe for the dust in the air, but he knew, even before he called out the punk's name, that he was alone in the room.

THIRTY

Michael turned off his walkie when he heard them shouting. Somehow, the sounds of his friends celebrating only made him feel more isolated and lost.

Somehow, he made it back down. When Maddie had touched him and then climbed on, leaving him shaking on the construction elevator mast, it was all he could do to cling in place, let alone find his way to safety.

After a long bout of trying not to die of panic, he managed to loosen his death grip on the frigid metal and painfully lower himself one rung at a time.

Unbearable anxiety continued to ride him until he could get to where he couldn't see outside.

And on the 183rd floor, he found a place.

Almost immediately, it felt strange. Opening the door, he stepped onto a floor that was not only sealed, but carpeted and painted, the rooms furnished and even equipped with a bar. Pushing through a set of double doors, he entered a plush conference room with walls of smoked glass, rows of upholstered chairs, end tables, and recessed track lighting. A massive Chihuly chandelier, an extravagant explosion of scarlet blown-glass blossoms, hung from the ceiling.

It felt exactly like the VIP area at Icon; not just finished, but used, when no other floor on the tower had been fully completed. The aroma of stale cigar smoke and spilled alcohol hung in the close air. No doubt, it helped sell the building to have a finished aerie where the glitterati could taste the rarefied air and try out the amenities before paying whatever astronomical sum secured one piece of this colossal eyesore.

Michael searched for a bathroom and found one with a gold-plated toilet and a stocked mini-fridge. *And now my bucket list is complete*, he thought ruefully. *Sure beats peeing in water bottles...*

He supposed he should feel proud of his friends, or at least relief that they'd successfully climbed this nightmare, and soon it would be over; but he didn't feel anything beyond the fear, fatigue, and residual shame from his collapse, up there. He should be angry at Cam and Maddie for leaving him behind, for dragging him out here when he wasn't up to it, but he only felt anger at himself for failing, for kidding himself he was ready in the first place.

Michael sat in a recliner, but its slippery silken cushions made it way too tempting to fall asleep; instead, he began poking around the spacious room. Soon he found a recessed door beside the entrance. It swung open at his touch, revealing a media closet. A console set into the wall controlled the lights and air conditioning. When he pushed one button, the black glass walls abruptly went crystal clear, revealing a panoramic view of the city below.

The unexpected sight triggered an electric jolt of high-test vertigo. Heart twisting in his chest, Michael quickly dialed the floor-to-ceiling windows back to full opacity. After some deep breathing exercises, he resumed tossing the room. Most of the drawers were empty, but he did find a few bags of spare connector cables and adapters, along with some slick-looking earpieces.

Someone was putting on a big show up here. Wonder what that looks like.

Returning to the media console, Michael activated the projector and pushed *Play*.

A cone of light sprang up in the center of the conference room, then resolved into a three-dimensional form. Holy shit, it was a hologram projector.

In spite of all the noise and worry, or perhaps because of it, his mind took refuge in the consoling reliability of technology. Noticing a row of input sockets on the projector, he fished out the mysterious thumb drive and plugged it in. The lasers hummed, the beam arcing across the room, conjuring a luminous ghost.

Standing in the open area, big as life, genuflecting to the empty chairs and speaking in a monotonous Russian purr, was a man Michael instantly recognized.

The balding but regally chiseled head, the padded shoulders, the aggressive hand gestures, were unmistakable. Michael had seen that form shaking hands with world leaders, tagging Siberian tigers, riding horses bare-chested, diving for ancient Greek amphorae, hurling enemies in judo tournaments.

Too bad you don't speak Russian, he thought.

The lights on the weird little earpieces were blinking, and he noticed a tiny cacophony coming from the half-open drawer. Holding a bud to his ear, he heard an oddly synthetic voice intoning the speech in Spanish. Another in Mandarin, then Arabic, before he found one in English.

"No man," said the hologram, "should be ashamed of his labor. No man should have to hide his success. We understand this, we always have. And we invite you to step out of the shadows and hold your heads high at last, as the masters of this world."

The hologram's eyes were beady little rivets, yet as they searched the room, they seemed to twinkle with forbidden wisdom.

"Why should you have to launder your wealth? Is it covered in shit? No, but you must pay and pay, for the sake of the West's hypocrisy. Your contribution to the global economy keeps their dying institutions alive, but when HSBC or Deutsche Bank is caught holding your money, they forfeit a fraction of a month's profits, while you lose everything. Here, that will never happen."

Michael felt as if he were resisting a hypnotic trance.

"We—I—make this solemn vow. If you entrust your wealth to the Black Bank, none will dare to shame or steal from you. Not only will we hold it in trust, but we will invest it as any bank does, but not in their markets. We will make your money work to build a better world for *you*. Breaking open new markets, softening resistance to your products, we will give you what they never could: legitimacy and influence.

"Let this grand new monument lift you up, out of the underworld to your rightful place at the top of creation. Dimiter is my agent in this venture. I invite you to direct any and all questions to him; he speaks for me in all matters. And I wish you every success."

The image deformed into a blurry apparition and swam around the room as the chandelier rocked in its mounting. Michael went back towards the media room. The hologram image cut out completely, and the chandelier's swaying became more violent. Michael turned back and ran for the stairway, wracking his brains for what to do, worrying about his friends.

The smoked glass windows shattered, flooding the room with wind and white light. The floor heaved like a rogue wave and flung him at the ceiling.

THIRTY-ONE

Maddie watched Cam run off the edge of the crane and leap, arms windmilling, legs pedaling on the air, across the gap between the two jibs. Amara clung to the struts at the end, following Cam with her camera. The jib shook with Cam's pounding tread. Maddie caught her breath watching, as if anything could go wrong. Cam sailed across the gap and landed in a tight tuck-and-roll on the #1 jib, where Rene and Zoe caught him by the hands.

Before Amara could get her in frame, Maddie ran up the slightly pitched jib, every step a ballistic clang on the sheet metal catwalk, and sprang off the edge.

The gap was a little over eight feet but, leaping between two shaky mechanical behemoths in high winds half a mile off the ground, a lot could go wrong.

The space beyond the cranes was a brilliant blur, the city so far below that it looked less solid than the clouds, the tower a concrete and steel island on a sea of mist. Time did not seem to slow down, but she seemed to speed up, to take it all in at maximum intensity as her body hurtled across the windy chasm.

She wished they could fly, that they'd brought BASE-jump gear; all too soon, she crossed the jib threshold and landed rolling. Cam high-fived her and tried to plant a kiss on her, but it glanced off her cheek. She was jazzed by the jump, but still upset with him.

Rene and Zoe did a little Fred-and-Ginger dance step up the catwalk of #1 and then sprang out into the void. Maddie gasped and clutched Cam's shirt, expecting them to simply drop out of sight, thinking maybe this was their plan all along; but they sailed effortlessly across the gap, stuck the landing with a cartwheel and a blown kiss to Amara's camera.

They were crazy but, Maddie had to admit, they were *good*.

Bhumi stepped up next, looking like a superhero in his streamlined wingsuit. The wind howled through the framework of the crane jibs, filling the wings and seeking to sweep him into its empty embrace. This would be the climax of the stunt, the twist that would leave the folks at home gasping for air.

Standing at attention with the wings furled, he planted his toes on the end of Crane #1, adjusting the streaming GoPro strapped to his forehead and the backup chute on his back while waiting for Zoe and Rene to get out of the way.

Zoe and Rene were dangling off the end of #2, mugging for selfies with Rene's camera, when the entire crane shuddered and bucked. Zoe caught Rene by his lapels just before he tumbled off the jib. His selfie stick slipped away, seeming to float just out of reach for a split second before disappearing into the scrum of low clouds clinging to the tower.

Maddie hugged Cam as the vibrations shaking the crane became sickly, relentless seizures that threw them from one wall of the jib to the other, as if the crane itself was a live, wild thing. She saw Bhumi waving his winged arms in the air, shouting, "Whoa, whoa, what the hell?"

On #2, Rene and Zoe flung themselves down on the catwalk, while Amara locked an arm around a strut with her camera up and shooting.

Maddie and Cam half-ran, half-rolled down the jib towards the ladder, when something in the crane's fundamental structure wrenched and tore with a deafening shriek. The entire jib swiveled on its mast, bobbing and swinging like the second hand on a broken clock.

Maddie was torn free of Cam and tossed headfirst down the caged safety ladder. Throwing her arms wide, she caught a rung that nearly dislocated her shoulder, leaving her teetering upside down over a ten-story fall.

Screaming for help, she saw Cam clinging to the struts of the jib just out of reach, too panicked to notice, let alone help, her. Rene and Bhumi flailed by their fingernails from the jib of #2 as the massive counterweight blocks on the elbow of the crane ripped free and dropped to the roof like bombs.

The shaking and swaying grew ever more violent. Maddie tried to flip herself upright on the ladder, but her overtaxed muscles gave out halfway through the maneuver. She slipped down several rungs, bashing her knee into a strut before she caught another rung with her toes and clawed at the safety cage.

The view outside whirled past as the crane spun, picking up speed. The end of the #2 jib hove into view again, but it was canted alarmingly downward. Bhumi and Rene dangled from the almost-vertically inclined jib, while Zoe tried to hang on and reach down for Rene at the same time. Amara hung halfway out of the jib, trying to climb up onto the exterior of the structure without dropping her goddamned camera.

Suddenly, the jib jerked upward and Amara was flung from #2 with such force that she actually flew *up*, arms waving and legs kicking. In spite of her own peril, Maddie's heart turned to ice as she watched Amara dance on the wind and then begin to fall.

The spinning jib of #1 swung past and smacked her out of the air like a flyswatter. Incredibly, she clung to the struts, but the camera strapped to her right hand was smashed to glittering bits.

Crane #2 was swinging even faster. Maddie was slipping again. Gripping the sides of the safety cage with both hands, she tried to kick her legs up to weave herself into the structure, but every time she got her feet around a strut, the crane kicked back. She caught an ankle around one strut just as her hands cramped and she was falling again; but this time, someone grabbed her by the sleeve and then the waistband of her jeans. She called out Cam's name, but it wasn't him.

Amara.

"I got you!" the journalist shouted, pulling her up out of the safety ladder cage and onto the jib. Maddie gripped the underbelly of the crane with her entire body.

On #2, Zoe reached through the bars and hugged her brother tight. He held on with one arm, his other flopping at his side like a rag doll. Impossibly, Bhumi stood alone, still poised on the end of the jib with his arms out. Shimmying and bracing against the increasingly erratic shaking, he kicked free as if to say *Fuck it*, leaping into space.

With his arms and legs clenched tight at his sides, he dropped like a hawk, plunging towards the roof of Korova Tower, spinning uncontrollably.

Maddie breathlessly rasped, "Come on, Bhumi, fly!"

She searched for him and saw him come around the cranes, skimming across the roiling clouds enveloping the tower, and then he was gone.

THIRTY-TWO

The hardest part of being Bhumi was making it all look so easy.

Spreading his corrugated wings, he bodysurfed the ferocious updrafts off the façade of Korova, settling into a spiraling descent. The fabric inflated with trapped air to become semirigid flaps which gave him an almost uncanny ability to glide on the buffeting breeze. He forgot the shuddering crane as he swooped down to the level of the roof and then dropped into a corkscrew spiral round the tower.

His takeoff had been as big a shitshow as every other part of this outing, but he rode out the roiling turbulence and slid down the face of the wind shear like the face of a breaking wave. In the tube, where all should be peace, he found himself fighting the old internal battle that he shared with no one.

Bhumi knew what people thought of him, and mostly didn't care. To look at Bhumi was to confront your own shortcomings as a human specimen. They hated him because he made the impossible look so easy. But what intimidated them about Bhumi was what they could not face about themselves. As far ahead as genetics had put him, it was his warrior-monk commitment that forced them to dismiss his superiority as an accident of birth, because it forced them to face how weak their own commitment was, how little they'd worked for what they wanted.

It galled them to see a warrior at peace with himself. They needed to see a flaw or write him off as an empty suit of armor, so mired were they in the tiny wilderness of their own egos.

In flight, he left all that behind, but it stayed with him now. The nagging monkey of his own ego, all but buried in his brain, sprang up and sank its rotten teeth into his bliss.

People always thought he had it easy. The son of refugee immigrants from Ghana growing up in the Netherlands, he had to suffer pasty Dutch kids with personal trainers complaining when he ran circles round them in soccer. As if he could shut off his gifts, or should slack off in his commitment. He left the world of competitive sport behind because there was no real competition. When he flew, he competed against gravity and himself, against that internal monkey who looked down on all his efforts with its own soul-sapping negative mantra: So?

He'd all but left that monkey behind, but it was on his back now, riding him down into the clouds when he most needed all his perception honed in on the wind, the only reliable indicator of where he was in relation to the tower.

Now he had no choice but to focus. Flying blind. The atmosphere like soup. Condensation streaming off his wings and the chill sucking the warmth and fluidity from his core.

So?

The grace that came with shutting out the self was denied him, so he had to muscle through it. Shut up, monkeys. All his consciousness consumed with keeping this impossible body aloft not because he feared falling or wanted to win, but simply because he was Bhumi, and nothing more or less.

Here, at least, was peace, if not perfection. Bhumi allowed himself a moment to revel in this act, to be nothing more than a bird, born to this rarefied space that no other human being could withstand, that no one in their right mind would seek out.

An unworthy stray thought lingered and smoldered in his

head before he could snuff it out. Cam had pushed him into this when he doubted himself. Perhaps that sad, broken-winged bird Michael had planted the seed that made him decide against the flight. Thinking back on that near miss when he'd confronted his outer limits and considered the very real chance of never flying again, he'd found himself trying on Michael's shoes, but he knew that way led to madness and failure.

Michael wasn't cut out for this. None of the others could do it, and he'd almost succumbed to the pangs of insecurity that made catastrophic failure a foregone conclusion.

This is what I am for, he affirmed until the other mantra fell silent. To be denied this rush would be a fate worse than death.

As if to drive this satori into his heart with authority, the clouds seemed to fall away above him, and he was at play amid great shafts of sunlight spearing through the clouds. The wind tore at him with new urgency, but he adjusted his yaw to take him wider round the skyscraper—

Which seemed to tilt alarmingly out of its alignment as if reaching out to swat him from the sky. He tried to roll away. The wind threw him back into its path, the buffeting updrafts like an angry sea of hands feeding him to his fate.

He had only a second to reflect.

This is what I'm for, he told himself again, just before he slammed into the outstretched arm of Korova.

This is what I did.

THIRTY-THREE

In all of Moscow's tumultuous, often tragic history, there is no record of a major earthquake. Nearly 500 miles from the nearest fault line, the modern capital of the Russian Federation has been spared the seismic upheaval that regularly plagues the Kuril Islands and Kamchatka, some seven time zones to the east.

But in the last two decades, a frenzy of oil and natural gas extraction using fracking techniques in the Ural Mountains and North Caucasus region, was observed by international geological surveys as destabilizing the Main Uralian Fault. These dire predictions were angrily dismissed by the Russian government as alarmist propaganda. Similar warnings from within Gazprom, the state-owned oil and gas monopoly, were suppressed by the nationalized media for fear of denigrating the prime minister's aggressive development agenda.

The earthquake's epicenter was in the Dyatlov Pass, several miles beneath the surface and nearly 200 miles from the capital. It registered 8.5 on the Richter scale and lasted one minute and five seconds. Natural gas pipelines were severed and wildfires broke out in the sparsely populated region; the shearing vibrations from the disturbance rippled out through the Eurasian tectonic plate. Though the tremor's destructive energy had largely dissipated by the time it reached Moscow, it abruptly lifted the city four inches above its mean elevation, then dropped it almost five inches. Already besieged by protesters and seasonal peat fires, Moscow descended into anarchy.

Of the city's 13.5 million citizens, 250,000 were out on the streets when the earthquake struck, forcing thousands of riot-ready police officers into the unlikely role of emergency aid. Brutalist Gothic structures that had weathered the upheavals of the Revolution and the Soviet collapse emerged largely unmoved by the tremor, with shattered windows, fallen shelves and isolated fires, many of which were set by ruthlessly opportunistic developers; but the most vulnerable building in the quake zone was also the newest, and the tallest in the world.

Like its neighbor, the Federation Tower, Korova stood upon a shelf of sedimentary rock separated by a thick stratum of alluvial clay from a deep but perennially depleted aquifer, which served as a perfect transmitter for the longest wavelengths of the distant quake to strum the skyscraper like a taut string. Built to suspend 190 stories of concrete, steel and glass on a minimal footprint with little consideration of seismic endurance, the skyscraper's tripod-shaped foundation core twisted against itself as if some greater force were wringing it dry. The shock waves resonated through the steel structure, sending fractal cracks through the concrete with each throbbing seismic pulse.

On the nearly completed floors of the lower section, windows popped en masse out of their mounts and rained cobalt panes of glass on the deserted construction site below.

Stairwells and elevator shafts screamed with the unbearable torsion and became clogged with avalanches of debris. Power surges ripped through the provisional electrical grid, maxing out circuit breakers and igniting fires in hastily insulated conduits. Electrical power shut down throughout the tower, but on the mechanical floors, badly damaged by runaway outriggers thrown off their mounts by the quake, the diesel backup generators automatically kicked in.

Near the crown of the tower, the fluid stabilizer tank, devised to counter harmonic resonance waves caused by atmospheric disturbances, swayed back and forth like an unstable cradle, a countermeasure now rocking in sync with the violent tremor, aggravating the catastrophic damage incurred by the earthquake long after it had subsided.

On the 183rd floor, Michael struggled to stay on his feet. Stance wide, arms spread like a novice surfer, his eyes squeezed shut as everything around him shook violently back and forth. Even when the terrifying rolling motion had fallen away, he still swayed and trembled, finally sinking to his knees.

Concrete dust floated in a thick, granular fog all around him, settling on his skin and spiking his lungs with every torturous breath.

Reaching for his walkie, he jabbed the *Send* button and called out, "Hello? Is anyone there?"

Maddie closed her eyes and screamed until the jib of Crane #1 finally stopped its drunken spinning. Throat raw, head ringing from multiple collisions with the steel framework, she stared blankly at Amara's offered hand for a moment before she moved to take it. The journalist pulled her back up onto the jib and squeezed her shoulder as if to assure her she was alive.

"You alright?" Amara asked.

Maddie just stared at nothingness until the words made sense in her scrambled brain. Her hands quivered so badly she couldn't make them move.

Amara rolled up Maddie's sleeve, sucking in a breath. Her forearms and biceps were mottled with fresh bruises and oozing cuts.

Maddie absently pushed her away, mumbling, "Where's Cam?"

Amara inclined her head to the left and above them. Cam clung to the struts of the jib an arm's length away, utterly oblivious to them or the fact the earthquake had passed.

That was what it was, wasn't it? Maddie couldn't bring herself to ask the question aloud, couldn't break the fragile silence that had fallen over them for fear it would all start up again.

From somewhere, a crackling like a fire and a muffled voice like a parrot called her name. She couldn't figure out where it was coming from.

She reached out and laid a hand on Cam's leg, which twitched away from her touch as if she'd shocked him. "I..." his voice was a hollow croak. "I'm good..."

Over on the jib of #2, Zoe struggled to drag her twin back up onto the catwalk. Amara crept down to the end of #1 and shouted, "Hey! You alright?" Zoe gave a feeble wave, and returned to her brother, who seemed unable to pull himself up.

Maddie was watching them, silently rooting for Zoe to rescue her brother, and almost gave a cheer when he flopped onto the catwalk, but right then, the entire length of the #2 jib dropped like a stone.

Cam, Amara, and Maddie could only watch as the crane folded up for lack of its fallen counterweights, collapsing on itself with their friends holding on to it.

THIRTY-FOUR

Painfully, slowly, Michael dragged himself up the wall and onto his knees, covered in cement dust, still calling into the walkie. "Maddie? Cam? Is anyone there…?"

He felt and heard it at the same time. A horrible subsonic groan and a staccato scream of twisting steel. Something dropped out of the sky to block the dusty sunlight and slam into the face of the skyscraper so hard that the floor canted treacherously, flinging Michael back into the opposite wall. Chunks and then slabs of concrete rained down on him, battering his arms as he kept his fingers laced over the crown of his skull.

An aftershock, It must be…

Aluminum ducts and light fixtures dangled into the room. The floor was webbed with fractures, exposing veins of steel rebar and gaps into the 182nd floor below.

Fighting every natural instinct, Michael stood up again and moved gingerly towards the exposed outer edge.

The jib of one of the tower's rooftop cranes dangled against the façade, which drooped alarmingly from the impact and the lopsided weight. Under his breath, Michael gasped, "What else…"

Searching the floor around his feet, Michael picked up the walkie and repeated his call, but got only static. He made his way towards the battered jungle-gym jumble of the crane arm, calling out, "Hello?!"

Nobody replied.

The wind ruffled his hair, lifting a halo of dust off his clothes. Unsure what to do, uncertain if there was anyone else left alive, he stood rooted to the spot, unable to move, to think.

Abruptly, the few intact lights on the floor switched back on, the exposed cables spitting sparks from the buckling ceiling. Restored power could be good or bad, if the electrical system was as trashed as everything else, but if they worked, a construction elevator could get down to solid stairs.

Michael tried his walkie again, but in vain. He picked up his backpack and slung it on his shoulder. He had to climb back to the roof to find his friends... but then he heard a faint voice crying for help.

It was coming from outside.

Tiptoeing back to the edge, he searched the wrecked crane jib as he listened for the sound over the wailing wind.

There it was. "Help!"

He saw her now, a tiny pile at the very end of the jib, about three stories below him. "Zoe!"

She clung with one arm to the struts, to her brother with the other. The strain was obvious in her voice. "Michael? Are you there?"

"Hang on! I'll..."

You'll what? He asked himself. *You couldn't climb this building before, so what can you do, now?*

"I can't," she cried. "I can't... hold him..."

There was no time to beat himself up. Michael rappelled down the stairwell to the 182nd floor and managed to force the door out of its crooked frame. This floor was not completed like the one above, the walls only bare steel girders and rudimentary electrical wiring. He could hear the ominous sloshing of the mass-damper underfoot and only then noticed how the tower continued to sway underfoot, still reeling from the quake. The wind gushed through the space, carrying the ragged sound of Zoe's voice calling his name.

His stomach roiled and his head swam with vertigo, forcing himself to approach the edge.

Zoe lay about fifteen feet away from the tower, clinging to Rene, who neither moved nor showed any sign of consciousness. His legs hung over the edge of the jib, waving in the wind.

"Zoe," Michael called out, "where are the others?"

She shook her head, somewhere between panic and shock. "I don't know."

He buried his fears and focused on the immediate crisis. "How's Rene?"

"He's alive," she managed, shaking with barely suppressed sobs. "He's not moving, Michael."

Looking up and down the crane arm, he forced himself to work out a plan. Muttering, "OK... OK..." he searched his pack, then turned and ran.

"Where are you going?" Zoe cried.

He shouted back, "Just hold on, OK?"

He double-timed back up the rope to the 183rd floor. Scoping the ceiling, he pulled a bundle of nylon climbing rope from his pack and looped it round a junction of two girders overhead. Paying out slack, he donned a harness and secured the rope through the carabiners on his chest.

So long as he busied himself with this familiar ritual, he could remain calm, could function without contemplating what he was about to do next. But all too soon, he was strapped in, the anchor tested. He walked out to the edge, trying to gauge the distance...

Vertigo set in again, the inescapable pull of the edge and the emptiness. He backed away from it, fear like black ice clenching his heart and spreading out to petrify his limbs...

"Michael?" Zoe's voice floated up from the end of the crane. "What are you doing?"

That's an excellent question, he thought.

"What are you doing, Michael? Where are you?"

He couldn't bring himself to answer it, let alone go through with it.

Pacing the space, he planted his forehead against the concrete core wall and pounded his fist against it, his fear turning to self-loathing.

"Michael? Are you still there?"

He shook his head, pushing himself away from the wall. Every moment he let himself wallow was a moment closer to too late.

Quit being such a pussy, bro, he scolded himself in a fair imitation of Cam's voice. *Just do it.*

He punched the wall again. *You can do this. You used to do this… How did you do this? You didn't think about it, you just…*
Do it!

Tears brimming in his eyes, he punched the wall again, then broke into a mad dash for the edge.

Focusing on the crane, he ran until there was no more floor, kicking off the threshold. He threw his arms wide and flew across the gap.

The crane smashed into him, knocking out his wind. His arms flailed at the struts, but he slipped and he fell away, into the gap and the wide, white sky.

Clawing frantically for the rope, he caught it in both hands and rebounded towards the tower. He spun clockwise as he swung towards it, an exposed and jutting floor slab about to smash into his face.

Michael tucked his knees tight against his chest, ducked his head and swung into the 182nd floor more by dumb luck than skill. His spasming hands lost their grip on the rope and he tumbled, rolling across the floor to end up in a heap against the fractured core wall.

"Michael!" Zoe cried out, sounding weaker, more distraught than desperate.

Lying breathless and battered on the plywood deck, he

could not manage a reply. He punched the floor and cursed his impotence. For just a moment, he'd glimpsed his old, fearless, reckless self. He'd almost pulled it off. But the moment passed. An epic failure. Bhumi definitely would've nailed it.

"Michael, you alright?!"

He rolled over on his back and just lay there. Feeling weak. Powerless to help Zoe and Rene, or even himself.

THIRTY-FIVE

Growing up in the Soviet Union, Vasily Sterankov never dreamed of being a *mycop*. Living under Soviet rule, where everything one might aspire to be was preemptively denied, Vasily wanted to be a rock'n'roll star.

Taking inspiration from the *samizdat* punk magazines and Sex Pistols bootlegs, they called themselves Ogrableniye Poyezda—the Great Train Robbery.

There was an old joke Russians told each other over the last of the vodka, when no Party apparatchik was listening. The Soviet Union, from the October day of its red birth, was a train that had run out of track far short of the glorious workers' paradise.

Every leader since had to find a way to get them there. Lenin summoned the passengers to build tracks out of his speeches. Stalin forged new track out of the bodies of the passengers. Khrushchev took up the tracks from behind the train to lay them ahead of it. Brezhnev drew the curtains and rocked the train so it only seemed they were moving. Gorbachev's great innovation was to admit that there were simply no more tracks.

While not overtly political, just being in a rock band was an act of rebellion. He and his friends made electric guitars with parts smashed and grabbed from public telephones. They released dodgy seven-inch singles pressed on recycled chest X-rays.

When Gorbachev declared the end of the Soviet era, literally everyone started a rock or a punk band. The Great Train Robbery enjoyed a summer of notoriety before the dream died with the collapse of the economy and the eventual realization that they kind of sucked. Vasily, who never learned to play bass half so well as even Sid Vicious, joined the army.

By the time he got out, Yeltsin had gone from heroic champion of democracy to hated scapegoat of failure, and Putin had come from nowhere to be the new vessel of Russia's hopes. The Great Train Robbery had long since disbanded, but now, the old joke was back with a new punch line.

In the new version, the passengers look for a way forward, when the new conductor dons a balaclava and declares, "*This is a hold-up!*"

When the earth had ceased shaking, Vasily helped his comrades who had sustained minor injuries and pitched in securing the police station. In the chaos, his suspect had managed to escape, but as soon as the power came back on, Vasily took to the street, setting out for the dingy industrial district south of Moscow, looking for his old bandmate, Boris.

The city was a horror show from the inner ring to the outer districts, though the police had taken advantage of the quake to clear the streets to admit emergency vehicles. Kettled in parks and plazas, the protesters chanted and waved their banners, but by mid-morning, the rest of Moscow had already put the disaster behind them and gone back to work.

Vasily had to put a dome light on the roof of his run-down Lada 4x4 to get out of the precinct. Once he passed beyond the Garden Ring headed southwest on Leninsky Prospekt, traffic had subsided to a manageable mess, and he passed dubious gated enclaves of single-family dwellings in Moscow Oblast wondering if they'd even felt it.

While the rest of the band knuckled under and got real jobs,

Boris the drummer disappeared into the weird new shadow country of the internet. From pirated software and counterfeit DVDs, Boris rose to preside over one of Russia's most prosperous web-hosting platforms, though you wouldn't know it to look at their headquarters. Big Idya, located in an old powdered milk factory across the road from Khovanskoye cemetery, maintained the disguise of a perpetually almost-bankrupt consulting firm.

In the new Russia—where companies were free to grow as big and as quickly as their cunning leadership could manage until someone bigger simply ate them up—Big Idya had craftily avoided becoming a Bright Shiny Object. Boris's genius with ones and zeroes was nothing next to his uncanny ability to recognize which, out of the sea of outstretched hands, he actually had to cross with bribes to hold on to what he had built. He cultivated the edgy air of a geek oligarch and covertly platformed dissident *demshiza* critics like Masha Zworykin, but he knew how to play the game, and seemed to do well enough, no matter who won or lost.

Poured concrete and exposed rebar and pipes gave the reception area empty-warehouse vibes. The receptionist ignored Vasily for half an hour before taking his handwritten note back to the boss. Another half-hour passed as Vasily watched a strangely hypnotic video on a wall of scuzzy Soviet-era Elektron 2-1 black-and-white TVs. The receptionist brought him a cup of coffee and immediately took it away before he could refuse it, telling him Boris had granted him ten minutes.

If the façade of Big Idya was a poor front for the tax police, Boris could not resist making his office a glowing showcase, with dizzyingly intricate parquet floors of birch and mahogany, bearskin rugs and video walls showing natural scenery that made the dim, cavernous space feel like the gallery in a natural history museum.

Boris launched himself from the vast island of his desk and came around it to shake Vasily's hand. "She was cold to you, yes? I apologize, but when old friends come knocking at the front door lately, I find I must first check who is waiting at the back door..."

They laughed a bit harder than the remark deserved. Boris offered Vasily a drink, which he refused twice, before accepting, in an old ritual. Seated in an indecently soft, creamy leather chair anchored just offshore of Boris's island, Vasily drained off more than he meant to of the glass—fine scotch whiskey—and set it down on a coaster Boris expertly threw into place from the far side of the desk.

The alcohol settled over him like a warm, heavy cloak. It would be more than rude to refuse the drink, and he assured himself that if Marina smelled it in his sweat, he would assure her that the herbal tea must be working, and all his deepest impurities were seeping out of his flesh.

Oh, if only, he thought.

"I'm not here to put the bite on you," Vasily said, which made Boris snort.

"But you are, old friend. You ask for help with this or that investigation, just a name, just a number, that you cannot pursue through official channels, and though I am happy to do these things for justice as well as friendship, sometimes, it costs me more than money. Would you like some money? The inspector from the National Logistics Committee was just here and took a shockingly low bribe. He must be new."

Vasily laughed indulgently. Boris liked to think of himself as a wit. They played at catching up, trading the fates of mutual friends as chips, anteing up to the laying down of cards. Ilya the guitarist was still a mail carrier, moonlighting in a jazz quartet to support a bad cocaine habit; Pyotr the singer still working as a local tour guide and trying to mount a campaign as an opposition candidate for Moscow's City Council, though he wasn't enough of a threat that he'd even been disqualified, yet.

Vasily let his old bandmate come around to talk of the earthquake. He was swimming when it happened, and the water lifted him out of the deep end and flung him on the concrete apron, can you believe that? Vasily waited for the inevitable, "And where were you?" before laying out his cards.

"We picked up a boy who was running from private security. You know those street gangs that do parkour and break into places, everything on video?"

"Of course," Boris said, refreshing his drink. "Narcissistic clowns. The world is theirs, and they make a jungle gym of it. I tell you, when we were young—"

"Yes, I told him, if he wanted to change the world, he should form a rock band."

Boris emitted a heavy sigh and slurped his drink. "Go on."

Vasily smiled, trying to take the sting out. Boris was the group's only true anarchist. When they used to argue, Vasily would maintain that a world of perfect freedom wouldn't last a day without perfect people.

"This boy, he's a tough nut, won't tell me anything, and the security company won't press charges; suddenly, they don't care about this kid. He won't talk, but his phone won't shut up. There's this site hosting a big live event, pay-per-view, and something like five million people watching."

Boris stared into his drink as if he'd much rather hear what it had to say.

"I believe this kid was hired as a distraction by the people putting on this event."

"What can you prove? Who is this boy?" Boris puffed up with his natural pugnacity, never more than a moment away from coming to the fore.

Vasily reached into his pocket. "All I have is his phone." He put the Android smartphone on the desk, inviting Boris to inspect it. "We can pick him up, but it's not so important now."

"What *is* important, detective?" Boris demanded, straining to rein in his annoyance. "To you?"

"The event in question, I only saw the feed for a moment before the damned earthquake, and since then, the site is down. But the kids who were doing this stunt, you see, they're Americans... and they're on Korova Tower."

"My God!" Boris grunted. "Fucking idiots, I swear..." Putting down his drink, he opened a panel in his desk that concealed a bespoke laptop the likes of which God might've used to create the universe.

"Yes, very foolish. But what can you do with Americans, eh?" They shared a short, insincere laugh, a necessary respite from what was turning into an argument. Ever since the last election, Russians, no matter their political persuasion, could make each other laugh just by saying, "America," and waggling their eyebrows.

"They may or may not enjoy the charmed lives they have been raised to expect," Vasily said. "But the real fool, I think the authorities will find, was the Russian company which hosted the site."

Boris shook his head at something on his screen. "Is not our responsibility to police content!"

"Tell that to the new inspector, when he comes back, and he will. Is the site still active?"

"No," Boris said, swiveling the laptop around so Vasily could see a window showing a *Page Will Not Load* error message. "It's not the earthquake, either. This is a DNS attack on par with the Research Agency trolls in Saint Petersburg. It's locked down—"

"But you have archives?"

"*I don't want to know this!* Why do *you* want to know this? I will plead ignorance and pay through the nose to be left out of it, and you should do the same." Boris reached into his desk and pulled out a fanny pack with a unicorn on it. He pulled out a sheaf of euros and rubles. "Take the money, Vasily. You were never stupid before, don't start when you're too old to recover from it."

"Why is everyone so scared of this tower?"

Boris looked around uneasily, then hit a button set into the console on his desk. The lights went out. The laptop blinked and died. A maddening, almost subsonic hum filled the room. "Give me your phone," Boris growled, "and that other one. You imbecile." Vasily handed Boris the kid's phone and his own. Boris dropped them in a padded foil envelope, then dropped them in a drawer.

"Six months ago, my best troubleshooter quit, quite abruptly. I try to convince him to stay, but he's going to work on very special temporary project. On Korova..."

"What is this man's name?"

"Igor Marinov," Boris answered. "Two weeks ago, he messaged me on Telegram, so of course it's encrypted, a lot of paranoid folk use it. Anyway, he told me some crazy bullshit about this project he's working on, how it's a gun pointed at the world's head, how he is trying to get word out, someone has to know... He called it the Black Bank. But I don't follow up, it sounds like nonsense..."

The agonized expression made it clear it was anything but nonsense. "But he goes missing. His apartment is rented out, his things gone. Phone disconnected. Like he never was. I know better than to push, but still... it bothers me."

Not enough to go to the police, Vasily thought. "Who was he working for?"

"It is a public-private venture, sanctioned from the very top. Vasily, you've got to believe me, I only learned of this recently, and I had no reason to believe... but if there are Americans up there, forget them. Let the system sort it out."

"You know what it is, Boris."

"Truly, I do not. And you don't want to know, old friend. Trust me. Anyone who knows, they can get to."

The silence unfolded between them. Looking at his hands, Boris went on, "One thing I heard... I know you are not a geek for this stuff, but you know everything in the news is AI this, AI that... The Black Bank is not just about money. Imagine if all those cameras pointed at us had an electronic brain that recorded every crime, every unpatriotic act or utterance. Imagine how large a prison you would need, to lock up all those imperfect people."

Vasily looked at his friend for a long moment until he saw this was no joke. "Easier to just change the doors on every home in Russia, so they lock from the outside."

"Just so," Boris said, and shuddered.

Vasily looked accusingly at the drink, put it down. "You know these American kids, they call themselves the Furies. Stupid, self-centered punks, yes, who do dangerous stunts at great heights, as if they could never fall. But they think they're changing the world with these acts of defiance. They're no better or worse than we were back then, no?"

"We didn't change the world, did we, Vasily? The world changed us."

"We didn't have a chance, but *they* do," the detective said. "I'm going to keep my head down and do my job, pursue the line of guilt where it leads."

Boris looked at his old bandmate for a long moment, then sighed as if something solid that had been lodged inside him all his life had vaporized and escaped. He took out a pad and a pen and scribbled on it. "This man was our contact for the website hosting. Does a lot of shady security work for would-be oligarchs...? Don't tell him I sent you."

Vasily took the slip of paper from Boris and pocketed it without looking at it.

"Now go." Boris's impatience, even in his inner sanctum, with electromagnetic dampers muting any bugs, was a frightful thing; but as he returned Vasily's phones and pushed him out the door, he braced him and pulled him close. "Of all of us, Vasily, how ironic that you turned out to be the only true rebel."

"I am only a policeman."

"Where the law itself is a tool of criminals, that is what makes you a rebel, old friend."

He shut the door in Vasily's face.

THIRTY-SIX

The sun hung high in the sky, benignly indifferent to the chaos below.

Rescue crews worked to evacuate unsafe buildings, treat wounded and restore order everywhere but at Korova Tower, which was, so far as anyone knew, uninhabited. Looming over the city like an accusing ghost, its shadow a chilled moat around its shattered foundation, the unfinished tower was already taken by many Muscovites as a sign of their invincibility. If it still stood, so they told each other, then Moscow and Russia would forge on undeterred.

But within the walls of Korova Tower, the portents were very dire, and growing worse by the minute.

The diesel backups on the mechanical floors had restored power to essential systems, but fuel leaking from hairline cracks spread across the floor, ever closer to a rat's nest of exposed and sparking copper wires from a toppled circuit breaker network.

The concrete core had weathered the earthquake, but cracks continued to worm their way upwards as if the quake had never stopped, the tension amplified rather than counteracted by the stabilization tank near the roof.

Fire crews and city building inspectors were turned away

at the gate, but the Korova Company's own surveyors refused to enter the building after the extent of the core damage was discovered. Until drones could be deployed to conduct a comprehensive external review of the tower, no one would set foot inside it; in the quiet corridors of power, the entire project was provisionally written off as a loss, and thus began the search for a scapegoat.

Michael sat against the core wall of the 182nd floor, walkie in his hand. For the hundredth time he pressed it to his lips and called to his friends. "Cam. Maddie. Is anybody there?"

When he finally heard a reply, the hairs on the back of his neck stood up. A woman's heavily accented voice spoke his name. "Michael, I wish to apologize."

"Who is this?" he demanded, when it suddenly snapped into place. "You were on the boat. You gave me the drive."

"Correct. We used you and your friends, and for that, I am sorry. There was no other way."

"I don't understand," he said. Pulling himself to his feet, he tried to push the confusion away. Zoe still needed his help, though he knew he was in no shape to try again. "I don't even know who the hell you are."

"My name is Masha. I have been working with some friends to bring the true purpose of Korova Tower to the world's attention. One of our number died to give us what little we know, but even with irrefutable proof, nobody would believe us. The world simply does not want to know, but we believed that, if Americans became involved, perhaps they could be made to see…"

"I don't get what this has to do with us. We just wanted to climb this stupid fucking building and get our picture taken, for Christ's sake…"

"You don't believe the things you say, then. If you truly cared about the ills of capitalism, then you would care about the Black Bank. It is a high-rise prison for the government's political rivals, and much worse. It is a total state machine, created to sow chaos abroad and impose absolute order at home.

"After Ukraine exploded in our nation's face, we became a pariah state, but even this was always part of his plan. Our deputy finance minister hopes to make Korova the clearinghouse for all the unclean money, and a fountain of disinformation to reshape the world in Russia's image. He will then lend this money below prime rate, destabilizing the international banking system—"

Michael spun around in bewildered fury, searching for someone to unload on. "It doesn't matter, why am I supposed to care? My friends are…"

"You stand on a missile aimed at everything the free world claims to hold dear," Masha said, grimly pressing on over his exasperation. "You Americans can only be made to act when one of your own is in danger. We hoped to draw attention to it by provoking an international incident, but with the earthquake, they will use the cover of disaster to remove you without anyone knowing."

He shivered with disbelief, then dread made him sink to his haunches. "You have to call for help. We're trapped up here…"

"When someone comes," Masha said, "it will not be to help you. We have gone into hiding with our families. Again, I am sorry…"

The channel clicked and only static answered when he cried out her name.

"Masha! Maddie! Anyone? Damn it…"

He nearly threw away the walkie in disgust, when he heard a voice coming from just behind him.

"I'm here."

THIRTY-SEVEN

Coming out of the stairwell, Maddie almost fell to her knees at the sight of Michael. She was beaten and shaky, but unbroken so long as the crew endured. His eyes welled up with tears and a shuddering spasm of relief ripped through him as he stood up, his bad knee nearly giving out, and hugged her.

"I thought you were—" he started, but she hushed him, enfolding him in her arms.

Cam ambled in behind her, looking ashen, his bravado utterly shaken, and Amara followed. Cam came up to him as Maddie broke their embrace. Looking down, his face dripping sweat, he held out his hand.

After a moment, Michael took it and squeezed, as much a competition as a reaffirmation of their friendship. *Same as it ever was*, Maddie thought, but it still felt good.

Searching her friend's faces, she sensed something off in Cam. A haunted fragility marked his features that she'd gotten used to seeing in Michael since the accident.

Michael and Amara nodded at each other. Her expression was grim, but not nearly as shaken as her friends'. "Zoe and Rene are out there," Michael said, pointing at the crane. "I tried to get to them…"

Maddie undid his harness and slipped it off his shoulders.

Climbing back up to the 183rd floor, she pulled the rope up, gave it a hearty jerk to test the anchor, and pounded across the floor to spring off the tower.

She executed the jump perfectly, catching the jib and alighting on it like a spider. Slipping through a gap in the struts, she quickly but carefully made her way down to Zoe and Rene. "I'm here," she called out, "I'm here."

"Thank you," Zoe said, "but I fear…" She sniffed back tears.

Rene's head was bloody, his eyes half-lidded. She checked his pulse—feathery and unsteady. Then she lifted up his shirt to reveal a wasteland of welts, bruises and discolored bulging in his abdomen—clear signs of traumatic internal injuries. Moving him would aggravate them, perhaps even kill him, but she couldn't see any other choice.

His eyes opened, looking at her. Oddly calm, almost serene, he smiled weakly as he took in their situation.

"Hey there," she said, straining to keep her voice calm. "How're you feeling?"

"Ready to get off this fucking tower," he replied.

Nervously, she laughed. "So, you *can* speak English. Alright." Looking to Zoe, she asked, "How are you?"

Zoe shrugged impatiently, but then admitted, "My arm," as if the compound fracture of her left humerus was merely an afterthought.

"Oh my God," Maddie gasped. She could feel the blood drain out of her head at the sight of splintered bone protruding from Zoe's sleeve.

"You have to set it."

Maddie shook her head vigorously. "I can't… I don't know how to do that. Do you?"

"No," Zoe answered.

"Great." No choice. Maddie composed herself, blocking it out in her mind, recalling long-ago first-aid training. Even the thought made her stomach flip-flop, so she proceeded with the deed.

Zoe took a loop of Maddie's climbing rope and bit down on it. Gritting her own teeth, Maddie took hold of Zoe's arm by the elbow, looking her in the eyes until Zoe looked away, then gave the arm a sharp, short jerk.

SNAP.

Zoe cried out as the bone grudgingly popped back into place within its sheath of flesh. Working as fast as she could in spite of rising nausea, Maddie bound and splinted Zoe's arm with compression bandages from her first-aid kit and a pair of permanent markers. It was flimsy, but it would have to do.

Next, she hauled Rene higher up on the jib and strapped him into the harness. Resting him so he rested in a gap in the struts, she looked up to Amara and Cam. "Amara, you ready?"

Amara knelt at the edge of the floor above, flashing an A-OK that the rope was secure. Rene gasped and gritted his teeth when the rope drew taut, lifting him off the crane to swing over empty space as Amara and Cam pulled on it, hand over hand, back up to 183.

Maddie watched, her heart in her throat until Amara caught Rene and lifted him up onto the floor. Next, they tossed the harness back. After a few hair-raising bad throws, Maddie caught it and secured Zoe for a repeat of the operation.

When Zoe's weight lifted off the crane, it swayed alarmingly, the mangled hydraulics protesting high above their heads. Zoe called out to them to work harder and faster, clambering onto the floor and stripping the harness off to go to her brother.

Maddie was on fire with urgency to get off the crane. When the harness fell into her hands, she snared an arm in it and jumped off the jib, which wobbled perilously before dropping out from under her foot.

Swinging towards the building, she kicked off the façade with one foot and eagerly climbed up onto the 183rd floor, laying against Cam until she caught her breath.

Nobody moved or spoke. The enormity of what had happened

seemed to seal each of them off from the others. Maddie crawled across the room and slumped against a girder beside Rene. It looked like he was vacantly staring off into his beloved void, but she realized he was really studying a vertical seam running up the core wall. He spoke to himself in French, but Maddie didn't need a translator.

"Her back is broken," he said, again and again.

Meanwhile, the others began, haltingly, to talk things out, trying to figure what happened to Bhumi.

"I saw him hold on as long as he could," Zoe said, all the while watching her brother. "I didn't see him commit, but when it was over… he was gone."

"I saw him," Cam said. His face was grave as he stared out at the sky, his voice unsettlingly solemn. "I saw him fall."

"He flew," Amara insisted. "I got pictures, but I lost my camera. I saw him fly…"

"He had a chute," Maddie said. "He could've made it. I mean, this is *Bhumi* we're talking about."

"We can't hang anything on that," said Michael. "Even if he made it, we can't count on him bringing help."

"Why?" Maddie demanded. "He'd never ditch us…"

"He might not be able to…" Michael's eyes were hooded, his head somewhere else, as his voice trailed off.

Cam looked at her. "Call for help."

Maddie shook her head. "I lost the phone," she said, ashamed of her failure, but nobody called her on it.

Amara searched the channels on her walkie for a local emergency frequency. "I still can't get a signal. What's the range on these things? Shouldn't we be able to talk to someone?"

"The earthquake," Zoe put in.

"We don't know what's going on down there," Michael said. "It's probably bad. We can keep trying, but we should probably start moving."

He looked preoccupied, even for Michael. Something else was bothering him, something more abstract than their immediate danger. She knew him too well not to notice it, but didn't know how to pry it out of him.

"I don't think we can move him," Maddie said, pointing at Rene. "He may be bleeding internally. Someone should stay with him while the rest go on for help."

"I'll stay," Zoe insisted, sliding closer to her twin.

"No," Maddie cut her off. "With that arm, if something happens, you won't be able to help him. I'll stay behind."

Maddie looked from Michael to Cam, expecting one, at least, to protest, but each was still off somewhere else, in their own worlds...

"I don't like that," Michael finally said. "What if another one hits? Aftershocks...? We saw what just happened. This is the *last* place we should be."

Rene, still staring at that crooked seam in the wall, started to speak. Zoe tried to silence him with a drink of water, but he persisted, and she dutifully translated. "He says it's not another earthquake we should be worried about. It's the wind."

"Why the hell should we care about that?" Cam demanded.

Rene continued, with Zoe translating, "Tall buildings are designed to trick the wind. If the core has been compromised, it will be more susceptible to wind forces. At this height, the building might not be able to withstand lateral loads."

"So who do we get to translate what *she* says?" Cam asked.

"The wind could be slowly tearing it apart," Zoe said. "Or worse."

"What's worse than that?"

"There is this... thing that can happen, when the wind matches the frequency of the building... the sway can become self-sustaining." She stretched out her hand and pressed it against the core wall. "You can feel it."

Maddie pressed her ear to the wall, and she imagined she could hear it as well, though it might just be her heartbeat. What else could that thudding pulse be, if not the runaway agitation of the water in the stabilizing mass-damper only three stories below them—the heart of the tower, beating a tattoo as the last dregs of adrenaline ran out in its blood?

"We've all been feeling it," Zoe said. "The seasickness. It's gotten worse since the earthquake."

True, Maddie thought. She'd blamed it on the altitude, but at such a height, a tower had to flex, rather than remain rigid and break. Now it was broken, and the floor beneath their feet undulated with every breeze like a ship on an uneasy sea.

With terrible, quiet finality, Zoe said, "It's called *resonance*."

The others exchanged grave looks and for once, no one could offer a retort.

THIRTY-EIGHT

Even among his peers in the upper echelons of the Russian government, Dimiter Zamyatin had earned a reputation for caution and discretion. His KGB training was not just a leg up because of the obvious rapport it gave him with the president, but a manual of survival skills in a uniquely volatile environment.

So it was that, on the morning of the earthquake, the deputy finance minister was planning to interview new candidates for the most critical role in his personal entourage, that of poison taster.

A difficult position to fill even at the best of times, but while Zamyatin had no reason to suspect that he might be subject to an active sanction, he had not held his position for so long without preparing for any scenario.

That was why, when the "seismic event" struck, he immediately began making plans to flee the country. The news was not even calling it an earthquake yet for fear of defaming the aggressive fracking operations in the Urals, and because earthquakes in Russia were like tsunamis in Saudi Arabia. Whatever they would call it, whether an act of God or man or mindless nature, Zamyatin took the message seriously. He was already set to meet his wife in Milan tonight for shopping and debauchery before their sons came back from their British prep schools for the summer. She had been pressing him about the paranoia that had twisted their lives, suggesting more than once that perhaps he should step down and retire to somewhere quiet, with no extradition treaties.

But after the quake had subsided, he made some calls to verify that the sum total of all his life choices up to this point was still standing tall over his beloved city, and went on with his day.

Say you are a career counter-intelligence operative who unexpectedly finds himself involved in politics, managing the economy of a shipwrecked superpower infested with crooked oligarchs and delusional, dead-end socialist reformers. Nearly a quarter of your population is now comfortably middle-class—too comfortable by far, drunk on their own self-importance, greedy for imported luxuries and meaningless political reforms.

The future looks bright—climate change promises to wipe out established coastal ports while opening Arctic Sea routes and turning Siberia into a breadbasket to dwarf the American Midwest—but to get there, one must trade on the last gasps of the dying petro-economy in a country that spans eleven time-zones with a GDP comparable to Mexico, while China and the United States surge ahead on every frontier, from renewable energy and automation to artificial intelligence and gene therapy. For a country poor in everything but avarice and empty land, what hope for the future?

A bewildering morass that had bedeviled sharper financial minds than Zamyatin's, to be sure; but he had moved seamlessly from stalking dissidents for the Soviet KGB to running down renegade oligarchs and recovering their exported wealth under the rechristened FSB before he seized the federation's purse strings. For one so expert at ferreting out hidden revenue, the solution was somewhat obvious.

It came to him when reading about how physicists heoryze that one half of the universe is composed of dark matter, though no one knows where this byproduct of the Big Bang ended up. These scientists didn't know how to find it, but were convinced that its discovery would lead to inexhaustible energy and perhaps even lift humankind to the stars.

Similarly, something like a quarter of the global economy flows through secret rivers, laundered piecemeal through offshore banks or fly-by-night cryptocurrency. Dimiter proposed the creation of a new kind of bank that would offer its own currency and a variety of financial instruments to its choice clients, from access to a global database of personal consumer data to a network of influence levers to sway public opinion towards acceptance of previously untouchable goods and markets.

It would be like Silk Road, Bitcoin, Liberty Reserve, BCCI and Cambridge Analytica under one roof, and it would lift all that dark matter revenue into the light. Any international legal obstacle to its ascendance would be greenmailed out of existence. The lines of economic power would be redrawn without hypocrisy, and with Russia securely on top: today, tomorrow, and forever.

As confident as he was in the brilliance of his proposal, he was stunned to find it not only warmly received, but front-lined as a pillar of the government's long-term fiscal strategy, married to another project that had languished for want of legitimate backing, that of a world-class skyscraper to proclaim Russia's dominance of the world to come.

To say that this project had consumed Dimiter Zamyatin's life since then would be an understatement; but more, it had forced him to become another Stalin, while appearing to kowtow to all the niceties of retail politics. He had overseen the construction of a building the likes of which the world had never seen, without cutting corners or stiffing crooked contractors and oversight authorities; threading a microscopic needle with a bundle of loose cables of dubious voltage in the midst of all the unpleasantness wrought by the Ukrainian Satanists.

The residential floors were alread" nea'ly seventy percent booked. While many oligarchs had purchased a unit merely to curry the administration's favor, others would be moving in as part of the new program to control morbidly moneyed interests who had become politically difficult. Rather than exile or sanction by traditional defenestration, which negatively impacted the government's image abroad, to imprison them in the tower made them an asset and a human shield against any direct action, once the Black Bank was fully operational.

This last bit, of making Korova into a high-rise gulag, was particularly delicious to Zamyatin and others who had marinated in the perverse irony and carefully cultivated class resentment of the last two decades.

That was the beauty of Korova, that it would bring the dark into the light; but the window of opportunity for its initial public offering was vanishingly narrow, with almost innumerable variables in play. During this vulnerable phase, the American media must be distracted with its own impending electoral crisis, the EU trapped between the hammer and tongs of fuel shortages, the refugees and the war in Ukraine.

Dimiter's Pakhan had always carefully made his most pivotal moves, from the wars in Chechnya and Georgia to the annexation of Crimea, in the shadow of larger global events that left the world community overwhelmed and apathetic. By the time they finally recognized the true nature of the Black Bank, they would be as powerless to stop it as they were to renounce the myriad vices which would be its lifeblood.

Uncertain about what to believe, they would ignore it, and soon enough, accept it. The day after that, everything would be business-as-usual, and the world would at last recognize Russia for its master.

But the timing had to be perfect...

There had been unforeseen threats, but he had crushed them all and kept any substantive investigation of Korova Tower's true purpose out of the public eye. His first thoughts upon waking this morning were not on the concerns of the day, but a true moment of contentment, a certainty that nothing could go wrong.

Almost as if God had overheard his self-prayer, the floor had begun to roll like the ocean and his priceless collection of Soviet Objectivist paintings to catapult themselves from the walls. It was almost enough to make one wonder if one were not doing something wrong...

But wrong or right, a man had to eat.

Whenever Zamyatin dined out—three-star Michelin-rated restaurants only, no traditional peasant slop—his taster would sample the fare under close watch by his most trusted security, and then submit to a short battery of physical tests to determine his well-being.

An archaic charade, to be sure, but too many enemies and two prominent members of the regime itself had succumbed to "food poisoning" in recent years. Zamyatin was beginning to worry that he might be *too* successful in his endeavors and begin to take on the aura of a rival to his superiors, never mind the class of people he now had to handle as clients.

The last fellow had resigned—that is to say, he attempted to escape—and the prospects lined up to replace him, so far, were not promising. One does not simply advertise on Avito for a poison flak, so Zamyatin had resorted to taking an option on the personal debt of selected specimens who fit his needs.

One was a vegan who refused to consume "dead flesh"; one was of such nervous temperament that he nearly choked to death on the first bite he took, and the last seemed to have no sense of taste whatsoever.

He had begun to despair, fearing that he would have to eat McDonald's take-out like an American president, or be certain to dine only with other senior political figures, which was a poison in itself.

But then the last applicant was brought in.

Fedor Dobrodeev was a student at a culinary academy until he was thrown out for violating the terms of his scholarship. He had gambling debts and an unhealthy internet porn problem, but a refined palate, a quick wit and a useful fatalism. He asserted that he could tell good wine from cheap shit at a whiff—a godsend in Moscow, which was plagued by vile counterfeiters of top-shelf vintages. He even agreed to look over a batch of headshots of Zamyatin, and pointed out the one that he said was the best and most flattering likeness. If he caught on that they were all actors made up to double the deputy finance minister in nigh-risk situations, he didn't let it slip.

Never one to resist a playful wager, Zamyatin bet Fedor ten thousand rubles he couldn't tell a 2006 Neuchâtel from a recent Italian vintage after finishing a cigarette. Fedor laughingly accepted the wager and held out his fingers as he was, alas, out of smokes.

The deputy finance minister took out his fresh pack of Silk Cuts and proffered a cigarette and a gold lighter with the old KGB insignia on it.

Fedor lit the cigarette, took a deep drag and lifted the first glass, but before it could touch his lips, his chest gave a hitching, breathless seizure and he slumped out of his chair, dead.

Zamyatin's security detail sprang uselessly into action, seeking to spirit him out of the kitchen, but the deputy finance minister waved them off and backed into a corner, looking from one to the next, then at the pack of British cigarettes beside the dead man's place setting.

Clearly, the cigarettes were dosed with cyanide, judging by the speed and symptoms of Fedor's demise. In all likelihood one or more of the three armed men surrounding him now had made the substitution, so how could he go with them and hope to survive?

At that moment, as if God had heard his silent question, his phone rang in his pocket.

He did not recognize the number, but he answered it. "Hello?"

"Dimiter, you sound out of breath. Perhaps now you will consider giving up those terrible cigarettes."

"I've just quit," he said.

"Excellent. We would hate to lose you…" He didn't recognize the voice, but he knew whoever he was speaking with represented the ultimate authority. The president's chief of staff, perhaps, or someone even more powerful, without the burden of official title or publicity.

You fool, Dimiter thought, *you've failed to kill me*. But now… what? "Is there something I should know… about the project?"

"It has become a complication. Foreigners are involved. They had help from within our house."

"All leaks have been sealed," Zamyatin said. "Only that one old bitch still dares speak ill of us, and she knows less than any astrologer."

"Nonetheless, there are people up there, even now… Americans posing as tourists, but who knows? Their interference should come to nothing, but they've worked very hard to draw attention to what you have built before it is ready. We can't just walk away from this, but what choice do we have?"

"Nothing they can know can hurt us. Who will believe these Americans if they talk? Nothing but fake news."

"If that's what you truly believe, maybe you should sit down and think things over. Have a cigarette."

"OK, I understand." If it had gone that far, then one had to be prepared to take it all the way. *Idiot*, he told himself. *You must be another Stalin. And how would Stalin handle such a challenge?*

No man, no problem…

"Whatever needs doing," Dimiter said, "let it be done."

"Excellent, I'm so *glad* you approve. Prepare yourself, if called upon, to issue a statement. These people frequently meet with accidents. We regret that they could not be saved, but we took every reasonable precaution. One cannot possibly protect such people from themselves, when they are determined to risk their lives for nothing."

"I wholeheartedly concur," Zamyatin said, but he was talking to a dead phone.

His heart, which might not have beat once for the duration of the conversation, at last resumed thudding in his chest. As if joining some kind of visceral argument, his stomach growled.

No more talk of fleeing now, he told himself. *For Russia, you must do your duty*.

He looked into the eyes of each of his security detail, wondering which, if any, if not all, of them had nearly succeeded in doing his own duty.

"Clean that up," he ordered, pointing at the poisoned poison-taster. "We're leaving in five minutes. And we're stopping… at a drive thru."

THIRTY-NINE

The nearly completed lower floors of Korova Tower were outwardly an oasis of calm in the beleaguered city. Wired, furnished and decorated, the business and retail floors looked ready to open for business the following Monday morning, but for the thin plumes of smoke streaming from the air-conditioning vents throughout the tower.

Smoke alarms blared on nearly all of the lower forty-eight floors, but the sprinklers only engaged on those closest to the reserve tanks. The water mains were severed, and the reserve tanks generated inadequate pressure to water a lawn, let alone suppress the inferno raging on the lower mechanical floor.

When they finally consummated their volatile courtship, the spilled diesel and electrical wiring ignited a firestorm that quickly engulfed the entire fortieth floor and pumped convective heat through the ductwork to fill the lower floors of the tower.

The intumescent paint on the steel beams supporting the mechanical floor's ceiling swelled into a protective foam as the fire attacked them. Without them, the mechanical floor would be a weak point in the tower's structure, but the heat required to buckle them would be impossible… if not for the unchecked flow of diesel feeding the fire.

* * *

By the time the sun had set, the crew had picked its way back down to the hundredth floor. Moving slowly due to their various injuries, the group was tied down by Rene, who limped along with his arm around Cam's shoulders. Cam struggled to keep him on his feet, but he did not falter, though his mind was clearly far away, fighting a private battle.

As they reached the ninety-ninth floor landing, Rene coughed into his fist and splayed his hand against the wall, leaving a smear of red. Up in front, Michael came to a stop. "Shit," he grunted.

Below the ninety-ninth floor, the stairwell had collapsed, the outer wall and ceiling meeting in a jagged rictus of crushed concrete and twisted rebar. Turning to Maddie, he said, "Let's backtrack, there's got to be another stairwell, or an elevator shaft we can rappel down..."

Cam let Rene sit down on the landing. Michael and Maddie forced the door open and searched the unfinished office space. They found another stairwell similarly trashed by the quake, but so far as they could tell, the elevator shafts, which bored through the inner concrete core, were intact and unblocked. Stray rays of ruddy sunlight penetrated a short way down the shafts, which Maddie's flashlight illuminated down to their gloomy vanishing points.

"Looks clear," she said. "I don't see any major cracks..."

One shaft had a black mast running down the opposing wall, a temporary installation for a construction elevator. "We can use this," she added. "Climb it like a ladder."

"But what about Rene?" Michael asked.

"We'll send help as soon as we get out," Maddie said, but as forceful as she sounded, nobody was convinced. Each of them had taken a turn assisting Rene down eighty flights of stairs and felt him weakening, his reflexes faltering.

But there was something else...

"I don't think they're just going to let us walk out of here," Michael said.

"What do you mean? There was a goddamned earthquake, they've got other things to worry about, and we're just trespassers. We'll appeal to the U.S. embassy—"

"It's not that simple," Michael retorted. "This isn't just a big, empty mountain we could plant a flag on. Didn't you wonder why nobody else has been up here yet? They don't want anyone to know until it's too late."

Maddie stared searchingly at Michael, who just looked at the floor.

Cam came over. "What's the deal?"

"Michael knows something," Maddie said. "Listen to him."

Michael clenched his fists, shook his head, trying to clear it. "When you decided to do this, didn't you wonder what this building actually *is*? Didn't your inside man tell you anything about it?"

Cam looked confused. Going on defense, he said, "You're the details guy, I'm the big picture. You didn't have any problem with it when I asked you."

"That's because I didn't know. Nobody did, and for good reason."

"Well, what is it?" Cam demanded.

"It's a bank," Michael said, turning away to look at the darkening night sky.

"Ooooh, scary," Cam mocked.

"Shut up. Ever since the Soviet Union collapsed, we thought they were trying to be like us, but they never stopped fighting the Cold War. We beat them with capitalism, so they turned capitalism into a weapon to beat us.

"Think of all the dark money that narcos, gunrunners, human traffickers, and corrupt governments generate. Where does it go? Banks launder it, hide it in real estate investments. But the Russians are going to run all that illicit money through here to build a better world… for the world's criminal class." Turning back to look at them, he added, "They call it the Black Bank."

Cam stood stock-still for a long moment, then blew a disgusted breath out and threw up his hands. "When did you get into this conspiracy bullshit, anyway? Altitude sickness screws up your head, man. It's just another big tower for rich assholes to look down on poor slobs, far as we're concerned."

Michael cut him off. "You know who told me? The people who set us up. One of them's been trying to get through to me since we got to Moscow. Your 'inside man' got thrown off this tower, and we're next. Didn't you wonder why they were so eager to help us pull off this stupid stunt? They risked their lives helping us because the only way to make anyone pay attention was by sticking some dumb Americans into the equation. We're the only people who still believe we can change anything without paying in blood. We danced right into it, making sure the whole world knew we were up here…"

"But we don't know shit!" Cam exploded. "We get caught, they'll just send us home, because that's how it works."

"That's not how it works here, and you know that." Michael paced, stopped at the threshold of the elevator shaft. Looking down into the narrow abyss, he braced his hands against the wall as if to stop his body flinging itself into the dark. "You saw the IT setup downstairs. That's godlike power, Cam. When it goes live, they can run the whole Eurasian internet from here. This place is built to service the worst people in the world, and we stumbled into it. Doesn't matter what we know, just that we die before we can raise a stink. They're never just going to let us walk away."

"But that's exactly what we're gonna do…"

"Because we're just another bunch of ugly Americans doing extreme misery tourism, is that right? I thought we were the Furies, the scourge of vulture capitalists and inequality. I thought we were crusaders, but in the end, we don't care at all, do we?"

Cam looked ready to knock Michael's teeth out. Maddie got between them, looking from one to the other and fighting for peace. "We just need to get out of here. Let's not… fall apart now, OK?"

They returned to the stairwell where Rene lay against the wall, wearing his parrot mask tilted up so he could smoke a cigarette. As the others broke out ropes and carabiners, Zoe knelt beside him and laid a hand on his arm, lifting him painfully to his feet and assisting him towards the shaft.

"Come on. I'll help you," she said in French. Her speech was slightly slurred from the codeine, stressed from the agony beginning to shine through the cloud of shock from her broken arm.

Rene shook his head, an affable smirk on his weary, pale face. "I can't climb that," he replied.

"Of course, you can."

He shot her a skeptical look and blew smoke rings out his nostrils. "No…"

He twisted away from her to take in the view. The smoky sky had turned to a gorgeous panorama of magenta, violet and orange as the sun set in the west.

"This is where I'll stay," he said with solemn resolve. "Right here."

Zoe slid down the wall beside him and took out a cigarette, clumsily lit it off the end of his. "Then I'm staying, too."

"*Zoeeee*," he moaned, trying to take the cigarette out of her mouth. "Don't be ridiculous."

She puffed and coughed. "You're allowed to be a stubborn ass, and I'm not?"

"Someone has to make it through. At least if you go with them, you can send help."

She knew it was, as the Americans said, *bullshit*. He wouldn't last until they could bring help, but the alternative was also unthinkable.

His face went hard and he spoke to her as he never had before. As if to a rude stranger. "Go. Fuck off. Beat it."

She stared at him, unflinching, forcing him to look away. As if *he* was the subject of *her* scorn, she abruptly turned her back, flicking her cigarette down the elevator shaft and walking off without so much as a "goodbye."

Maddie, watching the stairs, came over and knelt beside Rene. She didn't speak enough French to order a beer, but she knew what had passed between them. She dropped a water bottle from her pack in front of Rene. "We'll come right back for you."

"I won't be here, my friend," Rene said with a sickly chuckle. Blood rimmed his teeth as he coughed into his fist.

"Don't talk like that," Maddie said, though she wasn't even fooling herself.

"To accept one's fate is the only grace we can find in this world," Rene said. "To decide when one will die is our only real dignity."

Maddie couldn't meet his fading but steady gaze. Reaching out, she squeezed Rene's shoulder and then went with the others down the shafts.

FORTY

By sunset, order had been restored to most of the city, and the disaster put in the rearview as only grimly sardonic Muscovites could. Protesters found their way home and police returned to their respective districts on roads cleared of debris.

The news focused on the earthquake as a freak occurrence, while popular mystics and conspiracy-mongers on Ostankino and TNT, the leading national networks, solemnly speculated that it was the work of the Devil in retaliation for the president's forceful denunciation of the satanic West, if not of the diabolical Americans themselves, undermining Russia's strength and sapping her vital natural resources.

One prominent tabloid psychic cryptically announced that the quake was nothing more nor less than the Earth itself stirring in protest, refusing to bear any longer that which had been erected upon it, but when pressed to clarify, the psychic wisely clammed up and the program abruptly cut to a commercial.

Almost unmentioned in the coverage were the protests themselves, and though Korova Tower loomed in the background of nearly every exterior shot in the city, none dared speak its name, and no one reported that anything was wrong at the tower itself.

As he circled the Garden Ring with one eye on the phone clipped to his dashboard, Detective Vasily Sterankov had ample time to wonder what the hell he was doing. No one would fault him if he simply stood down and took Marina out to the dacha to wait until the dust settled.

So why, Vasily, are you out here, chasing these phantoms?

He told himself he was walking a fine line, as one always must, when the Law, bright and shiny and worthless, crossed into the darker and far more fatal territory of the Rules. If these Americans pulled a stunt on Korova Tower and Russians promoted and profited by it, then they had broken the law, and he would be remiss not to pursue it.

But if there was any truth to what Boris had told him, and he had no reason to doubt it—Boris had no problem lying to his friends, but would never let himself look weak, if he could help it—then the forces that enforced the Rules would take care of it in the shadows, and there would be no worrying about the Law.

Vasily kept flashing back to the expression on Boris's face when he told Vasily what he knew. For a man who reveled in his secrets and privileges, the naked fear evident in his old friend's eyes was truly unsettling. His palpable terror even of saying the name, as if merely speaking it aloud would release cyanide gas into his office, spoke volumes.

Everyone feared the figurehead, but none balked at calling him out as they did in the old days, so secure was he in his power for two decades. If Boris was afraid even of saying a name, it could only be one man.

Deputy Finance Minister Dimiter Zamyatin had made himself very valuable to the Federation. Some fifty billion dollars seeped out of Russia every year as oligarchs who acquired conspicuous wealth in the surreal casino of the new economy tried to bank their chips abroad. Zamyatin's department was so successful at clawing back fugitive funds and seizing assets, that some fifteen percent of those filling Russia's new gulags were legitimate businessmen locked away on trumped-up tax fraud charges—naively following the laws without playing by the *rules*.

Since those heady, chaotic days, Zamyatin had risen through the Kremlin hierarchy despite conflict-of-interest scandals that would have ruined any other politician; but in the last two years, he had been conspicuously silent. Around the same time, the ground was cleared and broken for Korova Tower.

Many in the city snorted at the building's delusions of grandeur, taking it for granted that the skyscraper was a swindle lining the pockets of the regime, but what if it was something more?

If this building was not as it appeared, if it was some kind of money-laundering operation, Zamyatin would be at its center, and anyone who shone a light on it would suffer. But if they were up to something so secret, could there be any more idiotic place to center such shady pursuits, than the world's tallest building?

But that's the way of it now, he told himself. What is done in shadow today, in shame and secrecy, will tomorrow be hailed as a bold innovation, and thereafter become the new normal.

But sometimes, Vasily had to admit, those shameful secrets were all they had. As proof, one need look no further than the black market app on his phone. A souped-up version of the various apps that let users track loved ones' phones via GPS, it had become a mainstay in any diligent policeman's toolbox. One had only to call the number to ping it and get a cell-tower triangulated location, accurate within three meters, or so they said.

He wasn't foolish enough to suppose it would just be that easy, and it wasn't. As soon as he was back in his car and pulling out of Big Idya's parking lot, he'd plugged in the number Boris gave him and called it.

It rang several times before someone picked up. "Hello," said a singularly unwelcoming voice.

"Good afternoon to you, am I speaking to Yuri Abramov?"

"Who is this?"

Vasily had to think fast, with only the fumes of Boris's excellent whiskey to speed his thoughts. It wouldn't be wise or politic to lie. "I'm an old friend of Boris's—"

"Sounds like a personal problem," Yuri grunted, and moved to disconnect.

"I imagine you have many problems yourself today, and I don't wish to add to them, but if you would give me a moment of your time, you would not need to look over your shoulder quite so often."

"Who are you? What do you know?"

"I know more than is good for me. I believe we can help each other, and I would like to meet—"

Yuri hung up. Vasily switched to the tracking app, but Yuri's phone location bounced like a ping-pong ball all over Moscow every time he hit refresh, and within ten minutes, the number went dead and vanished altogether. He'd expected no less from a self-professed counter-surveillance expert, but he wasn't without resources of his own.

Gribkov, the precinct's resident tech geek, ran Yuri's recent phone records for him, sending him a long list of outgoing and received calls. From these logs, Vasily winnowed out a pattern of calls to an American cellphone number over the last several weeks.

Requesting *that* number's call logs was a bit trickier, but the as-yet anonymous American had placed many calls through Moscow's network in the last week, mostly from the impressive address of the Ritz. These led to a whole raft of similarly foreign contacts, all of whom were currently touring the city in a group. Today, they had been to Nebo Trampoline Park, Lenin's Tomb, and the zoo.

Vasily was skeptical about this story, recognizing it for another phony alibi, like the punks who led the security guards away from Korova Tower. But whoever Yuri had hired to keep up the charade was nowhere near as cunning as his boss.

Picking up on the third ring, the voice on the line answered, "Hello," in the least convincing imitation of an American accent Vasily had ever heard.

"This is Yuri," Vasily said, in a fair impression of the tech nerd's phlegmatic voice. For once, the herbal tea helped. The tracking app showed the target at a shop called I Love Cake on Malyy Afanas'yevsky Pereulok. "Get to Arbatskaya. I'll meet you in ten. Look for a black Lada." He disconnected before the kid could answer.

Idling in the turnaround outside the Metro station, Vasily kept his eyes peeled, but somehow, the kid still snuck up on him. Pulling up on a light Kawasaki motorcycle, the phone courier circled around the Lada and knocked on the window, startling Vasily.

He was short and skinny, wearing a gray hoodie and a fully enclosed orange Bieffe helmet with the visor up, and a student's backpack slung over one slumped shoulder.

Vasily saw the courier's eyes widen when he failed to recognize the face behind the glass, and he bolted for the bike. Throwing his SUV into drive, Vasily lurched forward to knock the bike on its side. Without missing a beat, the kid jumped free and ran for the Metro station, vaulting over the turnstile like he lived to be chased.

For the first time since he had quit, Vasily had reason to be genuinely thankful he was an ex-smoker.

Throwing the door wide, Vasily jumped out of the Lada and ran after the kid, shouting, "Police! Stop him!"

A transit cop stirred from his long afternoon nap to emerge from his pillbox and stumble after the kid, blocking the descending stairs to the tracks. Vasily pushed through the turnstile ahead of an irate commuter who'd just swiped her Troika card through the reader slot, just in time to see the kid dart up the exit stairs on the far side of Arbatskaya Ploshchad.

The courier pushed commuters aside, sent several tumbling down the stairs to make an obstacle course. Vasily nearly tripped over a hobbling babushka and had to fight the reflex to stop and help her to her feet. His target climbed onto the handrail along the marble wall of the staircase. In the blink of an eye, he cleared the top of the stairs ahead of the crush of pedestrians and began sprinting away across the open plaza. Vasily's heart was a panicked crow in his chest, his lungs on fire, but he made a hole in the crowd shouting *"Police! Stop or be shot!"*

He spun on his heel at the top of the stairs, turning round and round without seeing the courier. He noticed people on the far side of the plaza looking over their shoulders and gesturing as if they'd just witnessed some outrage, so he ran in that direction.

A flash of orange caught his eye through the crowd, the gleam off the helmet of the streetlights as they came on in unison, all down the Arbatskaya.

The courier turned a corner onto a smaller side street, but when Vasily reached it he saw no sign of him. Turning again, he noticed the alley and went into it, but again, nothing. Dumpsters and parked freight trucks lined the back of a four-story commercial block. No sound over the rasp of his aggravated breathing.

Then he looked up.

What kind of herbal tea does this little bastard drink every morning? Vasily wondered.

The courier was climbing up the building almost as fast as Vasily could run, shinnying up a drainpipe with one hand, grabbing windowsills, satellite dish mounts, and seams between bricks with the other.

Already halfway to the roof, and Vasily had no hope of catching him. He could run to the other end of the block and drop down like a spider monkey anywhere that the exhausted cop wasn't...

Instinct ruled again as Vasily reached inside his jacket for the automatic holstered under his left armpit. He'd fired it only a handful of times before in the heat of an arrest, and never directly at someone. There was no shooting to wound when he trained with the weapon, only the hypothetical urgent defense of one's own life.

Perhaps no one would look twice at the incident report on such a day... but no. He was only a kid doing a shady job. He had no idea whom he served, or what was at stake.

"Stop or I'll shoot!" he gasped, but even he didn't believe it, and the courier didn't even slow down.

Vasily could not shoot him, but as his hand fell away from the gun, it brushed another weight in his front pocket.

Vasily took out the glass bottle with the horrid herbal tea in it, cocked his arm and hurled it at the courier's skinny ass.

The bottle shattered against the wall beside the courier's helmet with the hearty, terrifying pop of a lightbulb. Glass ricocheted off the glossy fiberglass, startling him into losing his grip on the drainpipe.

He gave a high-pitched yelp as he plummeted to Earth.

Falling maybe six meters, the courier seemed to float in the air long enough for Vasily to ponder if he hadn't killed the poor idiot, after all.

He landed flat on his back on the plastic lid of the dumpster, rolled limply onto the grimy asphalt and lay still.

Vasily approached cautiously, one hand again on his gun in case the courier had any other surprises. Stepping on the sleeve of his hoodie to pin his free arm to the ground, Vasily stopped and took the backpack. One of the phones inside it was ringing.

"You're not Yuri," the courier wheezed.

"Very astute," Vasily answered, unzipping the backpack and digging around inside. It was full of very high-quality phones, but that wasn't what he went for first.

"I am afraid I will have to confiscate these." Taking the kid's pack of cigarettes out, he stuck one in his mouth and lit it. After the first protracted coughing fit, he felt like a cop again.

* * *

The phone courier, a talkative, eager-to-please teenager named Semyan, knew both more and less than Vasily hoped he would.

His orders were to shuttle the phones around the city to lay down an alibi, as Vasily suspected. He sent off photographs and precomposed posts to the Americans' social media accounts detailing an ordinary tourist itinerary. It was adorable, the kind of play one ran to hide infidelity, but these fools never thought they would get into serious trouble. They thought it was only the world's tallest jungle gym, and never dreamt of what it would contain, or what it meant. They didn't set out to expose this Black Bank, but it didn't matter now.

Semyan expected to be done before lunchtime, but Yuri told him to maintain the charade: keep a low profile, keep the phones moving until further notice. Semyan watched the live stream on his own phone at the trampoline park, and had begun to think the Americans were toast, or they were too busy celebrating to check in. The phones had been buzzing in his backpack all day, especially the leader's. He thought someone was following him this morning, but he'd ceased posting on the phones and given them the slip on his motorcycle. The kid knew even less about phones than Vasily did, and thought he was safe.

"You are safer without these," Vasily told him as he walked Semyan back to his Kawasaki, still resting under the bumper of his Lada and a harried transit cop arguing with a traffic cop in the turnaround. After banishing them both, he told the kid to find an honest job, and tell him where to find Yuri.

"He's in the penthouse at the Ritz-Carlton," Semyan told him. "Where the Americans are staying. Or he was… I called him back after you called me… but he doesn't answer."

Tires squealing, Vasily set out on New Arbat Avenue, taking the phones out of the backpack one by one. He examined them, looking at the faces and profiles of the Furies.

All of them young, good-looking, healthy kids. He barely knew enough English to order a Big Mac, but he felt like he knew them a little by the time, one by one, he removed the SIM cards and threw the phones out the window, under the wheels of the oncoming traffic. The SIM cards, he dumped in his ashtray.

He had the sinking suspicion that he was no longer the lead detective in this investigation, but a person of interest, and if he was not very careful, or perhaps a victim.

The Ritz-Carlton was less than a mile from Arbatskaya Metro station, but the streets were thick with pedestrians. Cursing the protesters once more, he noticed belatedly that they carried candles, and some cradled photographs. They were on their way to a vigil to mourn their dead and demand the release of unjustly jailed loved ones. Just as well, he thought, to pray for the ground not to shake again tomorrow.

Vasily swerved off Tverskaya Street and pulled into the garage entrance alongside the Ritz-Carlton, jumping out of his car with the engine still running just under the curved, steel-reinforced glass canopy in front of Louvre Jewelers. A valet asked him to remove his car, but the rest of them stood around, pointedly ignoring the black Mercedes SUV blocking the valet drop-off lane.

Vasily was debating whether to call the room or just go up and knock on the door, when he heard a terrifying sound, from an unexpected direction.

He looked up just in time to see the body smash into the glass canopy.

A downpour of shards rained on the scurrying valet, and a moment later, a stocky bald man in a short-sleeved blue shirt, jeans, and sandals tumbled off the canopy to land prone on the sidewalk, almost at Vasily's feet.

Ordering the valets to call an ambulance, he knelt beside the body. There was no wallet, no phone, and no identification, but he had always been good at matching faces to voices, and he would bet a lifetime of drinking Marina's awful tea that he was looking at Yuri Zalmanovich Abramov.

Looking back up at the hotel, he expected to see... what, a sinister silhouette staring down on him from a high balcony? There was an open window on the highest floor overlooking the street, but he saw no one. Of course he wouldn't; when they did their work, it always looked just enough like an accident to provide cover for whoever would decline to investigate.

A crowd had gathered around the body. Vasily had to push through them to get back to his car. He would call the precinct and cordon off the hotel before whoever had left that Mercedes double-parked in front by the entrance made it back downstairs. He had witnessed a murder and this much, at least, they would answer for.

Climbing into the Lada, he'd pulled the door shut and had reached for the dashboard radio handset when he noticed the sinister silhouette sitting behind him in the car.

Then he noticed the gun.

It was down low, between the seats where no one outside could see it. The dazzling light from the luxury hotel's façade glinted off the muzzle as it seemed to wink at him.

"We can't be here when they come down," said the sinister shadow, which, he was surprised to discover, was a woman.

"It doesn't matter who they are," he said defiantly, though his weariness was a crack in his voice. "They murdered a man."

"It isn't murder," the woman replied, "when the state does it."

Vasily put the car into gear, but his eyes remained riveted on the Mercedes and on the revolving doors of the hotel, spinning wheels that could spit out a terrible fate at any moment. "Where is the state planning to not murder *me*?"

"Just drive," she said.

Vasily obediently slid the car into traffic, honking and nosing past the onlookers slowing to get a glimpse of the trouble at the fancy tourist hotel. Watching the gun in his rearview mirror, he slowly plugged his phone into his old factory-installed car stereo.

"You like homegrown punk rock music? No? Too bad. Shoot me."

The opening squawks of the Great Train Robbery's only recorded single, "Chernobyl Glow," filled the cabin of the Lada. Though it didn't sound half as good as when it was first pressed on a recycled X-ray photograph, it was still the sweetest song Vasily Sterankov had ever heard, because at last, he felt like he understood what it really meant.

FORTY-ONE

As night descended upon the city, the runaway processes set into motion within Korova Tower began to accelerate. The smoke from the raging fire on the mechanical floor had been pumped into the finished floors of the lower section, accumulating at the ceiling and pushing cooler air out, radiating energy to all of the fixtures and surfaces in the labyrinth of offices and shops.

Suddenly, all at once, the heat reached critical mass, and the floors ignited. The flashover phenomenon turned every floor into a brilliant furnace, even as the epicenter of the inferno continued to gnaw at the steep supports of the mechanical floor. As the protective foam fell away in charred flakes, the flames, supercharged by fresh air drawn in by the air-conditioning network, grew ever hotter.

Michael worked with the others on the ninety-ninth floor, chaining their ropes and checking their gear to start their descent.

Cam crouched against the wall, sipping his water, vacantly staring ahead. He still didn't seem to believe what Michael had told him, but his natural confidence was still gone, replaced by something unsettling. He should go and try to make things right, but he knew better. Cam would believe whatever he wanted to believe, whatever kept him at the center of his own world.

Maddie approached Michael with a new plan. "There's another shaft, around the corner. Probably for an AC duct. It's smaller, but I think Cam and I could maybe stealth our way, see where it goes."

"Split up?"

She shrugged as if it was no big deal. "Two options are better than one, right? If one of them doesn't play out, or something happens in there... We might have a better chance, this way."

Michael didn't like it, and he wondered if her concern for their safety wasn't just a cover for getting him away from Cam. But he had to admit, she had a point. Bunched up in the same shaft, they'd be more vulnerable. "Fine. But I think you guys should take this one, we'll take the other. You and Cam'll be able to move faster, give us a better shot."

Maddie looked at him skeptically. "You sure?"

Michael nodded. She started off, but Michael grabbed her arm. "Watch Cam. Something about him... His head ain't right."

She just looked at him, and he found himself holding her hand. It felt strong and vital, but also fragile, like a flower. He almost spoiled the moment by trying to tell her, but something in her eyes told him she already knew. Finally, she let go and headed off to confer with Cam. Michael watched as they entered the shaft and climbed down the mast.

Turning to Amara and Zoe, he asked, "Ready?"

Amara nodded. Zoe threw down her pack. "I'm staying."

He looked at her, trying to summon up in himself the conviction to make her come along. Her resolute expression didn't change.

He nodded. There was nothing else to say.

He and Amara went to the ventilation shaft and attached their climbing harnesses to the bundle of vertical pipes lining one wall. Just as he lowered himself into the shaft, he saw Zoe shuffle over to sink against the wall beside her twin, fish her pug mask out of her pack and slide it on.

Joined at the hip, to the bitter end...

In the much narrower ventilation shaft, Michael and Amara used flashlights strapped to their harnesses to illuminate the cramped confines and tricky footholds, clipping carabiners onto pipes and switching every couple floors, where the pipes were bolted to the wall. As they worked, striving to stay focused on each move, each gesture, and not to rush or panic, the tower around them groaned and trembled like an empty stomach.

With each successive floor, the darkness seemed to deepen, until it was a tangible substance before their eyes. Worse, they found the heat increasing, the air close and steeped in the stench of combustion. It felt like they weren't getting out at all, but descending, quite literally, into Hell.

Michael kept catching himself wondering if the shaft itself was not shrinking, constricting around them. The close, clipped echoes of every minute sound haunted him, forcing him deeper into his head. "I bet Syria's looking pretty good, right now," he said.

"I take back what I said earlier," she answered.

"What, about this stuff being easy?"

She coughed, trying to turn it into a laugh. "About being able to breathe in here. Is it just me, or are the pipes like really hot?"

"No, it is definitely getting hotter." Even through his gloves, he could feel the angry heat. The grip-pads on his fingers were tacky, half-melted.

"Maybe we're getting close," she said.

"Yeah, but close to what? We're still probably a quarter mile off the ground."

They paused to wrap their hands in socks, scarves, any spare fabric from their packs.

"What you said up there," Amara said, diffidently, "was it true? About the Black Bank?"

"As true as anything I've heard. You should be thrilled," he added, instantly regretting it. "You're sitting on the story of the decade." None of this was her fault.

"Some things are secret," Amara said, sounding both sad and wise. "But some things, the world simply doesn't want to know about. Kind of like some people. All of us, when we buy cocaine or save money because of cheap labor, we helped to raise it. When we get out of here, then will be the time to ask ourselves, if we can make them listen."

"*If* we get out of here," Michael muttered, but he confined his attention to the next handhold, the next anchor point, the unbearable, mounting heat.

Maddie and Cam made good time descending the elevator shaft. Green glow-sticks attached to their gear gave the pitch-black pit an eerie phosphorescence.

Maddie froze on the mast and cocked an ear, listening for something she thought she heard, high above them. A trickling sound steadily grew louder, adding creaks and crashes until it became a roar like a waterfall of stone, pouring down on their heads.

"Cam!"

Maddie hugged the wall, flattened herself against it as pebbles, then rocks, then boulders, came tumbling down the shaft, pelting her shoulders and back. Long after the deluge had subsided, the echoing thunder of the rockfall resounded up from the depths of the shaft.

Cam was silent.

"You alright?" Maddie asked, breath locked in her throat. She heard Cam stir on the mast below, but he wasn't moving. "I told him to do the jump. I knew it wasn't safe, and I pushed."

Maddie was knocked sideways by the solemn admission, but she switched gears quickly. "You're right."

She shone a dimming glow-stick down at his wide, staring eyes. He looked like a baby waking up from a nightmare, to find a far worse reality. Maddie was always his rock, his cheering section, validating every crazy scheme and backing every boast. But no longer.

"Because no one could ever say no to you. Not to Cam. People make choices. You can sit there and cry or you can—"

"No... no..." Cam cut in, floundering, "the building wasn't safe." He searched inside himself for something he'd never found before. "That's why they pulled the crews."

"You lied."

"...Yeah." She should've known better than to think he wasn't going to try to defend his bullshit. "But that's how the world works, isn't it? Nobody gets ahead by playing by the rules. People use people all the time. They were using us... so what? We were using *them* to come out on top. If we get out of this—*when* we get out—there'll be a book deal, sponsorships, branding opportunities... Shit, who do you want to play you in the movie? That shit doesn't happen just because you ask nicely, you know."

"I don't care."

That caught him off guard. He just stared up at her, awaiting judgment.

"People make choices. You didn't tell us this tower was unstable, you didn't even want to know what it really is. You used us, just like the Russians used you. Bhumi chose money, and he's never leaving here. You want to stay? Stay. But get out of my way."

Cam hung there below her. When he lifted a hand off the ladder, she briefly imagined he would just let go, and drop into the darkness. But he only wiped the sweat from his brow, let out a heavy sigh, and continued climbing down the mast.

FORTY-TWO

On the ninety-ninth floor, Rene lay with his head in Zoe's lap while she caressed his hair and stared off into the night sky. Every breath was a battle, bubbles of red foam popping in his chest and throat, his skin pale as morning mist. She laid a restraining hand on him when he tried to speak, but she relaxed as he began, ever so softly, to sing.

And if you didn't exist
Tell me why should I persist
To roam in a world without you

Zoe cried silently, but she smiled as she listened. He reached the end of the verse and then fell silent, searching for words, for breath, and finding neither.

She slid her hand up his chest to touch his neck, to feel for a pulse.

Nothing.

She thought of how they started out, doing what they did. For as long as she could remember, they were climbing doorframes, fire escapes or scaffolding as a game to snare their parents' attention, but when Mother couldn't be bothered and Father only laughed off their seeming death wish as a reflection of his own reckless nature, it became something for them alone, a way to feel danger in a childhood suffocated in comfort and indulgence.

A way to feel alive, to share something that ran deeper than love.

This was not the way they'd thought it would end. They always joked that they would go out together, simply falling to Earth hand in hand like autumn leaves, reveling in the unease their fatalism inspired in anyone who couldn't share their games. They were not fearless, but the fear of death was nothing next to the fear they could never admit, even to one another, which haunted them both.

The fear of being alone.

Now that it was upon her, she found any action was better than facing it.

Zoe tenderly separated herself from her brother's body, set his head down on the concrete floor, composed his hands across his chest, and covered his face with the parrot mask. The moment she broke contact with him, her movements became fierce and decisive.

She ripped off the pug mask and cast it into the elevator shaft, then tightened the sling holding her broken arm in place. Donning a climbing glove on her functional hand, she secured her rope to the valve of a fire hose mounted in the wall and dropped the bundle down the shaft.

She cracked a glow-stick and clamped it in her teeth, took one last look at Rene, and leapt into the shaft.

Free-falling in a perfect pencil-dive, Zoe dropped ten, twenty stories, until the sweltering miasma around her almost seemed to slow her fall.

She clamped the rope in her hand, feeling the nylon braid scream in her grip until fine smoke streamed out between her fingers, applying all the pressure she could muster, until she bounced off one wall to the other in the suffocating space, with less than a leg's length of rope below her.

For just a moment, she remembered what feeling alive was like, until it caught up with her.

Everyone had always observed that the Jardin twins were

one soul in two bodies, so what was left of her? Better to go forward and let the world decide, as they always had...

Kicking off the opposite wall, Zoe climbed onto the mast and resumed the painful descent. If she died, she would welcome it, but she would die moving.

Without hope, without regret...

FORTY-THREE

From its foundation to the crippled spires of its rooftop cranes, Korova Tower moaned, almost as if echoing Rene's final breath. Michael and Amara might have noticed if they weren't coughing so badly. The air burned their eyes and scoured their throats, even after they tied neckerchiefs over their mouths.

Michael spat down the shaft, purging the bitter tang of inorganic ash. He made conversation, searching for anything to distract from their plight. "Tell me about the DRC. Something you didn't print. Something just for you."

"This is *my* interview, now?" Her voice dripped sarcasm. That was good. If she could still dish it out, she was, at least, doing better than he was.

"Come on," he urged.

"What do you want to hear? You want to hear about the dysentery? That was fun. You want to hear about the camps, the children? I could tell you about them. Or soldiers, tortured, hacked to death..."

This was getting pretty dark, but he wondered what he'd been hoping for. A bright spot of inspiration, a field of wildflowers? "You saw that?"

She nodded, her face a pale phantom in the smoky glow of

her flashlight. "The fucked-up thing? I still don't know what's worse. That I saw what I saw, or that the only reason they did it, was because I was watching."

Michael was sorry he asked.

"No... the worst part... I was captured by these child soldiers... what you call tweens, but with Aks. They were going to kill me for taking pictures. They were going to..."

"What did you do?" The words a breathless croak he wasn't sure she heard. "How did you get out?"

"I did what I had to... You and your friends don't have a monopoly on sticking your head in the lion's mouth. But you're better off not knowing what you're truly capable of..."

Fumbling to change the subject, he came up blank, but she tugged his sleeve as she was wracked by a fresh fit of coughing. "Something's wrong. I can hardly breathe."

Michael nodded. He was feeling it, too. "We should go back up."

"Agreed—"

High above their heads, a booming implosion sounded. Michael and Amara froze and looked up into a downpour of tiny cement particles, straining to see what was coming out of the shadows towards them...

"Move!" Michael shouted, but he found himself paralyzed. The entire shaft was collapsing in on itself from the top down. The rain of dust became a hail of splintered concrete, then a meteor shower of cement death, cascading down the shaft towards them.

Michael unclipped his harness from the pipes and freed Amara. A rock caromed off the crown of his head, making him sag dizzily until Amara grabbed him by his collar and dashed water in his face. Recovering his wits, he grabbed her shoulder and they triple-timed it down the shaft, running on pure adrenaline, using only their hands and feet to slow their descent against the scorching pipes.

Overhead, the cement deluge grew thicker and heavier, a

constant barrage that battered their backs. Descending in a barely controlled fall, Michael looked down into the darkness, seeing no hope, thinking the spot of light in his vision was a trick of his dark-adapted eyes...

An opening.

A way out, but it was too far away. Michael clung to the pipes one-handed and let himself slide, inertia carrying him away from the wall and into the brunt of the falling rocks, catching himself as the pinpoint of light became a window, a door, an escape...

Springing off the scalding pipes, he flung himself sideways through the opening just as Amara came tumbling out after him amid a cloud of concrete dust. Behind them, the avalanche of rocks choked off the ventilation shaft, which collapsed at their backs like a crushed trachea.

For a long while, they lay side by side on the 74th floor, before stirring to cough, choke and rub their eyes. His gloves were in tatters, his hands skinned, blistered, and bloodied from the friction of the pipes.

They were back in the enclosed section of the building, a floor level encased in glass window panels, where the earthquake had not knocked them out. Rows of doors with ten-key pads beside them reminded Michael of a dormitory or a minimum-security prison, which it probably was. The luxury apartments upstairs would be filled with aging oligarchs who would require round-the-clock service, so they would need a population of cleaners, cooks, nurses, and personal assistants kept close by. These were, essentially, the slave quarters of a modern palace.

Amara was on her knees, trembling. He crawled over to her and cradled her face in his hands. "You OK?"

She was shaking so badly, he thought she was losing it, but her voice, though raw from smoke inhalation, was steady. "Did the building collapse?"

"No," he answered, more hopeful than certain.

She curled up on herself and began to cry with wracking, coughing sobs, showing a vulnerability he'd never have guessed she had in her. Michael felt shame for letting this woman be a vehicle of his anxiety, for never considering the possibility she might have her own breaking point.

"I thought that was it," she said with a nervous laugh, wiping her eyes.

Still holding her, he looked around for another way out, but he could see only the sagging, shattered walls, the infinite night sky. "The building's still here. *We're* still here…"

She rested her head on his chest, no longer fighting the tears. "…No matter how hard we try."

He felt a tear from her cheek drip down his ribcage, then a soft, startling touch. Her lips—

He felt giddy, faint. What were they doing? What else could they do? His hands pushed her back even as he swooned into her embrace. The scent of her sweat, mingled with smoke, dust, and concrete, hit him like a drug. Her hands clenched tighter, caressing the twitching muscles of his back. Her mouth trailed soft, wet kisses up his neck. Her mouth crushed against his, panting urgently.

He found himself trying to say her name when he realized she wasn't who he thought she was.

"Amara." He pushed her back until he could see her eyes, half-lidded, glazed with arousal. "What are we doing? It's not right, not now…"

"Oh, it feels right," she retorted. "I want to feel something real before I go. Don't you?"

She tried to kiss him again, but he turned away. "I just can't. We should… be looking for a way out."

"What do you think we're doing now?" The look in her eyes—steely, flat, and aggressive—deeply alarmed him, even if it did nothing to dispel his own arousal. It was like a stranger wearing her face… but how well did he know her, anyway? "We're not going anywhere. But we're not dead yet…"

He shook his head vehemently, but he couldn't see or think clearly. His head felt like it was spinning and spinning, and would soon come flying off.

She scooted back to unzip her pants and started to slide them off. Her speech was slurred, her movements jerky. "Just pretend I'm her. I want you to. I don't mind…"

"Don't, please," he said. He tried to tell her they weren't in their right minds, but he couldn't find the words. Even now, his body burned with the morbid urge to go out swinging.

Struggling to find his feet, he fell back against the wall and slid down it until he sprawled on the floor. He struggled to breathe, taking great gulps and yet somehow feeling with each breath like he was drowning.

Amara sagged against him, mumbling woozily into the hollow of his neck, "I get it… but sometimes… you have to pretend… it isn't… what… it is…"

FORTY-FOUR

How long they'd been climbing, neither could say. Maybe forever. Maybe they were already dead.

Maddie and Cam stumbled down the mast, extremely lethargic, their motions sloppy and slow. Beyond exhausted, too impaired even to wonder why they felt this way. Something was clouding their judgment...

Cam stopped moving, but he didn't realize it until Maddie stepped on his shoulder. He looked at her foot as if he'd never seen one before, followed it up her leg to her body and her own blank expression. Turning aside, he gagged and retched, expelling all the water and glucose and trail mix he'd managed to force down at their last break.

Major party foul, he told himself. "Sorry... I'm sorry... I don't know... what's wrong with me."

Maddie didn't even react, staring glassily ahead like an automaton. Cam rested his forehead against his arm. Just resting, not napping, not giving up, no, that wasn't his way, he was hardcore, he was... he...

"Cam," Maddie's urgent gasp cut through his delirium. "Don't stop. Keep moving."

Sure, no problem. Just keep going until they were dead. When would that be? Maybe soon... "Jus' a sec..." he slurred.

He heard something stir in the shaft above them and flinched in anticipation of more falling rocks. "You hear that?"

Maddie dangled off the ladder, looking past him. Their glow-sticks were already growing dim, but he saw a light in her eyes, a reflection of blazing orange.

"Whatchoo see?" he mumbled. "A way out?"

"Oh God…" she rasped. "Look, Cam… look down…"

That was crazy talk, he thought, you never look down, or that's where you'll end up… but he did, and what he saw blew the clouds of delirium right out of his head.

Something was coming up out of the darkness, ascending slowly towards them, bringing light and heat. He strained harder, blinking to see it more clearly.

"Shit," he moaned. *That ain't no welcome wagon…*

It was the construction elevator. Engulfed in flames and rising towards them.

It was beautiful…

"Cam." Maddie shook him. "Cam, wake up!"

Her hand slapped him, doing little to bring him around. Then a splash of wetness, a fleeting kiss of blessed coolness, as she dashed the last of a water bottle in his face. Suddenly, it all came entirely too clear, giving him a tiny boost of adrenaline, enough to follow Maddie as they reversed course and scurried back up the mast.

FORTY-FIVE

Michael and Amara lay together against the core wall, drunk on the fumes choking the air, each lost in their own world and rambling incoherently.

"Who were the rebels?" Amara mumbled, interviewing herself. "The Al-Nusra Front. And the kid... what was the name of that kid? Why can't I... think? This isn't right. This isn't..." Her voice trailed off into Arabic, pleading to or about someone named Yusuf.

Beside her, Michael mumbled through a rictus of gritted teeth. "That's what made it cool, if it wasn't like that, if everyone knew, then they'd probably tear it down..."

That was why you got into this, wasn't it? To see things nobody else had seen, to be part of the mystery. The danger, the companionship was icing on the cake, but you had to go further. How far was too far?

His idols were people like Philippe Petit, the wire-walker who conquered the World Trade Center, Alex Honnold, the climber who free-soloed El Cap in Yosemite, and Carl Boenish, the inventor of BASE jumping.

Petit survived his star turn and lived a full life trading on his fame, but the people who loved him most said that he changed after walking the wire, shed his friends and family like relics of an old identity, now that he belonged to history.

Honnold once submitted to an MRI that showed almost zero activity in his amygdala, where an average person reacted with sparks of anxiety just from being inside the machine. Whether he was wired differently or just so habituated to danger that nothing short of life-threatening peril could get a reaction out of him, nobody presumed to say. While the documentary about him sought to uncover the secret mutation that gave him his uncanny superpowers, Michael watched it repeatedly, seeking some connection that would validate his own commitment, even as the film made Michael's own amygdala sizzle like fat in a frying pan.

Boenish was a different animal, altogether. The irrepressibly cheerful amateur daredevil who parachuted off Half Dome in Yosemite refused to yield to the laws of society. When he found fame and secured a starring role on a televised *Guinness Book* TV special, he and his wife set a world record for leaping from the lip of a Norwegian gorge. He could have settled down and become a media celebrity; but the very next morning, he quietly went back to the gorge, to a more dangerous site the TV crews had judged as impossible to navigate, and he leapt from it to his death.

When Michael was recovering from his own catastrophic fall, he dug deeper into his other great love: computers and the people who hacked them. He'd found intriguing parallels between that dark, sedentary existence and the world of urbex and extreme outlaw sports.

Michael was born in '96, when the internet became a household word and less of a virtual Wild West where piratical hackers and phone-phreaks like the Legion of Doom, Masters of Deception and Cult of the Dead Cow traded wares and access codes to crack software and break into corporate and government databases. Some did it to stick it to the Man, but had gone on to become the Man themselves, with careers at Microsoft or the Pentagon. Others just did it to find some sense of self-worth and camaraderie beyond their lonely nerd-bunkers.

Michael had found common cause with those who burned to explore and maybe change the world through their crackpot experiments with ones and zeroes, but even there, he found a dark side that seduced and swallowed too many good people. Malware, troll farms, identity thieves, carders, child pornographers, Nazis, and at its shadowy core, amoral monsters who sought to spread the darkness and chaos in their hearts and wreak nihilistic vengeance on everyone who seemed to fit into the world that rejected them.

Where was the line? Was anyone who did what they did motivated by a healthy sense of risk, or were they all kidding themselves, playing at fame and fortune when all they were really seeking was a spectacular death?

L'appel d'vide, he said to himself, over and over—
NO.
I don't want to die. I want to live. I want—
Maddie—

Suddenly, he snapped out of it and sat up. Amara stirred beside him, but she had stopped talking. Her breathing was a sonorous, irregular rasp. "Amara…" He reached out, shaking her with hands curled into palsied claws.

She furled her brow in response, fluttered her eyelids, but did not awaken.

Michael slapped himself awake. He wasn't just punchy. The room was flooded with carbon monoxide. They would die here if they didn't get fresh air.

Michael struggled to his feet, looking out at the view. All the windows were somehow intact, the air stifling and unbearably hot. The effort of standing sent him backpedaling into the wall, and it was so tempting, so irresistible, the urge to just lie down and let go…

"Hang on," he muttered, more to himself than Amara.

He started moving, slouching towards the windows. Along

the way, he picked up a length of pipe off a pile of construction debris. Its weight dragged him off-balance, but he fumbled along the wall and soon found himself bouncing off the glass.

Hefting the pipe in both hands, he swung it at the nearest window. It bounced off the reinforced glass with a disappointing *thunk* and rebounded, sending him spinning away to fall flat on his ass.

The glass was barely scuffed. The pipe was too heavy to lift. The fog closed over his head again...

FORTY-SIX

Maddie and Cam climbed the shaft, trying to get to the next floor. The wall at their backs was lined with elevator doors, all resolutely shut, but if she strained, Maddie could make out a rectangle of light, maybe twenty, thirty feet above their heads.

But the flaming elevator was far closer, drawing nearer with every passing moment.

And they were so very tired, their brains saturated with poison. The end, when it came, wouldn't be so bad—

Come on, slugger, Michael told himself. Try again—

Using the pipe as a cane, he levered himself upright and twisted his body, brought the pipe smashing into the window with all his weight. The impact knocked him flat on his back again, with not so much as a scratch on the glass.

"And the crowd goes mild," he mumbled, cracking himself up. This wasn't funny, he had to do something, he was doing something, but he couldn't remember what it was.

Amara coughed and gagged in her sleep, body jerking and expelling foam from her mouth.

Michael dropped the pipe and threw his body at the glass.

* * *

Maddie and Cam had climbed to within ten feet of the opening, but the flaming elevator car was right at their feet, eating up the mast faster than they could scale it. They moved as if half-asleep, barely aware of the blistering heat, the licking flames, stretching up to touch their legs.

Maddie looked down, the apocalyptic sight paralyzing her where she dangled. A hand reached down out of the light to grab her by her collar, yanking her off the mast and pulling her over the threshold. She felt herself rolling across a bare concrete floor, then Cam was lifted out of the smoky shaft and fell choking and coughing beside her.

She lay watching the fiery pyre of the elevator ascend past their floor as Zoe flopped on top of them in a smoldering heap. Though her broken arm was in a sling, the pain and strain had overtaxed her completely.

Maddie stared with bewilderment long after the burning elevator had passed out of sight.

Did that really just happen?

Michael shoulder-rammed the glass with all of his might, and nearly went right after it when it popped out of its frame and tumbled into the night. Michael barely caught himself on the edge of the frame, reeling with the momentum.

The night air washed over him, flushing the cobwebs out of his brain, the filth from his lungs. He sagged against the frame, head thrust out into the gusts of wind, drinking it in until he remembered where he was, and what was at stake.

He turned back to Amara, stooped and grabbed her shoulders with both hands, dragging her across the floor towards the clean air. Light-headed with the effort, he half-lifted her until her head lay on the frame and the chill wind riffled her hair. She gave no response, no sign of life.

He smacked her a couple of times, bashfully, then harder as his desperation grew. "Amara. Come on, Amara."

Too late, you're too late to save her...

Finally, her eyes fluttered and focused on him as they did that first night, a thousand years or more ago, when she'd confronted him, chased him out of his office and his safe little life. He smiled in relief.

"Let's not die here," he said.

Michael reached out a hand to pull her upright. Just a few stories below, a massive explosion blew out the windows...

The whole floor shook and dropped out from under them. Zoe, Maddie and Cam flailed and fell with it, into the blazing ruin of the floor below.

Cam rolled over and rose up on all fours, casting around him for Maddie. They were surrounded by flames, which roiled with the fresh influx of air from outside.

"Maddie!" he cried out, but couldn't see any sign of her amid the jumble of rubble. Climbing over a tipped slab of concrete, he saw her writhing and clutching her knee as if it was broken. Flaming debris rained down on her, igniting her shirt. Cam leapt on her and rolled her on the floor, trying to smother the flames.

Though his legs were shaky, he scooped her up and staggered back the way they'd come. Zoe cried out, "This way!" She stood beside a door which opened on an office suite nestled against the core wall.

Cam shouted, "WAIT!" just a moment too late.

Zoe threw open the door and was swallowed up by a fiery backdraft. The concussion sent her spinning across the room, wreathed in flames. Before Cam could react, she rose up on her feet and ran, still blazing, for the only way out.

The window—

Cam screamed as she ran out into the night, arms waving, trailing crackling orange wings that only lit her way into the dark.

Cam stood rooted to the spot, emptily calling Zoe's name. Sweat streamed into his eyes and he shook his head to get it out, realized with horror that he still wore his streaming GoPro. For all he knew, the hideous death he'd just witnessed had gone out to millions of viewers on the 'net.

"*Yebat eto der'mo*," he growled. *Fuck this shit...*

Succumbing to weakness under Maddie's inert weight, Cam backed away from the open door, towards the windows. He felt the edge under his heel, the wind lashing at his back and fueling the approaching flames.

Cam turned and looked out at the view. Maddie stirred in his arms, took his hand in hers. They shared a glance that asked and answered the unthinkable question, whether to let the flames take them or to go out on their own terms. He was nerving himself up to take the next step when a bright, cold light speared out of the night and poured down on them where they stood.

"Oh, thank God," Cam said.

A helicopter hovered just a few dozen feet away from the face of the tower.

Hope swelled his heart and gave him breath. "Yo!" Cam screamed, "Over here! Help us—"

The helicopter dipped its rotors as if in acknowledgement of their appeal, but then rose up until they were level with the massive pod suspended by a cable from its undercarriage. Dipping its rotors again and pivoting away from the tower, the helicopter swiveled back so the pod came whipsawing back towards them like a wrecking ball. At the end of its arc, the bottom split open and a wave of water flooded the burning office floor.

Cam had only a moment for hope to turn to terror. He could only tuck his body protectively around Maddie as two thousand gallons of water swamped them and sent them tumbling back into the wreckage.

The wave swept them across the office towards the open elevator doors. Cam tumbled into the shaft and only caught himself by the doorframe, hanging on to Maddie with the other.

"Damn you," Cam roared, "help us!" But even as he raged at them, he knew that help was the last thing they could expect.

Though it hurt almost as much as admitting defeat, he had no choice but to accept that maybe, this time, Michael was right.

FORTY-SEVEN

"I think I know you," Vasily said.

"A lot of people think they do," she replied.

A squad car and an ambulance flew past, headed for the Ritz-Carlton. Vasily felt a powerful twinge of guilt at leaving the scene of a murder, but he had already gone so far beyond proper procedure already, destroying evidence, releasing an accomplice. It felt like a crushing, invisible weight dangled over his head, poised to smash him into the ground. Was this how it felt to be a criminal? To be Russian?

"I should text my wife," he said, reaching gingerly for the phone. When the gun didn't move, he thumbed out a brief message. *Working late due to quake. Drinking my tea. Love, Vasya.* When he looked up again, she'd put away the gun.

He turned left on Teatral'nyy Proyezd, passing Theater Square, where the crowds of pedestrians bearing candles and banners had gathered into a mob. "So... where are we going?"

"You should go home and see your wife," the woman said. Reclining in her seat, she pressed the bridge of her nose with her fingers. "Let me out anywhere."

He braked to a stop alongside the park. Ghostly, candlelit faces passed in front of his car, like disembodied spirits. "Give me your gun. If you're stopped with it..."

"Whether I have it or not, I won't be arrested. Did they arrest Boris Nemtsov or Anna Politkovskaya? Did your lot do anything for them? You couldn't protect them, you couldn't bring their murderers to justice, and you did nothing to make them think they couldn't do it again, to anyone who crosses them. You are standing on the same line as me, policeman. Cross it, and you can expect only a bullet in the dark for your trouble. Just look the other way, like you always do. Go home to your wife."

She opened the door and stepped out on the curb. The dome light in the back of the car illuminated her face, and he was both more and less sure that he recognized her. Careworn, deeply grooved with lines of stress and grief, the silver roots of her cheaply dyed hair made her look like a ghost. Vasily reached out and grabbed her arm. "So that's it. This thing you set into motion will kill some people, and the world goes on."

She shook her head angrily, but remained in the seat. "I hoped to convince Abramov to cooperate, but you saw how that turned out. I hoped to show the world the truth, but it will not see. The world... it refuses."

"Those Americans are still up there. Their deaths will be on your head."

"Yes, it's incredible, isn't it, what you can endure when your own life is forfeit? Why do you think you care, policeman? Did you care about the journalists the current regime assassinated after coming to power? Do you care about Navalny, who awaits martyrdom by the state you serve? What will you do, when they finally erase me? When it comes, nobody will dare to point the finger where it belongs."

Anger flushed his face as shame chilled his heart. He reached out a hand to take hers, then reflexively drew it back. "I am here, Masha. That's you, isn't it? I used to watch your program..." He trailed off, abashed at his own helplessness.

She shook her head, but her smile, though weary and sad beyond measure, was not unkind. "That was a long time ago, policeman. I have to go. You are no doubt being followed. You don't want to be caught with me. That could go badly for you."

Masha stepped out of the Lada and slammed the door. In an eyeblink, she had disappeared into the flow of protesters gathering for the vigil.

Vasily put the car into gear, but his foot wouldn't obey and step on the gas.

She was right. Why had he stuck his neck out so far? Was it because he cared so much about some privileged American idiots? Did he see a way to reclaim the broken promise of his youth by throwing away his career on this pointless chase?

Or was it just that here, perhaps, was something he couldn't ignore? A case that, if he just walked away, would haunt him every time he looked in the mirror?

He threw the door open and jumped out, making his way into the thick of the crowd. He bumped people who singed his hair and spilled candle wax on his sleeves, but he apologized and kept moving, searching for the sad, stony woman's face that still burned behind his eyelids.

He wasn't going to find her, and maybe he shouldn't. He should check in with the precinct and perhaps try Boris. He took out his phone to call Boris, but it never reached his ear.

A hand fell on his shoulder. Vasily twisted out from under it, turning around, when a fist pounded his liver, just above his kidney. His legs turned to rubber. He sagged against the man behind him, who frog-marched him to the open door of a waiting limousine, which screeched away from the curb.

Vasily tumbled into a suede seat softer than a dove's wing and found himself thrown against another man, harder than limestone. Ex-military, perhaps Spetsnaz. This one elbowed him up against the passenger-side door, rifled in his pockets and took his gun and his phone.

"Ah, Detective Sterankov," a voice said. "You can't imagine how irritated I am to have to make your acquaintance."

FORTY-EIGHT

S till groggy from the surgical gut-punch, Vasily rubbed his
  eyes to focus on the man sitting opposite him: a handsome
newsreader-type in a charcoal Armani suit with an expensive
silk tie that looked brand new.

Studying his artfully manicured fingers, the man said, "When
I reviewed your curriculum vitae, I said to myself, 'Here is a
man who would give his life for Russia. A true patriot, if only
someone would show him where his country's best interest lies.'"

"I love my country, yes," Vasily managed, "but I don't see
it here." As the car sped up, he craned his neck to peek out the
tinted window, but saw no sign of Masha.

The well-dressed man laughed impatiently. "You can relax,
policeman. Your friend will go free. She is more useful to the
state alive, and damaging to her own misguided cause.

"But I digress... You must be wondering why you are
speaking to me, instead of your superior officer. We asked him
to give you a longer leash when he reported what you were
doing today, in order to determine whether you were a member
of Masha Zworykin's impotent fifth column, or merely another
misguided patriot, looking for a hand grenade upon which to
throw himself.

"I have satisfied myself that you are of the latter class." He sat back in his seat, took a sip from a bottled water. Vasily had never seen a man so arrogant in his power, nor one so terribly frightened. Sweat stains seeped through his tailored shirt, glistened on his brow. Vasily concluded that this could only be the deputy finance minister responsible for Korova Tower, the redoubtable Dimiter Zamyatin.

Cocking his arm above his head, Zamyatin rapped on the partition between the cabin and the driver's seat. When it lowered to reveal a stone-faced chauffeur and another bodyguard, he snapped, "I'm out of cigarettes, stop at the tobacco shop on Butyrskaya. Not the BP station, damn it."

Zamyatin turned back to face him with a tired plastic smile. "Make no mistake, even if you have foolishly set yourself against the state you also serve. Even as poor Masha, in her pathetic attempts to frame us within her fantasies. Even as those young American fools you have become so fixated upon, while your city burns and digs itself out of the rubble."

The way this man talked, like the NTV newsreader unloading on a target of the regime's institutional contempt, gave Vasily a headache. "Millions know they are up there," Vasily said. "Dead or alive, you will have to answer for them. I am not the one you need to fear."

"Fear?" Zamyatin laughed harder, slapping his knees as if he couldn't bear the weight of his amusement. "I have just returned from a press conference at the Kremlin, where I briefed reporters on the brave firefighters attempting to control the conflagration still raging on Korova Tower and rescue those foreign saboteurs from the fire they quite likely set."

"You wouldn't dare…"

"I did! It almost needn't be said, but if the tower should fall, someone, as you said, must answer for it, and all that anyone will need to hear is that there were American saboteurs frolicking atop Korova when the earthquake confounded their nefarious scheme. I only told them enough to let them make up their own minds, where to focus blame.

"But this is no concern of yours. All that need worry you is the location of the telephones which belonged to the Americans." He checked his phone, licking his lips and shaking his head at disappointing news. "They are not in your car and you have not submitted them as evidence, so I have to wonder if you're not some kind of fifth columnist, after all?"

Vasily just shrugged. He thought of Alexei, that cocky kid who'd sucked him into this nightmare only twelve hours and a lifetime ago. He tried to project the kid's same carefree contempt.

"Anyway," Zamyatin went on, "I am on my way to the airport for a long-overdue personal holiday, but saw fit to attend to these matters personally because my only subordinates in a matter of such delicacy are so very indelicate. If Maxim, who is following us in your car, were to have to go to your home to search for them…" Zamyatin raised his eyebrows and affected an expression of operatic sorrow.

Vasily nearly lurched out of his seat at Zamyatin. He felt the man beside him tense in readiness, and made himself sit back. The phones, that's all they want, but if they had them, what guarantee did he have that they wouldn't deal with him, as they had Yuri Abramov? If they knew the phones were destroyed, would they kill him, or give him a promotion?

The only answer that he could conceive was that he wasn't important enough.

He was just an old cop, so used to keeping out of the way of power that he'd made a dog's breakfast of this investigation all on his own. If at any point today he'd become a real threat to them, they would have erased him. He had no doubt of that now.

No, he didn't matter enough, but the truth did. Let one of them tell it, at least. "I destroyed the phones, sir."

Zamyatin shrugged. "Well and good, I suppose, but what a remarkable thing to do."

"I had reason to believe I was being followed." He thought

about how he'd felt holding them, how scared. In all likelihood, the owners of those phones were already dead. He'd had in his hands the proof that they were pawns of a conspiracy, but in the end, fear had made him throw them away. He let Zamyatin see and believe that.

The deputy finance minister chuckled and sent someone a quick text. "Well, you may have to answer for it at the station, but this is none of my affair. Having them would have made it easier to drive the narrative... unless you're lying, of course, but why would you? We're on the same side, here."

Then he leaned in close, turning to the bodyguard and tapping on the Bluetooth receiver in one ear. "That thing play music? Play something loud."

He leaned into Vasily's ear and whispered, "It doesn't matter, Vasily Mikhailovich. Tomorrow, whether Korova stands or falls, my work is already done. I have been another Yuri Gagarin. This thing will lift this nation to its rightful place. You can only be a smear on the windshield of this great machine. Do you understand?"

Vasily could only nod.

They turned off the expressway to stop in front of Zamyatin's tobacco shop. He levered himself out of the seat and stepped out to intercept the bodyguard in the front seat, who'd started to go inside. "Get back in the damned car, I'll get them myself."

Zamyatin walked inside at a fast clip, looking at his phone. Vasily eyed the bodyguard beside him; he was also on his phone.

Vasily looked at his own hands, at his scuffed black leather shoes. He'd broken a shoelace, probably when chasing that damn kid. He'd set aside his already appalling caseload to run down a crime nobody had assigned him to, but still he'd done nothing outside his remit, nothing to merit the kind of treatment he'd received.

They wanted to scare him, but they wouldn't kill him. He

knew if he went along with this, they'd request his assistance with stitching up the Abramov "suicide," perhaps statements to the press in support of the American terrorist "narrative." Possibly, he could turn this to his own good, become a government spokesperson and tell lies for a living.

The thought made his stomach turn over. But still…

Finally, after an interminable three minutes, Zamyatin came back. The bodyguard slid over to open the door and the well-dressed man climbed in and sat down, looked at Vasily as if he'd never seen him before.

"So," Vasily started, studying the man's face (which he reflexively covered by running his hand through his hair), "where can you drop me off?"

Zamyatin said, "Anywhere you want, but I have a plane to catch. I hope you don't mind."

Vasily nodded agreeably, and covered his own face with his hand. He knew that he had only a fifty-fifty chance of being released alive, but he was as certain as he'd ever been of anything, that the man sitting across from him in the charcoal Armani suit and expensive but not-quite-so-new silk tie was not Dimiter Zamyatin.

At least, not anymore…

Note the weaker chin, the fleshier nose, the dyed hair… His mind racing, he turned to look at the bodyguard beside him, still on his phone. What did it mean? Whatever it might signify for Zamyatin, Vasily knew he was sinking in deep shit.

The limousine pulled out into traffic and then executed an illegal U-turn to head back towards the expressway. Vasily bumped the bodyguard so he dropped his phone. Cursing under his breath, he reached down for it and only then looked at Zamyatin. His lip curled as he came, to his credit, to the same conclusion Vasily had. It was written all over his face, but he was much slower in deciding what it meant for his immediate future.

When they stopped at the on-ramp light, Vasily leaned

forward as if to ask Zamyatin a question, but when he heard the motorcycle stop beside them, he threw himself onto the floor.

No doubt the manufacturers of the limousine's after-market safety features touted its glass as bulletproof. And perhaps it was, in the same sense that a waterproof watch can maintain its integrity up to a particular depth; but the motorcyclist pressed the barrel of his submachine gun against the glass as he fired, punching out the whole pane where Vasily had been sitting, moments before.

Gunfire raked the cabin before focusing on the handsome man in the excellent suit. The bodyguard drew his sidearm with one hand as he opened the driver's side rear door. He stood up and exchanged fire with the motorcyclist and caught a bullet in the shoulder. The motorcyclist threw something into the limousine and gunned his engine, taking off down the expressway.

Vasily crawled out the door and flung himself into the road. The bodyguard who'd been beside him paced backwards as he fired on the retreating motorcyclist, backing right into the path of an oncoming diesel semi. Vasily rolled with his hands around his head, counting backwards from three...

The limousine exploded with a staccato clatter; its bulletproof steel panels reduced to shrapnel. Clearing his head, Vasily stood up, patted himself down and found his badge. Waving it in the blinding glare of the passing cars' headlights, he made his way over to the red rag doll of the bodyguard. His eyes fixed on the burning limousine, he bent down and retrieved his phone and his gun.

He looked around. He was the only one left.

His phone rang in his fist. Numbly, he answered, "Hello."

"What the hell was that?" Boris sounded like he'd been running.

"What the hell was *what*? I was about to call you..."

"You did. You left the longest voicemail message of all time. Who was that lunatic talking to you?"

"You don't want to know," Vasily answered, "but please back it up somewhere, don't delete it."

Boris was talking, but Vasily could barely hear him. He took a deep, shuddering breath, realized he was still standing in the middle of the expressway. He dodged speeding, honking cars to the shoulder, cupping a hand over his other ear. "I've got something to do, but I'll call you later. I'll tell you everything else you don't want to know."

He hung up.

He didn't know how to feel about it, but he had something they couldn't erase, unless they erased him. He didn't know what he'd just witnessed, or what it meant; but he knew he had no choice now, but to stop the train and arrest the robbers.

A moment later, he came tumbling back to Earth.

Nobody would believe it, even if they heard it all. Even if you gave them no choice but to hear and accept it, they would forget.

If you let them...

He couldn't do it alone. Looking to the south, he saw the alarming sight of Korova Tower, glowing over the city like a colossal candle, burning from the foundations up. The only ones the world couldn't ignore were still up there.

But how long would the tower stand?

FORTY-NINE

"M agdalena!"

Maddie awakened to pain and smoke and fear and she was a little girl and the house was on fire. But then she opened her eyes. Cam was looking down on her.

"Thought I lost you, babe," he said, then he said it again, her birth name, over and over. The fear in his voice, the relief, was all she'd ever needed to hear. Cam was elemental, indivisible, and irresistible, but even in her most secure moments, she could never convince herself that he needed her, too.

Cam pressure-wrapped Maddie's knee and gave her the last of the codeine. The knee was strained but not broken, and he gently massaged it, promising that he'd support her all the way down.

She wished she could match his confidence, but she was completely tapped out. Staring glassily into his eyes, she listened and nodded, trying to believe, but this place was coming down around them. They were never getting out alive.

She didn't have to say it. Cam looked her dead in the eyes, laying a tender hand on her neck. "We're going to make it out of here, I promise. I love you."

It was the old Cam, the one she fell in love with. The forceful hubris was gone, but the irrepressible confidence, the unshakeable sense of purpose, flowed out of him and into all her empty spaces. She'd follow him anywhere.

"Listen," he said. "I found a way out."

He took her by the hand and led her through the wrecked office floor to the far side of the tower. A self-climbing crane, used to install windows, clung to the outside wall. Smoke billowed up from the lower floors, obscuring the view of the outside world. "We can't go down there," she muttered.

"I know," he said. "We'll take this up above the fire. Find an emergency channel on the walkies and call for help. We'll make so much noise, they'll have to come for us."

Maddie hesitated, hanging back. If what Michael said was true, nobody was coming to rescue them, but the whole world had to know they were up here.

Cam stepped out onto the crane's anchor, crossed it like a tightrope to stand on the mast. "See? Easy-peasy." He held his hand out for Maddie, like an invitation to dance.

She didn't realize she was still frozen until he said, "Baby, give me your hand."

It looked kind of wobbly when he walked across it. She didn't trust it; like everything else in this tower of shit, it had to be a trap. Recognizing her misgivings, he stepped onto the anchor and hopped on it a few times to prove to her that it was sound.

She started towards him, then froze, looking over his shoulder.

A roaring wind beat down on them as the helicopter hove into view. Its rotors shredded the pillars of smoke as it turned almost sideways so she could see a man on a bench leaning out of the open loading door, studying them through the scope of his rifle.

Cam turned to wave and shout, "There's our ride—"

She barely heard the shot over the roar of the chopper.

Cam arched his back. His chest exploded in her face. He threw his arms wide as if to catch her, and toppled off the crane.

She flinched like she'd been shot in the heart, tears welling up in her eyes. She backed away from the edge as two more muted reports sounded, punching fist-sized holes in the wall behind her. She felt no urgency, no relief when the chopper ascended out of sight. It didn't matter what happened to her.

Just like that, he was gone. After everything...

She walked to the edge and dropped to her knees, collapsed on her side when her bad knee gave out. Heaving sobs wracked her battered body. If they came back and killed her, so much the better.

Was that what Cam would do? If she was gone, he would forge on, find a way out, or at least go down fighting. Cam was dead, and so was Michael, for all she knew. Maddie might have nothing left to give and no reason to fight, but she was the F.U. Crew now, and the Furies never quit.

Finally, she wiped away her tears and set her eyes on that crane. She rose to her feet, tested her knee, then pressed on, crossing that anchor onto the mast.

Numbly, she poked at the controls until she found the right lever and threw it. The self-climbing crane lurched and began to ascend the side of the building.

Looking up, she saw the mast only extended up to the waistline of the tower. She didn't care. She looked out at the curtain of smoke and it was easy to imagine the whole world was on fire, and Korova Tower the last, safest place, the only place left.

FIFTY

Michael and Amara crawled painfully back up the mast of the elevator. The wet bandanas over their faces were encrusted with particulates, their heads buzzing with carbon monoxide poisoning, but their brains were not in control. Only a bone-deep instinct for survival drove them now, hand over hand, inch by inch, away from the smoke and heat.

Around them, the building swayed and shook. The rumble of floors collapsing, of fires raging, passed unnoticed.

Michael's mind squirmed like a caged animal, circling round his hopes, gnawing at his fears. If they could get above the fire, they could call for help. Maybe the live stream was still running, maybe there was already a campaign to rescue them. Maybe Maddie and Cam made it out and alerted the authorities, and the American embassy would send in the Marines...

He knew better than that. If what Masha had told him was true, the rot went all the way to the top, and the Russians would stop at nothing to make sure they died here.

The Furies had never relied on anyone else to bail them out, but everything they'd ever done was a joke, wasn't it? Clowning around, risking their lives for a cheap thrill and cheaper fame.

High on their own self-righteousness, their class warfare

message was nothing but a sad pose. What difference did any of it make? What blow had they struck against the inequality that raised these grotesque skyscrapers? Never more than a minor, unnoticeable nuisance.

In their tiny arrogance, they'd flown in the face of a giant who'd think nothing of swatting them.

You wanted secrets, he chided himself. *Now you've got one worth more than your life. What are you going to do with it?*

His mind chased itself in circles until Amara jostled him out of his reverie. Just above their heads, the shaft was blocked by a construction elevator, its bearings melted to the mast, so they climbed out of the shaft on the hundredth floor.

The wind howled through the tower's exposed, broken skeleton, and in the east, the indigo sky glimmered with the first livid bruises of the rising sun.

Morning already, though he couldn't recall what day it was. Michael picked his way across the floor to the edge. He thought he heard the growl of a helicopter circling the building, but he couldn't be sure.

He took out his walkie and pressed *Send* on all channels. "Maddie. Maddie, are you there? Cam. Anybody…?"

Maddie limped off the crane on the 109th floor, shuffling across an unfinished residential suite. Michael's garbled voice bubbled out of her walkie. She didn't react to it at all, but something else caught her eye and drew her out of her singularity of despair.

On the core wall facing her, big as life, was one of Rene and Zoe's murals.

It was all of *them*.

All of the members of the crew lightheartedly depicted as the Baseball Furies from *The Warriors*, Cam's favorite movie. Bats, Yankees uniforms, war paint and all, but she recognized each of their faces in the hastily sprayed stencils.

Maddie was drawn to the mural, her cloud of sadness and shock lifted. Up close, the fine cracks in the wall from all of the building's stress made the mural look like a relic from an ancient tomb, a forgotten history. She brushed her fingers over Cam's painted features, the unmistakable line of his jaw and sardonic, eternally winking eyes. She kissed it, and bits of paint crumbled away.

For a moment, she forgot where she was and what had happened, but it passed before she was ready. Her shock returned and she sank against the wall beneath the image of her crew as it once was, but never would be, again. All hope lost as the building moaned and bellowed its death agonies with ever greater urgency. It was no more than fitting that the Furies' final performance literally brought the house down.

She stretched out her legs, barely noticing the twinge of pain as her injured knee extended.

This is how it ends. All the hard work, the painful decisions, the sacrifices, the love, the family…

If this is all it got you, what was it worth?

Was it worth this?

The Furies had come into her life when she felt buried alive in her biological family, her class, race, and sex, and it had given her a new family, a new way to walk and talk, a new way to *be*—

And it led you here.

Was it worth it?

She bit her lip and kicked out at nothing.

Yes.

It was worth it, even if Cam and Michael and the others died without fully realizing why. What the Furies gave her wasn't just a way out of all the things that trapped her, it was the will to always find a way out, over, under or through, and never to give up. And so long as one Fury remained, she couldn't…

She kicked out again.

Her foot brushed something. She reached out and picked up a black plastic object.

It was a GoPro—shattered, but with part of a head-mount still attached. One of theirs. She looked around curiously. The floor above had partially collapsed, forming a ramp to the 110th floor.

She looked up.

A bat-winged silhouette hung suspended against the predawn sky. Forcing herself to get up and climb the ramp, she somehow had no idea what it was, until she found herself face-to-face with it.

Bhumi's body lay in a twisted heap, wings splayed out where he crashed into a pillar, like a dead bird.

By now, she was beyond shock. Maddie approached the body as she had the mural, so broken she could only bear witness. And yet something about it stirred the all-but-extinguished core of her being. Something about it restored a flicker of something inside her that had all but died...

Hope.

FIFTY-ONE

Michael and Amara sat side by side on the edge of the hundredth floor, watching the sunrise and sharing their last bottle of water. A crackling squawk made them both jump.

Their walkies came alive with the sound of Maddie's voice. "*Michael?*"

He jumped to his feet. Grabbing the walkie out of his breast pocket, he jabbed the *Send* button and wheezed, "I'm here."

"*Where?*"

"I don't know... the low 100s, somewhere. Where are you?"

"*Not far from you... Are you alone?*"

"I'm with Amara," he answered, looking sideways at the journalist, who appeared lost in her own thoughts. "You?"

He paced while he awaited her response, nervously shaking the walkie as if it could make her reply faster. A long, pregnant pause passed before she replied, "*Just me.*"

Oh shit, he thought. *Cam.*

Somehow, that, at least, was unimaginable. Cam was invincible, Cam was unstoppable; if Cam was gone...

"*They shot him, Michael. The helicopter. They* shot *him...*"

Michael searched for words, but the implications of what she said sent him reeling. "I'm sorry," was all he could manage.

"I found Bhumi," Maddie said. "His body."

Worse and worse. He barely knew Bhumi, but even if he'd kind of despised the jerk, he couldn't imagine him not succeeding. Their only hope for getting help from outside never made it off the tower. "Sorry to hear that."

"Michael, he has a *parachute*."

"*What?*" Michael spun on his heel, nearly dropping the walkie in his shaky exuberance. Even Amara looked up from her brooding. "Did I hear that right?"

He put a finger to his lips, hushing her. "Will it work?"

"*Yeah, I think so… He never got a chance to use it.*"

Michael felt a guilty stirring of hope deep in his heart. His nervous pacing had brought him close to one of the elevator shafts. He kicked a chunk of concrete into it, heard it rebounding off the walls all the way to the bottom.

"*I think one of us can get off this building,*" Maddie said, sounding tearful but resolute, making him want to go to her… "*We have a chance!*"

Now, he did smile. Turning to Amara, he said, "You hear that—"

But Amara wasn't sitting on the edge. She was right behind him.

She gave him a hard, two-handed shove, catching him completely off guard, sending him through the square opening and over the edge before he realized what was happening.

Amara backed away from the shaft, looking at her hands as if they'd simply acted on their own.

It was terrible, but not the first time she'd had to do terrible things to survive. In the Syrian war zone at Raqqa, the Al-Nusra child soldiers that held her hostage talked about how she would make them into men. They weren't just children, but they were going to kill her. They gave her no choice.

When one of them set down his rifle so he could rape her in a bombed-out post office, she went away into her head, but she was not helpless. It was as if someone else took over when she was assaulted, and she watched herself let him fumble at her until she could grab his gun and shoot him with it.

She watched herself hide from the insurgents who came to investigate the shots. She watched herself knife three of them as they came in the door.

A woman alone in a war zone had a brief life expectancy, so she changed into her victims' least bloodied clothes. All through the free fire zone and two checkpoints to the border, she reminded herself she was Yusuf of the Al-Nusra Front, delivering a dead journalist's gear to his unit commander.

She told herself that the person who'd done those things wasn't really her. She barely remembered it, as though it was a story she'd read, some other journalist, not her. Later, she was never quite convinced that the person in the mirror was not her shadow self, waiting for a chance to take over if she wasn't careful. She never quite believed that anything she'd experienced since that horrible night was real life. Any moment, she might wake up and find herself back in Libya... and she would have to be Yusuf again.

War was not about who was right, as someone once said, but who was left. And everything in life, if you got right down to it, was a war of survival. That was the story she'd never shared.

In her pocket, a tiny voice fought through waves of static. "*Michael. Are you there?*"

Amara slapped her face a few times. The deed was done; to fold now would be a betrayal of the act. Maybe she wasn't herself, right now. Maybe she wouldn't remember what she'd had to do, today. That would be a mercy.

"He's fine, Maddie," she said, amazed at the flat, vacant assurance in her voice. "He says to meet us on the roof..."

FINAL MOVEMENT

"I SINCERELY BELIEVE... THAT BANKING
ESTABLISHMENTS ARE MORE DANGEROUS
THAN STANDING ARMIES."

—THOMAS JEFFERSON

FIFTY-TWO

As the Monday sun rose over Moscow and the city began to recover in earnest from the disastrous holiday weekend, the death throes of Korova Tower reached a crescendo. The fire crews assembled in the construction zone watched the helicopters circling the blazing building and wondered who had commandeered them and for what purpose, and who the men abseiling from one of the choppers down onto the roof might be, but they wisely kept their questions to themselves.

The lower mechanical floor, once the heart of the tower, was now the agent of its death. The supercharged flames fell just short of 2,500 degrees Fahrenheit, the temperature to melt steel girders, but wherever Zamyatin's shrewd budgetary practices had cut into the quality of the building material, that standard was irrelevant. Slowly, the beams supporting the overtaxed footprint of the skyscraper began to soften and sag, adding thousands of tons of extra stress to the concrete core and setting the tower's swaying into a feverish, 190-story seizure.

As he fell, Michael final thoughts were not of the blank-faced woman who shoved him to his death.

He saw Maddie. Saw her as he did that very first time at Damen Silos, when she stood on the lip of a six-story smokestack as if she were waiting for a bus, as she turned and looked him in the eye for the very first time, and all his misgivings about this urbex nonsense had flown away and he'd simply decided that he would be as brave as he needed to be to win her over, and the feeling was like falling—

Falling.

He bounced off a concrete slab partially blocking the shaft, knocking the wind out of himself and bruising a couple ribs. He desperately caught hold of it, but it crumbled in his hands and now he was sliding...

He kicked away from the slab as he fell, rebounded off the opposite wall and was flung at the next open doorway. He hit the threshold and caught it with his arms, but the floor offered no purchase, and he was slipping again.

Scrabbling for anything, he caught a rubber extension cord and dragged something off its wheels with a loud crash.

He fell off the threshold, dangling by the cord as something heavy and metallic grated across the floor to wedge itself in the doorframe, holding him suspended in the shaft.

Painstakingly, gentle as a spider climbing a web, he wrapped the cord around his wrist and pulled himself up hand over hand, pausing when a god-awful coughing fit rang his ribs like the Liberty Bell.

Gasping, he pulled himself up over the threshold and crawled over the pneumatic bolt gun that had saved his life. "OK," he panted, "OK." A meaningless mantra, but it got him through it, got him ready for what came next.

He sat up, clutching his bad shoulder. He tried rotating that arm and nearly blacked out from the pain. It was dislocated. He pulled his knees up to his chest, gripping them with both hands, bracing his useless arm between his legs, and then violently extended his body backwards.

CRACK.

The head of his humerus snapped back into its rotator cuff with a burst of pure, electric agony. A ragged scream escaped his lips. He fainted, rolling over until he ran into the core wall.

The world went away for a little while, and that was nice. But then it came back, which wasn't so nice, but better than the alternative. Rubbing his eyes, tugging his ears, he forced himself back to full alertness.

The floor was barren, except for a surveyor's laser on a tripod, standing beside the elevator shaft. Then he noticed the trash. Then he noticed Rene, slumped against the wall beside the elevator shaft.

Then he noticed the helicopter hovering outside.

He started to move towards the edge, but there was a man with night-vision goggles and a sniper rifle sitting in the chopper's cabin.

They shot him, Maddie had said.

Michael threw himself to the floor as a fusillade of silent lightning bolts chopped the space he'd just occupied.

Rolling over and over away from the windows, he came up against Rene's pack. Reflexively, he tore it open, looking for a walkie to replace the one he'd lost in the shaft, but he found only a tangle of cables, packs of Gauloise cigarettes, so much stupid junk—

The green case at the bottom attracted him; he didn't know what it was, until he opened it.

Nested in crisp packing foam: an armada of the latest dragonfly drones.

Outside, the helicopter waited, suspended in midair while the tower itself rocked like a haphazard stack of cards.

Stay right there, you bastard, Michael thought. Unpacking the tiny drones, he switched on the remote and puzzled over the controls. He knew they'd been pre-programmed, he just had to remember how to initiate the routine. His thumb remembered for him, and the firefly fleet lifted off the floor, getting caught up in the sucking vortex created by the helicopter's main rotor. Just as they left the tower, Michael stabbed the *Show* button and every firefly lit up in a brilliant red display, only slightly muted by the approaching dawn.

What the pilot saw, Michael couldn't begin to guess, but he hoped to hell the message was legible, that the words *FURIES* and *F.U.* were blinking in his face loud and clear.

Whether or not he could read it, the pilot panicked and jerked back on the pitch and the throttle at the same time, pivoting into a power dive to get out of the way of what he thought was a red-hot incoming projectile. The smoky updrafts washing up the flanks of Korova Tower staggered the flailing chopper and its tail rotor clipped the building's façade. For a split second the graphite blades chopped steel and concrete like so much salad before they themselves were shredded and flew apart.

The crippled helicopter spun out of control, whipping round and round the axis of its surviving rotor, tumbling out of the sky to crash somewhere in the smoke and chaos, far, far below.

"FUCK YOU TOO!" Michael screamed into the wind.

FIFTY-THREE

Maddie climbed the stairs. She had abandoned her pack somewhere, and the weight of the parachute on her back was a tugging that threatened to send her tumbling ass over teakettle back down every time she stopped, so she didn't stop.

Her mind came and went, bringing her nothing useful, but keeping her distracted.

The record for climbing the most stairs in twelve hours was 33,000 feet by Chris Solarz of Philadelphia, USA. Solarz climbed 58,080 stairs. She may not have broken his record, but nobody was trying to kill him...

Every so often, when she could muster the breath, she called for Michael on her walkie, but got no answer. He and Amara would meet her on the roof. That was the plan, and it was the only plan they had, so she stuck to it.

"Michael?" she said, though she no longer expected an answer.

Then she heard someone above her. A low, unfamiliar voice, speaking a guttural, alien language.

Russians.

Her every instinct urged her to call for help, but who could she trust? They shot him, and they tried to shoot her.

She crept up to the next landing and stopped beside the door.

Above her, she heard a squeak of rubber-soled shoes on steel, and a whispered command. Tugging the door open, she slipped through it just as the men on the next landing opened fire.

The bullets punched through the door all around her. Maddie covered her head and ran, but where was there to go? She had no climbing gear, she had no other way out...

Then she heard a rumble and smash so loud it seemed the whole tower was coming down. The floor tilted beneath her, and she tumbled, splaying out her hands to stop herself sliding across the floor and right out the window.

She caught herself on a pillar as the tilting slowed to a creaking stop. The doorway was filled with a wave of water that all but drowned out the screams of the Russians as it swept them down the stairwell.

Water pounded over her, stopping her ears to the screams of men swimming past her and out into empty air. Maddie braced herself against the pillar until the flood had spent itself.

It had to be the damper on the roof. Even as she gave thanks, she knew if it was gone, the whole of Korova Tower could collapse with the next stiff wind. She was close to the roof, and escape. But she realized with grim determination that she would rather die than go alone, if there was any chance...

Please, Michael, she silently prayed as she waded into the flooded stairwell, *please find me...*

FIFTY-FOUR

Michael approached a construction elevator attached to the outside of the building on the 100th floor, sliding the red gates open and stepping inside. They'd avoided the exterior elevators when climbing up for fear of being spotted, and this one only descended as far as the middle section, which was engulfed in flames. But it could still go up…

No sooner had he stepped onto it, when the whole apparatus shook, the anterior mast tearing itself free of the crumbling concrete. If it fell, it didn't matter; he had no other hope.

The elevator was operated by a touchscreen console. It was still functional, requiring only a password.

Damn it.

This was a hell of a way for it to end.

He banged his fist on the console in frustration.

No… think. Anyone else, this could be the end, but you're a nerd. A coder. *Ones and zeroes, Cam…*

Michael wracked his brains, but guessing could lock him out of the system. But these things were designed for the average worker to operate. He held down the asterisk until all the buttons lit up, allowing him to recode a new password.

Baffled by the Cyrillic alphabet underneath each number, he entered 1-2-3-4, and hit the asterisk again.

Nothing.

Then he entered 1-1-1-1.

The elevator jerked. Michael threw out his hands to grab the nearest bar, though it wouldn't do any good if he found himself plunging 100 stories to the ground.

Grinding its gears in protest, the elevator began to ascend.

"Ones and zeroes, Cam," Michael muttered, "minus the zeroes."

It felt almost indecent, after all he'd been through, to just ride. He scanned the floors as he passed them, looking for Maddie.

For Amara.

It still stunned him, how the journalist had betrayed him. But it was of a piece with everything else he'd learned this trip, and he didn't have time to examine it any further.

As the car took him higher and higher, the elevator began to completely detach from the skyscraper, dismantling itself beneath his feet, its self-destruction pursuing him.

Michael dove off the car at the last possible moment, throwing himself back onto the building as the car and mast fell away into the sky.

He was on the 180th floor, almost to the roof. He circled the mass-damper tank, now broken off its gimbals and lying askew against the collapsed wall of its chamber. He only hoped he wasn't too late.

The floor was soaked in water. He noticed glints of brass, knelt and picked up shell-casings from an assault rifle. If armed security goons were in the building, he didn't stand a chance, but he'd done a hundred impossible things today, and still hadn't had breakfast.

He emerged on the 183rd floor to find it very different from the last time he was here. The lounge was a shattered ruin, walls askew and open to the elements. He picked his way through jagged mazes of concrete and rebar to the media room, hoping against hope that what he'd left behind was still there.

Kneeling before the projector console, he pulled the datastick free just as a red, luminous spot appeared on his hand. Snatching it back, he heard a deafening report and the console imploded. Crawling across the room, listening to every creak and groan for a sign of them…

There.

A man stood in the stairwell doorway with a rifle. There was nowhere else to go.

Out the window, he saw the dangling wreckage of the crane jib. The jib he'd failed to jump onto when he tried to save Zoe and Rene.

No time for doubt now.

He ran for it just as they came through the door, flung himself across the gap and slammed into the mangled crane arm.

Bullets zinged and ricocheted off the struts all around him. His hands clawed at the slippery steel, his legs flailing in thin air.

And that was when it happened.

Without thinking about it, he'd favored his bad leg through everything Korova threw at them, taking every step and unexpected jolt on his "good" leg until he'd almost forgotten which leg was the bad one.

Now his bruised ribs, his straining hands, his battered head all protested at the desperate effort, but they frantically rallied to save him, while his right leg picked this critical moment to simply give up.

The pain nearly knocked him unconscious. With a strangled moan, he felt himself slipping to the last rungs of the twisted ladder. His left leg kicked impotently at the jib, but his right leg might as well have been a rabid dog with its teeth clamped on his flesh, a spasming weight flashing blasts of pure agony as it dragged him down.

Stop, he told himself. *Breathe—*

Rejecting the pain and panic, the sucking void of despair, he tuned out everything and focused on his next breath.

It was sweet. It steadied his limbs and calmed his mind.

Worse than the fear of falling, far worse, was the fear of failure. Even before his accident, he'd let it cripple him. But no longer...

He let the breath out and took another.

His limbs stopped shaking. He pulled himself higher, dragging his left leg up until it caught the lowest strut on the jib.

Another breath, and he could see the crooked tangle of steel as just another challenge in his physical therapy, but with his personal trainer shooting at him.

Another breath—

Steamy vapor surging out through his gritted teeth, Michael forced his right leg to contract and catch the bottom rung, steadying his body and pushing him up into the safety cage, where the grillwork deflected the barrage of bullets. The pain was worse than ever before, but he pulled, rather than pushed, through it.

He climbed hand over hand, looking over his shoulder. When the gunman stepped into view in the window frames, Michael took out the surveyor's laser and aimed it right back at him. The gunman saw the red beam painting his face and darted back behind cover.

Michael climbed on, muttering to himself, "*Go get 'em, Spider-Man...*"

FIFTY-FIVE

M addie traversed the jumble of ladders, loose cables, steel beams, nets, ropes, and pipes that had made a lethal mess of the once-orderly construction site.

For Maddie, it was just another obstacle course that she handily climbed up onto the roof.

"Maddie!"

She spun around at the sound of her name, thinking it had been Michael, where was he...?

Amara stepped out from behind the pulley shed of an elevator. She was unharmed, but something about the way she carried herself made Maddie keep her distance.

No sign of Michael.... "Where is he?"

Amara pointed behind her. "He's hurt. He needs you."

Worried for Michael's sake, Maddie took a step towards the journalist, but then she stopped.

She didn't know this woman, and something about her never fit in. At first, Maddie was just jealous when Cam flirted with her, but no matter how bad things got, she never cracked, never betrayed a glimmer of fear or sorrow.

Amara saw Maddie's hesitation and didn't waste another breath on the charade. Closing at a dead run, she sprang at Maddie and took her down. The two of them rolled across the helipad, scratching and punching, but unable to land a decisive blow.

Amara raked her face with broken fingernails. Blood and sweat blinded one eye. Maddie tried to return the favor, but she'd always kept her nails sensibly short. Her fingers dug into the soft flesh of Amara's cheek, but Amara twisted and snapped at her hand, grazing Maddie's knuckles with her teeth.

They rolled off the helipad with Amara on top. Maddie hit her head on the concrete and her vision went blurry. Amara pressed the advantage, bringing down a knee across her neck and slamming her head to the deck once, twice, a third time.

Maddie was too dazed to fight back. Three Amaras loomed over her, with not a glimmer of humanity between them. "I'm getting off this building," she growled.

As Maddie scooted blindly backwards, towards the edge of the roof, Amara picked up a length of pipe and lifted it high over her head.

"*Amara, don't!*"

Amara turned, stopped in her tracks by the sight of Michael climbing up out of the wreckage of the toppled rooftop crane. Realizing how this must look, she lowered the pipe, but didn't drop it.

A conflict seemed to rage behind her eyes, the person she used to be grappling with the person she'd become, when she thought she had no other choice.

The conflict raged—and ended. Amara raised the pipe, resolved to do whatever it took. Maddie shielded her face, bracing for the end.

"AMARA!!!" Michael screamed, limping towards her, but he was too far away… when the building awakened.

The floor tilted underneath them, sending their bodies bouncing across the roof, towards the edge… then it tilted back in the other direction like a pendulum, steel beams snapping like banjo strings, concrete crumbling like soda crackers, as the tower went into its terminal spiral.

All they could do was cling to whatever support presented itself as the runaway cycle of harmonic resonance reached its inevitable conclusion.

While everyone held on for dear life, the entire tower swayed back and forth, swinging wider and more wildly with every spasm, until the tilting upper floor reached an extremity the lower floors could not match.

The whole rooftop subsided as the unmoored stabilizer tank rampaged through the unstable structure like a wrecking ball, smashing its way out of the tower and spinning off into space.

Clinging to the stairs of the helipad, Michael shouted at her. She could barely make out his words, couldn't process or accept them. "Maddie, jump!"

Still wearing the parachute, she looked at him and shook her head. Though she barely had a firm perch, she lifted one hand and extended it to him, beckoning.

"Not without you—"

A ladder fell off Crane #1, crashing down on her. She tried to dodge it, but it clipped her head and the world went black and very still.

FIFTY-SIX

Michael cried out Maddie's name and flung himself off the stairs, fighting the wild rocking motion of the tower to climb to her.

Amara lost her grip and began to slide while the tower was at the nadir of its tilt. She flailed, grabbing for anything, but none of it was locked down. She slid towards Michael, who reached out, but he was still several feet away.

"Give me your hand!"

For the moment, everything she'd done was forgotten. She was going to fall. She was a human being. He strained but couldn't get any closer without letting go of his own handhold, which wouldn't help anyone. A pipe rolled past. He caught it and thrust it towards her just as she began to slip again.

Amara looked at him with fear and mistrust, seeing the pipe and assuming he meant to do to her what she'd nearly done to Maddie. Instead of reaching out to catch it, she swatted the pipe away.

Before he could reassure her, she screamed wordlessly, sliding away across the rocking rooftop, a look of pure terror on her face... and sailed over the edge.

No moment to spare for reflection, Michael had to get to Maddie, who rolled across the roof like wet laundry.

Suddenly, the building seemed to stall in its erratic motion, creaking like a boat about to capsize.

Then it began to fall.

At ground level, the palatial lobby was suddenly and completely obliterated, the ceiling crashing down like a mouth snapping shut.

On the lower mechanical floor, the last stubborn steel beams snapped, and the mid-section of the tower tore itself free from both foundation and superstructure, cleaving the disintegrating skyscraper into three colossal modules, each falling in a different direction.

Maddie's unconscious body bounced and was flung free of the roof, falling full speed towards the edge.

Michael kicked off the roof and threw himself after her. Letting himself fly free of the tower that was suddenly a wall, then a collapsing wave, he began the half-mile descent to the ground.

The frigid wind buffeted them both, but did little to slow their fall. Maddie flopped limply in the updraft.

Michael made a missile of his body, slicing through the air to descend faster and catch up to her. She swam up in his tearing eyes, grew larger until the terrible emptiness in her face was all he could see.

He caught her in midair, throwing his arms round her waist and sending them both into a tailspin while the whole world seemed to fall apart around them.

"Just hold on," he shouted, embracing her tighter and reaching under her left arm for the rip cord.

The world spun above and below them and it felt almost like they might miss it and fall forever into the sky, into the rising sun, but the web of Moscow spread out with alarming speed, the Earth below never to be denied its due. The construction site, the whole of the park, was engulfed in spreading clouds of dust from the falling tower, and he still couldn't find the—

Rip cord.

He yanked it away from her body and she almost jerked out of his arms, whipsawing upwards with a surge of spent g-forces as all her velocity was broken like a Saturday night promise on Sunday morning. Swinging by the sleeve and collar of her windbreaker, Michael kicked and clung and cried all the way to the ground.

As they fell, so fell Korova Tower. While the lower section collapsed in upon itself, the midsection tumbled to the southwest to crash in the Moscow River as a rude new bridge. The uppermost section came down as a rain of steel and concrete over the river and the business park between the construction site and Federation Tower. The blocks immediately surrounding Korova Tower had been evacuated the night before, but several square blocks of business and residential buildings were crushed or razed by widespread fires caused by falling debris.

They touched down on the turf of the park alongside the river as a phalanx of security SUVs screeched up to surround them. Michael landed badly on his injured leg and rolled with his arms around Maddie, protecting her head. He heard men shouting and dogs barking and felt red laser dots crawling over his face like mosquitoes, but he had eyes only for the slack face of the woman in his arms.

A police car screamed into the midst of the circle of SUVs with its siren whooping. An older plainclothes detective jumped out with two uniformed officers, shouting in Russian and pointing his gun at the security guards, but what really held their attention was the GoPro camera in his hand. Somehow, Michael understood that what he was saying was, "*This is going out live!*"

Beyond the ring of cars, a crowd of protestors bearing banners approached, many pointing phones and chanting a slogan in which he could make out the repeated word *Korova*.

He looked back down at Maddie, who was looking up at him. Dazed, but conscious. Alive.

"What happened?" she asked. "Are we dead?"

"No such luck." Patting his pocket to ensure the drive was still where he put it, he held up a hand in surrender to the approaching police detective, while he held Maddie close with the other.

"We're going to be the Furies for real, now," he said. "And God help anyone who gets in our way…"

THE END

For more fantastic fiction, author events,
exclusive excerpts, competitions, limited editions and more

VISIT OUR WEBSITE
titanbooks.com

LIKE US ON FACEBOOK
facebook.com/titanbooks

FOLLOW US ON TWITTER AND INSTAGRAM
@TitanBooks

EMAIL US
readerfeedback@titanemail.com

ACKNOWLEDGEMENTS

No book is accomplished in a lonely vacuum, but this one came closer than most. Because of pandemic lockdown, in-the-flesh research opportunities were scarce, but websites like itsabandoned.com and urbexplayground.com provided crucial insight into the shadowy urbex realm. I am indebted to excellent friends Brian and Gwen Callahan, who introduced me to Portland's infamous Shanghai Tunnels, and to Aaron Costello for exploring Mount Laguna Air Force Station outside San Diego with me, back in less turbulent times.

Vertical owes its existence to the savvy negotiation of my agent, Janet Reid, and any polish and rigor it might possess to the inestimable editing skills of Jeff Conner. It would not have been completed without the kind hospitality of Alicia Graves, and the verdant support of Scott and Matthew Elsasser.

ABOUT THE AUTHOR

CODY GOODFELLOW has written nine novels and five collections of short stories, and edits the hyperpulp zine *Forbidden Futures*. His writing has been favored with three Wonderland Book Awards. His comics work has been featured in *Mystery Meat*, *Creepy*, *Slow Death Zero* and *Skin Crawl*. As an actor, he has appeared in numerous short films, TV shows, music videos by Anthrax and Beck, and a Days Inn commercial. He also wrote, co-produced and scored the Lovecraftian hygiene films *Baby Got Bass* and *Stay At Home Dad*, which can be viewed on YouTube. He lives in San Diego, California.